HEART TO HEART

♫

Mary Ann Nocera

Little Classics Publishing

Text copyright © by Mary Ann Nocera

Publication date – March 2015

Cover design by Mary Ann Nocera

Heart to Heart is a work of fiction. Characters, names and incidents are a product of the author's imagination. Any resemblance to the actual persons is coincidental.
Names of places, actual or real are used fictitiously.

ISBN-13: 978-0692392560
ISBN-10: 0692392564

♫ to my sons ♫

PART ONE

♫

the soul struggles to survive

CHAPTER ONE

♪

*S*haron was saying goodbye to the five other students and Dr. Wilhelm Kreutzer, after spending six weeks in Salzburg on the greatest musical journey of her young life. There were hugs and kisses and tears, but most of all she felt she would probably never see these new friends again. They were from different corners of the world, Japan, Vancouver, London and Rio. And yes they would write, but as time passed other important things would take precedent, and slowly their lives would meld into a new way and they would drift apart.

The loudspeaker announced the flight and with tears in her eyes, she boarded the large TWA plane for the first part of her journey home. Home presently was music school in Upstate New York.

She settled in her seat and put her hands over her face to hide her tears. It was hard to believe such a beautiful summer was over.

The stewardess stopped and with a quick glance at her clip board, "You're Sharon Heisendorf.

Is everything all right?"

"Yes, but it was hard to say goodbye."

"I know." She lightly touched her shoulder. "If there is anything I can get for you just let me know."

Sharon thanked her. She reached in her bag and pulled out her journal, that she had meticulously kept, to record her last day in Salzburg. She wrote August 28, 1960.

Sharon received a scholarship for her summer workshop from the music school she attend. She had also received a complete scholarship for her first two years at the school. This September she would be starting her last year. She was a very accomplished pianist and played jazz as beautifully as she played Chopin. She had a natural ability that exceeded many.

It was a long flight and she would have time to relive the past weeks, playing and listening to beautiful music, meeting new students and enjoying Salzburg. And she could not forget the many evenings at Dr. Will's home, as social gatherings.

She put her seat back and closed her eyes and the roar of the engine told her they would soon be airborne. Paris would be the stopover and then on to New York, arriving tomorrow morning.

After many hours of flying she was home. She was tired, hungry, her long raven-black hair disheveled, and her make-up had disappeared from her beautiful face into the pillow on the plane.

No one will be here to meet me she thought.

Tightly clutching her carry-on, as it seemed to give her strength, Sharon made her way to the baggage claim. As she waited for her luggage she heard a whisper, "Welcome home my Rose of Sharon."

She turned quickly, "Joel."

Sharon and Joel had become very good friends, when Mr. Jensen rearranged the high school band, seating Sharon and her flute next to Joel who played oboe. This started a long and close friendship. They dated and shared their love of music many afternoons at Joel's home. Sharon would play jazz or accompany him as he played the oboe.

After graduation, Joel went to the university and Sharon went east to music school. He visited her many times in the last three years and in the summer, when they were home, they spent much time together. Through the years, their friendship grew to a love that neither quite recognized nor acknowledged.

"Oh my!" Sharon called as she threw her arms around him.

Smiling, Joel put his hands on the back of her head and drew her near and kissed her lovingly.

"I didn't know you would be here, but I am so glad you are," was her warm and affectionate greeting.

"I saw you off so I thought it appropriate to be here when you came home."

"How did you know when I would arrive?"

"In your last letter you said today, so I drove up yesterday. I went by your studio earlier and you were not there so I came here, and was going to meet every plane today coming in from New York City. I didn't have time to answer, and I thought it would be a nice surprise. I thought you would be glad after the long flight to see a face that you recognized."

"You always amaze me." She hugged him.

"I wanted to be the first to hear about your amazing summer. It must have been wonderful."

"You can read my journal."

"I'd like that. You must be tired."

"It shows? I tried to sleep on the plane, but not much happened."

"We'll get your luggage and go to your studio and you can take a real nap, then we can have dinner later."

The drive home Sharon was too tired to talk so she put her head back, closed her eyes, and Joel tightly clutched her hand to assure her and that he cared.

Her studio was in a neighborhood of old Victorian homes at the edge of the music campus. Most were privately owned, some having small apartments for the students, as Mr. Heids, where she lived.

Sharon pulled the drapes, opened the windows and gazed into the colorful flower gardens below. Her thoughts went back to the gardens in Salzburg.

One side of the tiny studio was the kitchen, separated by an island, the other side, the everything room. She had a couch, small tables, another chair, lamps and a television. She had added blue and purple pillows and a dark purple shag rug. Her record player that Joel had given her as a present when they graduated from high school fit nicely in the corner. She treasured her newest piece of technology not only because Joel had given it to her, but she could listen to her favorite pianists and learn all of the nuisances of a composition.

The chosen colors for her small bedroom were

pinks and purples. A large window allowed a morning breeze to slip in easily. Tucked away in the corner was her tiny sewing machine where she made many of her clothes.

A bath also in pink and purple completed her living area. She had made it warm and cozy and home.

She looked around at her very casual studio and thought, another year then graduate school. She smiled at Joel.

"Glad to be back?"

"Yes, but you don't know how hard it was to leave. I have to remember how fortunate I was to get to spend the summer there and study with Dr. Will, as he was fondly called."

Joel sensed her sadness, took her in his arms and held her close. "I'm glad I can be here for you."

They held each other for a long time. Their relationship had been long and close, but never allowed them to become lovers. Why? Neither knew although there had been times....

"Want to rest? Planes can be very tiring although you aren't doing anything. It was a long flight."

"Do you mind if I take a shower and then a short nap?"

"Of course not." Joel kicked off his shoes and stretched out on the couch to wait for her.

Sharon excused herself, found a robe and on to the shower. When she came out she said, "I'll lie down for just a few moments and then I'll be better company. Then we can go get something to eat."

With the blinds closed and only soft light

shading her room she quickly fell asleep.

Joel let her sleep for a while, but eventually he felt the need to be near her. Even though the door was open, he knocked. With her head buried in the pillow, she said softly, "Come in."

He lay down beside her. "I missed not seeing you this summer. The first summer we've been apart. I just want to hold you."

As she snuggled close, her robe fell open exposing her soft light-tone body that told of French and Indian heritage. That was all there needed to be.

Joel undressed and lay next to her. He gently slipped her out of her robe and they were free for each other. They talked quietly.

"Why have we waited so long to make love? You know I have loved you since that first day in band when you sat down and said 'hi Joel.' My heart melted. I didn't even know you knew my name."

"I don't know why either, but we can't stop now," she whispered as she caressed his handsome face and ran her fingers through his dark brown hair. "Your love has been so much to me for so long."

"It's our love as it should be," Joel responded so very softly.

Their lips met again and again as they found each other completely after many years of waiting.

The emotion of love is a journey that travels freely until it finds a home in the heart. The emotion of love lies silently in a heart until a special moment, day or night, dusk or sunrise. Love opens like a lily or it can come as a flash of lightning. For Joel and Sharon it was the lily opening, days into years.

The quiet time after love is a hush, as special as love itself. They felt the aura that had closed around them to complete the circle.

Joel touched her face and felt tears on her cheek. He knew they were not sad tears but from the emotion they had just shared.

"Oh love, I never knew loving you would be so wonderful."

"I know," he softly replied as he held her close. "My Sharon, I love you with my heart and so much deeper than anything that I have experienced in my life. We can go forth with our lives with a contentment that we belong to each other. Life will be easier when you share, as we will."

He paused. "Our first real time together in the quiet and shadow of your tiny bedroom with pink and purple flashes all around will forever be etched in my mind. Purple and pink will be our colors. You pink."

They lay quietly as time seemed to stand still. "I'm glad our love happened today. Now we can enjoy each other every moment until I go. Seven days. It will be our moving of heaven and earth."

Joel pushed her hair that was splayed on her face. "We have been here a long time. Want to get something to eat?"

"Yeah, a little bit. I'd better see if Karen is home and tell her I'm back and that she won't have to put you up anymore."

They dressed and Sharon went across the hall and knocked lightly on Karen's door. She peeked out and then threw the door open wide and almost shouted. "You're back." They hugged and hugged.

"From your short notes, I thought you would arrive tomorrow. I wasn't sure what time you would be leaving Salzburg."

"I got in after eleven o'clock this morning and Joel surprised me. I didn't expect him, but I was glad to be met by someone, especially him."

"He's here?" Karen said softly and pointed across the hall. "The bedroom is a mess, but I'll hurry and get it in shape. He can bunk in."

Since they had lived there, Karen had kindly let Joel stay in her spare bedroom, when he visited Sharon.

"Well that brings up another thing," she smiled and hesitated. "He's going to stay with me tonight and every night of our lives. Anyway, that is where we are."

"Well, oh my, it's about time. You two have loved each other for so long and I wasn't sure either of you realized it. I'm glad you finally came to your senses."

"Yeah, me too. Is everything all right with you?"

"Good. Everything's about the same. We can talk later and I want to hear all about Salzburg. But now, I'll let you get back to Joel. Say hello for me."

"He is going to be here until Tuesday, so we can get together for a glass of wine."

They hugged again and Sharon went back to her tiny studio and to Joel.

On the way to an early dinner Joel said, "I want to hear everything that has happened to you in the last six weeks before I go home. When do classes start?"

"Wednesday after Labor Day."

"And I start the following Wednesday. So I'll go home Tuesday or maybe Wednesday morning and spend the week with Mom and Dad. They took a short vacation in July and I was in charge of the works. It was nice and I like doing that. After service I'll take over more and more." He hesitated. "Salzburg."

"Well, there were six of us and Sophia from London was very nice and we became friends fast. The guys were real nice too. And Dr. Will was an angel. He was very protective of us, even the boys. Monday through Friday we had a workshop of piano literature. We played and he was so good at helping us interpret. We would all work on the same selection or part of it. I learned some new Chopin, Scriabin. Weekends were lots of fun too. We went to recitals. Played recitals."

"Did you play any jazz?"

"I did. After Dr. Will talked about jazz and how it could someday fit into our repertory, he asked if any of us played. I got brave and said that I did."

"He looked at me and said, 'play.' So I did."

"How did that go over?"

"Great. He loved it, and he was amazed how I could switch from classical to jazz and so completely interpret both so well. Also in the evening at the lodge we all played. The other workshops were strings. I wish you could have been there."

"How you can switch always amazed me too. Isn't that little French restaurant in here somewhere?"

"Next street turn right. Every day I thank God for this talent and I really want to do good."

"Oh sweetheart you certainly have."

At the restaurant, "You need a glass of wine to relax you. How was the food?"

"Very good, although we only went out a few times. The lodge provided us with our meals and Dr. Will's cook was wonderful. We were there every Saturday evening. His wife was very sweet too. What are we going to do tomorrow?"

"You have the schedule. I'll get your car started, get groceries, and anything else I can do."

"I'll have to go practice. Call my parents. Call Mr. Kellogg at the country club and see if I still have a job for this winter. If not, I have to get busy and get another. I have to eat and the big one, grad school."

"You know if you need money just ask."

"I'm okay for now. Thanks. You're too sweet."

"I'll save the museum and the castle trips for tomorrow."

They enjoyed their dinner and were soon on their way home.

"Let's go for a walk. I have to get back to reality."

A hush lay on the evening. The sun was slowly falling into the night and the air cooled to pleasantness. The tall oaks and maples that shaded the old Victorian homes were still, tired from the day of motion and thought of sleep. The streets were still lined with gaslights that came to life as dusk silently crept in.

Most of the music professors and some of the students lived in this elegant old neighborhood.

Joel and Sharon walked hand in hand for several block. "I'm so glad you're here. I won't have that depressed feeling after such a beautiful summer.

Then school will start and I won't have time to feel sad. You know how it is."

"I do. Every time I leave you."

Sharon acknowledged with a quick kiss on his cheek.

"When I go practice I want to check the schedule and see if there are any changes. It was all done before I left. Are you staying at the same place this year?"

"Yeah, I like it there and it is close to school and everything else. Saturday my sisters are coming for the day. May I tell them that we are engaged?"

"No, let's wait for a while. It just happened. We have another year in school. Are you going with me while I practice?"

"Yes, first I will listen and then I'll read. I brought several books."

"We can cross on the next side street and be home"

"I think you have forgotten that you just got off the plane this morning after a very long flight. We'll get a good night's sleep after we make love, again." And he looked at her lovingly through the glaze of dusk.

"I hoped you would say that."

♫

CHAPTER TWO

♫

*T*he morning started as yesterday had ended. They loved passionately and without reserve.

Softly, "It is so much nicer waking up here than over at Karen's. She was so good to put me up."

"I can't believe these few beautiful days are going to end so soon," Sharon whispered.

"We have to make up for lost time."

"Let's not think about that now."

"First break will be Thanksgiving. What is your schedule like? Are you going home?"

"I don't know yet. I might have to work, or have a recital. It's a short time to spend that much money. Wait until it gets closer."

"If you don't, I'll be here, or let me get you a plane ticket."

"Wait until later and we can talk about it."

Joel shifted and pulled her closer. "I'd rather stay right here and hold you all day, but it is getting late. Let's have coffee."

"Okay," Sharon said as she went to make it.

When she went back, Joel had the shower going and they enjoyed another close time together. Over coffee and toast they planned their day.

"I have to unpack and do laundry."

"Does your car need an oil change?"

"I don't think so," she wrinkled her nose, "but can you check. Cars aren't my strong point. Let's get groceries and after lunch I'll go practice. Is that okay?"

They went about doing as they planned and after a bit of lunch they decided to go to school so Sharon could practice.

"I usually ride my bike over, but I only have one so let's walk over. We don't have to hurry."

Sharon gathered her music and Joel his book and they were on their way.

"Tell me about the castle."

"Hohensalzburg. Oh! It was awesome. From afar it looked like a great protectorate of the city. Like Zeus watching over. Up close it was so big it was intimidating. We had a recital there on a Sunday afternoon. I mentioned that in a letter. We had our farewell recital at the Mozarteum. That is where Glenn Gould played last summer. All the workshops performed. The hall just made the music sing."

"What did you play?"

"A Schubert impromptu and a Brahms ballade. The one you like so much. Afterward there was a reception. It was well attended by what seemed to be important people. All very formal. The ladies in long dresses and gentlemen wore their tuxes. They congratulated us, if they spoke English. Those that just shook our hands and nodded probably didn't. But our music was understood by all, no language barrier."

"I'm sure you looked beautiful and played the same way, my Rose of Sharon. I wish I could have been there," he said as he pulled her hand to his lips.

"I took pictures in and outside at the castle and my journal pages are full. If the pictures come out I'll match them up for you."

They reached the large campus. Each musical group had their own building. The other buildings were dorms. This is where Sharon had lived her first two years. In the main building, there was a large auditorium and a small recital hall where she had permission to practice.

They entered the hall, turned on the stage lights, and Joel helped her remove the cover from the grand piano. She seated herself and Joel beside her.

"This is for you." Light and playful to begin and about halfway through her short piece it became very melodic and sounded like white silk waving in a soft summer breeze. She turned and kissed him lightly. She play for a few more moments and it ended as soft and gracious as a touch with her finger tips on his face.

"Oh god it's beautiful and you wrote."

"Yes, it was an assignment and I could only think of you, so writing it was very easy. I'm so glad you're here and I could play it for you so soon."

Joel easily turned her head and kissed her. "Play it for me every day we come here because I want to go home with every note imprinted in my heart."

Visibly moved, Joel got up and said, "I'll let you practice."

He sat down in the front row very close to her,

as the stage was not high, so he could hear every perfect note as well as the not so perfect.

"I'll go for about an hour."

"As long as you want. My book is rather big," and he held it up for Sharon to see.

Sharon was in the middle of her warm-up exercises when she stopped quickly. "Did you hear that? It sounded like a door opening and closing."

"Yeah, I don't know where it came from," he looked around the dark hall. "No one else is here."

Sharon continued for a while and they both heard the same sound again.

"Maybe it's a vacuum moving the doors. You know how that happens," Joel reasoned.

What they did not realize that someone had slipped in and out, making the noise they thought was created by a vacuum.

She had practiced about an hour and said, "That is enough for now."

Joel again sat down beside her and said, "Please play my song again."

She gazed into his big, brown eyes until she reached the last note. As the music filled the air, it traveled from heart to heart.

"When you're far away I'll play it and you'll hear it. It will be our togetherness when apart."

"It's our song, truly."

Joel whispered, "I love you."

They covered the piano and flipped the light. In the hall Sharon said, "I would like to see if Dr. Bernard is here and just say hello and that I'm back and had a wonderful time."

The lights in his office were on but he did not seem to be around.

"We'll stop in tomorrow."

As they walked home Sharon asked him what he was reading.

"*Churchill, Roosevelt and Stalin.* Really interesting times."

"You should have been an history professor."

"Yeah, but my father's business is well established and it would be too bad not to keep it going. And there is only me. My sisters want no part of it. I like the work."

Joel's father has a very large and lucrative contracting business, residential as well as commercial. They planned that Joel would become part of the business and take over when his father retires.

"Tell me about where you stayed."

"Okay. It was a large lodge near Untersburg Mountain. Not far from the city. All of the workshop students stayed there. Each group had their own van and driver. It ran on a schedule or rather it was on our schedule. We planned our days. In the evening we had a great time. Everyone was very serious about being there, but it was a way to let down a little. The groups played for each other in the evening."

"Did you play jazz?"

"Oh I sure did."

"And."

"It was a hit. One evening I played with a group that had been playing together for a while. It was an impromptu jazz session and oh my, that was so great. Everyone sat around and didn't want us to stop. They wanted me to go home with them."

"Did everyone speak English?"

"Most everyone did rather well, but that didn't seem to matter. A few gestures to me and to the piano and you didn't need words. We spoke the language of music."

"A perfect example of music being universal."

"The lodge was new and they planned to have the cable car up the mountain open next spring. One Saturday our group decided to go hiking. When you get up higher you can look back on the city and oh, the hills! The view just took your breath away."

"In your letter you said that you had your own room."

"Yeah, we all did. There were twenty-two in all of the workshops, so there was enough space. But playing with the strings group was the best. It gave me such a feeling of freedom. Here they don't acknowledge jazz in school. I don't want to bore you so I'll save some for tomorrow."

"Sweetheart, you never bore me. It is so wonderful that you had this experience. You deserve it. You have worked very hard."

"I don't consider practicing hard work."

"But it is. I hear you go over passages many times until you get exactly what you want."

"I thought you knew how much I loved doing that."

"I guess I did," and he smiled at her.

As they walked on, they noticed the air had cooled and that was a welcome change. The tall trees that were normally still had created a steady breeze and stirred the fragrance of the flowers.

"This is so refreshing," she said as she put her head back to accept it on her face. "It even looks like it might rain."

As they got closer to home Sharon took a deep breath and said, "There is so much more to tell you. Old Town. The gardens. And Dr. Will was so special."

Inside he asked her, "Where do you want to go to eat? Remember it's out every evening for dinner."

"How about The Kitchen Place?"

She took his hand. "How about food for the soul?"

"Yes," as he cuddled her in his arms. "I was really moved when you played your music for me. It is a special gift that no one else has or will ever have. It's like our love."

In Sharon's bedroom of pink and purple they undressed each other. He lay down, pulled her on top and held her close and they both felt the warmth that love brought to their bodies.

"I've imagined this hundreds of times and wondered if it would ever happen. My Rose of Sharon, now that it has, dear god there's no end."

They came to each other as if they had been together forever, and in their minds they had. There was nothing shy about what they said or did to the other. It was the best of feelings that each could give. Each touch was gentle, each move was sensual, each kiss overpowering. And when the fire of passion was all it could be, she reached for him and guided him to the special place that had become his to caress, to

26

touch, to kiss and to make them one.

They remained one in body as their hearts silently came to rest. They fell asleep with love lingering in their souls.

The breeze that fell on Sharon's face earlier became a bit heavier. It brought the clouds that carried the rain. It was gentle and easy and lasted through their sleep. It passed as quickly as it came. The new fragrance that followed slipped into her bedroom.

Joel moved slightly and she too was awake.

"Is it morning?" she asked.

"No, thank goodness, I can love you again tonight."

"Oh yes," and she rolled over and kissed him passionately.

After a shower, they found their clothes in little heaps where they stepped out of them a while ago.

"Food," she said with a smile.

On the way Joel asked, "Tell me about the museums."

"Well, the Mozart was special. It was not very big but it had old instruments, furniture. It was sad knowing how his life ended. His museum is his memorial. The Old Town was absolutely beautiful. I don't know anything about architecture, but I heard it was gothic and baroque. Michael Haydn is buried in St. Peter's cemetery churchyard. The graves were decorated as if the person had just been buried. There are a few private museums. The one in the castle has many musical instruments. Oh, I'm skipping around. My brain is outworking my words. And the people love their festivals."

"You have certainly whetted my appetite. We'll have to go back someday."

After eating a large dinner, they realized how hungry they had been.

"We have a few hours before bedtime, what would you like to do?" he asked her.

"It might rain again, we have to do something inside. Let's just go home and watch television."

"Okay with me. Or we can play records."

"Did you bring any records with you?"

"No and you probably haven't bought any new ones lately. So that brings us for something to do. Where is the closest record shop?"

Sharon didn't have to think long and she guided him easily. They bought a Glenn Gould, an album of Chopin etudes, and an easy listening of strings with romantic selections.

At home they had a hard time deciding what to listen to first, but the Glenn Gould won out. After that it was the strings.

Joel changed the record and went back to the couch with her. "What are we going to do tomorrow? Although I want to keep hearing about Salzburg."

"Okay," she whispered, "but for now, I want to tell you how much I love you. And then I want to show you. We have to make every minute count."

After loving, they listened to the soft rain as it lulled them to their sleep.

♫

The next day they woke to a new sunrise. In the

freshness of the morning Joel said, "Before coffee let's start this day right."

It was another hour or so before they were ready for coffee.

"I'll make it this morning," he told her.

She lingered in the shower and Joel soon joined her. With closed eyes, they touched each other everywhere and the feeling was unbroken. Each sensation was whole. Each passion was complete.

Over coffee they decided how their day would go forth. A little later Sharon called Mr. Kellogg and he said to come over and talk about her playing for the winter.

Later they drove to the country club and entered his office and Sharon said, "Mr. Kellogg, this is my friend Joel Steiner."

They exchanged greetings and handshakes and Mr. Kellogg motioned for them to have a seat.

"When we have a little more time I want to hear about your trip. But this is what I would like to schedule for the winter. Saturday evenings from six until ten o'clock, which means extending your playing time by an hour. At ten the orchestra would begin for the dancing until closing. Karl wants you to fill in again if the piano player can't make it. I also want to add a couple hours on Sunday afternoon, two until four. Where people can sit and listen and have a drink and enjoy your beautiful playing. Little different from last year. I'd like to try this. How does that sound?"

"Real good. It won't interfere if I have to play at church."

"And the best news, I have had permission to

increase your hourly salary. We hope to get started next weekend, the seventeenth. Hopefully you can be here?"

"Yes, I'm anxious to get started."

They said their goodbyes. Joel and Sharon were on their way home.

"That is three extra hours a week. That is so good. I won't have to count every penny. With tuition and I spent a little money in Salzburg, my bank account is pretty low.

"One more year of keeping my jazz playing a secret at school. At least no one has said anything. I might be reprimanded if they knew. I can't believe Dr. Bernard would dismiss me. It is like Dr. Will said, someday the schools here will accept jazz as a musical form."

"Well if they put you out just call me, and I'll give them a piece of my mind and take you home with me," Joel said in a half-joking manner. In a more serious tone, "On the way we'll get married."

♫

Their next few days were very full. A movie, a gallery experience and always, dinner out. She went every day to practice while Joel read. Again they heard the sound of what seemed like opening and closing of doors, but after a while they didn't pay much attention to it. Each day she started and ended her practice with her song for Joel.

Most of all, they enjoyed their new-found love for each other. Each time seemed to be new and different. It would be soft and gentle, another it would be passionate with strong desires. They shared their aggressiveness and boldness, but whatever, they both enjoyed their moments together.

Sharon experienced emotion that she did not even know existed and she wanted them only from Joel, forever.

Friday afternoon after practice they found Dr. Bernard in his office. "Oh dear girl, my wonderful pianist it is so good to see you and know that you are home safely. I want to hear everything," he said as he gave her a big hug. "Did everything go all right?"

"Better than all right. I can't begin to tell you how wonderful everything was. Thank you."

"I want you to give a little talk at the first piano department meeting."

"I'd love to."

"Dr. Bernard, this is my friend Joel Steiner."

"Wonderful to know you. Do you play the piano?"

"A little. I played the oboe."

"Beautiful instrument, one of my favorites."

"We won't keep you, but I was here to practice and thought I'd say hello."

"Dear girl, check in with me next week."

Joel and Sharon walked leisurely home.

Saturday Karen asked Sharon, "Would you and Joel like to go with me and Jim Monday to the lake for a picnic?"

"We'd love to. You can visit with Joel since I have kept him to myself."

Joel had only bunked at Karen's once since she

and Jim had been dating. Jim was a little confused until Karen convinced him that Joel was Sharon's long-time boyfriend, but they didn't stay together, until now.

♫

Monday morning the girls filled the picnic basket and the four of them were on their way to the lake in Jim's car.

They set up their volleyball net and decided to take a quick swim before playing. They stripped down to their bathing suits, Sharon grabbed Joel's hand, and they ran to the water and plunged in. The water was cool and refreshing on this warm September day. They swam and rolled in the water until Karen called, "Let's play volleyball."

There was a continuous back and forth for about a half hour, with sand flying and arms waving, until they exhausted themselves.

"Let's cool down then eat," Jim suggested.

All four raced to the water again. They swam, played and continued working on their appetite.

Karen and Jim went back to the beach so Joel said, "Let's join them."

"Everyone hungry," Karen said.

"Yeah, we are," Jim responded.

"I hope you two made enough food."

Everyone pitched in, table set, food arranged and ready to indulge.

After eating, Jim and Karen sat on the blanket and talked while Joel and Sharon decided to walk along the beach.

A little strained Sharon asked, "Are you going tomorrow?"

"I don't want to leave at night. Maybe I'll go early Wednesday morning."

"My first class is at ten."

"Would that be okay with you? I can love you two more nights. It has to last a while."

"I feel better that you're not leaving tomorrow."

With their arms around each other, they followed the beach until it became rocky. They sat on an old log smoothed by time, with waters from far and near. They watch the shore birds fly in and out with the waves. They listened to their mournful caw and watched the seaweed wiggle at the water's edge. The air was cooler and Joel felt Sharon slightly shiver.

"Are you cold?"

"No. I'm just a little overwhelmed by what has happened in the last few days. Coming back from Salzburg. Making love to you after all of these years. Talking about getting married. A new school year."

"You're also probably still tired."

They held each other close as the evening was searching for twilight. The sunrays reached toward the heavens and were turning its reds to gold, reflecting sharply on the water. The water was gently meeting the sand only to quickly leave it behind. Everything was far away. They savored these gentle moments of closeness.

"Let's go back, they may want to go." Joel suggested.

"I'll race you."

♩

The new day was quiet for them. It was hard to laugh or be silly because this was the last day they would be together. Joel took her to the grocery store and bought her as much as her tiny cabinets would hold.

"I have to keep my future wife strong and nourished."

"I can keep my head above water for now. With the extra hours of work, it really helps."

Lunch, and Sharon went to practice. As they walked home, she told him as much as she knew about the coming semester.

"At our winter concert I will be playing the Paganini with the orchestra. There will be choral groups, strings and maybe one other piano. It will be near the Christmas break and I hope you can come up."

"I'll be here."

"Tonight I want to take you to a real nice place for dinner. You choose."

"Huntington Place? We went there last year."

"I remember, and that's a good choice."

"We're going to have to get dressed up. And better call for reservations. Tuesday, not a problem."

They were seated on the patio in the midst of a perfect evening. The satin blue sky dipped and rose with the faraway hills. The sunset was on the other side so they could not witness the passing of their time together. The fragrance of the flowers on the rock terrace added to the sweetness in the air.

Joel took her hand and said," This is not an end, it is only the beginning."

"I know, but this time is different. I'll have to sleep by myself."

"Me too," and they both laughed.

After enjoying the great food and an aura of love around them, they decided to go.

"I have one more thing to tell you about Salzburg. Dr. Will."

"As we drive."

"Dr. Will. Probably to date, the sweetest man I know. Dr. Bernard comes close, but … he called us, 'my children.' I don't think he and his wife had children so music and their students are their children. His wife was very nice too and she played the viola. One Saturday after dinner they played for us. They were truly one in spirit. You could not only see their closeness, you could feel it. It was so wonderful."

Sharon thought. As much as I love Joel, I will never have that nearness with him.

"In our workshop, we each had a piano. He was so physical and mentally vibrant. He had more energy than all six of us together. And he was that way with the music. The emphasis he would give a note or a passage was with such enthusiasm. And he could convey it to us so easily with his words.

"After he played for us, we offered what we knew about the composer and then he would fill in. Then he asked us to write what it said to us, just a line or a few words. Was it happy, sad, dark? Chord changes, patterns, harmony. He wanted us to understand the interpretation while we were learning the notes. We studied the markings, hands separately, then together."

"Does he only teach?'

"Now he does, but he was on the concert stage for about ten years." She paused. "We've done many of the things he presented, but he took it to a greater depth. It was awesome and I can understand why his workshops are in demand. I'm so fortunate to have been there.

"One day we did a Bach and I thought he was going to come out of his shoes. You just had to smile as well as listen and he certainly was infectious.

"You worked through a piece with such unbelievable feelings, so vibrant and yet so relaxed. He would praise you when you played and say 'do it again just that way' or he would say, 'not that way' then so lovingly offer how.

"And you should have heard him about Glenn Gould. He attended his recital last year and he loved him. He played a recording of his "*Goldberg Variations*" and we talked about it. He thinks he plays Bach better than anyone to date. I agree.

"Oh, we're almost home and I've been talking all the ways."

"But I love hearing every word. And it was so much fun watching you relive those moments, eyes closed, expressing with your hands. Those days are embedded in your soul just the way it was intended. You're beautiful telling me, and it was so vivid that I felt so much too.

"Sweetheart, you don't know how glad I am for you that you got to be there this summer. Knowing the wonderful impression it has made on you and how much you have enjoyed, it was worth giving you up this summer."

At home they watched television for a while in each other's arms and then decided for an early bedtime.

This last evening they left their passion for another day and loved each other with gentleness and tender care their hearts felt. Soft words to be remembered for the empty days to follow. A touch to be felt when far away. Longing for a sensation. Reaching in the night to find. Knowing without asking. Knowing without telling. Not wishing time away but closing that space until they would again be in each other's arms.

Morning, and before dark was gone and the sun appeared, they loved one last time. "Leaving this time is different and so very special." Joel told her. "Every night I'll pretend you're next to me."

Sharon smiled. "It's real happiness along with such contentment. Your loving me was the greatest homecoming gift I could have received."

After coffee and toast they gathered for her classes and for his long drive home.

"Let's get your bike."

Outside they held each other and he kissed her lightly. "Bye love, my Rose of Sharon."

Sharon watch as Joel drove out of sight and everything had been too wonderful to be sad.

♫

CHAPTER THREE

♫

*T*he crisp morning air passed quickly on Sharon's face as she rode to school. Even this early in September the coolness was felt, especially morning and evenings. In between those hours, it just could not decide to rain or be fair or pure sunshine.

Three years ago there was a different first day. Moms and dads were helping unload stuff. Neither Sharon's mother nor dad were there. Her Aunt Katy had brought her all the way from Missouri. This had caused a lot of tension in the family. Thankfully it had been temporary and at the moment that was a long way back. Her struggles were almost over. There were times when she thought they would never begin. Like all pain it can be forgotten when there is a treasure at the end.

In high school, Sharon worked hard with her piano instructor to develop her natural ability and learn classical literature, developing technique by playing Hanon and Czerny. Performance was her goal.

From time to time college would come up as a

discussion with her parents and she told them she wanted to go to music school. With casual words and a laugh they would dismiss the subject. Weeks and sometimes months would go by and Sharon would bring up the subject again. Over time she became aware they were not taking her serious and she became concerned and addressed the subject head on.

Kindly but firmly her father had said, "We are not going to send you to music school. You know it would be a waste of your time and our money."

Her mother added, "You will get married and it will all be in vain. There is a good business school in the city. Secretaries always get good jobs."

"But you sent Allen to school and he became a minister."

"That is what we wanted for him."

She thought, was it his decision or yours?

A running discussion ensued between her and her parents and each time it became more evident she was not going to persuade them.

Her dreams seemed to be dashed. At a breaking point, she confided in her Aunt Katy and she offered hope although Sharon could not see. She also talked it over with her friend Joel and he suggested a scholarship. That was the best thought of all. She discussed this with her music teacher at school and they started the process. Their effort was realized when this famous music school in Upstate New York offered her a two-year complete scholarship. It was a beautiful beginning. Her parents said it was ridiculous and would not take her. Aunt Katy stepped in. Here I am today beginning my fourth year and graduate school on the horizon.

She arrived at her Advanced Theory class and there were friends that she hadn't seen since May. Everyone wanted to know about Salzburg.

Dr. Chamberlain asked her, "Would you say a few words about your experience."

Sharon offered a few words about Dr. Kreutzer and the impression he had left on her as an individual and as a musician. Her next class was much the same.

Sharon and several of her friends had lunch at the picnic table in the courtyard. She was especially glad to see Glenna. They had been roommates the first two year and remained close friends. After that she went to practice in the recital hall. Again she heard that sound of the doors, but thought nothing of it. An hour passed and she stopped and walked around the stage to give her body some relief from sitting. Practicing could be very intense because she gave all the strength she had to learning new literature. Her concentration could overwhelm her. She knew when it was time for a moment of rest.

I would like to break into some jazz. It helps to relax me, but someone will hear. After a few minutes she defied her better judgment and played for about five or six minutes. I can always say I was just exercising my fingers. Then she went back to her Bach and concerto and another hour passed. On her way out, she stopped by Dr. Bernard's office and his secretary, Dorothy said he was out but had left a message for her.

Sharon read the note. "It's about Monday's department meeting. He mentioned that when I saw him the other day."

Sharon paused, "Is everything getting off to a good start?"

"Everyone is back and we have two new string professors, a resident piano composer and instructor and a new janitor, rather a maintenance man. And as far as I know everyone is well."

"I'm glad to hear that. I'll see you Monday." As she left she grabbed a copy of the school newspaper and stuffed it in her bag.

Sharon found her bike and was on her way home. Her tiny studio seemed empty, but she played the romantic strings album and then the Chopin etudes. She curled up on the couch and was giving the music undivided attention when her phone rang.

"I just got home and safely."

"That's good. I was just thinking you would be calling soon."

"How was your first day?"

Sharon went through a few things she thought he would be interested in, "But the best thing is happening right now."

"I wish I could have stayed another day. I was looking at the calendar and maybe I could fly up on Columbus Day weekend."

"Yeah, I didn't think about that. I won't have classes but I will have to work."

"Sunday I can nurse a soda for a couple hours at the bar."

"Oh Joel, please come if you can."

They talked a few more minutes and then it was a loving goodbye.

She pulled the blanket over her and relaxed.

When she woke she saw the sunrise. A fresh breeze came through her window and with it the promise of a cooler day. After the hot summer it was a welcome change. Sharon had missed most of the unpleasant heat. It was cooler in Salzburg and on several days it had rained.

She would begin the day with her piano instructor, Professor Shepard. Along with Dr. Bernard she was instrumental in getting Sharon the scholarship for her summer in Salzburg. When she arrived Professor Shepard was waiting.

"I want to hear all about Salzburg, although I hear Dr. Bernard has asked you to say a few words Monday."

"Yes, I am gathering my thoughts and consulting my journal."

"Let's talk about it for a few moments. I know it was a wonderful experience."

Sharon elaborated briefly.

"It certainly sounds like you have been totally enriched, musically as well as personally. Well let's get to what I have planned for you this semester. This group of compositions will give you a broad study of many things. Patterns, expression, developing your technique in different ways. Also we'll work on your concerto for the winter concert and soon we must choose the music for your recital in the spring. Over the last three years, you have learned a lot of piano literature. First let's look at the Bach "Partitas" and consider them for your recital. Then we'll go over the concerto and also a Chopin. That should be a full week's work," Professor Shepard concluded.

Sharon had two more classes and then went to the recital hall to practice. She worked on her Bach for about a half-hour and was just beginning to look at her new Chopin when she heard a sneeze. She stopped abruptly, turned toward the sound, and there in the shadow sat what looked like a young man. His presence frightened her and she stared at him.

"What are you doing here?"

He got up and walked out of the shadow and she could see he was dressed rather casually, his plaid shirt and khakis wrinkled. Old sneakers gave him an unkempt appearance. His unruly dark blond hair didn't help, but as he came closer she saw that he had beautiful dark blue eyes. The new janitor she thought. They can be nice looking too, but he is big and that's scary.

"What am I doing here? I am listening to you play."

"I have permission to be here and this is a practice session not to be heard by anyone."

"But it is intriguing how you..."

She interrupted and answered again with strong expression. "But I don't like anyone to hear me while I am practicing."

"There was a young man with you and he listened, so why can't I."

"He's my friend and I don't know you. Would you please leave? Now! You have been here before. Please go and don't come back," and her gaze with those dark eyes went right through him.

"I'm sorry I have disturbed you. Please forgive me." He turned and left.

She did not like the way he looked at her.

Kind of young for a janitor, maybe a little slow and that's all he can do. The thought frightened her even more, realizing that he had been here before. He saw Joel.

At home she decided to study her concerto and music for her other classes. She thought it would be a good time to catch up on everything because next weekend I will be working.

♪

The Saturday had been long, but she felt she had accomplished much and decided to start her new novel when the phone rang. Of course it was Joel.

"Hi love. Everyone just left and believe me, it was a busy day. My sisters' kids are good but together they are active. Uncle Joel got a real workout. It is a good preparation for our kids."

"You're going too fast. That is a ways off."

"I miss you my Rose of Sharon."

"Oh honey, I miss you too. All summer I've been so busy and constantly with people. And you being here. Then all of a sudden I'm alone. Such an abrupt change. I don't like it. Even Karen went to visit her folks this weekend."

She proceeded to tell Joel all she had accomplished. Reluctantly she told him about the janitor sitting in on her practice sessions.

"Those sounds we heard and thought it a vacuum, well it was the new janitor coming in and listening to me practice. He saw you and asked me who you were. I told him my friend and my voice wasn't so sweet."

"That doesn't sound very good."

"I told him to leave and not come back."

"Good girl."

"Although he didn't seem like a bad person, he apologized and left. If he bothers me I will have to tell Dr. Bernard or somebody. Wait and see."

"I'm not happy to hear about this and me far away."

"Please don't worry, he's new and probably just likes to hear music. But a practice session isn't the most pleasant thing to listen to." She changed the subject. "Our winter concert is December seventeenth and I hope you can come up."

"Right now I am going to say yes, I'll manage somehow. Don't forget about Columbus Day weekend."

Their conversation went on for a while and then they said goodbye with love in their heart.

♫

CHAPTER FOUR

♬

*A*fter a lonely but busy Sunday, the hours passed and Monday morning opened with a sunrise. Sharon felt refreshed and the semester was off to a good start.

As she rode her bike, she rehearsed what she was going to say at the piano department meeting.

Dr. Bernard opened with a welcome back for his faculty and, "I thought I would introduce our new composer, Dr. Craig Jamieson, but he had an emergency. His mother is quite ill. She lives in Albany and he took a quick trip down to be with her. We hope for her quick recovery and I'm sure he will be back soon. His credentials are vast and impressive and I will introduce him properly at next meeting. Perhaps some of you have met him. He was here last week, also a new maintenance man, Mr. Sanderson."

Sharon thought, I've met him!

Dr. Bernard went through the important business he knew about the semester. "Our winter concert is December seventeenth and there will be a reception at Lombardi's after. Our Sharon will play the Paganini "Rhapsody" with the orchestra and that is all I know about the program at this time. Dr. Melrose needs the complete program by September thirty."

Dr. Bernard spoke about a few other things and, "Now, as you all know, Sharon spent most of her summer in Salzburg and I have asked her to say a few words about her experience."

Behind the lectern she began, "I'm not a speaker so I'll just consider that I am conversing with my friends. Being in Salzburg was even more wonderful than I even imagined. I won't talk about the city because many of you have been there. What I loved most was Dr. Will, as we fondly called him, and his approach to a composition."

As she spoke her demeanor went back to where she was describing. She was looking at the group, but there was a depth in her eyes that was far away, playing a recital, Dr. Will, new piano literature, Salzburg. She was reliving those moments the same as she had told Joel. Her expression put a smile on everyone's face and the feelings transcended to those listening. They understood because they knew the emotions and had felt a similar experience.

Her talk seemed to be enjoyed by all and Dr. Bernard closed the meeting by thanking her for taking us on the journey that so inspired her and sorry that Dr. Jamieson could not be here.

Sharon finished the day with two classes and a practice session and then biked home.

The next two days were much the same, memorizing her concerto, other studying and practice.

Thursday she found a note in her mailbox from Dr. Bernard's secretary, please come to his office Friday at one o'clock.

The next day after practice, lunch in the courtyard with friends, she made her way to Dr. Bernard's office.

She heard voices as she knocked lightly on his half-open door.

"Come in."

Sharon gasped softly. "Do I have the right time?"

She was startled for there sat the new janitor. He was dressed more neatly in a short-sleeved shirt, tie and the unruly hair, better. She stared at him and wondered why he's here too? It must be something about what I said in the recital hall.

She tried to recall the not-so-nice things and hoped that he didn't remember either.

"Sharon, thank you for coming. I'm not sure you two have met. Dr. Craig Jamieson please meet our very talented pianist, Miss Sharon Heisendorf."

Startled, Sharon put her hand over her mouth and gasped. Instantly her face became flushed exposing her discomfort. Dr. Jamieson stood up and said as he extended his hand, "It is a pleasure to be introduced properly." His face held a broad and mischievous smile.

Sharon offered her hand and stammered. "Yes, to meet properly. And I'm sorry…"

He stopped her words. "It's a pleasure to meet and more of a pleasure to hear you play. You're very talented."

"Thank you." She managed to say.

Dr. Bernard did not seem to notice the uneasiness between them and went on talking.

"Well Sharon, you are not here to just meet Dr. Jamieson, but as you know he is our new resident composer of piano literature. Hence, he presents his work at competition, which he has done several times. The competitions that he is interested in this year will not let him perform his own work. He heard you all last week and discussed it with me, and he would like for you to play his music at the competitions."

She looked at him, eyes wide. "Me!"

"Yes, you have command of the keyboard, beautiful control. I know, I heard you at practice and these attributes certainly stood out. Also Dr. Bernard tells me you can memorize very fast. A talent in itself."

"Yes, I seem to be able to do that." She knew why, the same way she could play jazz and many other things, as they say, "by ear." But that is my secret.

"Would you be interested in doing this for me? The two competitions are close geographically. We can try it and if we both agree that it isn't working out, we can take another route. But I would like for you to try." And he looked at her with his expressive blue eyes wide and head tilted forward awaiting an answer.

"Well, I am surprised. Perhaps I should look at the music first and when is the first competition. I also have a work commitment and other classes."

"The first one is November seventeenth in Albany and the next one not until February in Ohio. It is a new one as of last year and I expect it to become prestigious. We'll have more time to prepare."

"I don't know what kind of music you write."

Dr. Bernard mentioned, "You will be exempted from your classes should it interfere. So why don't you two take this discussion to your office, Dr. Jamieson, and give her all of the information and then she can make a decision."

As they walked to his office, he asked, "Where do you work?"

"I'm a waitress at the West Side Country Club."

"Sounds like a good job with good tips. I did lots of jobs getting through school."

"It can be," she responded nervously.

"Dr. Jamieson, first I must apologize for being so abrupt with you when I was practicing. I didn't realize you were our new professor. I thought you were someone else."

"I'm the one that should be apologizing. I was the intruder. It is forgotten," and he smiled, "and since were going to work together, I'm Craig and may I call you Sharon?"

Trying to relax, "Of course."

As she entered his office, a painting caught her attention. Gazing around the room she noticed others. There were some leaning against the wall.

"Are you an art collector?"

"Collector, no. I buy what I like, whether print or original. I'll tell you how I use them sometime. Have a seat and I'll show you the two compositions that I would like to present this year. It is such a short notice so if you are able to learn one I'll be happy, two ecstatic."

He opened a folder and handed her one of the pieces. He stared at her as he had in the recital hall that day he presented himself by sneezing.

"You spent the summer in Salzburg."

"Oh yes, and it was a wonderful experience."

"It is so good that it happened early in your career. You can carry the knowledge and memories as you go through life. Probably a question you've been asked many times, what impressed you most?"

"Without a doubt, Dr. Kreutzer and his approach to a composition."

"I've heard so much about him. You're so lucky."

"Oh yes, I am very grateful."

While they talked he didn't take his eyes off her. He thought, she is delicately beautiful.

She noticed this and it didn't help her to get her uneasiness under control.

She looked at the score entitled "Rhapsody Op...."

"You have no dynamics."

"Not on this one. I would like you to play through and I'll listen. I have them on another copy, but first I would like to hear you play the notes."

As Craig gathered his music he said, "Let's go to the recital hall."

In the hall he said, "Play and I will sit here and close my eyes and listen."

Sharon played through the unmarked score and thought, rhapsodic in form. Overall not too difficult, just a few passages would need a lot of work. When she finished and before Craig could say anything, she asked, "May I play it again? The first time is always not so good. I like it."

"Certainly, but you sight read very well."

She played it again and she found many places to insert expression and dynamics.

"Oh, that was so much better."

"Second time, wasn't a surprise," she answered. "I'm playing "Rhapsody on a Theme of Paganini" for the winter concert, so I have been studying the rhapsodic form."

"Our timing seems to be perfect," and he handed her a copy with the dynamics.

"This is how I would like for it to be played and you had much of the same expression that I have. Play through and then we'll talk about it." He hesitated, "Here I'm talking about all of this and you haven't said that you will do this for me."

"If you're willing to take, I'll try, for an answer, then I will. If not, maybe you should choose someone else."

"Dr. Bernard and I discussed that and he said if you are not able to, there is no one else. I will accept, I'll try. Are you free for a while?"

"Yes, I'd like to get started and do you have the other piece with you."

"I do, but first let's look at "Rhapsody." Let me play it for you."

Sharon listened carefully and followed along as he played, trying to grasp as much of the expressions as she could.

"It's unfortunate that you can't play your own composition, because you play beautifully."

"Thank you. You back at the keyboard. Let's look at the first page. I want this part to be free, up to here. Maybe even loose, not sloppy, but I want the melody in the right hand to sing over the bass, as if it was flying. And more emphasis where I have marked, sort of a waking up, an oh ... feeling. A happy emotion. In these first few lines we have to grab the listener. It takes both of us, the music and the performer."

They spent the next hour working through several pages. He explained what he was trying to say with his music, so she could interpret. Also they briefly went through the second piece, but decided to concentrate on "Rhapsody."

"We've been here a long time. I hope I haven't kept you from anything. Do you work this evening?"

"No, just Saturday evenings and Sunday through the cocktail hour."

"I won't bother you Saturday, but would it be all right if I stopped in on Sunday? I want to be sure you are off on the right track. Then I'll leave you alone for a few days."

"By then I'll probably need some directions," and she relaxed and finally broke into a big smile.

"I'll leave you now and you can continue. See you Sunday at nine o'clock."

She nodded her head as he left her to work on the new composition and her other assignments.

On her way home she thought, I hope I can do this for him, I'll feel bad if I can't.

At home she talked to Karen, fixed herself dinner and settled down to one of her many projects.

She hoped Joel would call. He had started school Wednesday and she wanted to hear all about what he was doing. And she wanted to tell him about the "janitor."

She had originally thought this year was going to be quiet, but so far it has proved to be just the opposite. She actually liked the challenge because she found much of her music rather easy to learn.

While eating she pulled her music out of her bag and looked at the newspaper that she had grabbed earlier.

"Oh my," she read aloud, "a profile of Dr. Jamieson. Received doctorate. Was in Texas before coming here. Has won two prestigious events for composing. Twenty-seven years old. Interesting. Voice major as well as piano and composition."

She thought he looked young, but probably older. I think I could like him. So far he doesn't appear forceful. Nice enough. I'll do my best.

While deep in work her phone rang. "I hoped and knew you would call. How was your first week?"

"Okay, my business classes are light this year. I'll be done with my requirements in December, so I added a class that I really like. European History. Hopefully I can get home and help Dad on weekends. He can teach me so much about running our business."

"Well, you will be relieved. The person that I thought was the new janitor is our new composition professor."

She went on to tell Joel about playing his compositions at competition.

"Yes, I am relieved, but that's really funny."

"I was embarrassed and I apologized for my harsh words. He seemed to smile through it all, so I believed him when he said it was forgotten. I didn't tell him that I thought he was the new janitor."

"Are you going to play?"

"I told him that I would try and he seemed to be satisfied. It will look good on my resume."

"Is it all right if I make reservation to fly up Columbus Day?"

"Yes. Oh yes. I wish you were closer."

"I've done this for three years. I certainly can go another. Check your Thanksgiving schedule and we can talk about it later."

"What else has happened?"

"I came up Tuesday. Just getting started. You start work tomorrow?"

"I do."

"I want you to say that to me real soon, my Rose of Sharon."

She smiled, even though Joel could not see. "I will but, we have to get through this year and don't forget you have service and me graduate school."

"I know love, but that I can make love to you makes the wait a little better."

"I love being closer now." She paused. "I start work tomorrow. I am looking forward to doing this one more year. I don't want to make a career of playing like this, but it is fun for now. We'll see how the Sunday cocktail hour turns out. I hope my car lasts."

"Sweetheart, if you need to, take it to the garage and send me the bill."

"Honey, you're so sweet and thank you, but I have tiny savings in case I have a problem. The nice thing, my rent is so reasonable. Mr. Heid has always said he wasn't trying to make money, but help us music students through college. He is a sweet man."

"Karen isn't a music student."

"She is an artist and she told me someone recommended her. We share our trials once in a while and cry in our wine," and she laughed.

"Well sweetie, it is getting late and I'll call you Sunday evening and you can tell me about the cocktail hour. I love you."

"Love you too Joel."

♫

Sharon spent the next morning at practice, concentrating on Craig's piece because she wanted to be as prepared as she could by Sunday.

In her studio she studied and readied herself for the evening at the country club.

Arriving, she felt at ease and went to Mr. Kellogg's office to let him know she was ready for the dinner hour. She had a break of five minutes after each hour, if she remembered. She would get so involved with playing and then ten o'clock would come soon. No playing with the orchestra tonight. At home she went right to bed and slept very soundly.

Sunday morning was cool again. It was a sweater and jeans day. When she arrived at school, Craig was waiting in the lobby. He saw her park her bike and opened the door.

"Riding your bike over. A great idea. Maybe I should do that. I have an apartment on the other side of the campus. Let's get started."

In the practice room, Sharon played for him what she had worked out. He mostly liked it, but clarified his intentions in several places.

"I won't keep you long, but I wanted to make sure you are on the right track. I am going to drive down and see my mother when we finish here. My mother and my girlfriend vie for my time. One lives in Buffalo and mother and stepdad live in the other direction. That doesn't make it easy."

"Dr. Bernard said your mother was ill."

"Yes, she's okay, but I thought I would spend today with them. They live north of Albany. I was fortunate to get this position and be so close. You work this afternoon."

"Yes, just a couple hours."

"I'll let you practice and I'll be on my way. How about meeting next Wednesday. This will give you time to make progress. How about one? Come to my office first and I'll give you an overview of how I composed "Rhapsody." I believe it will help you to interpret."

Craig was gone and Sharon was relieved that she could practice all of her work. Although I do need his input on his music. Perhaps I can relax after I know him better.

On her way home she smiled to herself and thought about how she interprets a composition.

Early in high school she had been developing this little journey technique. She became aware of it one day when she was reading a biography of Schubert. She dropped her book and thought so deeply about what she had just read she didn't hear her mother call. From that day on she thought, why can't I get that deep into a composer's soul when I play. She felt their spirit lives in their music and she wanted to reach that spirit to pull it into herself and play as they had wanted their music played. So she went on a little journey. Biographies helped her to find where they might have been when they composed, understanding their demeanor. Chopin with George Sand. Brahms falling in love with Clara Schumann. Scriabin in the north country.

Craig is here. I can touch him. I don't have to wander to find his spirit. He is my journey.

She thought about his music and how it could possibly relate to him. His music was stirring but he seems gentle. But he did get excited when he was explaining how he wanted a certain passage played, but yet it was in a quiet way. He seems to know what he wants and can explain it well. I feel bad I was so harsh with him. That's over. And so were her thoughts about Craig and his music.

I'm glad Joel is coming up in a few weeks. Oh how I miss him, more than ever. Loving him finally happened. The surprise was how wonderful he made me feel. I know that it is not the only thing that love is about, but it was so very wonderful. Now the cocktail hour, and her thoughts faded as she put her bike in the shed. A bit of lunch and she was on her way.

The piano in the lounge was a grand, but smaller. Sharon played the two hours. People came and went, others stayed for the whole time. She took her tips, stuck them in her purse and was on her way.

She spent the remainder of the evening studying. She counted her tips and was amazed. Thirty dollars. That will take me a long way. The phone rang and jolted her out of her financial thoughts.

A ripple of excitement went through her body. She knew it was Joel and she thought of his nearness.

"Hi love, my Rose of Sharon. I think of you every moment of the day."

"Our thoughts will have to do for now."

"How was your session with, what's his name?"

"Dr. Jamieson. We worked for about an hour. He is good at explaining things and how he wants it played."

"And how did the cocktail hour go?"

"Wonderful … I got thirty dollars in tips."

"That's good. Several persons or just one? If it is one I am going to be concerned."

"I really don't know. I don't think so."

"That I have all my requirements by December, I was thinking, what if I enlist and not wait to be drafted so I can get this over with and back to life."

"Really!" Sharon responded a little surprised although she knew he would have to fulfill his duty. "I thought you would go after graduation."

"Well I did too, but thinking about us and our future and Dad needs me." But most of all I want us to be married so you can be with me."

"It is something to think about and discuss."

They talked for a while and then said goodbye.

Joel's words distressed Sharon. Yes I want to marry him, but I want to go to graduate school. He doesn't seem to hear me when I say that. Two years in the service is a long time.

♫

CHAPTER FIVE

♫

*W*armth was in the air this mid-September, but there were sign that a new season would soon present itself boldly. Touches of color changed among the greens and the sky grayed often. The fragrance of fresh cut grass was fading.

The new week found Sharon working hard on her piano music and Craig's "Rhapsody." Everything was going very well and she had started to memorize.

Wednesday arrived and she went to Dr. Jamieson's office.

"Sharon." He smiled and offered his hand in a welcome. "I asked you to meet me here because I wanted to explain how I came to my "Rhapsody." Here is its companion," and he pointed to the painting hanging behind his desk. "My inspiration."

"Inspiration," she said softly. Craig's words caused a bewildering look and she just stared at the painting, then turned easily and looked at him.

"This is a Vlaminck print entitled *Landscape,* as you probably know."

"I'm not well versed in art."

"If you would get out your music, you can follow as I explain."

"You know the musical form of the rhapsody. Free flowing. The earth beside the houses flow from nowhere to nowhere. The roof of the houses and the yellow grass have the same freedom. Look at the clouds and you can see into the universe. The color of the sky has a high contrast and is unsettled, as does the tones hovering over the piece. There is a vivid boldness, sure of themselves. My notes put into a pattern provide a sense of color and the tones are likened to the hues in the painting." He pointed to several passages in the music and then went on. "The chords and melody are arranged to be emphatic."

He paused only to take a new breath. "Since "Rhapsody" is a one-movement form, we can't separate it into parts. Although it could easily be done in the painting. So, the houses, earth, and the sky exist for each other and because of each other, so they can be thought of as one. The light poles certainly connect the earth and the sky to make them one." He paused again.

"So this is my "Rhapsody" briefly on a canvas. Now that you know how the music was conceived, it will help to understand it better. I have allowed you to look into my mind. I don't let many people do that."

"Beautiful—just beautiful," Sharon responded softly still in awe.

"Color creates a mood. Music creates a mood and for me it can cross the spectrum from happy—sad—sensual."

She smiled and nodded her head slightly, while continuing to be deep in thought she stared at the painting and as the music was going around in her mind. This was the first time she had truly connected these two art forms and it fascinated her.

"What a beautiful way to come to a composition. So very creative." And Sharon thought, it opens so much of him to me.

"How did you come to this method?"

"Years ago. My mother paints. They are nice and she liked to go to the art gallery and I frequently went with her. And when I was around eleven or twelve we were at the gallery and classical music was playing and something caught my attention and I thought it sounded just like the painting looked ... and that was how it started."

"You started piano before that?"

"I started lessons at seven. Voice in high school. Then I started writing music officially in high school theory class. But that day in the gallery, the music and the painting are forever etched in my being."

"Do you have your students use this technique?"

"Yes, but I also try to have them find their own way, just as I did. Sometimes we have to look for things, but for me it just happened. So I try to impart they notice and listen to what is around them."

"This is such a beautiful approach. So creative. Your profile in the school newspaper said that you are also a voice major."

"I am. Singing is as much of a pleasure as

playing the piano. I'm going to start studying with Dr. Westmore soon. I don't want to be a great singer and I don't think my voice would ever develop to that, but I want to be able to sing in church, events. And one of my friends in Texas has asked me to sing at his wedding in April, so I have to get back in shape. Maybe you would accompany me."

"I did a lot in my first two years here."

"Let's talk about you. You are very talented and creative."

"My talent was just there and I developed it. I didn't have to go looking for it."

Craig did not make the connection of a natural ability.

"Have you ever written music?"

"In class, just short assignments." Sharon thought of the little piece she wrote in Salzburg for Joel. That was just for him and she did not want to play it for anyone else.

Craig broke the wonderful conversation of art and music. "Well, let's go play. I want to hear what you have accomplished since last time."

He seated himself and listened as she played through "Rhapsody" starting and stopping in a few places to correct notes or phrasing. He added comments and then said, "You're doing very well. Have you memorized any yet?"

Closing her music, she played several pages.

Craig was amazed, "You have only had this music a short time. That is fantastic. By November and even before you will do very well."

She smiled, wanting to keep her secret.

"Well, I'm not going to bother you until next Wednesday. But if you want any guidance just stop by my office or leave me a note." Craig thought that is a long time not seeing this new friend. But I can't seem too anxious. I really like her and she plays piano so very beautifully. If only Eileen played or showed some interest in music, we would be a good match.

Craig and Eileen met at a mutual friend house party about two years ago. When he came north to accept the new professorship, he wanted Eileen to come with him. The closest place where she could get a first grade teaching position was Buffalo. So she took it. Although Craig felt that he loved her there was an emptiness between them. They thought they would soon work things out and be married.

Every moment of that week Sharon devoted to practice and classes. The following Saturday morning she received a call from the Bethany Baptist Church. Would she be available to play for service tomorrow?

She had never played at this church, but she knew it was a black missionary church. Baptist had been her faith of her youth, but she had not been faithful to it since starting college. Although she knew she would feel at home and she accepted.

♫

CHAPTER SIX

♫

*T*he Sunday was bright and cheerful and as she drove to church, she thought, I'll be spending most of this day inside. Joel is far away so, I'll work.

She entered the small brick church and not knowing where to go, looked round. Just then a large man approached her and said, "You must be Miss Sharon Heisendorf."

She smiled and said, "Yes, am I in the right place?"

"You are. I'm Deacon Ely," and he extended his hand in a welcome. "I've been waiting for you. Our Mrs. Geller is very ill and we need someone to fill in for her. Come with me. The auditorium is just through these doors."

It had a vaulted ceiling and held a feeling of reverence. There were many people already there for the service. The whisper of conversation melded into a soft lull as they spoke quietly to each other or prayed aloud so God would be sure to hear.

She followed Deacon Ely to the piano at the

side of the auditorium.

"Here is the program and hymnal and I have marked the pages for you. You can start in about ten minutes and play while everyone gathers for the service. We will sing all four verses of the three songs. The choir director will give you all of the cues that you need. You will play while the offering plate is being passed."

"I brought a short quiet piece for that."

"I believe that is all and after the service, please stop by my office and I will pay you."

Sharon thanked him and seated herself near the piano to wait a few minutes. She had played for church services, funerals and revival meeting at home.

After the service, several people came and thanked her and said how much they enjoyed her playing.

At Deacon Ely's office, "Miss Sharon, that was beautiful. And I'm going to get ahead of myself, but would you be able to take this as a full-time position at least until Mrs. Geller is well? It would be just Sunday mornings."

"Yes, I would be interested to help out."

"That would be good and we won't have to look further. We will see you next Sunday and have a good day."

On her way home, she thought, extra money will come in handy for graduate school. I hope I'm not taking on too much. It is not far so I'll be home in time to eat and go to the country club.

The afternoon hour of playing was much the same as last week. In the evening she worked on memorizing music. After eating she called Joel, but he wasn't there and she left a message. About an hour later he called and she told him about playing at church and it being a steady job.

"I made reservations to fly up Friday afternoon on the seventeenth and then back on Monday."

"I'll be so happy to see you. I've been busy and the year just started," Sharon replied with a bit of stress in her voice.

"Sharon, please don't overdo it."

"I won't. I love being busy, but sometimes it gets a bit overwhelming until it's over, then I think, that wasn't so bad."

"How is everything going for you?"

"Busier than I thought, but okay. I don't have classes on Friday and that's good, when I come up to see you or go home and help Dad. They are working hard to get several projects done before the weather turns."

"When you come up I have to work."

"That's okay, I am going to bring books and class work."

They talked for a long time not saying much, but just the nearness of hearing each other's voice, a laugh or a sigh. Sharing what each day had brought and would bring in the next few weeks. Distance was overcome with soft words.

"We've talked ourselves out, so honey, I love you and will say goodnight."

"Oh Joel, I love you too, I can't wait two weeks."

She hung up her phone and rolled herself in the

big heavy blanket and pretended that he was near. She lay quietly waiting for him to hold her close and kiss her. But she awoke from her little dream to reality and realized he was far away.

♫

CHAPTER SEVEN

♫

*I*n this new week, just after lunch, Sharon went to practice and shortly thereafter Craig quietly slipped in, sat down, and motioned for her to keep playing. He watched her with his heart. Her long black hair fell randomly off and on her face as she worked passages of his "Rhapsody."

After a few moments she stopped and smiled at him. "How am I doing?"

He didn't answer but just stared with a tender smile locked on his face. A moment passed and Sharon waved slightly to break his thought that appeared to be very deep. She thought he was listening and didn't stop when she did.

"Oh," he finally said.

"Is something wrong?" she quietly asked. "You looked so far away."

"Oh no, nothing is wrong, but so right. You just pulled me right in." Sharon missed what he meant.

"I have a few minutes, let's check page three."

They worked through the page several times

and then he said, "Could I intrude on you Saturday morning and we can cover more."

"Sure. Morning is fine."

"How about ten. Since we can't use the hall, why don't you come over to my house? My piano arrived and they tuned it yesterday. With you playing I can hear it from across the room."

"No. I wouldn't want to interrupt your morning and I will have to practice for quite a while."

"That's not a problem. After we go over "Rhapsody" you can have the piano all to yourself. I have compositions to grade and a test to prepare. Much to do."

"I'll disturb the other people in the house."

"That is not a problem either. My landlady is older and she is the only one there besides me. My piano is on the ground floor and all of my living space. You can look into the garden. It's losing its color, but still a nice setting. It will provide a beautiful scene when the snow falls." He paused, "I'll come and get you and take you home when you're done playing."

"Sounds so much better than one of those little rooms."

"Is that a yes?"

She smiled calmly and saying to herself, you have won. "Okay." She tilted her head.

"May I have your phone number in case something comes up? But I plan to be here all weekend." However he really didn't.

Craig pulled out a small tablet from his pocket and wrote her number then his and handed it to her.

"Now, where do you live? Somewhere close."

"Cumberland Street 921. I have a tiny studio on the second floor."

"I like this neighborhood, the old homes."

"Me too. So much better for studying. I lived in the dorm the first two years."

"It is a nice place to go to school and a nice place to work." He glanced at his watch and said, "I have to get to my class. Will be in touch before Saturday. It will be a much better practice session."

Craig left feeling satisfied that he would see her in a nicer setting, his own little home. I really like being with this girl. She is sweet with such a gentle way, but so dynamic at the keyboard. And so enjoyable to look at. Not tall, not short, pleasingly in between.

♫

Friday came fast and Sharon went to practice early. She was thinking of all of the things that were suddenly on her itinerary.

As she rode home she could feel the air had turned cooler and today there was no sun. Fall was making its appearance in a kind and gentle way, but demanded notice. The remainder of her day was deep in music.

It was later than usual when she finished her light dinner so she decided to relax and watch television before going to sleep. But the phone rang and changed her plans. She thought, is it Craig or Joel?

"Sharon it's Craig. Are we still on for practice tomorrow?"

"If you're sure you want me to intrude."

"Again, no problem. How's a little before ten."

Shortly thereafter her phone rang again. Of course it had to be Joel.

"Hi love." He started the conversation.

"Where are you sweetie?"

"I'm home. I worked with Dad today and will do so tomorrow. If I stay at school it is a waste of time. The guys drink and chase girls. I'm tired of those parties and I have a very special girl. Anything new."

"Same stuff, music, music and more music."

They discussed their week and what they could do next weekend other than love each other.

"I'll be there around noon. So can you pick me up or should I get a cab?"

"I'll be there. I'll practice and then come out. There is a lot to do. The art calendar is full, but no faculty recital that weekend. Everyone will be gone or just quietly resting at home."

"How is the competition piece coming along?"

"I think I can learn it in time to play."

"We just finished dinner. Dad and I were late tonight. So now I am going to read and tomorrow go with Dad again. I'll call you when I get back to school. Sweetheart, hold that pillow tonight and pretend it's me."

She laughed. "But you are not that soft. I'd have to stretch my imagination."

"I suppose you're right. Anyway, I love you Sharon and will call Sunday."

"Love you too Joel."

♫

Saturday morning Sharon was up early and her second cup of coffee completed her steps to waking. She quickly dressed, jeans and sweater, and did some studying before Craig would arrive. A little before ten she went down to the front porch, where the air was fresh and the sun was bright. She thought, I don't know what kind of a car he has.

Soon a black Chevrolet drove slowly down her street and stopped in front and Craig got out.

Sharon walked to the car.

He said, "Good morning. You are very prompt."

She only nodded her head slightly and wondered if she was doing the right thing. Little late to turn back.

"This is a beautiful street. I love the gaslights. They are on my street too."

"In winter it is so picturesque. The snow creates a wonderful atmosphere. It's quiet and you can see the horse and carriage if you look. And in the summer everyone plants colorful flowers."

"You lived here last year?"

"Yeah. I did. I was lucky to find it. It's small, but I don't need a lot of room."

On their way to his house they talked about the neighborhood, the campus and how it melded so well.

"It is a little world all of its own," Craig offered.

"We call it the Music Box. There is entertainment at school. Four blocks over there are

74

small restaurants, a few shops and a movie theatre. We wouldn't have to leave this area for four years." Sharon laughed and appeared a bit more relaxed.

Hardly five minutes passed and they were at Craig's. He opened the door for her and said, "Come on in. The place is in good shape, yet."

This house too was an old Victorian with the ornamentation of the times. Lovely carved woodwork framed the large door. Inside the outer foyer Craig said, "Down these stairs is my little home for now."

He unlocked the door at the foot of the stairs and it opened into a living room, comfortable with mismatched furniture. The soft blue walls were bare of decoration. Sharon quickly noticed a large sound system and many records and a bookcase, full.

"I live rather casually and I haven't had a chance to get anything on the wall. I'll show you around. Over there is the kitchen. I don't cook very well, but I am doing better. An eating nook." And he pointed down a short hall. "A bedroom and bath."

She followed him through the living room and into a larger room. "This is where I have my piano."

In the middle of the room was a beautiful old Bechstein, presenting itself like a jewel.

"Oh." Sharon gasped. "It's magnificent." She walked to it slowly. "Am I dreaming? Is it real?"

"Very real." He smiled so warmly.

She touched the woodwork and then lightly played a chord. Softly she asked, "Where did you get it?"

"My mother found it when I entered high school."

"I hope you have its history."

"We do. Made in Berlin and it came to Texas in 1932 with a wealthy family from Germany. It stayed with them until 1947 and no one in their family wanted it. My mother was there and bought it for me. It's here now. I hope to stay here for a while. It is a nice home."

"You are so lucky and your mother is so nice."

"She is a nice mom. Play it for me."

Sharon sat down and thought for a moment. What will do justice to this wonderful instrument … my Bach, that I just finished memorizing?

Craig watched as she immediately lost herself in the notes that were written long ago. Little black symbols had become sound to transcend time. Her solid touch, with feeling, brought the music and the instrument together as one. Craig closed his eyes and thought he was in Bach's studio, but soon realized he was here and this beautiful girl with the face of an angel and long black hair was creating this heavenly music.

When she finished he could see that she was with him again. She lifted her head and smiled playfully as if she had done something special.

Craig thought that she had.

He shook his head. "You don't know how wonderful you made my piano sound."

"Thank you. I just finished memorizing it."

"You played it superbly. I know that "Partita" and I could not find a thing wrong with it."

"I'll probably play it for my recital. They are so wonderful to play and listen to."

"It's wonderful to hear it played."

Sharon relaxed and glanced around the room. The walls were the same soft blue as the living room. Several framed prints of the masters hung with dignity. A van Gogh, a Pissarro, that she recognized, others she did not. A quaint old desk and two comfortable chairs, she was sure, for reading. And by their side another large bookcase filled with what looked like a conglomerate of books and music. On the floor was an oriental rug of deep blues and reds. Beyond the double French doors was a garden that had passed its prime and ready to slip into another season.

"This is a great room to play and for you to compose. You have your paintings and a garden to look into. It provides a real live scene. You could make a four season composition."

"I have a similar one."

"No one else is here but you?"

"Just me and Mrs. Zachery. She taught at school for years and realized that some of us professors needed a piano. She was in contact with Dr. Bernard and he told me about it. I was really lucky."

"Let's get to work on "Rhapsody" and then I'll let you practice for as long as you want."

Twelve o'clock came fast and she thought, I had better go home. This has been the best practice time in all my years. This piano is a treasure. If only I can have one like it someday.

She called, "Craig."

"I'm here," he said as he walked in the room. "I just finished grading papers."

"It is twelve o'clock and I had better go home."

"Okay, but first I fixed a little lunch. I'm not a

cook, but I made us sandwiches and I have a salad. After we eat I'll take you home. What would you like to drink, coffee, soda and I have milk."

"You shouldn't have," she said as she got up from the piano bench.

Looking bewildered. "You do eat lunch?"

She replied only with a smile that grabbed his heart.

"Well, I was a little hungry, thought you would be too after that workout at the piano."

She only smiled again. Craig thought, if she keeps doing that any longer ... so innocent and yet so seductive.

"Your playing is like a painting. It has so many levels. You have such command of the softs and louds. Your arpeggios are so clear and even."

He walked over to her and took her hands in his, "Your hands are not large and they look so delicate, but they are so strong. I'm just in awe of your playing. Each time you go over a passage I can hear improvement."

"That's good, because sometimes I'm not sure."

"Come on to the table."

He pulled the chair for her and she sat down to the lunch Craig had prepared.

"It's so nice of you." Sharon did not know how much to say to him, for she felt she still did not know him very well.

"What's on your agenda for tomorrow?"

Sharon wondered if he wanted to get together again. She realized that he was anxious to make progress on his composition. We don't have too much time.

"I'm going to play for the Bethany Missionary Church morning service, then work in the afternoon."

"Is playing churches another job?"

"This is possibly long term. The lady that usually plays is ill. Deacon Ely talked like she would not be able to come back. Although he didn't say what was wrong."

"You could play in bigger churches."

"Most have organs and that is not my strong point. I'm listed at several for piano, but I don't always get a call. The pay at Bethany isn't much, but it's steady. I have to save for graduate school."

"I can relate to funds. My father died just before I graduated from high school. Although, he had set up a trust fund for my sister and me for college. And we both worked and we made it."

"I'm sorry to hear that you lost him in your young life. Was it a surprise?"

"He had cancer. It came and went fast. It jolted all of us. But my mother remarried and her new husband lives near Albany, so she moved there."

"It is bad at any time to lose a parent, but you were almost an adult and that probably made a bit of a difference."

"It did somewhat. My stepdad is a great guy, he's a lawyer. I was glad to get a position near them. Your folks help you?"

"No. They thought going to music school was a waste of their money. Other than gifts or clothing, they haven't contributed at all. But they contributed a lot to my brother who went to divinity school."

"He's a minister?"

"Yes, he has a Baptist church in southern Missouri. He is six years older than me."

"And you're all of twenty-two."

She gave him that smile again.

"Do you resent their partiality?" He asked with great concern.

"Sometimes, but it is unconventional in some ways. I suppose I respect their decision. Do I have a choice? My Aunt Katy doesn't agree with my parents and sends me money occasionally. She is my favorite aunt and her son, Jack, is quite well off, so she shares with me. So when I got my scholarship I was a happy little girl. I took it and ran."

Sharon thought I am telling this person about things that I usually keep to myself.

"You certainly did, all the way to graduate school."

"I am not there yet."

"You'll make it. You have talent and determination. It is a combination for success."

They finished their lunch and Sharon thanked him warmly. "I really enjoyed playing your piano. I must go because I have some theory to do before I go to work tonight. I'm going to be busy all day tomorrow."

"How do you get there, a cab?"

"No, I have a car. I only drive it to work."

Craig thought, I can't offer her a ride.

On the way to her house he asked, "Can we get together Tuesday, perhaps?"

"I will practice from nine till eleven."

"I have a class from nine to ten, so if it is all right with you, I'll stop in. I don't believe you will need me for a while after that. I am going away the Columbus Day break and will see you sometime after that. I am going to visit with my friend. Are you going to stay here?"

"Yes, I have to work and it will give me time to practice on my music."

"Without me bothering you."

"No, you don't bother me, you help me," she said happily and with a smile.

I'm glad he won't be around, because I want to spend all of my time with Joel.

As Craig drove away, his thoughts were confusing to him. I really like being with this girl. I thought I loved Eileen, but now I'm not so sure. If only she cared about music. Sometimes I'm not sure she hears what I play for her. The emotion just isn't there. But with Sharon I feel there is an attachment and we both love the same thing and share so very well. But I have just met her. I'm not going to think about anything other than, she is going to play for me. Yeah, what about that guy I first saw her with. I haven't seen him around. Just a friend. And it wouldn't be nice if I asked her. She might tell me that it is none of my business. I remembered how stern she was with me that day in the auditorium at the beginning of classes. Those dark eyes were as strong as lightning bolts. I thought I had better get out of there before I get fried. She didn't realize that I was an instructor and he smiled to himself.

Craig went back to his house, gathered a few things and was on his way to Buffalo to visit Eileen for the remainder of the weekend.

♫

CHAPTER EIGHT

♪

*F*riday morning after practice Sharon went to the airport to get Joel. She was bubbling with excitement. Her heart was filled with the real and imagined passion for him. They caught sight of each other as he came off the plane. Meeting, they held each other, their eyes closed and exchanging silent and unseen love between them.

"Love you my Rose of Sharon," he whispered, her hair hiding his words for only her to hear.

"So glad you could come up."

They broke their embrace and just smiled at each other.

"Anything other than that?" She pointed to his carry-on that he had dropped when he took her in his arms.

"No."

She handed him her keys and they were on their way to her car.

"How has it been running?"

"Good. I only drive it to the country club. I

have to work this weekend."

"You mentioned. I brought work with me. I have two papers to write."

They drove home and in her studio they took off their jackets. She took both his hands and walking backward leading him into her bedroom. "I don't want to wait until tonight."

"Neither do I."

As they undressed each other they were playful. "How I have lived this moment and now it is real. To touch you, to kiss you, to feel you next to me."

It was a passionate togetherness, the only way they could be. Time lost had to be recaptured and then they slept in each other's arms as the day moved on.

At dinner Joel brought up marriage again. "Can we get engaged at Christmas and then get married after you graduate?"

"But Joel, have you thought about the two years in service and I want to go to graduate school."

"I have, that is why I want to talk about it. I've thought about not going back to school in January. I can graduate in December and then enlist."

She looked strangely at him but he continued. "We can get married after you graduate and you can go with me or stay at home, whatever you want to do."

Emphatically, "I want to go to graduate school."

"My love, I want you to be my wife. I've known that for so long."

"And Joel, I want to be your wife."

"Well then what is wrong here?"

"I want to go to graduate school because I want

to play recitals, or get a job in a college and without that I won't be able to. You knew that was my goal all along."

"Dad wants me to take over his business as soon as I can. I can't do that until I'm home. Honey, we'll have a nice life. There are a lot of places at home where you express your talent."

"I know, but Joel one more time, I have to go to graduate school, at least. I have to be in one place to do that. I can't follow you around the world."

She saw on his face the most distressed look she had ever seen him display. "Well, I suppose we had better talk about this. Looks like I have some convincing to do."

Sharon wondered if he had heard her at all. She was surprised at his planning, because he knew what she wanted to do, but didn't seem to consider her beyond getting married.

"I don't want this weekend to be bogged with serious stuff. I just want to love you."

"What do you want to do tomorrow?" she asked, trying to bring the conversation back to a better tone.

"First let's think of tonight."

♫

A gentle touch and a passionate kiss opened this bright and sunny October day. The freshness had a new fragrance. Long after the sun was up, Sharon and Joel were still nestled in each other's arms.

Coffee and a small breakfast were delayed but

they enjoyed it just the same.

They went to school so Sharon could practice. It had to be in the small room, but Joel stayed near. In the afternoon, they went for a walk and to the art gallery. After an uneventful dinner, without marriage discussions, he took her to work at the country club. He did not stay but went back to her studio and worked on his two papers for school. Around nine o'clock he went back to get her. He nursed a Coke until she was through playing.

They made their way home and met the night in a most awesome way.

♫

Sunday Joel went to church with her. Baptist was not his faith, but he had attended church with her many times.

Sharon and Joel stopped at Deacon Ely's office and she introduced Joel. Deacon asked them to sit down.

"I know that you are a student and I would like to put a proposal forward. We have a number of young children, age's seven to eleven, in our congregation and they do not get any musical training. We deacons were wondering if you could spend a couple hours on Saturday morning imparting musical knowledge. We would leave it up to you, just something to broaden their knowledge. Of course there would be a small salary for your services."

"Oh my, I would like to think about this."

"That is good. I was afraid that you would say

no for some good reason."

"Let me think it over and talk again."

"Wonderful. Is your career toward teaching?"

Sharon smiled at Joel and thought I don't really know where my career is headed.

"I hope to perform as well as teach."

"Well, let's talk about this next weekend, and you can say yes or no and have some ideas. Nice to meet you Mr. Steiner and do come back. We welcome you with Miss Sharon."

As they drove home, they discussed the pros and cons of a job like this and at this time.

"I'm really going to have to think hard about this. I would have to prepare something that would interest all those ages at one time. He didn't say about how many children there are."

"No he didn't. Honey, I can't make a decision for you, but it seems like you have a lot going on. I don't want you to get bogged down."

"I know that. One thing I don't have is a social life or do any partying." And she laughed. "You are my social life and you are far away."

After a quick lunch, Joel drove her to the country club for the Sunday hour. He had decided to stay and listen to her play.

They walked hand in hand into the lounge.

"I'm going to play for you today and you will know that because you will be able to feel from across the room. They are going to be love songs."

"I can recognize that feeling because you have done this for me so many times before."

"Maggie is serving today. She is real nice."

"Hi Shar," Maggie said.

"Maggie, this is my friend Joel and he is going to wait for me."

"Oh I have just the spot for you. That chair in the corner. It's comfy and you can listen. What can I get you?"

"Nice to meet you. Just a Coke. Thank you."

She looked at Sharon, "Honey what do you want for your break?"

"Just water, please."

"I'll be back and I'll stop over and keep you company when I'm not busy," Maggie said to Joel.

"My piano is waiting." She squeezed his hand and he went to the comfy chair in the corner.

One solid hour of love songs followed. She played them all in the same key as not to interrupt the flow to the listener. She would weave one song into another. She would pause occasionally and accept a gentle and warm applause. Quietly she would say, thank you. At the end of the hour she slipped off the bench and joined Joel for a quick rest and sip of water.

At the end of the two hours, she glanced at Joel and played the song she wrote for him in Salzburg. He knew and smiled in acceptance.

They said goodbye to Maggie and were on their way home. There was a comfortable silence between them as they drove.

"Do you want to change into something more casual before we eat? You look so beautiful and I look so casual they would throw me out."

"Yes I would. It will only take a moment."

At dinner they again started talking about their

future. "How do you feel about my enlisting in December?"

"It comes as a surprise, so I haven't thought about it yet, but perhaps it might be a good idea to get it over with. I need you, your dad needs you. Have you talked it over with them?"

"I mentioned it briefly and they said think about it. Sounded like they hoped I would forget."

As they ate, talking about their future ceased.

Back at Sharon's studio they both delved into some studying before closing the day with love.

♫

Morning came quickly. After staying in bed half of the day they slowly met the hour of twelve. Breakfast or was it lunch. Lightly nibbling at the nourishment, their conversation was casual and somber. Both felt a heaviness because of the parting that neither wanted.

"Have you decided on your recital program?"

"Mostly."

"When is it?"

"Late. First part of May."

"If I enlist, I may not be here. Not good."

"I know."

"But I am looking forward to the Christmas concert. Have you started practicing with the orchestra?"

"This week."

"When is the competition?"

"The seventeenth and eighteenth. Week before

Thanksgiving. It goes until Saturday, but I play on Friday at ten, so we have to go down the day before. I'll only miss classes on Thursday. That is all I know."

She did not tell Joel that she had practiced at Craig's house. She did not think that it was important. She wanted to be with Joel and not talk about other things.

"What about Thanksgiving?"

"I have been thinking about it and I think I will fly home. We don't have classes Wednesday and I'll come back Saturday morning. That way I won't miss work. I haven't been home since July. It will be nice to see everybody. We can make the rounds together."

"Let's check about reservations when we go to the airport today. Then I will know when to come and get you. Your mom and dad will probably be working."

"Yeah, good idea. I will have to come back Saturday morning. Remember I have two jobs. Maybe I can get a late Tuesday flight."

Joel thought, I can pay for her ticket and she won't have much to say about it.

"Speaking of airports, I had better get things together. Dad is going to pick me up and I'll go home and get my car and go on to school."

"How much did you get accomplished with your papers?"

"More than I expected."

As they drove to the airport neither said much. They just held hands and had an almost sad smile for each other.

There was a Tuesday flight at four-fifteen.

They made reservations and Joel pulled out his wallet and Sharon gave him a look. "Put that away."

Softly, "You don't want to make a scene."

Her big eyes flashed, but he just gave her a look saying, I won.

"Honey, you think yourself clever."

"You can't be mad at me now, I'm leaving."

She relaxed her demeanor to warm. "No, I'm not, how could I be."

"Sweetheart, I see how hard you work and I am so proud of you doing it all by yourself."

They stepped away from the ticket counter and he put his arm around her and whispered, "I love you, and I want to do for you all I can."

"That's the call to board. I am going to have a lot of making up to you someday."

They waited for a few more moments. Not caring who would be watching, he turned and kissed her very tenderly, but passionately.

He walked toward the tube, turned and gave her one last wave and a smile.

She threw him a kiss with a smile.

As she drove home she was still warm from his last embrace, but there was uneasiness in her heart. Tears hung loosely in her eyes. She tried not to think of their problem. It was counter to what she wanted and what Joel wanted as their life together. She thought, we just went along falling in love and not even talking about how our lives would fit together.

♫

CHAPTER NINE

♫

*E*mptiness swelled in Sharon's heart, but she spent the remainder of this holiday week doing the usual, studying, memorizing. Friday she went to practice early because in the evening she wanted to go to Professor Billings' piano recital. This was the first of the year. Every other Friday there would be a faculty member playing and these events were very popular with the students as well as the public.

After her long day, she made her way back to school. She decided to walk. There was a chill in the air and the smoke from the fireplaces told that fall was here. Each day brought more gold and reds to the trees. As she walked, she thought of Joel wanting to get married before she finished graduate school. If we get married I may never be able to. He just doesn't understand.

The recitals were in the small auditorium where Sharon practiced. She walked in and saw Glenna and she motioned to her to join them.

"Professor Billings is so popular, he gets a big

group and not just from us students," Sharon said.

"I hear he is going to retire," Kay added

"Really, I haven't heard that."

"There's Professor Jamieson. You're playing his competition?" Glenna asked.

"He is so handsome. I just want to run my hands through that blond mess," Kay softly said. "Is he nice?"

"He really is," Sharon added, "and he is quite considerate and explains things really well."

"Kelly is in one of his classes and she likes him."

About that time he spotted Sharon and made his way to her.

"I haven't seen you all week. How is the piece going?"

"Very well. When do you want to get together?"

"How about tomorrow. I'll talk to you after the recital," he said just as they lowered the lights.

Sharon was the envy of all of the girl piano students because she had Craig's attention.

She settled and relaxed, ready to listen intently to every note that Professor Billings was going to play. That didn't happen. Her thought immediately went to Joel going into the service and soon. I won't get to talk to him when I want to. I won't be able to see him as often. I have to go to graduate school. Nothing is going to stop me. Getting married. Playing for Craig. All of my commitments here at school.

Sharon was jolted out of her thoughts by the applause that ended the recital. She wasn't sure how much she actually heard, but she joined the applause.

Oh, I have to talk to Craig she thought. She said goodbye to her friends and looked around for him. Just then he caught her attention.

"He plays so very wonderfully. I don't need to ask how you liked it." Craig asked.

"He's one of my favorites here at school."

"He plays with such expression."

Sharon nodded her head yes and smiled while Craig stared at her.

He realized what he was doing and said, "Did you ride your bike over?"

"No, I walked. I thought I needed the exercise and it is such a nice evening."

"Well, let me drive you home. I know that it is not too far but it's dark."

She laughed, "I don't want to put you out."

"Come on, it won't be putting me out."

As they walked to his car he said, "Do you want to meet tomorrow morning?"

"Tomorrow, okay."

"How about at my house again. I really loved hearing you play."

"Well, I planned to spend more than two hours so that would really disturb you."

"No it won't, because I have several hours of student work and that would force me to get it done. We can go over "Rhapsody" and then you can play as long as you want. All day if you like."

"Oh Craig, are you sure? I do love your piano."

The drive to Sharon's house was short and she thanked him and said, "If you insist I'll see you tomorrow. Want to start earlier?"

"I'd like that. Nine."

♫

She was ready and waiting Saturday morning. On the way to his house she told him what Deacon Ely had asked of her.

"What did you tell him?"

"Nothing, but that I would think it over. It sounds like a big group and different ages could cause a problem. It would have to be something that interested all ages. Listening to classical music would not be ideal for all. I would like to have your ideas."

"Let's talk about it when I fix lunch," and he smiled mischievously.

Her only response was, "Craig."

Inside he said, "Let me have your jacket and we can get to work on "Rhapsody" and then I'll leave you alone."

She made her way to the piano and he couldn't take his eyes off her. He thought this girl is so special.

After working, Craig said, "I think you will do okay. We still have four weeks."

"I have it pretty well memorized, but it needs some polishing. You are a good instructor," and she smiled at him.

It warmed his heart. "Thank you."

While they were having their lunch Craig asked her about Salzburg. They had not talked about it. Getting his composition perfected had taken all of their time. They also talked about what the deacon had proposed, but decided to discuss it more, later.

In the early afternoon, Sharon decided that she had worked enough and asked Craig to take her home. He did and was on his way to Buffalo to see Eileen.

It was a busy afternoon for Sharon, and after a small dinner, she was on her way to the country club. While driving her thoughts, again, were troubling. What if Joel says no to graduate school? Would I give him up?

The country club was crowded for dinner and Sharon delighted them with wonderful piano selections. She kept them at a slow or medium pace and reserved the jazz for the cocktail hour. She did not have to play with the orchestra, so she made her way home at ten o'clock.

♫

The next week she did not see Craig until Thursday and he asked, "Do you have a moment? I'll give you the schedule for Albany."

"I have an hour to be exact."

"Come on in my office."

He sat down at his desk and motioned for her to sit also. He opened a folder and read her the schedule.

"You will play on the seventeenth at ten o'clock and we can leave soon after. Since you play early, we will have to go down the day before. We'll drive down. Leave in the early afternoon, have dinner and get a good night's sleep. I have made hotel reservations for us for the one night. After, I am going to visit my mother for the weekend. I will put you on the train at two-twenty for home. Get a cab and I will reimburse you. It might be a little late. You can go with me to visit my mother if you want."

"No, I'll come home. I have to work."

"I would like to start polishing "Rhapsody." Do you work in the evenings?"

"No, just weekends. Nor do I have any commitments on Friday. I usually study and practice."

"I have one class at ten. We might do something then. Now that I know your schedule, I can intrude, if you let me. So can we work in the evening?"

"That would be fine."

"I am going to be gone the next two weekends."

Craig's girlfriend, Eileen, had been upset with him because he would arrive so late on Saturday, so he decided to be a little more generous with his time.

Sharon did not give any thought to Craig's plans. I don't always need him.

"How about Tuesday and Thursday evenings next week and then see how much time we need? At my house."

♫

The next week they worked very diligently, smoothing passages the way Craig wanted them played. They were both very satisfied with the overall progress.

Sharon went to work on Saturday evening at the country club. Craig also decided to check it out.

He walked in the bar around nine o'clock and

wondered where she would be working, the lounge or waiting the dinner tables. He sat at the bar and ordered a drink. I'll just wait here and listen to the piano player. Moments passed and he didn't see her, but he was very much enjoying the music. He listened and thought how beautiful. This guy is very talented. That jazz is so delicate and the soft selections were rich with arpeggios, the chords so full. He listened for a while longer just analyzing his playing. Who is this guy? He decided to look in the dining room. "Oh my god," he said aloud, but softly. "A waitress! Just wait!"

At ten o'clock Sharon quit playing and the orchestra struck up a few notes for dancing. She exited down a long hall.

I hope there is not a back door and I'll miss her. He waited and shortly she came through and he said, "Excuse me, may I have this dance?"

Startled, she stopped short and gasps, her hand over her mouth.

"What are you doing here? You said you were going to be away."

He smiled. "My plans changed so I thought I would come out and have you serve me a drink. Did you finish your tables and then just casually go play the piano?" he asked with a slight smile.

"I don't do any serving. I just play."

"And it sounded wonderful, especially how you play jazz."

"Oh Craig…"

"Let's dance and then you can talk to me."

She conceded and they walked to the floor and were immediately lost among others.

Craig thought at last I can hold this beautiful girl close. I've wanted to do this for so long.

"Why are you here?"

"I came out to see you." And he could feel that she was stiff.

"Relax. It's okay."

"Please don't tell anyone that I play here. I need to work and I'm not sure school would like it."

He pulled her a little closer and he could feel that she had relaxed somewhat. His lips met her forehead and he kissed her.

"I'm not sure anyone would care. It is the school that doesn't accept jazz as musical form. And that brings up the subject—where did you learn to play like that. I listened to you for almost a half-hour before I knew it was you."

"Oh Craig it's natural. I play by ear and as you know I have been trained classically."

"Oh, of course. Why didn't I think! That you play so well and memorize so fast it all makes sense now. You don't know how beautiful you make that instrument sound. Especially mine."

"Dr. Jamieson..."

"Craig—please."

"Please keep this a secret," she said softly but emphatically.

"I would never say anything you didn't want me to." He said as he gently pushed her head on his shoulder and he snuggled his head next to hers. "I want to talk about how you developed your jazz, but for now, I want to enjoy dancing."

The orchestra stopped after a while and Sharon

said, "This has certainly been a surprise, but now I have to go home. I have a busy tomorrow."

"Would you like to get a coffee or something?"

"No. Some other time—maybe."

"If you drove out, I'll follow you."

At home they parked their cars and found the porch swing comfortable.

"This was a surprise for both of us."

"It sure was. You were the last person I thought I would see at the country club."

"And you were the last person that I thought would be playing piano there."

"How long have you been doing this?"

"Beginning of my first year here and have been doing it ever since. In September Mr. Kellogg started the cocktail hour on Sunday afternoon."

"I am astounded again. When I first heard you play in the auditorium I knew that you were special and now even more so."

"Oh Craig," and she turned to him, "it comes so natural, otherwise I can't explain it."

"When did you first discover this talent?

"My brother started lessons and I would mimic what he played. When I was about seven mother started lessons for me. When I was eleven I changed teachers and she encouraged light jazz or something like. I learned to modulate and use chords, but she also introduced me to classical literature and I loved it. I did theory in high school against my parents' wishes. It was a good thing my mother worked because I was not allowed to play jazz at home. They thought it was too wild, or not God's music."

"Oh my," was Craig's response. "And couldn't they hear your talent?"

"Well I guess they did, but thought it wouldn't be a way to a good job."

"I respect your parents, but they are so wrong."

"This is nice just talking to you, but I have an early morning so I had better get to bed."

Oh my Craig thought. "I'll be on my way. How about Tuesday and Thursday this week and maybe Friday during the day? Then we'll have just one week after that."

"That's okay. I have to start working with the orchestra for the Christmas concert."

"I'll stop in and listen."

"Do that."

"I am going to start voice lessons with Dr. Westmore next week. He knows that I am spending a lot of time getting "Rhapsody" ready. We don't expect to get much accomplished but we want to get started. Maybe one evening when you're at my house you would play for me. I keep asking so much of you. If you don't want to, I'll understand."

"No, I'd love to. I have accompanied a lot."

"Just a piece or two for now."

Even in the darkness he could see that she smiled softly at him.

"I'll go."

They both got up and he kissed her lightly on the cheek. "Thank you for the dance."

♫

The next week when he picked her up she felt a bit apprehensive. She didn't say much on the way to his house.

He felt that she was uncomfortable and at the piano he sat down beside her and turned her face to his. "Smile for me." And she did. "That's better. I'm sorry if I have made your uncomfortable, but it's all right. We're friends, friends share. You have become special to me."

Softly she said, "Thank you. I will relax because I want to play perfectly for you."

After Friday practice they talked about the Saturday musical session at the church. Craig said, "I have a suggestion. A choir."

Her eyes lit up. "I don't sing, I play piano."

"But I know all about directing a choir."

"Oh Craig."

"I wouldn't ask to be paid, because I have a salary. You could play and I could direct a little children's choir. Singing, all of the children could participate. And we could do other types of musical instructions, something related to the music that we are singing. How does that sound?"

"I like that. Do you want me to present it to Deacon?"

"Would you like for me to go with you and we'll talk to him together? I'll explain that I'm a choral director and sing and would volunteer my time. Since there would be the two of us, we could divide the children into like age groups and do something else on occasion."

"Want to go this Sunday? He will probably

have to think about it too."

"Yes. The Baptist Church I have never been to. From church to the cocktail hour is quite a jump."

"It is and my parents would think this evil."

"Do they think you are a waitress as I did?"

"They do and don't even approve of that. I have to pay my rent."

After the service, they talked to Deacon Ely and he liked their proposal, especially the choir. He said he would present it to the other deacons and perhaps talk to some of the children and get their reaction.

On their way to her house he asked "How do you like playing the cocktail hour?"

"It seems to be working. There are always people there listening. It's fun and the extra money goes for grad school."

"This week, if you can, let's spend some time every evening and then we can judge what to do next."

"I'll do my other practicing at school and we'll devote all of the time to "Rhapsody.""

Craig left Sharon to the remainder of her day and went to enjoy his piano alone.

♫

CHAPTER TEN

♪

*F*all was everywhere. Leaves were making their last appearance in color before a gentle drift to their final resting place.

Sharon and Craig were totally absorbed in polishing "Rhapsody." They worked every evening of the week. It was a casual togetherness and both were lost in what they loved best, music.

The weekend passed on schedule and the first days of the important week arrived.

Wednesday, Craig picked her up for their ride to Albany. She invited him up to her little studio.

"So this is where you hide away."

"It's small, but perfect for me."

"You have a lot of records too."

"Mostly classical piano."

"That is the best. Could I look through them when we have more time?"

"Of course. I noticed that you have a good collection too."

"I do, and sometime we'll have to spend an

evening playing either yours or mine."

"Hopefully we have different ones."

On their way they talked about nothing but music, especially form.

He asked her, "What are your plans after graduation?"

"I want to go to graduate school."

"Here?"

"I hope so. I am going to apply soon."

He laughed a bit. "You'll have no trouble getting accepted. It is the best and you're the best."

"Are you going to stay here next year?"

"I am going to teach here as long as they will have me."

They drove in silence for a while and Sharon put her head back to relax. She said, "It's not fair that I relax and you have to be so alert."

"You should relax, you are the one to perform. But I don't want you to miss the beautiful trees. Some are passed, but there are patches that are breathtaking."

Soon the tall building of Albany came into view. Craig wove his way among traffic and they were soon at the hotel.

"I made reservations here at the Belleview because the campus is just a few blocks away. It is also very nice."

He checked them both in and he walked with her to her room. "I'm just a few doors down. Would dinner at six be okay?"

"Yes. I would like a light one."

"Me too. They have good food here."

After dinner, Craig suggested they get their

coats and go for a short walk.

"Just display windows around here, but it will give us a little exercise."

He took her hand and they strolled slowly for several blocks, and then went back.

"Shall we call it a day? Check-in time tomorrow is nine and just a short drive."

At her door, he took her hand in his and they smiled at each other.

"You don't know how much I appreciate you doing this for me. Name it and I'll repay you."

"Nothing. It has gone well, but it's not over."

"Everything going to be just fine." Craig slipped, "Sweetheart with you at the piano, we can't miss." Sharon heard him, but it registered only as friendly words of endearment.

♫

After a breakfast of coffee and toast, they drove to the campus and were taken to their room to wait her playing. He tried to say things to keep her calm although she did not seem nervous.

"When you leave to play, I'll go listen."

She knew he would be in a state of anxiety for her. "Don't worry, I feel very confident. I know this composition really well. You have been a wonderful guide to get me to this point."

She truly put him at ease and he noticed the effect she had on him.

Sharon was called and they parted with a deep gaze into each other's telling eyes.

She played, as Craig listened in the sparse audience and was extremely pleased with how it sounded. He hoped the judges felt the same way.

He went to meet her.

She took a very deep breath and asked, "How was it?"

"You played beautifully. I couldn't have asked for a better performance."

"It felt good as I was playing." Her voice was tight and tears came to her eyes. He could see that she was about to let go after those long weeks of stress.

He said, "Let's walk." They went down an empty hall and he took her in his arms. A few tears rolled gently down her cheek.

"I'm not unhappy, just glad it is over. I wanted it to be perfect for you."

"And it was."

"This is the first time I have done anything like this."

"Your heart and soul were in your playing. Believe me, it was wonderful. I heard it. I wrote it." He wiped the tears from her cheek with his fingertips and kissed her. She liked his nearness.

He held her for a few more minutes, and she said, "I'm sorry."

"Nobody is here but me, and I understand. I like consoling you."

Sharon too was rather surprised. She had never quite thought of him in this role in her life. In those few moments near him, she remembered all the times that music had brought them to this closeness.

"You did your part to perfection, now we'll see

how they view mine."

She gathered herself and again apologized.

"No words."

He hugged her again, tipped her face up and again kissed her on the lips, and she too offered hers.

"Let's get lunch before I put you on the train. The invitation is still open to go with me to moms."

"Thank you—work."

At lunch, "I know it is a strain because I have played too and you have every right to let go. At least I was there to comfort you."

After lunch he drove her to the train station.

"Here is my mom's phone number if you have a problem. I'm going to come back Sunday. Maybe I should let you rest, but we have to start working for Ohio. It is much more difficult than "Rhapsody.""

She smiled, "I want to start working soon and I like that composition very much. You'll have to tell me how it came to be."

They hugged each other and he kissed her lightly on the lips.

As Craig left he felt her nearness go with him. He thought I wanted so much to kiss her the right way. But now I have to go and get her something for helping me in such a special way.

In her seat she put her head back and relived the tender moments with Craig. We have developed an attachment over these few months. She thought of Dr. Kreutzer and his wife and how they played as one. You could see it and you could feel it. Their eyes would scan each other and a hint of a smile would carry them into the world of the beautiful tones they were making.

Are we reaching this place in music?

Playing someone's composition when they are sitting in the room is different. You know they are following every note, every phrase, soft and louds. They are in your heart helping you express. Her thought went to Craig's emotions. His heart is in my fingertips as I depress every key. This brings us together. We are becoming a part of each other. I am reaching into a creative soul and making it mine in another form. Craig allowed me into his inner self, by explaining how he creates. His notes on a page have connected him to me and I make them come alive.

With these beautiful thoughts about Craig and his music and how it has affected her, the gentle movement of the train allowed her to drift into a light sleep. Sleep made the train ride shorter.

She arrived and took a cab home. She had just got into her casual clothes when there was a knock on her door.

"How did things go?" Karen asked first.

"We think great."

She stepped back into her room and brought out, "Mr. Heid said they came for you."

"Roses," Sharon said softly.

"A dozen deep red. You know what that means. Did something happen?"

"Oh no. They're just appreciation."

Sharon read the card aloud. "To Sharon. Thank you. Soul mates in music. Love Craig.

Karen raised her eyebrows.

"He's really nice. We have been spending a lot of time together and he rather grows on one."

"Put those in a vase and come on over for a glass of wine. I'm fixing a late dinner for Jim and me, would you join us."

"No, but I will have a glass of wine. I need it."

She told Karen all about what had happened but she loved Joel very much.

Karen did not know what to say, but she could see that something had happened between them. Maybe it was just the music they were so passionate about or something else. "Life has a way of rerouting sometimes," she told her.

Jim arrived and after a brief hello she went to her studio.

As she fixed soup the phone rang. "Sharon it's Craig. Just wanted to know if you got home okay?"

"I did and the big welcome was the roses you sent. They are so beautiful. Thank you."

"I'm the one that has to say thank you. Roses aren't enough."

"Yes they are. They will be beautiful for days, and then I can make potpourri and that is forever."

"May I stop by Sunday for just a moment? I should be back around six. I'll call you first."

Sharon went through the weekend and Sunday around six Craig called.

Shortly she went down to let him in and then back upstairs.

"I don't want to take any more of your time, but I have a little appreciation for you." He pulled a small box out of his pocket and opened it, pearl earrings. "Thank you." And he handed them to her.

She saw they were expensive, "Oh Craig, so

thoughtful of you. The roses were appreciation enough. I loved doing it for you."

"Yes it is necessary. No more said. I won't stay because I'm sure you have to catch up on things. I'll call you this week if I don't see you at school."

She went back downstairs with him and in the foyer he turned and kissed her lightly on the lips. It was so quick she did not have time to return a warm response, but she smiled.

Joel called later in the evening and she told him all about her first playing at competition. She did not tell him of her "meltdown" after, because she did not want to discuss Craig with him. He liked when she reminded him that she would see him next Tuesday evening.

It seemed to Joel that Professor Jamieson was very nice, the fatherly kind, probably older. That was all he thought about him.

♫

CHAPTER ELEVEN

♫

*T*hanksgiving week, and everyone was excited about a respite and home-cooked food.

Sharon was looking forward to going home, even if it was just for four days. Monday evening Craig called and asked about her holiday plans.

She told him she was going late Tuesday afternoon. "When will you get your information from Albany?"

"Because of the holiday, probably next week."

"After we get back, I'd like to start on "Opus," as they called it. At least we have a little more time."

"Not working on "Rhapsody" will be like losing an old friend."

Craig was pleased that he had reached her so deeply.

"Are you going to your mother's for Thanksgiving?"

"I am." He didn't share that Eileen was going with him.

"When are you flying out?"

"Tuesday, late afternoon."

"Let me take you to the airport. I'll just be hanging around."

"I can't believe that."

"No, I am going to practice piano and voice. I'll miss you not playing my piano." In thought, wait for Eileen.

"What time do you want me to pick you up?"

"I seem to lose all of my little disagreements with you, so three will be okay."

On the way to the airport she told Craig that she was coming back Saturday morning. He said he would return Sunday.

Just before she boarded, he kissed her lightly and said "I'll miss you."

"Thank you. I'll miss you too." She thought we have spent so much time together.

On the plane, head back and engines roaring she relaxed for the first time in days. She did not quite realize how she had woven herself into Craig's heart. She felt a connection, but thought it more musical than emotional.

In a few hours she would be in Joel's arms. School, New York and Craig would be far behind.

♫

"Love you Rose of Sharon."

"Love you Joel."

On the way home they told each other what had been happening at school. Then Sharon asked, "How are we going to make love?"

"I have a plan," smiling mischievously.

He drove her home, stayed and talked to her parents a while. She told them about the competition, playing in church. They weren't too interested in the competition, but church perked them up.

The next day at Joel's home they played records, piano, and danced, just being together. In the evening they drove out to the old nook in the woods, on his father's property, that they knew well.

"This will be no fun in the car after your sweet little bedroom."

"We'll have to modify things."

"He took her in his arms and said softly, "Let's see what we can do.""

They touched each other and made sure they would reach a feeling that was better another way. They caressed and talked softly. "We did our best."

"You had better take me home. My father will be waiting for me."

"Really. Still."

"Under his roof…"

Thanksgiving Day Sharon and Joel had dinner with their families. In the evening Joel went to Sharon's and enjoyed dessert with her family.

Before he left he said, "Tomorrow my mom and dad are going to the business gala and we can watch television at my house … alone."

"That sounds like a plan."

"It's my bedroom tomorrow."

♫

In the morning Joel caught his father's ear.

"Dad, I'm going to bring Sharon over to watch television and..."

He looked at him with apprehension. "You mean you want to love her."

"Yes, and I was—wondering what time you and Mom—would be home."

He instantly wanted to lecture him, but probably a little late. He knew that he had made many trips to visit her in New York.

"Well, you must be careful. She is a nice girl and you don't want anything to happen. Her parents would kill you."

"We're okay Dad. If anything did, we would just get married sooner than we have planned."

"I know you have loved her for so long. She is a beautiful girl in every way. She'll be welcome in our family." He paused, "I'm sure we won't be home before midnight."

"Thanks Dad."

Later his parents went to the gala and Joel to get Sharon. She seemed disturbed and was quiet.

He noticed and asked her why. "My parents were at me all day about wasting four years in music school. They were not going to help me at all."

"Don't they realize that you have been helping yourself since high school and doing all right."

"They keep hanging on to the same old thing, be a secretary. I haven't been home since summer and they have to treat me like this."

"Honey, put it behind you. I want to enjoy tonight. We'll not see each other until the concert."

She smiled. "I want to enjoy tonight too."

At his home, they fixed hot chocolate and went to watch television. It wasn't long until they were in each other's arms.

Joel said, "My bedroom."

Sharon was a little concerned. "What if your parents come home?"

"They would find us in bed." They both had to laugh. "My father assured me they would not be home before midnight. We can love several times."

He had convinced her and they went to his bedroom. He closed the door. She turned and said happily. "Get naked for me."

He smiled. "I thought that was my line."

"You can use it too."

Playfully, he picked her up and gently placed her on his bed and was on top of her. "Get naked for me."

They both laughed again. They got naked for each other in a caring and loving way and then it was all serious.

"I want to do things to you that will last until Christmas," he said.

"I'll remember every moment," and she closed her eyes to accept his touch.

He fondled her breasts and to her stomach and then with her legs apart he kissed the softest part of her body. She caressed him so he too would have the desire that she had. They made their passion one to remember.

"Oh Joel, what could be better than loving you."

"Truly belonging," he answered softly.

She thought, please Joel don't destroy these wonderful moments we have together by talking about our future.

She just wanted to be near his warm and awesome body that made her feel like heaven had touched her.

"What time is it?" Joel looked at his clock.

"Doesn't your dad want you home again, like you were a teenager?"

"I don't really care. I'll be going back to New York tomorrow and then, do they pick on each other."

They dressed and had some cheese and crackers and he took her home.

"Love, your plane leaves at ten? How about if I come to get you at eight and we can spend time together."

♫

On the way to the airport, Joel told her that he was going to enlist and would probably leave as soon as school was out in December.

"I won't get to talk to you so often or see you."

"If we were married it would be different."

"Joel, hear me, graduate school."

He heard her many times and began to wonder if she wanted to get married at all. She doesn't want to even get engaged and all she talks about was going to graduate school. I wish she could think beyond that, but it seems that her mind is stuck there.

"Seems like every time we go to the airport

we're growling at each other. We never did that before."

"I know, it's when I bring up getting married."

"You'll have your own business and it will be very rewarding to carry on what your father has started. I have to have something too. I haven't come this far to give it all up. That is what you are asking me to do."

"No, I'm just asking you to marry me when you're through school."

"And being done with school ... well I don't want to say it again. If I get pregnant, then what?"

"We'll have a beautiful baby girl," and that brought a smile to both of their faces.

"We're almost to the airport. I don't want this to continue. Let's think long and hard and at Christmas make decisions," he suggested.

"I don't want to part this way either."

"Growling. No." That too made them laugh. "Soon as you are on the plane, I'll get my ticket for sixteenth and when do you want to fly home?"

"How about Tuesday? That will give us some time together, alone. Once home loving isn't so easy."

"If we were married we wouldn't have to worry about that."

"Oh Joel." She paused. "I have to be in New York for New Years. That was part of the agreement, that I be there for holidays. Christmas an exception. You can come back with me."

"Yes I'll do that."

'I'm looking forward to hearing you play with the orchestra."

"It is a great experience. There is a reception after. It's going to be at Lombardi's. That is just a few blocks and we can walk and you can meet everybody."

After check-in at the airport they just walked slowly around, holding hands. He put his arm around her and whispered something and she smiled and nodded, yes.

And then she was gone.

♫

CHAPTER TWELVE

♪

*T*he plane landed and Sharon looked out the window. There was snow, lots of snow. For her it made the air fresh and clean. For the trees and bushes it was a protection and decoration to cover the drab that fall had left behind. For others it brought a silence that the other seasons did not know.

The cab took longer to get her to her studio because of the snow. Once there she felt lonely. She felt something was happening between her and Joel. It must be that he is going away, but I have to accept it. He'll come home and we'll pick up where we left off. Now I have to work tonight and tomorrow.

At school Monday, everyone was active and spirited after the holiday. It had given them energy for the days to come. Soon Sharon found herself sharing this energy.

At home in the evening she was deep in study and her phone rang. It was late so it had to be Joel, she thought.

He didn't wait to tell her the bad news. "I've

enlisted and have to report on the twenty-eighth of December."

"Oh no, we can't even spend New Year's together."

"I know. That's bad. The first since we have been together."

"Joel this is not going down well." She choked up and started to cry.

"You could've made it different."

"I don't want to hear that."

"I'm sorry."

"You're still coming up for the concert?" she managed to say.

"Sweetheart, I'll be there."

She was crying so hard she just hung up the phone without saying goodbye.

He called her back immediately.

"I'm sorry," she apologized softly.

"Honey, I don't know what is going to happen, please don't cry, I can't be there to hold you."

"We can cry together when you get here."

"Okay, but I don't want you upset for the concert and I want Christmas to be special."

They closed their conversation in sadness. Sharon thought the worst, whatever that could be.

I want to sleep. It's a place to hide from what I don't like to hear.

As the week went on she grew accustomed to the reality that all of the young guys had to face. She and Joel were not alone in this demand.

She practiced each day but hadn't seen Craig and was glad. She did not want him to see her upset.

Thursday he did slip in as she practiced and she did not hear him. He listened and after a while he faked a sneeze and she turned quickly.

"Oh you startled me." And she laughed. "But this time I won't ask you to leave."

"You were so focused I felt that I would just listen and not interrupt. Your Chopin sounds great." He walked out of the shadows of the hall.

"It is not the easiest, but I guess it is coming along. I would like to play it for my recital."

"How is "Opus" doing?"

"Okay."

He sat down to listen.

"I need to give you some directions. Are you busy Saturday morning?"

"No. If it's early."

"I can do that. Nine."

She nodded in agreement.

"I'll pick you up and we'll get right to work. And you can stay and practice as long as you want."

Sharon thought. Okay. It doesn't seem to bother him or he wouldn't keep asking me.

♫

He was there Saturday morning in all of the snow.

When they got back to his house he said, "I got my competition review. I received an honorable mention. It carries a small monetary award and that is always nice. They liked it but thought it too ordinary." He handed it to her to read.

She studied it carefully, then, "Craig they didn't say anything bad and they liked it."

"The others I received went into more depth, and I felt they had taken more time to study the piece. With an honorable mention I thought they would have said more."

"You have two prestigious ones to your credit, so let's look ahead to the next one."

"You're right, so let's get to work."

He took her hand and they went into his piano room. They spent much time working on "Opus." While she practiced her other pieces Craig fixed a small lunch. After they ate, she practiced another hour.

As Craig drove her home he said, "It's too bad you have to work tonight. You could stay and we could play records. You are going to like some of them. My collection shares piano with voice."

"That would be nice, but rent and eating just seem to get in the way. Probably won't be too many at the country club tonight."

"Before I forget, Dr. Westmore is going caroling next Friday evening with the double quartet and I'm going along and I am asking you to go along with me. Afterward warm drinks. I have been helping him get ready for the concert. I'm practicing with the girls' glee club. He's very busy with the opera."

"That would be great. What carols are they going to sing?"

"Dr. Westmore is going to bring the music. He likes having a real choral director around even though I'm not officially in that capacity. I like doing it for him and just for myself."

"We're all going to be very busy these next two weeks rehearsing. Do you think we can squeeze in an evening to work on "Opus," he said before he reached her house.

"Tuesday."

"Okay. How about if I fix dinner for us?"

"Craig."

"That sounded ominous. Well you should be afraid of my cooking. So let me get some stuff and we can fix something together. I feel that you are a good cook."

"Maybe."

"That didn't sound quite so bad." His mischievous smile was so captivating.

She thought again, I never win so I'll just say yes.

♫

Tuesday, Craig arrived promptly at five. She was waiting for him in the foyer and went to the car. As well as her bag of music, she had a box.

"And what is in the box that smells so good?"

"Cookies. I baked them last evening. I gave Karen some and we can have the rest."

"Home baked cookies and a glass of milk, that's the best. I sound like a little boy."

She thought, but I don't think you are.

"Cookies are quick and easy."

"I hope you like cheeseburgers. I got stuff to make them."

"Everybody likes that."

In his kitchen she found the only things that he had were meat and cheese.

"We need an egg, onion, and a few bread crumbs and some seasoning."

"I have eggs but no seasoning."

Sharon took over. She made bread crumbs and mixed all and cooked the burgers. Craig fixed the table.

Their first cooking experience was playful and full of discussion about music, the winter concert and the life around the campus.

"Before we start to work on "Opus" let me tell you how this was composed. He took her hand and led her to the piano room. He turned her around and placed his hands on her shoulders and said, "This is it, a print of van Gogh's *The Peach Tree*. I saw a little color, shades of light pink and green. Delicate, but intricate and compact. Light, but full. I have included a lot of embellishments." He continued his explanation.

"Let me play it for you." He sat down and said, "Sit here and you can watch the music."

"It's beautiful. The approach is light, the middle more determined and the end light."

"That certainly is an overview. Let's look at page one. You play," he said as he moved over and she moved to the center.

The clock went from seven to nine.

Sharon said, "This is more complicated than "Rhapsody." More intricate embellishments and surprises. I'll have to spend a lot of time on these."

"Yes, but you will do fine. At least we have more time."

"I like how you interpret color."

"I like that too." He smiled and gazed directly into her dark eyes.

"I suppose it is the way with all creative things, some you like better than others." Sharon glanced at the clock. "You must be tired, I am. Want to take me home?"

"Yeah, tomorrow is a busy day for me, but would you please play for me?"

Her smile was a yes.

Craig reached for his German Song Book and placed it in front of her.

She played and he sang in German.

"Ah so beautiful. This is the first time that I have heard you sing. You can sing for me anytime. Your voice is wonderful." She was very moved.

Although Sharon did not read German she knew it was a love song, she followed the words in English. Was it a random choice or….

As they walked to his car, her scarf slipped off. Craig reached and helped her pull it up. With his hands he drew her head near and kissed her so very tenderly. He stopped and then kissed her again and this time she responded nicely.

At her house, "Don't forget caroling Friday. We're to be at Dr. Westmore's house at six-thirty."

"He doesn't live far from here. Why don't you drive over here, park in our driveway and we can walk over."

"I'll do that. I won't bother you these next few days. Maybe I'll slip in just to listen."

Craig did stop by briefly and listened and then

126

said, "I'll be over tomorrow around six. Dress warm."

Her eyes widened in an expression of approval.

Friday he arrived at six and she said, "Come on up while I get the rest of my winter gear on."

Karen and Jim were leaving so Sharon introduced everyone. Craig said, "You're braving the cold too."

"Not like you two, we're going to a movie."

Inside Craig played with the tiny ornaments on her little tree.

"I had to do a few. It brings the season closer."

"I don't have any. Maybe I should get a few little things. Go with me to get some? Maybe after practice tomorrow we could stop at the craft store."

"I like to pick out stuff like that, especially Christmas."

"If you help me pick things out, you have to help me put them up. You work so much, when?"

"Sunday afternoon I finish playing at four."

"Come right from the country club and I'll fix dinner for us. I'll work very hard to make it good. We had better get to Dr. Westmore's."

They walked briskly down the snow covered walks. The gaslight flickered and the houses were gleaming with lights of red and green. He held her hand through her mitten and his heavy glove and their conversation was quiet as the winter air around them.

Everyone was just getting there at the same time, and in a joyful and festive mood. Sharon knew the entire group. Craig was addressed, "Dr. Jamieson." He had insisted that Sharon leave that behind.

Dr. Westmore briefly explained the route and it

would be about two hours. "Afterward hot drinks here."

They were on their way and at each house they rang the doorbell and offered a big "Merry Christmas" and then they sang. Craig and Sharon snuggled together at each stop. She held the music and he held the flashlight and her.

Back at the residence it was off with coats and hats. Craig took Sharon's hands and rubbed them vigorously then he kissed a fingertip. That did not go unnoticed. Jenny Westmore had mulled cider, hot chocolate and little sandwiches ready for the group. After the food and warmth, Dr. Westmore asked Sharon to play a few Christmas songs on their grand piano and they all sang again.

He told Craig that she played for him the first two years she was here and, "I was amazed."

Craig thought, if you only knew what else she can play you would be astounded.

It was a quick, quiet and pleasant evening.

In the midst of lightly falling snow they walked back to her studio. Craig put his hand in her mitten. She invited him up but he declined. "It's late and I have too many clothes to take off and put back on," and he realized that didn't sound right. He amended, "You know boots and coats."

She tried not to smile but it happened anyway.

He couldn't help himself and he reached for her and held her close and just smiled. Still holding her, "The fresh air and walk is a recipe for good sleep."

He kissed her softly and she responded so naturally.

Oh my, she thought is something happening?

"Tomorrow practice, shopping and you work. A busy day. Good night now."

♪

Sunday after church service, Deacon Ely told her that they liked what she and Dr. Jamieson had proposed, especially the choir. Perhaps they could start in January.

After playing the cocktail hour, she went directly to Craig's. She found herself anxious to get there.

He greeted her warmly.

"Hope you have something good to eat, I'm famished."

"I called Mom and asked her what I could fix."

"You didn't."

"She liked that I am getting domesticated."

"What did she suggest?"

"Just baked chicken. And I think it turned out okay. Are you brave enough to try it?"

"May I change? I brought jeans and a sweater."

"Come on in my bedroom. It is presentable."

He led the way and closed the door and went to get the food on the table. On his dresser she saw a picture that had been turned over. She resisted the temptation to look.

He looked lovingly at her as she arrived back in the kitchen. "Feel better?"

They enjoyed the baked chicken. After, they decorated with the few things that would bring

Christmas to his little home.

"Done. How about I play a Glenn Gould?"

Craig put on the record and said. "Come on, let's curl up here and just listen."

She sat on the couch, Craig next to her and put his arm around her. "Comfortable?"

"Very."

Comfortable and together they listened to each note struck by this famous young pianist.

When it was over Craig said, "I've got to check his concert schedule and see if he is going to be near. We'll go."

"Oh that would be special."

"We're coming up to the big concert of the year. Are you and the orchestra ready?"

"We are. How are your groups coming?"

"The quartet is good the others need work in my estimation. We're rehearsing every evening except Friday. Could we get together before we all go away?"

"I have plans Friday."

"Oh." Craig seemed surprised. "Also Saturday, because I have to be with the groups early, you probably don't want to come over that early. Or do you?"

"That's okay. It is so close."

"I'll try to get away before you play to wish you well. We'll go to Lombardi's after."

Oh my, she thought, am I in trouble?

"I assume you are going home for Christmas."

"I am, Tuesday afternoon."

"Not till Tuesday. I am leaving Sunday morning early for Texas to visit my friends. Then I am coming back and spending Christmas with Mom and Bill and my sister and her family is going to be there. It will be so nice." He paused again, waiting for her to offer her plans. She didn't.

So he asked. "When are you coming back?"

"I'm not sure, but I have to play New Year's Eve at the country club."

Sharon thought, Joel has to leave before then and I'll be all alone.

Music over, she decided to go home.

Heavy coats on, they went outside. Before she got in her car, he turned and put his arms around her.

"Hold me too," he whispered. She willingly yielded to his request. It was a warm and almost passionate kiss that said goodnight.

♫

CHAPTER THIRTEEN

♫

*T*ime had brought more snow in December. Time had also brought the holiday season and the biggest event of the school year, the winter concert.

This week was also the end of the semester and for many only one more before graduation. Sharon was in that group, although she would stay on for graduate school.

This week was very demanding. Students had to complete course work. Professors had to complete their grading. And to add to this, many were rehearsing every spare moment for the concert.

Sunday everyone would be leaving and not be back until January. Sharon had lunch with her friends Monday. Glenna asked, "Are you and Professor Jamieson dating?"

Surprised, she responded, "I don't think so."

"Someone at caroling noticed that you called him Craig and he kissed your fingertip. Kelly saw you two at the craft store."

"Oh! Oh!" was all she could say.

It caused awareness in her mind. It had flickered in the back, but Glenna's question brought it very forward. She thought too, the way he has kissed me.

Glenna smiled. "Hey girl, we'd all like to be in your place. Take it and run."

"I don't know what to say. We worked together for his competition piece and got to know each other and seemed to enjoy each other, that's all."

"That's enough, but what about Joel?"

"Yeah, and he is coming up for the concert."

She thought, they will probably meet. What will I do?

Lunch over and what was said completely engulfed her mind. We're not dating, we're working together. She remembered there were a couple times that she was anxious to get to Craig's, but I was hungry. This can't be happening with Craig. Well maybe it isn't. I let the girls put false ideas in my mind. But good friends don't kiss like we have. Oh lord. I love Joel and have for so very long. I am making love to him.

The next few days she couldn't let these thoughts go away.

Wednesday evening, she practiced with the orchestra and got home late. She rushed to the ringing phone.

"Hi sweetheart. Just called to say that I turned in my last paper today and I am done with my four years."

"That must be a good feeling."

"It is, and I can enjoy my time until I leave.

From one commitment to another."

Sharon did not want to answer him or even think about it.

"I'll be there to pick you up and then I have to go back to school in the afternoon to practice with the orchestra, one last time."

"Can I go with you?"

"Of course."

"It is kind of sad I won't be here in May for graduation. They'll just send me my diploma. It all comes down to a piece of mail."

"Won't they let you even come home for that?"

"I didn't think so. I won't even be there for yours."

"Cancel it."

"Yeah. We did talk about it and this is what we decided."

"I know. I don't like it."

"I am going to pack up and go home one last time. I'll see you Friday morning."

"Bye Joel," she said with a heavy voice, as was his.

Thursday melded into Friday morning and Sharon went to get Joel.

He took her so gently in his arms and tears came to her eyes. Life for many years had been very steady, but now it seemed to be changing. After a very loving kiss and whispers, they went to her car.

"I have to go straight to school."

"That's okay, I'll just tag along. I can hear the orchestra early. Can I take you to dinner tonight?"

"Let's go somewhere special where we can

hold hands and be close. Go home and make love."

"Do we have to wait?"

"No," and he smiled lovingly at her.

♫

Craig was home Friday evening and Saturday wondering why Sharon could not see him. Maybe she just wants some quiet time before the concert. I would understand. Well I'll see her after the concert and we'll go to Lombardi's. It will be our last time together until January. That's too long for me to go without seeing her. I'll get her phone number at home and talk to her.

♫

Saturday early Sharon and Joel fixed a light dinner and they ate at her island. Candlelight flickered and made it special. Later they dressed, Joel in his black suit and Sharon in black lace over black silk. The sleeves were long and the neckline round and low. She pulled her hair back slightly to show the earrings that Craig had given her.

The winter concert was always well-attended by students, professors and many from the city.

Sharon and Joel went to the room where the orchestra had just finished warming up. Sharon was busy saying Merry Christmas and introducing Joel. Time was closing in for the start of the program and she hadn't seen Craig.

"Go with me backstage while I wait."

"We have about twenty minutes."

135

The orchestra was making their way on stage one by one and Joel and Sharon talked softly. Even though she did not seem nervous, Joel tried to keep the conversation light.

Almost lost in the sea of black attire, Craig came through the stage door in tuxedo and blond hair almost in place. Sharon smiled at him as her heart fluttered.

Ignoring Joel he took her hands in his, "Thought you would be here," and he kissed her on her cheek. "I just had to get away for a moment to wish you well. You look beautiful." And he glanced slowly all the way to the tip of her long dress.

Joel stepped forward to join the conversation.

"Craig, this is my friend Joel Steiner, Joel, Craig Jamieson."

They were both a little surprised, but shook hands in a polite way, but no nice to meet you.

Ignoring Joel again, "I had better get back I am going to conduct the girls tonight. Dr. Westmore said I have been rehearsing with them so much they might not respond to him as well."

"That's great. I'll be watching."

"It's nice to get recognized in this area. And you know I am playing for the double quartet."

"Yes."

"Going to Lombardi's?"

"Yeah, we'll be there."

"See you then. Good luck," and he kissed her again on the cheek.

Joel looked bewildered and said, "That's Dr. Jamieson. He's not forty."

"Who said he was?"

"Well I got the impression that he was fatherly."

"No!" And she looked away thinking of the times that he had kissed her in a much different way.

"You called him by his first name."

"He asked me to. I'm not in any of his classes."

Joel didn't want to say any more that might upset her before playing.

As Craig walked back to the room he thought, I believe that is the same guy I saw her with at the beginning of school. Where has he been? Is he over at the big campus and I have just missed him. She hasn't mentioned him. Well I suppose I haven't mentioned Eileen either. I wanted to spend the evening with her! Is he more than a friend? The only way to find out is to ask. Right now I have to keep my head on straight.

With the girls he said, "If you want to hear the orchestra, there is a little break after, we can slip out very quietly. If you don't, stay and we'll all be back."

Lights were lowered and a hush came over the audience. Dr. Peterson and Sharon came on stage and received a warm welcome.

Baton high and everyone's complete attention, the first notes became real. Craig sat where he could see Sharon's face and he felt that she was completely relaxed. He could see that she had closed her mind to everything around her and was completely engrossed in her playing. When you have her talent and her discipline you have it all, he thought. She performed beautifully and the audience acknowledged with a hardy applause.

She bowed lightly, threw a kiss to her audience and acknowledged the orchestra and Dr. Peterson.

Someone presented her with a bouquet of red roses. She whispered a thank you.

Craig watched for a moment after she received the flowers and then slipped out to join his girls' glee club. He thought her performance was excellent.

Joel watched as she received her second bunch of red roses and he had troubling thoughts. Who else would do that? Sharon left the stage and Joel went to be with her. Before she could thank him, he said, "I only sent one."

"Thank you so much," she said sweetly. "How was it?"

"Beautiful, very beautiful. At rehearsal it sounded choppy. I suppose there were so many starts and stops, but tonight, just beautiful."

"It felt good. Let me put these in the orchestra room and we'll go listen to the rest of the program." She eased the cards from the tie and put them in her little velvet bag.

Craig's glee club was in the last half and she didn't take her eyes off him. This was the first time she had seen him conduct. She thought, he's so energetic and expressive, so talented. He is all music. Again she thought of Dr. Kreutzer and his wife and the bond that music had created between them. Would it do the same for Craig and me?

When the program was over Sharon heard, "Beautiful. Best concert ever. Very moving." She was pleased that it had been a success. Everyone had worked extremely hard. Devoting time to their music was a great love of the students and they were rewarded.

Lombardi's was not far, but they didn't say much to each other as they walked. Sharon talked about Dr. Peterson. She confessed to Joel that she was glad it was over, because she didn't like the way he works with us. "He is so distant. He doesn't talk to us much, he just gives directions. There is no warmth between him and the orchestra."

"You're not playing with the orchestra any more this year."

"No, I'm done."

"This Craig, doesn't he teach composition. Why did he conduct the girls?"

"I didn't know until tonight that he was going to. He has been rehearsing them for a while. He was helping Dr. Westmore and you heard what he said. Although he is a coral director, not officially in that capacity at school. But he could be."

They reached Lombardi's in a few minutes. She excused herself to go to the ladies room where she opened her tiny bag and pulled out the cards. From whom she suspected. Craig wrote, *Dear Sharon, Soul mates in music. Love Craig*—Joel's read *I love you my Rose of Sharon. Love Joel.*

She found Joel and squeezed his hand. The atmosphere was festive. Everyone was happy that the concert went so well and glad that it was over. The music for dancing had begun and the light buffet was ready for enjoyment. Joel and Sharon gathered their food and drinks and joined Glenna, her date Tom, Emily and others. They were all discussing every mistake they had made, every note missed and trying to laugh them away.

Sharon said, "I thought I was off at measure fifty-five, but I wasn't. Dr. Peterson gave me a strange look. I don't know what he was trying to say."

Mike said, "I saw that and wondered too, because you were right on, and with a look like that it could have thrown you off. He's strange."

About that time, Dr. Jamieson came over and said, "Could I join this group?"

They all said, "Of course."

He squeezed in next to Sharon.

She asked him, "Did you hear us play?"

"I did, all of it and it sounded absolutely wonderful. Your expressions were right on. Your control was perfect and that piece is demanding." Craig went on with a few more statements about her playing, as well as the orchestra. Everyone was very interested in Dr. Jamieson's comments except Joel. He just heard it as wonderful.

After a discussion of the performing groups, Craig said to Joel, "Would you excuse Sharon and me? I would like to discuss "Opus" with her so she can work on it during break." He turned to her and asked, "May I have this dance?"

"Excuse us, Joel," she said.

Sharon's girlfriends took a deep breath.

Craig took her hand and they walked to the crowded dance floor.

"What about "Opus?"

"I don't want to talk about "Opus." Drop the o p and that leaves us."

"Us!" Sharon said softly but firmly.

"Who is this guy? Is he a boyfriend or more? You haven't mentioned him."

"Why should I. You don't talk about your girlfriend."

"We'll discuss that later. One thing at a time. I like you very much and if there is someone else in your life I would like to know."

"I'm not sure right now. He is going away and things seem to be going bad."

"Where is he going?"

"Army. Enlisted."

"I'm glad I have that behind me."

"I wasn't aware that you liked me."

"We have spent a lot of extra time together and I kissed you and you kissed be back. Was that your buddy kiss?" His smile was playful and mischievous. "If it was, your passionate kiss must be overwhelming and I want you to try it out on me."

"Oh Craig. I am so confused. I really don't want to discuss Joel with you."

"I'm not asking you to, I just want to know where I stand because I really like you—I really like you. I missed you this week." And he drew her close and her body fell into his. "We're going to be apart and when we come back I want to know. I don't want to waste my time or yours unless it means something."

He stopped talking and pulled her even closer.

"I'm leaving for Texas very early in the morning. Can I say that you will accompany me in April at the wedding?"

"Craig, that is a long way off. I can't say now."

"I'll tell them yes and if something happens, Judy can find someone to play for me."

As they danced Craig's heart filled his whole body, I can't lose this girl, he thought. Maybe I have never had her. She has been warm, playful and generous with herself. We have a wonderful connection to music and I love her as a person.

"What are you thinking about? You seem far away."

"No, I'm right here and very aware that I am holding you. You look absolutely beautiful tonight. Your dress is exquisite." His eyes fell slowly to her small breasts, wanting to fondle and kiss them.

"Also I noticed that you are wearing the earrings I gave you. They're perfect."

"I like them too. Thank you for the roses."

"It is so appropriate for such a wonderful performance." He was unaware that she had received a second bouquet.

"Regardless, will you still play "Opus" for me?"

"Of course."

He couldn't help himself, he kissed her on the forehead, hoping no one noticed.

"I'd rather kiss your lips," he whispered.

"Me too." Softly.

"Maybe I'd better get you back to the table with your friend." He said rather curtly.

She detected his abrupt words. "Craig."

He took her hand and led her back. "We discussed a few points about "Opus" and I have her back." He said to Joel. "It has lots of embellishments that I would like played differently."

Sharon thought, he sounds so convincing. "Merry Christmas Sharon," and he kissed her on the cheek and to the others, "Merry Christmas. See you all in the new year."

Sharon's girlfriends again took a deep breath.

He turned and walked away. Sharon wanted to turn and follow with her eyes, but she didn't. She brought her demeanor to her friends and Joel, smiling at him.

The hours grew late and the gathering was beginning to disperse. She found Dr. Bernard and a few of her other professors and wished them happy holidays.

At home they both seemed exhausted and went to sleep in each other's arms.

♫

Morning brought a different feeling. They woke to a passionate togetherness and seemed to leave school, concert and especially Craig behind.

Sharon felt guilty that she liked Craig. How could this happen? Is it the music? It had happened so fast she could not explain. Hopefully time will give me an answer. For now, she knew Craig was far away and she was glad because she did not want him to know that Joel was staying with her.

The day before they were to fly home, they spent it in a loving manner, Sharon sometimes tearful and Joel consoling. Thoughts of their first big parting loomed heavy and they both were apprehensive about what it had caused between them, emotionally and physically.

That night they made their love very special. Words and touch that would have to last a very long time.

Joel gathered all of the things of his that were in her studio and packed them. "I might not see you for a while. You might move and I don't want you to have to lug them around." That brought more tears.

"You'll have enough of my stuff around some day. It is not the end of the world."

Tuesday they boarded their flight and were home in a few hours.

Their parents were there to meet them. Loving hellos and loving goodbyes were exchanged and Joel said to Sharon, "I'll be over later."

Until Christmas Eve they were together each day. Joel was bitter that she did not want to be engaged, yet, and let her know his feelings.

She tried to explain, but he did not hear.

Christmas Eve, after festivities at Joel's, he did not take Sharon straight home. They went to the nook in the woods. After loving each other in the best way they could, Joel reached in his glove compartment.

"My love, Rose of Sharon, I have your real Christmas present for you."

She opened the little box and there were a pair of round diamond earrings.

"Not just one, but two and I give these to you with the greatest love that I have known."

"Joel, I have loved you for so long, thank you.

Words are not enough." She was so choked she could hardly talk. The embrace that followed was filled with passion.

"You know I wanted to put a ring on your finger so the world knows that we belong to each other. You sent the message that you were not ready. What I am going say is very hard … very hard," his voice cracked, and it gave Sharon a horrible feeling. "I am going away for a long time so I am going to release you to your music. I don't seem to have any other choice."

Sharon could feel her body, getting hot and then cold, to the reaction of his words.

"What are you saying?" she stammered.

"That we don't have to make any decisions about our life together. Seems there might not be one. That I'll be gone for so long I don't want you to feel obligated to me. You have graduate school that you seem so determined about and I have two year of service. That puts us far apart. At the end of two years, if we find each other our love will be even stronger, but for now and until then it's a farewell to a long and close relationship."

Her tears were flowing, "I just can't believe it is all going to end this way. It can't Joel!"

"Me either. Well don't think of it ending, but a pause, and then we'll have all this behind us and maybe just pick up where we left off."

"You sound like it will be a blank two years."

"Yes that is what I am saying. Each going our own way and see what happens at the end."

"Joel you're saying goodbye to all that we have

145

been. How can you?"

"That is the message that I have received from you. I have asked you to marry me and you more or less said no." Rather emphatically, "I don't see the need to go on."

His words had so startled Sharon that she could not stop crying. She was so upset that she could not think or want to continuing talking.

Joel too had tears in his eyes as they held each other, and said, "We still have three days."

"Will you go to church with our family tomorrow? Dinner and gifts."

"Yes. I will."

The day after Christmas they spent the day at Joel's home. They talked about many things. Sharon played his piano. She played her little composition that she had written for him and as before it affected him deeply. They had lunch with his mother, went for a long walk and she stayed for dinner.

Joel had always loved when she played for him, but this time his feelings were of resentment. He felt that music had driven them apart. He knew her love for music was innate, but it had overwhelmed her and nothing else seemed to matter. It had pulled her in like a habit. I feel she forced me to make this decision.

On the way home they drove again to the little nook that held their many secrets. They made their last time together unforgettable.

The next day he went to get her and they would all take him to the airport, his parents, sisters and Sharon.

Everyone was tearful and he kissed his sisters,

mother and a big hug for his dad. Then he took Sharon in his arms and kissed her long and whispered, "I'll always love you, my Rose of Sharon." He turned and walked onto the plane.

Sharon did not see him leave because her eyes were so heavy with tears, but she did not stop her gentle wave goodbye.

Joel's mother lovingly said to her, "Honey, he is gone, but he will be back for you."

♫

PART TWO

♫

the soul finds a home

CHAPTER FOURTEEN

♫

*T*he cold and loneliness of winter had crept into Sharon's heart. Her emotions were like a tree stripped of its beauty or a shadow without a form. She realized she had reached an end of a wonderful time in her life. But deep in her mind, it wasn't real.

With a heavy heart, she arrived back in New York the day after she and Joel had said their sad goodbyes. It was a physical and mental parting that left her confused. She thought it seemed so sudden, although it had played out over the last several months. It was sudden compared to the years we have been together. The most confusing of all, Craig has entered my life. Had Joel been my childhood sweetheart and will Craig my grown-up love? Perhaps I am searching too hard for an answer, just let one drift in. I'm sure I will recognize it.

The ride home from the airport she thought how cold out and how warm in the cab. Just like my heart, half warm and the other half cold. It seems to represent the past and the future. What about the now and she realized there was no present in her heart.

It was early in the evening when she arrived at her studio. It too was cold and lonely. She wondered if Karen was home, but she didn't have the desire to talk, just thinking exhausted her soul. She curled up on her couch in the big heavy comforter and she thought, when I sleep bad things go away.

She woke to the sound of a distant siren and realized it was morning. How emotions can exhaust a body. This is life and I am going to have to make the best of what the future brings. If it brings Craig, that will be wonderful, or maybe someone that I don't even know at this time.

After coffee and a few stretches, she went to the cellar to do her laundry. I must get food for the week and get ready for New Year's Eve. It will not be festive for me, just another twelve o'clock. I'll hide away in sleep.

Later in the day as she was bringing her laundry upstairs, she met Karen coming home from work. They hugged. How was your Christmas? Did Joel come back with you?"

That moment, Karen could see the sudden sadness in her eyes.

"No he left on Wednesday, and I don't know what to think."

"Why? Come on in." And the wine glasses came out.

Sharon told her everything.

"I am so surprised that he would say that. I know how much he loves you."

"I know, I don't understand either. What am I

supposed to do? Wait for him when he is not coming back to me? He didn't say that he would write or call." And tears came to Sharon's eyes.

"Oh my, I don't know what to say."

"And to complicate matters, Craig, at the reception after the concert, said when we come back he wanted to know where he was in my life. He wanted to know who Joel was."

"That does present a dilemma, or does it? Maybe fate is working out something for you that you aren't able to."

"It is hard to imagine being with anyone other than Joel, but when I am with Craig I feel comfortable and I really like him. I have a connection to Craig that I don't have with Joel, music. I never dated anyone else much, it was always Joel."

"You have been spending a lot of time with Craig, so you both should know if you want to start something."

"Apparently he does. We'll see what the next few weeks bring. I know he has a girlfriend, he mentioned her once. If he asks about Joel I suppose I have a right to ask about her."

"You definitely do. You both have to put all the cards on the table if you are going to start something."

"I'll just have to wait and see. I had better let you get your dinner and I have to get stuff put away. Thanks for listening to me."

"Oh Sharon, you did the same for me when Ron and I broke up. That's what friends are for. Are you doing anything for New Year's Eve?"

"I have to play till ten and come home."

"Do you have plans?"

"We're going out but I don't know where."

♫

New Year's Eve, Sharon drove to the country club to play for those enjoying their dinner before the long and passionate kiss at midnight.

She played as many love songs as she could find in her songbook. Tonight was to be gentle and sensuous for those listening. She felt in a mood to impart her emotions through her fingers. She started her last hour. Soon she could go home and not have to see the happiness she would not be a part.

Craig arrived around nine o'clock and sat at the bar and listened to her play. Her playing excited him so much because of her technique, also knowing that she was near excited him more, but was she alone?

She left the piano just as the orchestra struck up its first chords for dancing.

As she went down the hall she heard someone. She turned, "Craig!"

"It's me. Are you alone tonight?"

"Yes," and ever so softly, "very. You're not with your girlfriend?"

"I am with my girlfriend. I hope she is with me."

She gave him that knowing smile.

"Let's dance so I can hold you."

He took her hand and they walked to the crowded floor. He took her in his arms and she gently laid her arm on his shoulder.

"If you're my girlfriend hold me close."

She moved her arm closer and ran her fingers along his neck.

"I knew those beautiful fingers had more use than playing piano. You make me want to whistle." And they both laughed quietly as he snuggled her.

"Whistle. I never heard that before."

"I just made it up," bringing big smiles.

They relaxed in each other's arms and Craig sang softly to her as the orchestra played "I'll Be Around."

Sharon thought how foretelling. "I like when you sing to me. How did you know I'd be here?"

"You told me that you had to play tonight."

"I did, didn't I."

"I came home Thursday and called you several times. I was afraid that you hadn't come back."

"I got back Thursday too. I was out doing stuff. I talked to Karen a long time. Out for groceries."

"How was your Christmas?"

"Bittersweet, and that is all I want to say. How was yours?"

"Texas was nice. I got together with many friends. Got the wedding plans. Weather was good. I flew back to Albany and spent Christmas with Mom and Bill. My sister Beth, brother-in-law Josh, and their little boy were there. Her baby is due in March. That is exciting."

"How wonderful. You're going to be an uncle again. How old is their little boy?"

"John is four. Beautiful little boy."

"It is always nice to have Santa visit."

"I want you to meet all of them and soon."

"I'd love to."

He pulled her even closer and whispered in her ear. "You look beautiful tonight. You look scrumptious in white." He paused. "It is nice to have you near me to welcome in the new year."

"I know," and she thought how sad she had been these last few days, but all of a sudden, it seemed so different and the sadness was quickly drifting away.

They danced ever-so-close until the orchestra stopped. He asked, "Do you want to go somewhere else. Are you hungry?"

"You're being here comes as a surprise. I hadn't thought about it, although I didn't eat dinner."

"You need to eat."

"If you want, I'll ask Jack if he has a table."

Jack guided them to a small table in the lounge where they enjoyed a mix of light cuisine. Neither ordered alcoholic drinks. They sat near each other, talked and even had a few laughs.

Just before midnight Craig said, "Let's dance so I can hold you when the hour is here."

The festivities gained energy and the ball dropped, and in each other's arms their very passionate kiss lasted for moments.

He took her face in his hands and softly, "Sharon, this is our year. We have each other. We have our music to share. That's the whole world."

She smiled and he knew she was with him.

The loudness of the breaking into a new year settled down and the orchestra played for those in love in a most sensuous way. Sharon and Craig fell into the spell around them as they held each other and danced.

When the music stopped Craig asked her, "Do you want to go or stay?"

"Let's go before the roads get too crowded with people having too much to drink."

"If you drove out, I'll follow you home."

At Sharon's they parked their cars and she asked, "Come up and I'll fix coffee."

"No coffee. I won't sleep tonight and I haven't had anything heavy to drink."

"How is milk?" and she laughed.

"Milk it is. First let me get out of this dress."

"First let me look at you. You're beautiful in a strapless." And his warm hands gently swept over her soft shoulders.

She fixed warm milk and a side of cookies.

"This is so much better than being inebriated," he said to her as she placed their childlike treat on her coffee table.

As they sat close, Craig said, "I was so afraid that you would not be alone tonight."

"It was a nice surprise. I was going to come home and roll up in this blanket and sleep the night away, taking twelve o'clock with it."

He cradled her and kissed her again and she with her whole self returned the closeness. "We can still roll up in the blanket." So many times these months I have wanted to do this, he thought and more.

Softly she said, "I really didn't know."

"You just liked my piano," he said jokingly.

She was lost for words. "I do like your piano, but I really didn't think too much beyond that."

"Now you know and you can have both of us. We have fifteen days before school start. Let's do something every day. After that, we'll both have to share our time with classes. Dr. Westmore wants me to continue working with the girls and the quartet."

"I watched you conduct and you have so much energy and feeling and the girls respond nicely."

"I'm glad to hear that. I thought they did."

"It's only natural to respond to a handsome, blond conductor."

"No. No. They are beautiful voices. You are the only one I want to respond to me. School is locked. You will have to practice at my house. We can get a lot done with "Opus" and you can work on your recital pieces. Let's get started tomorrow."

"I have to play at church, but there is no cocktail hour."

"May I go to church with you? That will be a great way to start the new year other than holding you and kissing you."

"I'd love to have you go. The service starts at ten."

She went downstairs with him and again he pulled her close and they molded into each other.

"You have made me very happy. Happy New Year sweetheart."

"Happy New Year Craig, my soul mate in music."

♫

This New Year's Day Sharon and Craig went

to the little missionary church. After, they talked to Deacon Ely and he thought they could start with the children later in the month. They told him they decided to start with just an hour and see how that worked out.

"We also thought we might divide up the age groups and do something appropriate for their interest. Sharon would you like to relate some of your ideas?"

She spent the next few minutes explaining what she had in mind. "If something doesn't work, we'll try something else."

"We also thought after a month or so we would evaluate and if it isn't working, we'll just stop."

"I like what you have proposed, and you both are taking a very practical approach. And I am excited and I talked to some of the children and they liked it too. One thing they told me, they liked Miss Sharon and how she played. Big."

Deacon told her how much they would pay and thanked him, "It is kind of you to ask."

They all shook hands and wished a happy new year. Craig and Sharon drove to his home, excited about their new venture together. "We work together very well, "Rhapsody" proved that. Now this and "Opus."

After being together all New Year's Day, in the evening they curled up on Craig's couch and listened to Rachmaninoff's "Second Piano Concerto." When the music stopped, he said, "Remember yesterday when I said I'm with my girlfriend."

"I remember."

"Well, I was very serious. I am asking you to be my girlfriend, only for me. I want you to know that I am yours body and soul." And he smiled happily. "I was very much attracted to you from the moment I saw you. As I got to know you I really liked being with you. I loved the way you played the piano. I think you are very special and want our relationship to go beyond friends. Being close and belonging to each other. Sharing. My life is music and I have to be with someone whose life is music too. I found that in you."

Her heart was beating wildly. "Oh Craig, I didn't realize any of this. I just thought we were working on your compositions and enjoying each other's company."

"And we were."

"There were times when I was anxious to get here, but I thought it was because I was hungry."

Craig squeezed her, "Oh you sweetheart."

"I began to relax when I was with you and looked forward to practicing with you." She ran her fingers around his face. "I was having lunch with Glenna last month and she asked me if we were dating."

"I know Glenna. What did you say?"

"That I didn't think so."

"But now you know that we are."

"And it got me thinking. Also it was noticed that I called you Craig. I'm sorry. I didn't think."

"But sweetheart, I asked you to call me that. It can give the students something to gossip about. If we're the only thing they have to talk about, things are rather boring."

"Here in the Music Box we're all very close and know all about each other in a caring way."

She cozied up very close to him and again ran her hand over his unruly blond hair and said, "You are a beautiful man and I would love to be your girlfriend. My life is music too. Hold me close Craig."

He nestled her tightly in his arms and kissed her gently. "This makes me very happy."

After a while Sharon asked him, "Should we keep it quiet that we're dating?"

"Why? We're both adults. We don't have to hold hands at school, but I don't see why we have to hide our relationship."

Craig knew that he was falling in love with her, but for her it was a little new and he felt he had to give her time to adjust to his presence, his attention to her, his life of music, and yes his body.

Later he took her home and said. "To the next fifteen days."

♫

Each evening they prepared something and ate by candlelight in Craig's dining nook. Sharon confessed she had cooked a lot for her mom and dad. Craig said he and Kevin never got past short-order stuff, but he was willing to learn.

Another afternoon they embraced the cold and visited the art gallery. Craig looking at the Impressionists said, "I can always get new inspirations."

"I wanted to take an art history class, but there was no time for it."

"Sweetheart, you have a lifetime and there are

millions of books. Which one do you like best?"

"A big question. Gauguin is firm and bold. Monet offers assurance and Degas you can see the wind blowing through. I like them all. Do you have compositions that are not inspired by paintings?"

"Yes, some from poetry, nature and the Psalms. My notebook is very diverse."

The next evening at the art theatre they held hands like teenagers and were lost in the music and romance of *Song Without End.*

Craig took her home and she said, "Come up and I'll fix warm milk."

He laughed and replied, "The popcorn was enough. I'll just stay a moment or two."

Jim and Karen were coming home also. Karen asked, "We thought we might have a glass of wine, will you join us?"

At Karen's cocktail table the conversation took off. Jim and Karen are artist, but work for different companies. They design and do illustrations for books and magazines. It was a lively discussion how the arts are so entwined. An hour passed and Sharon and Craig decided to say goodnight.

Every day they were together, sometimes out, other days at home. Regardless of what they did, they practiced. Craig piano and voice as Sharon played for him. Sharon just piano. They made "Opus" their priority.

To end most of these cold and snowy days they cuddled on his couch. The warmth of the big comforter, the lights low, the music playing brought them closer in body and spirit.

"I can't believe how contented I am. Your love, together with music," Craig whispered.

Sharon hesitated to say, but she thought, your love and your music are just what I wanted from this beautiful life. Please let it mature to a perfect togetherness.

Trying not to think how close they were he asked, "What have you decided for your recital?"

"Bach Partitas, Chopin Etude. That's all for now. I am anxious to hear your faculty."

"It is supposed to be an hour and a half, and you can help me decide which ones to play."

"Okay." She said softly as she could feel his warm breath on her neck. It was a nice delicate feeling that didn't stop there.

"Do you have any classes on Friday?"

"Yeah, this semester I do, but at nine. The rest of the day is free. I like that."

"Me too, one class but it's at ten."

He kissed her neck softly and between her breasts as he gave a little sigh of contentment.

This closeness happened several evenings, but they managed to quell their feelings for a later time, as Craig thought, it has to be love, not just desire.

The last day before classes started for the last semester was Sunday and Sharon had to play for the cocktail hour. When she got to Craig's, "You're all dressed up."

"And since you are too, I thought I would take you out to dinner this evening."

"Oh, you're such a sweetheart," And she gave him a hug and a big kiss.

"I made reservations at Rudolph's."

He cradled her and said, "I am so glad we had this time together so your love can catch up to mine."

"Oh Craig," and she gazed deeply into his eyes wanting to say ... but she felt not just yet.

"Reservations are for six. If you want to freshen up, I'll loan you my space. I'm not one on fashion, but you have another beautiful dress, where do you get them."

"Well," and she hesitated, "I make them. Some are a couple years old."

"Really! Girl, what else do you do well that I don't know about!"

She just gave him that smile. She got her bag and went into his bedroom and to the little bath. She felt close to him even though she was by herself.

This is his intimate space. When will I share it with him she wondered? She knew that she was falling in love with him, but the closeness of Joel was raw and still present. It was fading into what had been a beautiful past. So strange how you can love for so long and have it fade away so fast, or has it. Apparently it wasn't meant to be. Craig and I are much more compatible. She also noticed the picture that had been turned over was gone.

When she came out she told Craig, "My Aunt Katy sends me money and I buy material and sew. I make something plain then decorate it with a scarf or something. But I bought my dress for the winter concert."

"A great choice. You looked absolutely beautiful and I only got to dance with you a short while. Not what I planned."

"Last year is behind us. We have had a real good beginning."

After a delightful dinner of small talk and warmth they decided to go. On their way out they met Dr. Bernard and his wife.

"Professor Jamieson and Sharon, my two beautiful musicians. You have just finished dinner?"

Craig answered, "Yes, we just finished."

"Too bad, you could have joined Carrie and me. We would have had a spirited conversation about music."

"That would have been great, but we just missed each other."

"We'll all be back tomorrow. And good night to both of you."

Craig could feel that Sharon was uncomfortable.

"Remember we are both adults and not attached. We're not the first professor and student that fell in love."

She smiled and accepted his words.

"I'll take you home. I am sure you have things to get ready for tomorrow, I do. Want to get together a couple evenings this week and work on "Opus" and Saturday. It will be the last time before we start working with the children."

"I'll do my other practicing at school."

At Sharon's they cozied on her couch.

"These days with you have meant a lot. Eating, shopping and cooking together. We have so much to look forward to. We will let everything fall into place

164

as we go through the days. It will be naturally."

"That's the best way."

"I'd love to stay, but I promised you I wouldn't. Walk downstairs with me."

A warm embrace ended these wonderful days together.

♫

CHAPTER FIFTEEN

♬

*T*he second semester started in the middle of a very cold and snowy winter. The world was white, the air was sharp, and giant icicles hung from the houses. Sharon dressed warm and walked to school. When she and Craig's schedules were compatible, he would pick her up in the mornings. After classes, most days, they would go to Craig's, fix dinner and practice. A routine was falling into place.

The early part of the second week Craig ran into Dr. Bernard in the hall.

"Dr. Jamieson, do you have a few moments? I've wanted to have you stop by."

"I do, my class is not until eleven."

In Dr. Bernard's office he asked, "Are things getting off to a good start? Any glitches in scheduling?"

"Everything is going smooth."

"Good to hear. I am anxious to know if you are planning to stay with us next year. There will be a formality, but I thought I would ask you friend to friend. I would like to do some planning."

"I would like very much to be asked again."

"That's good news. We want you to stay. You have much to offer in both piano and voice. Dr. Westmore likes how you handle the two groups you're working with. Although they are not officially on your teaching schedule, they will be next year if you would like. We can work things out later."

"This is a great school and I am honored to be here."

"You and Sharon are going to Ohio in February during break. You did well with "Rhapsody" and how is "Opus" coming?"

"Sharon recognizes that it is more difficult, the embellishments, and she is so devoted to get each one perfect."

"She is a talented young lady. Professor Shepard thinks she has a natural ability."

Craig was a little surprised and did not know how to answer because Sharon didn't want it known.

"Perhaps."

"You know she has applied for graduate school."

"Yes, she told me she applied."

"It won't be a problem accepting her. We're not even going to ask her to audition. We're just going to stamp her application. We know her well."

"She will be happy about that."

"In the future maybe she will join our faculty. With her talent we can't let her go."

"Her big goal right now is getting through graduate school."

"I know she will have to answer, but I'll mention it to you. I have a request from the film department. They are having a film festival in March at the Millard Auditorium. Among other things they are showing two silent films and want a pianist to accompany one of them, just like in the old days. Sharon would be the perfect person. I am going to ask her if she would be interested."

"That would be a lot of fun. I think she would like to. It's different."

"Well, I'll have her come in."

Dr. Bernard hesitated for a moment. "Perhaps I shouldn't ask, but are you two dating?"

"We are," Craig answered happily. "I find her very delightful to be with."

"I wish you well, because you would complement each other beautifully."

"Thank you."

"It is almost time for your class. I'm glad we talked. All good news. Thanks for stopping by."

"My pleasure."

♫

The next evening Sharon asked Craig, "I have a note so see Dr. Bernard Friday at one. Do you know what he wants? Is it about us?"

"We had a long talk yesterday and he wanted to know if I was planning to be here next year. We talked about competition. The vocal groups."

"What does he want with me? Do you know?"

"I do know and it is not about us, although he

did ask if we were dating, and I said yes. What he wants to talk to you about, they are going to accept you in graduate school, but you knew that."

She said happily. "Relieved but I thought so."

Craig also told her what Dr. Bernard had said about the film festival.

"I am so glad you told me. That sounds exciting. I have never done anything like that before. What do you think?"

"Sweetheart, it is your decision. You can always make something up if you have to. You're good at that."

"Do you know what the films are?"

"He didn't say."

Later they snuggled on the couch. "It is so cold this is the best thing we can do." They needed a respite from music, "How about TV?"

They didn't watch it for long. He pulled her on top and they nestled close and forgot the world.

♫

Friday, Sharon went to Dr. Bernard's office to hear the news she already knew. She told him she would love to play for the film festival. And she also expressed thanks for being accepted into graduate school.

"On your way out tell Dorothy to make an appointment for you to meet with the film people."

The next morning Craig and Sharon arrived at the church to meet with the young people. Deacon Ely met them in the foyer and there were warm greetings.

"It is a cold day to be out and I appreciate your both coming. We have twelve children here today, mostly older."

Craig said, "An older group might be good to start with."

"Let's go in and meet them."

There were introductions and they talked to each one of the children.

Deacon Ely spoke to the group that was rather lively. "You know Miss Sharon and Mr. Craig is a choral director and they are here to introduce you to music and help you learn to sing. You will be on your best!" He said emphatically as his eyes popped.

When they all settled down, Craig asked, "What would you like to do first?"

They all called out, "Sing."

Sharon nodded her head yes and smiled.

"Let's get our chairs in order, boys in back, girls in front. What would you like to sing?"

"Let It Shine," was almost unanimous.

She quickly found it in a songbook on the piano and gave it to Craig and started to play without music. Craig sat down in front of them. He didn't want to stand just yet, but wanted to be at their level as he started to work with them.

"First, let me show you some hand signs for when I want you to sing soft or loud."

They sang several songs while Craig made an effort to lead.

Sharon played "big" as they sang.

After that, Craig asked if anyone would like to sing a solo. Two boys raised their hands.

Craig was pleased to find two beautiful young voices willing to sing for him.

Then he asked, "How many of you can read music?"

Only one hand went up.

"If we are going to have a young choir we have to learn to read music. Would everyone be willing to do that?"

There was an anxious call of yes.

Then they all played a musical game with cards that Craig and Sharon had dreamed up.

When they finished Sharon said to the group. "Let's ask Mr. Craig to play the piano for us. He plays very well."

They all gathered around the piano and Craig played two short and happy songs. They all listened very intently and thought that was very nice.

"That is all for today. I am so proud of all of you and you sang so beautifully," Sharon told the group and they became a bit more active.

Deacon Ely was there for the hour and showed satisfaction. "These are young voices ready to change, but now they can produce some angelic tones. I hope they stay interested because we could have a nice little children's choir," Craig expressed.

"I believe the congregation would love that. We all love to sing."

"I'm with you. It is a beautiful way to express yourself."

"We'll try to hold their interest and work within their attention span," Sharon said.

♫

After the cocktail hour Sharon went directly to Craig's

He kissed her lovingly and she returned the welcome.

"Come in the kitchen. I have everything about ready. You want to change first?"

"Yeah, I brought a sweater and jeans."

"Go ahead while I finish up."

Sharon changed and came back to help him.

They sat down and Craig served.

"A seafood casserole, very good."

"You can tell what it is?"

"Honey, it's great."

They chatted about classes, the children and other musical topics.

They had just finished the dishes when they heard a terrible crash upstairs. They both looked at each other. "That didn't sound good. Is Mrs. Zachery home?"

"I saw her this morning when I left for church."

"Let's go see what happened. She could be hurt. Or is someone breaking in?"

Quickly they ran upstairs, but found the front door locked.

Craig called, "Mrs. Zachery—Mrs. Zachery." There was no answer.

"Let's check the back door."

It was also locked and again she did not answer.

"We had better call her daughter."

They went back downstairs and called. She told Craig there was a key on the back porch in the blue flowerpot, for the back door.

They ran to the back and opened the door and through to the front and found that a bookcase had fallen on her. Sharon called an ambulance and then her daughter back, while Craig removed the bookcase.

"Please lay still Mrs. Zachery, Craig and I are here and the ambulance is coming. Isabella is going to meet us at the hospital. Please be very still, you might have a broken bone. They will know how to move you. We'll stay with you and," she turned to Craig, "I'll go with her and you drive over."

Shortly the ambulance arrived and they were on their way to the hospital. Craig found them in the emergency room and soon Isabella arrived.

At her bedside, Isabella asked her mother if she knew what had happened. She could barely speak although a few words sounded like she didn't know.

Craig said, "We heard the awful crash and found her. I got the bookcase off while Sharon called the ambulance and you."

"Oh, I am so glad you were home. She could have laid there for hours."

"Oh gosh yes. You remember my girlfriend Sharon Heisendorf. She came with your mother in the ambulance."

"Yes, we met before Christmas once. It was so sweet of you to do that."

Craig asked, "Is someone else coming to be with you?"

"My sister Catherine. She lives further out."

173

"We'll wait with you until she gets here."

As they talked, the nurses were getting her vitals and said they would be taking her to x-ray shortly.

Catherine arrived and Craig and Sharon decided to go. "Please let us know as soon as you hear something. Also I locked her house and I'll be there."

They went to his car. "Honey I brought your coat. You left without one."

"Thank you, you're so good to me," and he took her hand and he could feel that she was trembling.

At home they discussed what had just happened.

"She looked so sad lying there. How long has her husband been gone?"

"I don't know exactly, but she implied a long time. Come, I'll make us some hot tea," he said as he took her hand and noticed that she seemed quieter.

"It is so sad when one has to give the other up. It changes your life completely."

"If she has broken bones, she may have to go where she can get constant care. She could have had a stroke and grabbed the bookcase and over it went."

"Her eyes were a little glassy and she wasn't too responsive. My grandmother Heisendorf had a stroke and my grandfather took care of her for almost a year. We all lived close so we helped out. It was terrible to see her suffer, and my grandfather too."

"That is devotion."

"They were."

"Mrs. Zachery is in her late eighties and has been mostly caring for herself. Her daughters take her out. This is a big house and I know she has a cleaning lady because she asked me if I wanted her to stop down. I said I could do that. That is when she gave me her daughter's phone number."

"You make a mean cup of tea. It really makes me feel warm," she said softly, trying to ease the situation.

He returned the smile. "Why don't you play for us? That will help too. Music can do so much. It heals, it make you sad and happy. It takes you away from the bad moment and finds a better one."

They went to the piano and Sharon said as she played gently, "It's not bad to use music, especially playing as an outlet. When I was younger I remember doing that."

She played softly without music for about fifteen minutes while Craig sat beside her with his arm around her. They both knew what was happening between them and held this quiet time in reverence, what love expected of them.

Craig said softly, "Time will be very fast and that is why we have to do the things we love and with the one you love." He turned her head and kissed her tenderly.

She stopped playing and touched his face. "I so agree."

Their minds were slowly exiting the trauma that had just happened.

Craig said, "I think it is late and I'll let you go. Are you okay to drive?"

"I feel better now that I've played and a warm cup of tea. It's close, and I'll call when I get there."

"You're sure you are okay?"
"With you near I will always be all right."
Holding each other close, they said good night.

♫

CHAPTER SIXTEEN

♫

*T*he week went as scheduled and Friday morning Isabella called and said her mother had died late last evening.

Craig expressed his condolences and said, "Please let me know the arrangements when they are complete."

He found Sharon practicing later in the morning and quietly slipped in. She did not hear him, so he sat for a few moments listening to the love of his life play, even if it was just a passage over and over.

"Hi sweetheart," he said rather solemnly. She detected his demeanor and asked, "What's wrong?"

"Mrs. Zachery died last evening."

"Oh no." And she put her hands to her mouth.

"Isabella said she had a stroke and multiple broken bones. It was just too much for her frail body."

♫

After working with the children on Saturday

and a light lunch, Craig and Sharon went to the funeral home to express their sympathy.

She had been a string teacher in the earlier years. None of the students remembered her and not many of the professors.

Just as Craig and Sharon were leaving they met Dr. Bernard. "She wasn't here when I started, but I knew her from casual meetings."

"Her funeral is at eleven Monday. I don't have a class so I think I will attend. I'll tell Dorothy I'll be out."

They talked quietly for a few more moments and then went their separate ways.

"I'll be over for church tomorrow."

♬

The excitement for the coming week was Craig's faculty recital. One evening earlier when they were eating he asked her, "Could I bore you by playing through my recital material and get your opinion."

"Hearing you play your beautiful compositions is never boring."

"When?"

"Tonight. Now."

Sharon settled in one of the big comfortable chairs. It was dark so she could not see the winter garden. She listened very intently to his every note.

When he had completed his program, he made eye contact with her. "How was it?"

She sat down next to him.

"Beautiful. Your sonata is like a bell curve. It

178

starts so seemingly simple and then climbs to a height through modulation and then it comes back in degrees of such speed you are unaware when you've reached the bottom. I love it. I want to play it at recital sometime." Her gestures matched her words.

"That was really fun to work out. Sometimes you get an idea and then you find it is hard to work. "Sonata" was not like that."

"Did you name "Woodland Fantasy" before you wrote or after?"

"I named it first. It was motivated by a park where I was stationed while in the army. I would go there and read and take notes and this is it."

"Then you played "Virtuoso in E." That is a big piece and lot of everything."

"I am thinking about playing that at competition sometime."

"What about "Interlude?"

"Just what an interlude is, a respite. After "Virtuoso," ones needs a short and mild and melodious group of notes to rest the hearing. Then "Rhapsody" and you know that well."

"I am so glad I was here to do it for you. And I like it a lot."

"Evocation of Emotions," Craig said, "is a part thing. Short expressions of its name. Happiness, in a major key and little up and down. Elation is wild and all over the keyboard."

"And I chased every note."

"Then there are tears. Lot of ascending chord in different keys. Apathy is depicted in very close harmony. Passionate, big and smooth. Sensitive is light with staccato here and there. Poignant streams into a nothing at the end. This one won me the best recognition."

"It is beautifully varied and so very well structured, and it sketches the emotions exactly. Worthy of the award you received."

He looked at her and said, "I think you're going to be my best critic."

"I am being honest. They are all wonderful. "Seasons: A Suite."

"I set up four Pissarro prints, went to the keyboard. Winter is heavy and full chords but in a major key. Spring is light and colored in pastels sounds."

They both laughed at his interpretation.

"Summer is bold and autumn is quiet and knows that it will soon give way to sleep or death."

"Your last one is really dark. Were you unhappy or did something happen?"

His eyes fell and he thought for a moment.

"If you don't want to talk about it, I didn't mean to pry."

He took her hand, "No love, I will share anything with you because I know you will understand. It was a dark time. As I mentioned before, my father died right at the end of high school. I was heartbroken for losing him and seeing my mother and sister so sad too. So many things in life you have some control over but not death. It creates an awful feeling, so helpless. I wrote an undeveloped version of it at that time. Later I completed it and, each time I play it, my dad is with me."

"He would be very proud of your accomplishments. Your mother and sister are here to enjoy them." She smiled softly through each word. "My darling man, how I love you and feel so much a part of you through music. Playing is one thing, but to express yourself by creating and putting feelings into notes that become a beautiful sound, dark or happy, is a very special talent and you have that talent."

"You are so kind with your words."

"Well, the judges thought so. You have awards to prove it. The recital order seems perfect and I am sure everyone will enjoy."

♫

The day of Craig's faculty recital arrived. He and Sharon went back to school early to check that everything was in order. As all of the faculty performances, it would be in the recital hall. They mingled backstage as the crowd gathered.

"There seems to be a lot of people."

Sharon said, "I'll go see."

She came back and said, "It is almost full and we have fifteen minutes to go. I'll have to stand."

"You have already heard the program."

"I'll go now and let you have a few moments to collect yourself."

Sharon wanted to give him a quick kiss, but she knew that would not be appropriate.

She went in the back of the hall and Glenna caught her attention. She motioned to come and sit with us.

"Were you backstage?"

"I was, to give him support, as if he needs it."

The lights were dimmed. Craig in his professional and stately manner, entered to a warm applause that he graciously acknowledged. He sat down at the piano and paused a moment and then began to play.

It was a beautiful extended hour of his expression in sound as he heard and saw and arranged the notes on their home, the staff.

The applause was so long that he had to play an encore. Then, as he was saying thank you and smiling, a young person brought a bouquet of white roses. He was surprised and thought they must be from Sharon.

When all appreciation calmed, Dr. Bernard came on stage, "A beautiful selection of Dr. Jamieson's own compositions. We thank him for sharing. He will be in the outer foyer, and if you so wish, you can stop by and thank him personally. Good evening and thank you for coming."

The lights came on and the crowd slowly started to move about.

By the time Sharon, Glenna and Kelly got to the foyer the girls' glee club had surrounded him. Others came to express how much they had enjoyed this beautiful hour.

Sharon saw Karen and Jim and they hugged.

"I haven't seen you much lately."

"We have been working on tonight's program and "Opus." His landlady died. Been really busy."

Quietly Karen asked, "Have you heard from Joel?"

"Nothing. No letter, no phone call. Nothing."

"It is so hard to believe, but Craig seems so perfect for you."

"We have the same interest and that seems important. Come on over and say hi."

"Karen!" and he kissed her on the cheek, "it is so nice of you to come. Jim," and he extended his hand.

"This was a fantastic program. Love your compositions," Karen said.

"Why don't you two stop over at my place and have a glass of wine? It is close and we won't keep you too late."

Jim said, "We'd love to."

They all arrived at Craig's and Sharon said, "Who sent the beautiful roses?"

He looked at her rather shyly. "They are not from you. That is why I said thank you in the car, I just assumed."

"You had better check the card."

They all waited. "Oh my, from the girls' glee club."

"Oh how sweet," Karen expressed.

"I didn't thank them because I thought they were from you." And he looked sheepishly at Sharon.

"I would have sent red. In all of my four years I have never seen flowers presented at a faculty recital. Do you have a vase?"

"How nice of them. No, all I have that will hold them is a jar."

As Sharon put them in the jar she said, "If you will get the wine, I'll get some cheese and crackers."

"This is a great little place you have here. Sharon told me your landlady died. I'm sorry to hear that."

"Thank you. I really like it here and hope I don't have to move."

The evening was short but pleasant and they offered to take Sharon home, but Craig said, "I'll do that later. I believe we have to get organized for the children tomorrow."

After they left, they prepared for Saturday and then Craig lowered the lights and put on soft music. "Well, how did the evening really sound? I value your opinion."

"It was very, very nice. The order was perfect and you looked wonderful and handsome, and so very professional and you played beautifully."

"I haven't done many recitals, other than playing my compositions for the judges. But I liked doing it. Where I was before we didn't have this. I like this school so much better. Its own little campus and it's so much better for music. In Texas we were lost in academia. There, when you struck up a conversation you might be talking to a chemistry professor and always having to identify yourself. Here you know."

"And the girls love you. I hear the buzz."

"That is nice, but I am only interested in one girl loving me," and he pulled her close.

"I didn't want you to go home with Karen and Jim because I wanted some quiet time with you."

"I wasn't about to."

She curled up in his arms and he kissed her long and passionately.

She whispered, "Craig. I love you."

"Oh my beautiful Sharon, I too love you so very much."

♫

CHAPTER SEVENTEEN

♫

*T*he snow fell softly and gracefully throughout the days. The outer world was silent and white. Wood smoke curled above the housetops and scattered into the unknown. The ominous sky held its secrets, changing from hour to hour. Outside Craig's piano room, the little garden was deep in sleep. The statue of the little girl holding her doggie was frozen in time. No leaves dangled and red berries were numbed by the cold. The grasses were shades of wheat and their lacy tips moved delicately with the rhythm of the gentle winter wind.

Sunday evenings had become special for them. There was no practice or homework for either. The past week was slowly becoming a memory and the new week was yet to begin.

Sharon arrived after playing. After a warm greeting and at dinner they discussed their week. "I want to spend every extra minute working on your Opus."

"I'm glad we don't have to miss classes.

Honey, you're so prepared in every way."

"Memorizing is never a problem. Just making my fingers do what I tell them."

"Also I have been thinking about what Mrs. Zachery's daughters are going to do with the house. We'll just have to wait and see, but now it's quiet time.

♫

Monday evening Craig said, "I told my composition classes they could have the week of recess to work on their piece. If they take advantage of the extra time that will be good. Most of them will. There are two that probably won't. I don't see either of them as serious composers. But hopefully they are enriched by the time they have been with me and they learn a lot from the other students. We all learn from each other." He paused, gazing gently into her eyes, "I have learned so much from listening to you practice. How you play my music. The wonderful world of music and you in my life, makes it perfect."

"I don't want to be anywhere else."

Finally Sharon said, "The winter dance is Friday."

"Yeah, I saw the poster. Do the faculty members go?"

"They do. I have been to most of them, if I didn't work. The professors and their wives come and go home early. It's chaperoned and we have never had any trouble. The music students are a serious bunch. It is like a big family here in the Music Box. If we don't have classes together we live together. The professors

187

are concerned about the students personally as well as their musical education."

"I have noticed and have tried to be concerned without seeming to be nosy. If you want to go I'll be your date."

She gave him a pleasing smile. "Well let's wait until later. We have a busy week."

"But I'll only dance with you. Promise not to leave me alone. Those girls in glee can be … well."

"Do they know you belong to me?"

"I'm not sure."

I'm glad we're going to Ohio Monday and getting back Wednesday, then we have the rest of the week to get ready for, whatever," Sharon said.

"We can sleep late Monday before we go to the airport."

"It is a beautiful composition with so much expression and if I do well, you should get the top award."

"We can hope. I know you will do well. How about a little practice time and then I'll get you home.

♫

The week, with all of its activities and classes passed without incident. They had a short practice with "Opus" every evening. She was home early, because she too had classwork to complete before Friday.

With all of the work done, they decided to attend the winter dance. It was at Wagner Hall in the strings building.

When they entered there were several faculty

members arriving too. Dr. Harrison asked Craig, "Is your new composition ready for the world?"

"I believe so. Sharon has it mastered."

"We all wish you well. I enjoyed your recital immensely and find your work superbly structured. I am sure this one is also. Enjoy the dance."

He wanted to take her hand, but said, "Let's walk in and begin to dance."

As she gazed into his eyes, it was hard for him not to pull her close and kiss her lovely face that held the smile that said so much.

"We'll probably have to dance with someone else, but try not to leave me alone too long," he whispered. Just then Jody and her date Will came by, and Will said, "May I, please?" They exchanged partners.

Craig started the conversation, "Are you pleased with how your glee club sounds this semester?"

"Oh yes. We sound very special. You somehow bring out our voices, unlike Dr. Westmore. We like him, but we all like you better."

"Thank you Jody, but Dr. Westmore is a wonderful instructor and very talented and we have become good friends. You are graduating in May?"

"I am."

"What are your extended plans?"

"I want to go to New York and audition for some things. I want to see what I can do."

"You do a lot of work in the area now."

"Yes. I have sung for a lot of events these four years."

"I wish you well. Keep us up on what you are doing. I believe your date has come to claim you."

Sharon back in his arms, "Will is a nice young man but you belong here."

She whispered, "This is where I want to be."

Craig pulled her as close as he could being among students and professors. "Our friends know that we are dating. Dr. Bernard knows, so who is left? As I said before, we are not the first student and professor to fall in love."

Sharon squeezed his hand and looked lovingly into his expressive blue eyes.

They continued to dance and talk softly as the band played a group of slow arrangements.

When it stopped he suggested they get a cool drink.

They made their way to the refreshment area and Craig got sodas.

Some of Sharon's friends and their dates were also there.

"Hi all," Craig said to the group. "Is everyone going home or staying around and relaxing?

Glenna said, "I am going home."

"Where is home?"

"Pittsburgh."

"The music school there is a real good one."

"But here is top of the list."

"You are right about that. Sue, going home? I believe you told me you live in Virginia."

"Yes, but I am staying here and working on things. It is a nice quiet time and can get a lot done."

Will joined in, "And we can go to a movie or

something else without feeling guilty. Extras don't fit into our schedule very well. And the practice rooms are open."

Craig knew all of the students and they continued their casual conversation as they finished their drinks.

He turned to Sharon. "May I have this dance?"

After a few more they decided their evening was over.

At Sharon's, "I am glad we went. It is nice to mingle among the students other than the classroom."

"I got acquainted with many of the girls while I lived in the dorm. We were all new together. Glenna and I were roommates for two years and still good friends. Want a cup of tea?"

"No thanks. We have the kids tomorrow. I am pleased with the way they are learning to read music."

"I am too. They have a good teacher."

"Are you enjoying working with them? If not, we'll just say we have too much to do."

"No, I like doing it. They are good kids and so far they seem interested."

He reached for her and she walked into his arms. "I could hardly wait to get you away from all of those people so I could hold you." His hand on her back he moved her even closer. After a passionate kiss that made them both weak, he said, "Tomorrow."

♫

Sunday evening they worked on "Opus" for the last time before the competition.

191

"You have mastered these embellishments perfectly."

"I feel comfortable. The judges will note the composition and not the person that plays."

"I think they are both important. I met you at the right time."

Craig thought, not just to play my music, but to fall in love. Eileen and I were pretty serious. I am so glad I waited. A comforting thought.

They read over the notes they would need for tomorrow. "Plane leaves at two, gets there around four. We'll have dinner and then get you to sleep. I want you to be well-rested."

At her house he stayed only a few moments.

"See you tomorrow at twelve."

Alone Sharon finished putting a few things in her bag and decided to shower and sleep.

In the dark of her bedroom with only the soft moonlight easing through the blinds, she tried to let his composition play through her head, but it fought with Craig the person that she had fallen in love with. He shares his love of music in every way. He draws me into his soul. He wants his music and me to be one. I suppose this is why we work so hard to interpret Bach so long ago and Craig is here and can tell me the feeling he wants me to put into it. He seems to step outside of my being his girlfriend. As he instructs he is very respectful and considerate. The girls in glee say he is that way with them. He explains so easily and clearly. That is why the kids at church are beginning to sing so nicely. He knows exactly how he wants something played or sung and can express it so well. I love his energy and strength. I saw it in his conducting. When he sings his emotions show as when he kisses me. Oh, to make love to him has to be the most wonderful thing I will experience. Let it slip gently into our lives.

♫

CHAPTER EIGHTEEN

♪

*T*he morning was crisp but clear and it was a good day to fly. They boarded the plane and take-off was shortly thereafter. He held her hand until the plane reached its height. The two hours passed quickly and they landed and a cab took them to the designated hotel for those participating in the competition.

"Why don't we get settled and then have dinner or a walk first?" Craig asked her.

"Let's go for a walk to stretch and get acquainted with the surroundings. It doesn't seem as cold as when we left New York. I suppose being a little south makes the difference."

"I'd like a walk too," he answered with a smile.

They went to their rooms, which were only four doors apart. He came back in a few minutes and they were on their way to explore the area. Hand in hand they strolled along, looking in the windows of the boutiques on this busy street.

"Have you been here before?"

"No, but I looked into what they offered for a

composition major. This is a highly rated school, but at the time, their composition department didn't have the classes that I thought would be necessary for the making of a good composer."

"Did you ever consider coming to New York?"

"I did, but it was a little too expensive and I thought I could get what I wanted in Texas. I wanted a complete curriculum for piano, voice and composition and it offered all of that. I have to admit it was closer to home. As I said, my dad had just died so it was nice to be near my mother for a while. I would shoot home on weekends as often as I could, taking my roommate Kevin with me."

"We just passed a little French restaurant. Let's check it out."

They went in and were seated ready to enjoyed French cuisine.

"I don't want to have any wine. Maybe tomorrow if we like it here, we can come back and have a toast," Sharon expressed.

"I won't either. We'll just enjoy the food and go back and get a good night sleep. There is a shuttle every hour, so what time do you want to go over?"

"I play at three, so one will be early enough. I would like to sleep late and eat later too."

"Anything you wish my dear Sharon. Again, I don't know how to say thanks for doing this for me."

She took his hand. "You are so sweet and no presents, Craig. I'm your girlfriend now and want to do for you. This is a nice change of scenery. As you know, us students don't get off campus very much."

They had finished their dinner and noticed that

it had grown dark. "Want to get back?" he asked.

"Yes. And thank you for the wonderful cuisine."

They walked back even slower than before, talking about tomorrow. He tucked his hand in her heavy wool mitten.

"These mittens are really good for keeping warm which is a must for playing," he said as he squeezed her hand.

"My Aunt Katy made them for me when she knew I was coming north."

"Maybe she could make me a pair. They are really great. You talk about her a lot."

"We're very close. She has always been attentive. She supported me when I wanted to go to music school. My parents did not."

"You proved that parents are not always right."

"Well, I don't have a job yet."

"But you have supported yourself for two years and ready to go on to graduate school."

"And they think I'm a waitress, which they are not happy about."

"I just don't understand their thinking."

"Does your Aunt Katy know that you play at the country club?"

"Oh yes. I can share with her. We can't forget the scholarship made it all possible."

"Did you go to work immediately?"

"Yes. I knew I would have to pay after the two years so I had to start working immediately. I saw an ad in the newspaper for a piano player at the country club so I made arrangements and went out. I played for them and they hired me on the spot. I have been there ever since, except last summer when I was in Salzburg. And when I went home for a while in the summer."

"You so deserved Salzburg. Sweetheart, you are special in so many ways."

She gave him a loving smile for those words and whispered. "Thank you and so are you."

At her door in the hotel, "I am going to say goodnight here and you said about eleven you would like to eat."

He looked lovingly at her and kissed her once, "Happiness and contentment are is on our side," he said, "and good night my love Sharon."

♫

At exactly eleven he knocked lightly on her door.

She opened it immediately and they greeted each other warmly. "I'm glad to see you. I am a bit hungry."

After a half-breakfast and half-lunch they went back to their rooms, and gathered their things and caught the one o'clock shuttle to the campus. With direction they found the check-in. They went to a room where Sharon could warm up and play for a while. The attendant said, "I'll call for you when we are ready for you to play. It should be close to three."

They thanked him and she sat down at the piano to do her warm up exercises. Craig gazed out the window as he heard every note she struck.

After completing her exercises she played

through "Opus" and when she completed it, she looked at Craig for approval.

"Perfect. Play it that way." He paused. "Come and look out the window at this beautiful park." He took her hand. "Everything about you amazes me and you are so relaxed."

"I am. I have played out for a long time. Although this is special and I want it to be perfect."

"Do you want to play some more?"

"No I feel fine, and just being near you gives me strength."

They enjoyed the park below and waited for the attendant to return.

A little after three he came for her.

No words were spoken, only their eyes locked upon each other. Sharon went to play and Craig went to listen.

Another attendant came on stage and asked her if she would like to play a short selection so she could get the feel of the action. She played the selection that she had composed in Salzburg. After getting the feel, she relaxed and put herself in the state of mind that she always called on when she played. Today it was to engage Craig's inner soul, just steps away.

Craig met her as she came off stage and had nothing but praise. They walked back to the room, just smiling at each other.

"We did it again. Rather you did it," Craig said happily.

"Honey you composed it and I think it went well. I was relaxed just like at your house. The piano was very accommodating."

"Thank you love. It was a lot of time and stress and I will be ever grateful to you. Are you okay?"

"Oh yes, but it is a weight off my shoulders."

"Would you like to listen to a few of the others?"

They gathered their things and went to the auditorium. They listened until just before six o'clock and then caught the shuttle back to the hotel.

"The French restaurant again."

The shuttle arrived at the hotel and Craig said, "Let's freshen up and I'll be back in about fifteen minutes."

They walked to the restaurant and chose a small booth. The waitress came and said, "It is good to see you back. Are you here for the competition?"

Craig answered, "We are and it's very nice."

"I wish you well and what can I get for you?"

He ordered a carafe of wine and hors d'oeuvres. They made their selection from the main course and then relaxed.

"What we heard this afternoon was good, but it didn't seem very intricate," Craig said.

"I didn't think so either. The embellishments were in patterns and they were not exciting. I liked yours so much better."

"But what was that little selection that you played before you started? I didn't recognize it."

"You wouldn't. I wrote it."

"It was beautiful. Why haven't you played it for me?

She just looked at him and it told all.

"It was an assignment in Salzburg."

"Was it for someone else?"

She said nothing but just gazed into his wonderful blue eyes.

"I didn't mean to pry, but it was excellent."

"That's okay. I had forgotten about it until he asked me if I wanted to get the feel of the piano, and that came to mind. I didn't want to start a Bach or something."

Sharon felt his concern and put her hand on his thigh, telling him that all was well. "What kind of wine is this? I like it. A carafe is just enough. So what did you think of the second piece we heard?"

"Frankly, I did not like it. The structure was all messed up as I heard it."

Their conversation continued about the new music. After a tiny crème brûlée, they slowly walked back to the hotel.

"Our plane doesn't leave until twelve, so we don't have to hurry. And we have the rest of the week, maybe we can go to a movie. Speaking of movies, when are you going to meet with the film festival people?"

"Monday, he's coming over at four."

"Would you like to use my office?"

"Oh yeah, that would be good."

"Also what do you think about driving down so you can meet my mom? Weather permitting."

"We're free until Saturday."

"I'll call her when we get back."

"Come on over to my room," she said as they got off the elevator.

She unlocked the door, took his hand and

pulled him in and closed the door. She turned and took his other hand and gazed into his velvet blue eyes, offering that little sensuous smile. She said softly, "I thought it over and there is a present you can give me."

"And?" His eyes widened.

"Yourself—Craig I love you. Stay with me tonight and make love to me."

He took her in his arms and warmth traveled between them. "One thing more beautiful than music will be making love to you. You will be the song in my heart. I love you so much Sharon."

He released her and with a quiet tender smile on his face said, "I love you with all my heart. I want to know that our love is real. Do you love me enough to marry me? If you do, I will stay and make love to you way into the night and we'll watch the sunrise and know it's a new day and our new life together."

"Oh Craig." Tears rolled down her cheeks over a happy smile. "Every part of me loves every part of you, and more than enough to marry you. When I found you, I found complete happiness."

He embraced her and held her so tightly. "This is what I have wanted to hear for so long, and I don't want to ever let you go. You stir my emotions more than music and I never thought that would happen, to love you now, even more."

Sharon thought, I will give him every part of me. He will kiss my breasts as he did before, but not stop. He will touch me and make me wild and I will let him kiss every part of me as I will him. He will be mine body and soul. He is the perfect happiness of my dreams.

Craig mirrored her thought of desire. Don't be shy when I love you. Offer yourself to me. Let the thrill of my body reach yours and let us reach our passion together.

"My love, our first love will not be blessed with music, our passion will be the music in our hearts. It will be as we have never known."

The music of the universe sang for Craig and Sharon. The stars smiled and played in the heavens as they opened their hearts and bodies to each other without pause. Love that had gathered in waiting for these special moments was at last released to one another. It was a love they both had hope for and now they found.

Their love lasted long into the night and they fell asleep in each other's arms.

They awoke to a new day and they lay close. Craig said, " 'Love comforteth like sunshine after rain.' "

♫

CHAPTER NINETEEN

♩

*C*raig opened the morning with, "This day is special because as we go forward. I know you will be my wife and I your husband. I will eternally love you."

"Oh Craig eternity will not be long enough for us to love each other."

"Let's think of now" He said as he moved closer and whispered, "and we have a little more time, and I have a good idea as to how to spend it."

As they kissed each other passionately, the moment passed into an hour.

"Sharon darling, we have a plane to catch and there are thousands of days before us to love each other. Now we have to get dressed and meet the timetable."

"I know sweetheart. Loving you for the first time was so special, I don't want it to end."

"Our love will never end."

He took her hand. "Let's go. I have to take a shower and get dressed."

"No you don't. Shower with me."

The warmth of the sprinkling water on their bodies brought a rebirth of their feelings. One more time they shared sensations that left them in awe of each other. Drying each other with the heavy white towel ended their first time together.

Craig said, "Why don't you get everything together and go with me to my room?"

What had been enough time in the morning to catch the plane had turned into, we are going to have to hurry along. After a quick breakfast, they were on their way to the airport and soon on the plane to New York.

Again, he held her hand as they took off and when airborne he just gave her a big and beautiful smile. She responded by laying her head on his shoulder. "Love you Craig," she whispered.

"Love to you my Sharon. What a wonderful life were going to have together."

They relaxed and then Craig mentioned, "I have to think about my next composition."

"I was going to ask you about that."

"I have several ready, but I need to pull them together. And now I have a new emotional strength."

"Your new pieces will explode."

"You called it exactly." And he had to laugh. But more seriously he whispered. "You have certainly awakened emotions in me that I never thought existed."

"I am so glad it was me."

"I remember the day in Dr. Bernard's office, I had doubts that anyone could do what you did in such a short time. Not too many could have."

"Yeah, that day I discovered..." and she

quickly paused to catch her words.

"You discovered what…?"

"Oh nothing."

He kept looking at her, waiting for her answer.

"Is it that bad that you can't tell me?"

She paused again. "No, just funny. Promise me you won't take back any of the last twenty-four hours."

"Nothing would cause that. I promise."

"Well, that day I first saw you in the recital hall, I thought you must be the new janitor."

Craig had to laugh. "The janitor! Why?"

"Your shirt and khakis were wrinkled and your hair was unruly. You had on sneakers. I knew there was someone new and I just thought you were him and had slipped in to listen to me play. As you know I didn't want any one there. But you were nice when you talked to me and I felt a little bad. Then when I found out who you were, I really felt bad."

"I remember how those dark eyes of yours flashed. I wanted to get out of there. Oh you funny girl, I love you so much." He had to laugh again. "I do apologize for looking so bad but most of my stuff had not arrived. I didn't have an iron or most of my clothes. This is too funny."

"I'm glad you think so. Again, I am sorry."

He put his finger on her lips to stop her words.

"It is a beginning that we can look back on some day and laugh again. I could see that you were surprised when we met in Dr. Bernard's office and I didn't realize it was twofold."

"You being there made me nervous, especially a big muscular janitor."

"You know me now."

She smiled so warmly. "And oh so much."

Their plane landed to a bright and sunny afternoon, although still cold.

On the way home he asked. "Will you stay with me tonight?"

"I will but I have to get some things."

"I'll call mom when I get home and will know if she has any plans for tomorrow and the next. We can get an early start."

Craig got her bag and said. "I will call you before I come back so you will know if we're going to Albany. You want to practice?"

Craig called back and said that his mother was very excited to have us.

"So gather what you need for the next couple days and I'll be over to get you in about an hour."

"An hour will be good."

"We'll go out to eat tonight since we won't be here for the next few days. When we come back we can get ready for next week. But tonight my girl, you might not get much sleep."

"I hadn't planned on it."

♫

After Craig and Sharon had breakfast and practiced they were on their way to visit his mother. As they drove their conversation was mostly about music.

"You'll be finalizing your graduate recital, but have you thought about recitals for the public?"

"I thought graduate school over first."

"Sweetheart, you have the repertoire, and I would get going on that soon. I'll do some research for you. Also Dr. Bernard must have contacts. I can be your agent."

"If it is not too soon, I'd like that. That's been my goal beyond graduate school."

"Honey you don't have to wait. You are ready now."

The drive was pleasant and not much traffic.

"There doesn't seem to be as much snow down here as we have at home." She said observing the landscape.

"I was noticing that. The weather promised to be clear for a few days. We'll leave early tomorrow afternoon and be home before dark. Saturday we'll be back with the kids at church and you work."

"This week has been wonderful. It went fast and I was anxious to meet your mother and now I am nervous."

"Oh you don't have to be. She will love you. I told her we would be there shortly after lunch so we'll stop soon. I didn't want her to fix lunch and dinner."

"She was ill at the beginning of school."

"She had the flu and it was serious and they thought that something had happened to her heart, but it didn't and she is all right. That is why I didn't make the first piano meeting, where I would have met you. And I missed your little talk about Salzburg."

After a quick lunch they arrived at Craig's mothers.

"Oh, dear children, do come in."

Craig gave her a quick kiss on her cheek and

said, "Mom, this is Sharon and she has said 'yes' to marrying me. Sharon my mother Helen."

She hugged Sharon and tears fill her eyes. "Oh, I am so glad to meet you and so happy for you. He is a good boy."

"Oh mom you're biased."

"Of course I am, but you are. I knew you would find that special girl. And you have."

"She is special and plays the piano like an angel"

All the while Sharon smiled.

"Bill said he would try to get out early. He had a meeting with a client this afternoon."

"Has he been busy?" Craig asked.

"Very, the entire group has been. But first, why don't you get your things out of your car and show Sharon to the large guest room and you can take the one in the corner."

While Craig got their bags Sharon noticed the painting. "Craig told me you paint. Are these some of your work?"

"Did he tell you? Yes, I did those two. It is just a passing hobby."

"Beautiful. I love the way you use color."

"Thank you dear. Craig tells me that you have a natural talent as well as being trained in the classics."

"I do and I have worked very hard to develop that along with the Bach's and Beethoven's."

"I'm back with our stuff, just for overnight."

"Take Sharon and show her, then come back and maybe she will play for us, and you too Craig."

They went upstairs to deposit their bags and

after a big hug and kiss they went back downstairs and joined his mother in the living room.

"How did the competition go?"

"It went well and we're hoping for a good recognition."

"Please play it for me."

Sharon looked at Craig and raised her brow.

"You," and he pointed to the piano at the far end of the large room, "play better than I do."

She played "Opus" with love in each note.

"Oh honey this is the first time I have heard it. It's wonderful, Craig as the composer and Sharon playing."

"Mom she plays everything that way."

"Thank you both." Sharon went to sit by Craig.

They continued to converse when they heard the front door open.

"Bill is here and it's early."

They all went to greet him and introduce Sharon and share the good news.

They continued their conversation in the living room. Bill asked Sharon about graduating, graduate school and if they had set a date to get married.

"No, we'll work it out soon."

Helen asked, "Craig are you going to stay in New York?"

"At least until Sharon finishes graduate school. I have been asked for another year. All of that is a ways off. How is Beth?"

"She is doing well."

"How is John? Does he know there is another baby coming?"

"No. They thought soon they would tell him. A month is still a long time for a little one to wait."

"He's a sweet child." And he glanced at Sharon.

"Bill, why don't you serve wine, and I will get some things to nibble on."

A glass of wine was the perfect choice to take them to dinner.

Craig told them about Mrs. Zachery, and he didn't know what they were going to do with the house.

"I hate to ask her. The piano is the problem. Everything else I could put in boxes and go. It is such a great place, I would hate to move."

Helen asked Sharon, "He's been cooking for you."

"Yes, and they have been wonderful."

"We mostly eat together and I share in the cooking and cleaning up," Craig added.

"Oh I am so glad to hear that," his mother joined in, "most men won't get near the kitchen except to eat. Bill cooks every Sunday."

"I like it too. It is a break from reading briefs."

Dinner was long, and Helen served cake and coffee in the living room. She also asked Sharon to play "Opus" for Bill.

"I think it has been a long day and I believe we should retire," Helen suggested.

After the good nights, they all went to their rooms. Sharon took a shower, put on her long sweatshirt and started to get into bed when she heard a light knock on her door.

"Who is it?"

"The janitor."

She quickly opened the door and playfully pulled him in.

"I'll probably never live that down."

"Not soon," he said as he took her in his arms. "You didn't think I was going to let you sleep alone."

"Your mother might not approve."

"They won't even know. Their bedroom is down stair. And what was she thinking when she sent us both up here?"

He looked at her. "We are mismatched. You have the shirt and I have the pants. Let's do something about that. He dimmed the light to low and then took off her sweatshirt as she untied his sweat pants. He picked her up and laid her on the bed and cuddled beside her. They talked softly for a while and the desire for each other took the place of soft words.

♫

Morning and Craig asked softly, "Are you awake?"

"Sort of."

"I'll go get us some coffee."

Craig came back. "Mom and Bill are having a bit of breakfast and he said he would wait for us to get dressed and come down before he left. I'll go to my room to shower. Mom will think the bath is too clean. If I stay and shower with you, I'll get distracted. I'll be back in twenty minutes."

Craig and Sharon went down to the kitchen and

enjoyed a few moments with Bill before he had to leave for his office.

After breakfast, Sharon played the piano and Craig sang for his mother.

"This is the nicest morning I have had in a great while, although Saturdays and Sundays with Bill are very nice. It's our time together."

Later Craig said, "I think we had better be on our way. The sky is not as clear as yesterday and we have to get food when we get home. I hope it isn't snowing along the way."

"Let me fix you a lunch before you go."

"Mom thanks, breakfast was big enough to last all day."

They gathered their things and after loving goodbyes, they were on their way home.

The drive was clear of snow and in the early afternoon the sun made an appearance. When they reached home they went straight to the grocery store to replenish Craig's refrigerator for the coming week.

"Stay with me tonight, and after the kids I'll take you home. I think I will skip church because I have to get some things done before Monday. I have to be ready for compositions. It takes time to go over them. But come over after you play Sunday."

♫

CHAPTER TWENTY

♫

*T*he week that had just passed was a memory, but a special one for Craig and Sharon. They had shared their love and vowed to become life partners. It had brought a special happiness to their lives and within their world of music.

For everyone else it was back to classes until the next break, but there was always an energy that reflected a fresh start.

Near four o'clock, Sharon stopped by Craig's office and said she was going to the lobby to wait for the person from the film department.

"Do you want me to stay?"

"Oh yes, you can help me remember all about it. I am excited about doing this, but some reservations."

In the lobby and amidst students coming and going a young man came in with a large folder, stopped and looked around.

That could be him. She approached and asked, "Are you from the film department?"

"Yeah, are you Sharon?"

"I am, and you are?"

"Dave, and so glad to meet you. You are going to play for us?"

"Perhaps. Come on in and Dr. Jamieson has generously offered his office so we can talk."

"Great. Who is Dr. Jamieson?"

Sharon wanted to shout, the love of my life and the one I am going to marry, but she just offered, "He is our resident composer and professor."

Dave thought some old man that is out of touch with reality and the famous picture of Beethoven leaning into his music came to his mind.

They walked into his office and Dr. Jamieson stood and offered his hand as he introduced himself.

Dave said, "Thank you for letting us meet here." Thinking he is not an old Beethoven at all.

Craig said, "I am anxious to hear all about the festival and the silent movies."

Sharon added, "I am too, tell us all about it."

"Our festival is March twenty-third, fourth and fifth, and were going to start with the film that we hope you will play for, *Cyrano de Bergerac* but we thought this one everyone would know. Probably read in high school and might like to see it in another medium."

Sharon and Craig both nodded yes.

"The other is *Sunrise*, late, from 1927 and Dr. Grayson has orchestrated for a small ensemble, but won't have time to do *Cyrano* and that is why we're asking you so late. But he did a lot of preparations."

Sharon asked, "Do you have the music?"

"Maybe somewhere." And he smiled. "That is

the problem in many of the silent films, a person would just play popular music or classical. They would improvise to mimic the action on the screen. Most local theatres had a person that would play. What they used, if they had anything, was called a cue sheet with music and notes, telling the action. Professor Grayson has music and he made cue sheets."

He opened a large folder on Craig's desk and showed her the sheets.

"Oh my," she said.

"It probably looks strange but it really isn't. I play piano and I sat with him at one showing and I could follow, so you being a piano major would do okay. Also, Professor said if you wanted to use other music that would be okay, but it has to be composed before the film was release, which is 1923."

"What kind of a piano is at Millard?"

"An upright, like they used in the old days. But it is in real good condition. I played it. No missing ivories."

Craig asked, "What else is included in your festival?"

"It is entitled, 'The Progression of the Film as Entertainment.' We're including *Citizen Kane* of course. Musicals. A talk on the history and acting techniques. We have a lot of pictures of early actors and actresses. Lots of good stuff.

"Music is a big part, starting live and how it was added as background. Another group is preparing a booklet with essays about the growth of the film industry, and that is going to press in a couple of weeks so we have to know whether you will do this for us.

We need to add your name to the credits."

As Sharon was looking over the cue sheets, Craig noted a list of silent films in Dave's open folder and said, "Here is a film called *The Janitor*."

It surprised her, and she almost lost her composure. "I suppose it's real funny."

Dave not being aware of the humor between them said, "It is a comedy."

It was very hard for both of them to refrain from laughing.

Dave continued, "We'll understand if you say no. It really is a short notice. Would you like to meet and have a run-through then make a decision?"

She looked at Craig and then David, and said, "I would really like to try. It sounds like so much fun and I can improvise pretty well."

"Oh great. We wanted to do two because we had hoped to generate interest in the silent films and perhaps run more. We'll set up a practice run and Professor Grayson and the silent group will be there to give you support and then we can all decide."

"Briefly, what is your schedule like?"

"Friday afternoon and any evening. Leave a message with Dorothy, our secretary and I will get it."

"Very good, and thank you Dr. Jamieson for letting us use your office."

After Dave left, Sharon said, "Wipe that smile off your face."

"Oh I couldn't resist. And be prepared, I'm sure I can find a lot of good janitor jokes."

"I shouldn't have told you."

"No, I'm glad you did, now I have something

to tease you about."

She squinted her eyes tightly and pulled her lips together and thought I'm going to have to be really alert.

"Can we go over the cue sheets tonight?"

"Sweetheart, of course you can. Remember body and soul I am yours and now I add my piano."

They smiled lovingly at each other.

Craig asked, "If you're through for the day, let's go home and get on with our evening."

♫

One evening in the middle of the week when Sharon was practicing and Craig working on students' papers, his phone rang. Being in his dining nook, Sharon could not hear the conversation, but it was lengthy. She began to wonder if there was a problem, a student, his mother or sister, or maybe that ex–girlfriend in Buffalo. There would be long pauses and then she could hear Craig's voice but could not make out what he was saying.

When he finished, he came into the piano room and took her hand and said, "Come and sit with me."

"Oh Craig is something wrong?"

"Oh no, I didn't mean to alarm you, but it is a big matter."

They sat down on the couch and he put his arm around her. "That was Isabella."

Oh no, Sharon thought he is going to have to move.

"She called to talk about the house. No one in

217

the family wants it. She and her sister have their homes and their children are scattered or not interested, so they are going to sell it and she wanted to know if I had a glimmer of interest. She said her mother wanted it to stay in the musical family from school. I told her that we were going to be married although we didn't have a date, but a house would be something we would need. I told her I would talk it over with you. She will take us through Saturday afternoon and tell us about everything, if we are interested."

"Oh Craig, it does sound wonderful, but it is a big decision."

"It is, and that is why we have to discuss it."

"Honey, I don't have any money, only enough for graduate school."

"She gave me a tentative price and I would have enough for a down payment and I am employed. I didn't commit to anything other than going through on Saturday. The price seemed reasonable, but I will check other values of homes in the neighborhood and compare. Or—honey would you rather live out of the area. I am not adverse to that but it is really nice here."

"I really like this area, school and the homes are all one big campus. Also, do you want to stay teaching here?"

"This school is one of the best, and so far I really like it here. The city is also very musical. We're close to many big cities if you want to give recitals. Dr. Bernard also said he hoped you would consider joining the faculty. You can get your doctorate here. And after all of that one thing that we haven't talked about, a family. Then we would definitely need a house."

She smiled so contentedly. "Yes, I want to have children. Your babies will be so special. Lots of blond curls." And she ran her hand through his unruly mop.

"Or black wavy."

He turned her head and kissed her lightly. "We're going to have to set a date to get married."

"Yes. First, let Isabella take us through Saturday. We'll have a few days to think about everything."

"This area would make a great studio for private piano and voice lessons."

They spent the next days talking and weighing many aspects and questions to ask Isabella. They were looking forward to Saturday, but Friday brought the best news of all.

♫

Friday after classes, on their way to Craig's, Sharon told him that the run-through for the movie was going to be Monday at six o'clock.

"I hope you can go with me."

"Monday, yes."

At home Craig picked up his mail and they went in.

"Oh honey! Ohio! It has to be my review."

They couldn't get their heavy coats and boots off fast enough.

"Let me hold you and send good vibes."

"Should we eat first before we open it?"

"No, let's do it now. I know it is good. We can

be giddy while we eat."

Craig slowly opened the large envelope and pulled out the certificate with word announcing the highest recognition of the competition. Attached was the monetary award.

They looked at the beautiful certificate together and the check. Sharon happy with tears in her eyes, "I knew you would because what you wrote is so beautiful. Oh Craig. I am so happy for you, you so deserve it."

He just smiled. "Oh thank you, thank you."

He read the letter of congratulation. The announcement would go out Monday to colleges and newspapers and his own school.

"Honey, this check is enough for our down payment on a house, wherever."

"Call your mother."

"I will after we eat."

"Oh Craig, you have given us such a good start and I don't have anything to contribute."

"I don't want to hear that. You bring yourself and that's all I want."

"I love you Craig. You are a beautiful person and you are mine," she whispered softly.

"I'm pretty excited, and I think before we eat we need comfort for the body now that the soul is cared for."

Her contented smile told him yes.

♫

Saturday, after an hour with the children and a

quick lunch they met Isabella.

"Congratulations to both of you. You are both in the musical family, and that makes everything so wonderful. If you are interested, timing is perfect. My sister and I grew up here. It seems like yesterday yet a long time ago."

She unlocked the large double doors into the main foyer. Beautifully carved woodwork throughout told of its Victorian splendor. The staircase was to the left and to the right was the living room, which was large.

"The fireplace is in good working condition and this mantel is walnut and the small room over there we used as a library, the fireplace also good. We have always helped her keep everything in good condition. Sadly we knew this day would come."

They walked on. "And this is a dining area and on back just a big room where Dad would sit and read the paper while Mom fixed dinner. The kitchen, pantry, and back here a mud room and a bath. You can come back here from the foyer also."

Craig and Sharon were looking and listening to her and forming their own thoughts.

"There are back stairs to the cellar and upstairs, which is nice."

On the second floor there were four large bedrooms, two smaller rooms and the baths for each bedroom. "This hall is wide enough that we would spend more time playing here than in our own rooms."

"It is unusual for an older home to have a bath for each bedroom." Craig observed.

"After Dad died she had them installed and

221

rented rooms to her students at school."

They went downstairs to Craig's apartment.

"Catherine and I have taken all of the furniture and small things that we want. I am going to leave you with the key, and you and Sharon can look around again and if there are any pieces of furniture you would like, we'll just add it in. We'll clean the rest out."

The three of them talked a while longer about the house, neighborhood and school. Then Isabella said goodbye leaving Craig and Sharon alone.

The first thing they did was walk into each other's arms and take a deep breath.

"And I have to go to work this evening."

"I will skip church again, but come over after the cocktail hour."

♫

CHAPTER TWENTY-ONE

♫

Sharon arrived after playing and Craig was dressed up. She looked at him wondering, what tonight.

"I think it is time to celebrate a lot of things, a house, our winning Ohio. It is a beautiful winter evening and I didn't feel like cooking."

That made Sharon laugh as she tenderly embraced him. "Love you."

"I made reservations at Mirabella's. But you probably want to freshen up first."

Outside Craig said, "Let's walk around the house and we can talk about it over dinner."

The beauty of the late afternoon was its calm, an interlude from the falling snow. The winter sun was easing slowly from the ice-blue sky, but it stopped and rested on fields of red and gold streaks near the horizon.

Craig said, "It feels like we're alone in the universe. It is so quiet."

"We are alone in our little universe."

He took her hand that wore the heavy woolen mittens and they walked around the house.

"They're nice bushes on this side and the window from the staircase is really charming with its stained glass," Sharon remarked.

"They are nice." Although he didn't even look.

"I especially like the carving above them."

He didn't answer and appeared to be uninterested.

She thought, he is acting a little uneasy, maybe he is having second thoughts about the house. Over dinner he'll tell me.

She tried to interest him by commenting on the back porch. "I especially like this. We can eat here in the summer. I like the yard that it goes way back and we can have a vegetable garden."

"Your hands are not going to get in any dirt."

"Oh Craig, I've always grown vegetables."

They walked on and ended up in the winter garden just outside of Craig's piano room. It held a beauty, even deep in sleep. Nature had decorated the sleeping bushes with red berries. The small evergreens held touches of yesterday's snow.

Sharon said, "Of the whole yard I like this garden the best. In the spring we can have colorful flowers and it will be beautiful from the piano room."

"I like it too, and this is why I brought you here."

He looked into her contented eyes. "I wasn't sure I would even find someone that I could love as much as I love you, and who would be so beautiful and share the love of music as I do. Our love and music

224

makes us one." He paused and looked into the far away sky for a moment and then took her face in his hands.

She could feel that he was trembling very slightly.

"I have been blessed in my career and now a special love you give to me. I will treasure you and our love as the days pass by. That you have consented to be my life's partner, I want everyone to know."

He took her left hand and took off her mitten and reached in his overcoat pocket and pulled out a little ornately carved wooden box. He took out a large emerald-cut diamond ring, and as he placed it on her finger. "Darling Sharon, I give this to you with a heart so filled with love there are no words to say enough, so I will spend a lifetime showing you, being at your side, caring for you and forever being true."

Her heart was out of control and tears were waiting to flow as she said, "Craig, I'll be your love through life and eternity. I couldn't love you more. I want to grow old loving you more each day. I love you, you beautiful man and so proud to be your wife."

They held each other in the winter garden and the warmth of their hearts and their love folded them into one.

Craig looked into her eyes and wiped the tears of joy from her face and cleared his throat as well.

He smiled lovingly at her. "We have a candlelight dinner waiting for us at Mirabella's."

"This is a real surprise and one that made me cry, and yet it was the happiest." She paused, "Can we go in for a moment?"

They went in and she asked, "When did you do

225

this?" As she looked at the obviously expensive ring, flanked with two smaller emerald cuts on each side. "It is so beautiful."

"It is a family heirloom, my grandmother's engagement ring. It has been destined for me and has been in my mother's care until I found the special girl. She gave it to me when we were there."

"It was your grandmother's. What a wonderful symbol of love."

"The story goes that my grandfather gave it to her one summer day under the large oak in their yard. I want us to be married before the summer days. We also have the bands that are braided white gold."

"Oh Craig, it makes it so special and we'll carry on the love they started."

They held each other one more time.

"I need to fix my face a little before we go."

At Mirabella's they were ushered to a private room filled with red roses, and one red rose on their table between two lighted tapers. Soft music made everything complete.

"Oh Craig, you are so romantic and I love you so much."

"Sweetheart, these days are to be remembered so they have to be special in every way."

The waiter brought champagne and poured it for them.

He reached for her hand. "Sharon to you and our long life together."

"A long life with you, my love." And their glasses gave a tiny ring as they toasted to their love.

"The garden is now special. It has to be our."

"Are you saying that you like the house and want to buy it?"

"I do like it a lot. I want you to want it too."

"Let's go through it again and look at every corner and then make a decision. Now our dinner."

"Honey, I'm not sure I can eat after this wonderful surprise."

"The champagne will relax you, and listen to the music and then you'll be fine. I need to relax too. It's not every day that I ask someone to marry me."

As they were nearing the end of a very special day Craig said, "I have one more request."

"After this, anything."

"Stay with me tonight and the day will be complete."

"A very easy request to fill."

♫

CHAPTER TWENTY-TWO

♫

*E*arly, Sharon went back to her studio. She saw a light under Karen's door and the fragrance of coffee filled the hall.

She knocked lightly. Jim answered and said, "You are early."

"I was at Craig's. Is Karen up?"

"Yeah. I'm here."

Sharon held out her hand.

Karen's eyes got big. "Oh god it's beautiful," And they hugged each other vigorously. "Congratulations."

"He gave it to me last evening. It is a family heirloom, his grandmother's. And were considering buying Mrs. Zachery's house, or rather Craig is, I don't have any money. And Craig received top award at Ohio."

Rather loudly Karen said, "All this wonderful news. I'm overwhelmed. And we have news too. We're going to get married too."

That brought a louder response from Sharon. "I

love it. I love it." More softly, "We're going to wake up Mr. Heid. But that is great news. Congratulations to both of you," and she wiped a tiny tear from her eye.

"You two are so good for each other. I have come to the conclusion that two people should have like interests. You do and Craig and I do."

"Do you have a date?" Jim asked.

"No, but Craig said he wanted to before summer. And you?"

"Tentatively fall," Jim answered, "and we're going this weekend to pick out rings."

"This is all so wonderful. A good way to start the week. We're going to have a run-through at Millard tonight. You are still coming."

"Oh yes." Karen and Jim answered in unison.

"I'd better get going, we all have a clock to meet." And Sharon turned to go.

"Tell Craig congratulations for winning Ohio."

Jim followed. "And winning you."

"Thank you so much. I will."

At school Sharon went to the cafeteria for a cup of coffee. Glenna was there and she sat down and held out her hand.

"Oh Sharon, it is so beautiful. When? I just knew this would work out for you. Congratulations."

"Thank you." And she could not stop smiling. "Well—he asked me in Ohio, but proposed again last evening and gave me the ring. He was so romantic."

"You two make a good pair. You're both so talented. I can't imagine your kids."

They both took a deep breath from the excitement and Glenna asked, "You are still going to graduate school next year?"

"Oh yes, and Craig is going to be here too. And you will be here."

"Yeah. Have you heard?"

"No, but we should soon. We're going to have a run through of the movie tonight."

"That sounds like so much fun. We're all planning on going."

The day moved on and after a quick dinner Sharon and Craig went to Millard. Professor Grayson and three other film students were there and Dave introduced everyone. Professor Grayson asked Craig, "Are you Sharon's piano instructor?"

"No, she plays piano better than I ever will."

Embarrassed, Sharon shook her head, no. "Dr. Jamieson is our resident composer and plays beautifully."

"And she is my fiancée."

Everyone smiled and nodded happily. Dave thought, well that ends that, I was going to ask her for a date.

Professor Grayson looked at Sharon. "Have you ever played for anything like this, and how did you like those cue sheets?"

She had to laugh. "No, and the cue sheets were strange at first, but they got better."

"She improvises better than anyone I have known, so I think she will do a good gob, plus her classical repertoire is vast."

"I read *Cyrano* in high school and I did another quick read this week to help refresh my memory."

Dave spoke up. "Does anyone have any

questions?" There were no vocal responses just nods of no.

"Jack, why don't you start the reel?"

As Sharon started for the piano she said to Craig, "Take notes for me. Anything will be helpful."

In the darkened theatre with only the music that Sharon created, and the silent expression on the screen, is a timeless story of love realized too late.

The heart withdraws after a love is lost, but to stay in that state is unfair to the soul, to deprive it of physical and mental intimacy.

These poetic words about Roxanne and Cyrano written so long ago could be from the pages of today.

About halfway through the film Jack stopped and came down from the projection booth.

"I thought I would give you a rest," he said to Sharon. "The first time can be very intense. How is it going?"

"I think okay, but ask the others."

Professor Grayson spoke up. "I think it sounds wonderful. Sharon you do improvise really well and I detected touches of classical." He turned to Craig. "Really nice, don't you think?"

"Yes. It sounds great and I was enjoying it."

"Next time everything could be played very different."

Professor Grayson asked the others, "Do you have anything to add?"

They all shook their heads no.

Jack said, "Let's finish."

With the last hour behind, the lights went on and everyone seemed to come awake, even though no one was asleep, just memorized.

Craig had scribbled a few notes for Sharon in the dark and hoped he could make out what he had written when the lights came on.

Professor Grayson went to talk to Sharon. "Your interpretations were on with the action. And when you changed with the action you had such a beautiful transition." He paused. "The big question, would you like to do this for us?"

"I would really like to."

"Professor Jamieson, how did you like it?"

"I thought she did wonderful. I would hire her in a moment."

"Come on over," he motioned to the others.

They all discussed the film and the music and came to the conclusion that Sharon's music matched the action beautifully

Bruce said, "We should do this all of the time. And you didn't even have to practice."

"Oh Bruce, there is a lifetime before this moment."

"Well spent," Dave added.

They all concurred that Sharon had the job.

When she said yes there were moments of relief among the students that they could run two silent movies.

Craig asked Professor Grayson, "Your other movie is *Sunrise* and Dave said you orchestrated the music for a small group."

"I did and we practiced a few times."

"Were you a music teacher?"

"Oh yes. I went to music school a few years

back, but film has been my bigger interest and we have a wonderful film department here."

"You must have command of all of the instruments."

"A good working knowledge, but slow, and that is why I only finished one. Hopefully it sounds okay. The students like it." He paused, "Well, the evening is getting away from us and we all have other things to do. So with Sharon in agreement, we're opening at four o'clock on the twenty-third and *Cyrano* will start at six. Also Saturday at Lombardi's, there is a reception for all who participated and both of you are invited."

Craig thanked him and Sharon nodded.

They all acknowledged their new friendship and bid goodbye.

On the way to Sharon's Craig said, "I would like for you to stay with me every night, but I know you have things to do so I'll get you home."

"I want to call my parents and Aunt Katy and my brother."

"I assume you want your brother to marry us."

"I would. We always got on together. He looked after me, rather than any sibling relationship. He was off to college when I was about twelve. Then he got married and I never got to know Carolyn very well. We talk and she was always nice. He never objected my going to music school."

"It would have been a terrible waste if you hadn't."

"I was talking to Glenna this morning and we thought we should be getting our acceptance soon."

"I can tell my parents that too. Aunt Katy will be happy for me."

When they reach Sharon's studio she said, "Come on up and we can talk about the movie and your notes."

They sat down on the couch and Craig said, "My notes. You probably noticed much of what I wrote."

"You can put it in perspective for me."

"First, you really don't need a lot of big changes in style. I thought about three. Until the love scene it could be gentle. A lot of walking. Could be light. Then the love scenes need love music, more smooth and connected and that goes on for a while. The battle a little more spirited. And I noticed when there was a change, there was a little warning."

"Oh, that's great to look at it as a whole. When I was playing I was going with the moment. Your observations are really helpful. I can make my own cue sheets."

She put her arms around him and pushed him down and kissed him lovingly.

"Are you trying to start something? This beautiful girl has attacked me and what am I to do."

"You know what to do," she said softly.

"I was going to let you work."

"It is a little late to start anything, but…" She took his hand and led him to her bedroom. They undressed each other in the shadows of the late evening. After sharing their love they snuggled closely under the covers and fell asleep.

Much later Craig woke and looked at her clock

and realized it was morning. "Honey it's morning and I had better go."

Sharon jumped up and got into her robe.

"Why don't you get the shower going while I make coffee."

♪

The next evening at Craig's, Sharon called her Aunt Katy and told her about their engagement. She was very excited for them and asked about graduation.

When she hung up she relayed the conversation to Craig. "They are all coming for graduation. Jack, her son and Sue his wife. She asked if we had any wedding plans."

"Before we make any more calls, let's talk about a date."

"You sound like you have a suggestion."

"I do."

"You said you would prefer to get married here and not at home."

"Yes I believe so. My friends are all here and my family will come. Your friends will have to travel regardless."

"That's all right with me, but it is your decision and if that is it, consider—you will graduate on the twenty–sixth and all of our families will be here, so how about the next day or Sunday."

"That is a great idea, and I think I like it."

"We will have a house, somewhere."

"Then we would have all summer for a honeymoon and get settled."

I like it and something to work with."

"I'm taking you home. A guy has to have a little rest."

He looked at her with his mischievous smile and thought it had been non-stop.

♫

The school day over Sharon went to Craig's office.

"Come in sweetheart, I'll be through soon."

She sat quietly while he finished his write-up for one of his students. She looked at the pictures on his wall and thought of "Rhapsody" and how so much had happened since that day in the recital hall. She thought of the "janitor" and smiled. He looked up just then and said, "Yes?"

She just shook her head no. She didn't feel like reminding him, maybe he has forgotten.

"I'll give this to Dorothy to type for me and then we'll go. The contractor is going to meet us at five o'clock."

They arrived home just in time to get their heavy coats off and go back upstairs.

"Where did you hear about this guy?"

"Dr. Westmore told me about him and said that we could trust him for an accurate evaluation."

They welcomed the contractor and for the next hour or more they walked through the house. He explained all of the things he was checking. After they were through, they ended up in Craig's apartment and discussed a few last things.

"Overall, the house is in great shape, all but those few windows that I pointed out. That would not be a costly fix. The basic structure and the big appliances are in good shape and some rather new. The back porch needs some repairs that you could do easily. It is a very attractive buy. You are close to school and your music students."

"It's good to have your professional opinion."

"If there are no further questions, I will leave you to your dinner."

They thanked him and when he was gone they fell into each other's arms with a sigh of relief. Craig looked into Sharon's eyes. "Should we?"

"Oh yes, I feel so good."

"After we eat, I'll call Isabella and tell her that we have decided to make it our home, continuing the musical tradition that her mother had wanted."

"I'm so glad the fireplaces are in good condition. The one in the library is so charming and the mantel in the living room is beautiful with all of the woodwork. I can't wait to get it going."

"I noticed a woodpile out back, but it's rather covered with snow. I'll bring some to the porch. What furniture do you want to buy from her?"

"The dining room. I like the oval table."

"I like the chairs."

"I like the china cabinet, you can store dishes at the bottom and display at the top."

"It is quality furniture and we can find living room furniture to coordinate. The beautiful beams connect the two rooms so well, right to the library door. The atmosphere is so old-world."

"Do you like the library table?"

"Yeah and the bookshelves."

"There are some chests and bed frames upstairs. They would be a good start for the bedrooms."

"Yes. I agree."

"We can leave mine downstairs for guests. We can buy living and bedroom furniture for us. We will have until May and that will be plenty of time."

"I can bring my sewing machine over and make curtains and drapes, and we can paint and polish in our spare time, as if either of us have any."

"It is too bad that you can't just move in with me now."

"That would be frowned on by a lot of people. Best of all, you don't have to move."

"I'll call Isabella now, and it is about seven o'clock in Texas so I'll call Kevin and tell him I have a fiancée."

"Will he be surprised?"

"No."

"I'll watch television while you talk."

Craig went into his dining nook and called Isabella and then Kevin, and talked to him a long time. When he came back he had a strange look on his face.

"Is everything all right?"

"I suppose so." He sat down next to her and pretended to be watching the show, but Sharon knew different.

"What has happened? Is something wrong with the wedding?"

"Nothing, but I suppose you will know

eventually. But first, Isabella said Saturday she would send a truck to collect the furniture that we do not want. Keep anything we did and there would be no additional charge."

"Oh Craig that is so sweet of her."

"She also said to start doing whatever we wanted such as painting and dusting because it would probably be several weeks before our lawyers could close, and if we waited that would be time wasted. I thanked her and I'll send a note of appreciation."

Craig ended his conversation and pretended again to be watching television.

"And Texas."

"You knew I had a girlfriend in Buffalo."

"You mentioned that once. I thought it none of my business."

"Yes that is right, but she will be at Jeff and Sara's wedding. She and Sara are good friends. When we finally decided that we were not compatible we called our relationship over. End of story."

Sharon stared straight ahead and though of Joel and how they ended things. Finally she said, "If it would be too uncomfortable for everyone I won't go."

"Oh no! You are going with me."

Continuing to stare ahead, "That is what happened to Joel and me. I wanted to continue my career and he did not want me to. So it ended."

"Darling Sharon, we were out there searching for each other and we both could have taken different paths and not been happy. We found each other and I am never going to let you go."

She took his face in her hands. "I love you and

I know we have done the right thing. I know we were meant for each other," and softly, "beginning of story."

"That first day in the recital hall, I was in there several times before that fateful sneeze gave me away, and I knew it was more than the way you played the piano that attracted me."

♫

At weeks end Dr. Bernard popped in Craig's office all excited. "I found this on my desk when I came in." And he held up the letter from Ohio telling about Craig's award. "You must have known."

"I received the information last Friday."

"Oh Professor Jamieson, this is so wonderful for you, and we will send out a press release and it will be in the arts section next Sunday and Dorothy told me that you and Sharon have become engaged."

"Yes." And Craig had a very big smile.

"My most sincere congratulations to both of you. You are a beautiful couple."

"I will announce this at Monday's department meeting and bring Sharon and maybe we could go to the recital hall and she would play it for us. Everybody has been waiting for the news. And how did the silent movie go?"

"She is going to play, and the movie is *Cyrano de Bergerac.*"

"I must get to that. Have a good weekend, and I'll see both of you Monday morning."

♫

Saturday afternoon Craig took care of emptying the house of the unwanted furniture and Sharon practiced, then he took her home. She gave him a quick kiss. "I'll be over after the cocktail hour tomorrow."

She ran upstairs and sorting through her mail, she stopped abruptly and her body turned cold. A letter from Korea, from Joel. She was glad she was alone because she did not want Craig to see it. She was not sure she wanted to see it. Why now? She ran her finger over his name in the corner as if to connect.

Their love had ended so abruptly and with a finality that almost didn't seem real. A few words from Joel and it was over. Seven years disappeared like the tone from a note of music.

Well maybe it is just a friendly hello, but then what if it is not? Should I read it now or wait? I have work to do and I don't want to be distracted. Just getting a letter is distressing enough and the contents could be worse.

Sharon, so able to focus, did her class work while the unopened letter lay glaring on her island.

After the dinner hour she was asked to stay and play with the band until twelve. She called Craig.

When she got home, it was after twelve and her phone range. "I couldn't sleep till I knew you were home okay."

"Yeah, I'm here and safe and very tired."

Their conversation was short and she was quickly in bed. She propped herself up on the pillow and opened her letter.

It started *My Darling Rose of Sharon,* and she knew what the remainder was going to be like.

…after basic I was home for a few days and tried to call you several times but obviously no answer. I had to get back to Georgia for the long plane ride to Korea. There isn't much happening now, just watching, but that is not what I want to say. It is so much I can hardly get it on paper. I am so sorry I ended things the way I did. I just don't know why. College over, going away for two years. You not wanting to get engaged. I felt at some level you wanted a way out and I had no choice but to give it to you. But maybe you will forgive me and be my love once again. I miss you so very much. I miss you like a flower misses water. I can't enjoy the beautiful sunrise nor the sunset that falls so slowly to replenish for another day. A new day is not new, just the same old yesterday. I can't look forward to a new day until you are mine again, until I can hold you and kiss and love you. Happiness is gone from me. I see things that I should be laughing at but I only stare and think of you. I relive over and over the afternoon you came back from Salzburg. I didn't realize what being away from you would be like. I can't explain what I said at Christmas, please forgive me and I hope it is not too late to make amends and so sorry that it had to be in a letter.

My Rose of Sharon I know that I will never love anyone else should I live for an eternity. It is all of you or nothing. I love you. I love you. I love you.

When I get a furlough you could fly to San Francisco, I will too and then we can start anew or…

Exhausted, and tears streaming down her cheeks, she looked up from the plea of written words. They totally and emotionally disarmed her. She turned out her light and slid down under the covers and cried herself to sleep.

♫

Sunday morning her first thought was what she fell asleep with, emotional pain. I have to right my mind. I have to work. So glad I will not see Craig until later today. But worse I have to answer those heartfelt words. Oh god, have I done the right things by going to Craig so quickly? I know I love him so very much and I know he loves me. I was with Joel so long, that has to mean something. I told him so, but he didn't seem to hear and now he has put us in a very precarious position. Someone is going to be hurt. Choosing when it is such an important matter. I will have to do it all by myself. I'll come home early tomorrow and talk to Karen.

All through the cocktail hour, her thoughts were clouded with Joel's words and the many years and fun they had together. Their first date when he was almost shy and it took him five dates or so before he took her hand and very shyly kissed her. I remember how I wanted him to kiss me with some feeling, but it took him a while. Once we broke the teenage ice we were very comfortable with each other and life carried us together through college and that afternoon when we didn't stop, as we had so many times before. He made me feel so beautiful and that we belonged to each other. I'm not sorry that I loved him, but in some ways I wish that I had waited for Craig to be the first to love me. I don't want to hurt Joel, but what can I say? What do I really want to say?

The hands on the clock traveled fast to four. I hope my playing was more organized than my thoughts. In a daze, she drove to Craig's.

Arriving, she caught a whiff of something really good that he had prepared for their dinner. He is getting to be a good cook.

He kissed her lovingly.

"I want to change into something more comfortable," and she looked at him softly. "I need you Craig, will you make love to me?"

"Your eyes asked before there were words and I was ready for you." In his bedroom her thought were only of Craig, everything else was as far away as the moon.

He sensed her need, but felt that she was only very tired from working all weekend. Afterward he whispered softly, "You are mine darling, and I want to always be here for you. If you need a kiss, I'll find your lips. If you need a loving glance, I'll look your way. If you need my touch in some special place, I'll find where. If you need all of me, I'll give my all."

♫

CHAPTER TWENTY-THREE

♪

*A*ll welcomed the little break in the long cold winter. The melting snow exposed the tiny bushes that had been covered for so long. A small reminder of what was to come.

Craig picked Sharon up Monday morning and asked, "Are you rested? You look better. You must have been very tired."

"I was very exhausted and yes I feel rested. You helped to relax me."

"Anytime love."

She only smiled contentedly, but thought how upset she had been and it wasn't over.

They went to the piano department meeting and everyone congratulated them on their engagement, and Craig for his competition award.

Dr. Bernard started their meeting with both announcements and that Sharon had agreed to play Craig's composition for them.

"Let's all go to the recital hall and afterward come back here and we will have our meeting."

As they made their way to the hall, there seemed to be more students and professors around than usual. The word had got around and everyone was anxious to hear their Professor Jamieson's newest work.

Sharon went to the piano and Craig sat down in the front near her. Just before the lights were lowered in the packed hall, she turned and smiled at him and he responded with a tiny wink and a slight nod. She closed her eyes and when she opened them, he could see that she had slipped away.

Craig knew well her way of retreating to where it was just her and the instrument over which she had such wonderful control.

In the silent hall she played his composition with such love that it brought tears to many eyes, even her own. She held everyone spellbound until she laid her hands in her lap, raised her head and smiled again at Craig. A very loud applause rose from the crowd.

Craig went to her and took her hand and said, "You played it even more beautifully than in Ohio, and that is saying much."

Before she could thank him, they were surrounded with students and professors, the girls from the glee club, students from Craig's classes, Dr. Westmore, and several professors from strings. There was excitement for the next fifteen or twenty minutes with colleagues and students. They were all very proud of Dr. Jamieson. Motivation was in the air.

The excitement ceased and everyone went to their classes and the day continued as any Monday.

That evening Craig mentioned he got the

wedding music from the library. They added that to their schedule of practice.

"The week of the wedding is spring break, so instead of coming home, let's fly to your folks and stay a few days. We should meet before our wedding."

"They did ask when they could meet you. That sounds like a good plan. But no slipping into my bedroom. My father has a shotgun." And she laughed but Craig only smiled.

"Are they really that strict?"

"They are."

"We're staying together in Texas, so I will be a good boy when I get to your house. We'll fly to Texas Friday morning and the wedding is Saturday. Monday we can fly to Missouri. By then we'll have wedding plans."

"I like what you said about one of the days after graduation. Everyone will be here. And I was thinking it could be in our little garden where you gave me my beautiful ring."

♫

When she arrived home she saw the light under Karen's door, and knocked lightly.

"Hey, you're home early."

Sharon glanced behind her and in a whisper, "Are you alone?"

"Yeah."

"Come on over if you have a minute or two."

Sharon got out a bottle of wine and two glasses and Karen knew something was wrong because this scene had played out between them before.

Sharon asked, "Did you get your rings?"

"We did and they are being sized and Jim says he has something special planned."

"Can't wait to see them. I am so happy for you two, it is so uncomplicated."

"What happened? Please don't say you broke up with Craig."

"Oh no! I got a letter from Joel."

"Oh—oh—now!" and Karen knew from the look on Sharon's face that it had upset her.

"He's in Korea."

As she took big gulps of her wine, she read most of the letter to Karen with tears in her eyes.

"What do I do? I have to hurt him and that hurts me so much I don't know what to do."

"Why did he wait so long? Almost like he couldn't decide if he wanted to. He was in the states a long time, no calls, no letters. Maybe he is just lonely that he's so far away."

"He is messing with my head."

"Did he know that you and Craig were spending so much time together?"

"He knew we were working together, but never really asked about him. He thought he was older."

They just sat both staring into different areas of space.

"Well, remember Christmas when he said that he would free you and you went on with your life and he's sorry for what he said. Well it's too late. He should have thought more about what he said. You two had been together for a long time. It wasn't like you met a month ago. You had years."

"That is the problem, we were together a long time and I don't want to hurt him."

"But he hurt you almost without reason."

"I didn't want to get engaged yet."

"Maybe subconsciously you knew you didn't want to marry him. Now you met Craig and you two are a perfect couple."

"We are soul mates, especially in music."

"And you love each other."

"I didn't have that with Joel. Although it was music that brought us together."

"The problem is that I have to tell Joel that I am going to be married. Out of his life forever."

"You seem so upset. Are you sure, really down deep that it is Craig you want to marry and live with for the rest of your life?"

"What would have happened between me and Craig if we hadn't broken up?"

"I believe you would have gone with Craig anyway. Sooner or later you would have realized that you loved him and you were really meant for each other. Which I think you are."

"I have feelings for Joel and don't want to hurt him."

"Feelings are different than loving him. I got to know Joel and really liked him. I don't know Craig as well, but he seems so very nice and considerate and so very talented and so nice looking and no doubt he loves you very much. It's obvious."

She paused. "You didn't answer. Is it Craig for the rest your life?"

249

"Yes. Yes. I didn't hesitate when he asked to marry me. All I could say to Joel, let's wait. Don't diminish that I loved him."

"If you are sure, just write Joel a letter. Say as much as you want, but I would make it short. You are not obligated to say anything more than you are going to be married. You're not writing him a Dear John letter, that part was over at Christmas. The sooner you let it go from your mind the better. Write, and everything will start to fade. Go on with Craig like nothing ever happened. You have so much with him."

"I will, I'll do it soon. You make me feel better by talking about it. I just don't like doing it. It will seem so final."

Between the words, they managed to empty the bottle of wine, but it didn't put a glow in their demeanor. It just dampened their soul searching.

♫

CHAPTER TWENTY-FOUR

♫

The next two weeks Craig and Sharon were very busy with school and with their house. They decided on a new master bath. They also chose bedroom and living room furniture. Sharon worked on curtains and drapes throughout the house. They gathered their books for the library. Craig moved his sound system upstairs. It sounded much better in a more open space.

They set up two bedrooms for guests and planned to do the others later, but before their wedding.

Although Sharon was very busy, Joel's letter shaded her thoughts and she kept telling herself, later.

The twenty-third appeared on the calendar and that meant it was time for the film festival. Sharon had been practicing many different ways to play, but she decided on the way they first talked about, three main themes. She felt too much intricate or elaborate music would take away from the story. Craig agreed.

They arrived for the opening talk. There was a

large crowd of students and those who were not students. The big attraction was the displays:

Someone had persuaded Jerome Cannon to display his collection of autographed photos of film stars. He was offering little stories about how he had acquired them, some even personal...

A woman from the museum was explaining how they dated an image, by dress, background, or paper it was printed on...

A display of the restoration techniques at Millard, and how they work every day to preserve old films that are stored in the Library of Congress...

A chronology of film history on a large filmstrip that ran in a wave along the wall...

A display of books from local bookstores on film that could be purchased...

Another of film music, old cue sheets and old sheet music that was probably played at silent films...

This interested Craig and Sharon, and he said, "My mother has a lot of old music and she said anytime I want it, it's ours."

Saturday, student films would be shown and everyone was invited to view and write a brief critique.

Sharon and Craig mingled among the crowd and she chatted with Karen and Jim and some of her other friends. Glenna and Kelly came over to say hi and good luck. Craig was talking to professors as well as his students. Many had never seen a silent film. The interest was infectious.

Promptly at six the theatre lights were dimmed and the film rolled. The beautiful words, written so long ago, with music were brought to life once more.

Sharon could feel a hush settle over the audience as they were being pulled into this love story.

When the lights came on an air of contentment floated easily throughout. Everyone seemed to need a moment to bring them back to reality after being in deep emotion of love found, but all too late.

The evening proved a success. Craig and Sharon accepted the invitation to have wine and cheese at Karen's.

"We enjoyed the film so much," Karen said, "we're going to see *Sunrise*."

"This was the first silent film I've seen," Jim offered. "I loved it and I hope they show more."

"*Sunrise* is tomorrow and we're going, Want us to pick you up?" Craig asked

"We'll do that," Karen quickly responded.

After discussing the film and the music, they turned to information about getting married.

"We're going to have our house in pretty good order soon, at least livable."

"Wonder if Mr. Heid would be interested in selling. We could just move downstairs, like you two moved up, aye Karen."

"If not maybe something else will come on the market in the spring. We like it in the Music Box."

"We'll keep watching," Craig added.

Another wonderful time had passed and Craig suggested to Sharon, "I'll drop you off across the hall." They all laughed.

"We'll see you tomorrow for *Sunrise.* "

"Good night, and thank you for the good company and the nibbles."

Sharon closed her door and walked into his arms.

"Did it sound okay?"

"It really did. Your three themes were the best. They were so much a part of the story, but never overshadowed. Your talent just amazes me."

"I have other talents that I would like to share. I feel exhausted and need quieting down, will you stay with me tonight." She said softly as she held his face.

"An offer I can't refuse."

"Let's go now. By the time we get to sleep it will be late."

"An offer I can't refuse."

♫

Craig woke to Sharon's little alarm clock. I'll make coffee for us and wake her in a few moments. He opened the cabinet door and a letter fell out onto the counter. His eye caught my Rose of Sharon and without touching it, kept reading. A knot hit his stomach. What is this all about? How long has she had this? Did she answer it and what did she say? Was I supposed to find this? Maybe this is why she has been so … whatever lately, and I thought she was just tired.

He went back to the bedroom, dressed and she got up and said, "You seem in a hurry. I'll make coffee."

He threw her a robe and then took her hand and led her into the kitchen and pointed to the letter.

Sharon froze.

"I have not touched it. It fell out when I opened

the cabinet to get the coffee."

"Oh no! You shouldn't read it."

"I can see why. It is a little upsetting. It's quite a passionate plea. You left it almost in plain sight. Did you intend for me to find it?"

"No Craig, it is nothing like that."

"Have you answered it?"

"No. I just didn't have time."

"Time for what, another decision."

"No Craig. It is not like that. Honey I love *you*." She emphasized you.

"You should have answered it and threw it away unless you intended for me to read it."

"Craig, I have been practicing and we have been working on our house. I have been busy for us."

"I'll have coffee at home and when you have made a decision, please let me know."

"Craig, please don't leave like this. Craig!" And tears rolled down her face as he gently walked out and softly closed the door.

♫

After classes Friday she went to his office and he said, "We had better go with Karen and Jim tonight, but I'll be over to your studio to get all of you. See you then."

She turned and walked away without saying a word.

She walked home alone and her thoughts were troubled. Is he going to break our engagement? I am not, I have no reason. I should have answered Joel's letter. Oh why didn't I throw it away? Oh god, don't let this break us up. Please let him believe me. The walk seemed long, and when she reached her studio she wanted to cry, but she knew she just didn't have time. She fixed herself a bowl of tomato soup from the can, and as she waited she looked out the window at the snow scene below.

When he arrived he said, "We'll just go to *Sunrise* and not let our feelings get in the way of a nice evening. Karen and Jim are nice and I don't want to act like a couple of teenagers having a fight. Okay?"

"Then why are we?"

He just looked at her and thought of those big dark eyes that day in the recital hall.

They went to the film festival, Craig and Sharon met the criteria of, as if nothing had happened.

Afterward Craig explained, "We have to meet with the kids at church tomorrow morning, so we're going to call it a short evening. We'll catch you for wine and cheese at our house soon."

Sharon wondered if he meant it or was just assuaging those words for now. The only thing he said to her after they went in was, "*Cyrano* and *Sunrise* themes are not just made up but taken from real life, like ours. I'll see you tomorrow morning."

She curled up in a fetal position. I don't know how to prepare for what he is going to say. The stress had exhausted her and she fell asleep to hide from her distress.

♫

Saturday morning she thought, this can't go on. I will explain what I can. We're going to settle this problem and not let it linger. This is not the way we should act. On the way home I will have my say and then I will hear him.

At church they sang for a while and then he asked her, "Do you think they could sing for Easter Sunday?"

"I think they sound really good and they would like that. Should I go ask Deacon?"

"Yeah. I will play while you go."

She came back in a very short time smiling, "He was elated because he thinks they sound very good and knew they would like to."

Craig talked to them and asked if they would like to sing for Easter? They got all excited and he knew the answer.

"We'll talk to Deacon and he'll tell us one or two songs."

Immediately they wanted to know what to wear and Craig told them to look nice. "A shirt and tie if you have one. If you don't have a tie that's okay."

Sharon said to the girls, "I'm sure you have already decided on something and that will be all right."

"Deacon Ely said to meet in his office before service next Sunday and Mr. Craig will be there and I will be playing." Sharon told the group.

On the way home they talked about the progress the small choir had made. "They will be excited to work harder knowing they can sing for the service."

Abruptly she changed the subject knowing he had to listen.

"Craig, we are not acting like adults. Yes, I should have answered the letter, but as I said, I didn't have time and kept putting it off."

"I know I shouldn't have read it, but it landed in the middle of our love affair with a jolt and seems you needed to make another decision. When I saw him at Christmas I knew, and it was a big surprise because I had not an inkling there was someone else in your life and to find out he is still not gone."

"Craig he's gone from my life. I made a decision in Ohio and it is still the same. Do I have to bare my soul? I had a life before I met you and so did you. I never questioned you about your friend in Buffalo or anyone else. Everything was before I met you and I accepted that and you should too. You read it, he wanted to get married and I always wanted to wait. I believe I was waiting for you. When you asked to marry me I did not hesitate one second. Oh Craig! We were waiting for each other, don't destroy it now. We started over together and you said yourself this is our year. I have not written or received any other letters or phone calls from him. He is out of my life. I was going to write and tell him that we are going to be married. If you love me you will trust me. The end."

They arrived at her studio and he had not said anything further, but he had to listen.

"Are you coming over tomorrow after playing?"

"I'd like to."

Upstairs she did not know what to think. His

258

lack of words was stronger than if he had lashed out. Was he going to break up tomorrow? He'll have that big house all to himself. He heard my side of things. She rolled up on the couch and took a nap. I have to work tonight.

When she got to the club she thought he might be here, but the hours passed and in her five minute breaks she looked but there was no Craig. At ten she went home and maybe he'll call, but he didn't. Should I call him? No. He asked me over tomorrow so that could be the end. Oh god no! I love him so much. He can't just stop loving me like that. That I had a boyfriend before him is bothering him. Not that he didn't. All right for him, but not for me. I'll do my best. In a day he will think differently, maybe.

After playing for Sunday service, she went home and wrote a short letter to Joel.

After the cocktail hour, she drove slowly to Craig's, not because of the weather or traffic, but she was not sure what she would be facing.

He met her at the door and said, "Come on down."

She took her coat off and pulled out the letter to Joel in one hand and said, "Read it." In the other hand she had a "million" little pieces of paper. "Take this."

"No," he said quietly, "I trust you."

"Should I change?"

"No," he responded, and she turned cold.

He took her hand and led her into the piano room in front of the doors and they looked out into the cold little garden.

Oh no! She thought. It began here and is going

259

to end here, but he put his arm around her.

"Sharon darling." And he gazed deeply into eyes, "Please forgive me for acting so badly. Some of the words broke my heart."

She started to cry.

"Don't sweetheart. Everything is all right. I love you so much it was hard to imagine that you had ever been interested in anyone before me. That was selfish and I will never do anything like this again. It wasn't so much that there had been someone else in your life, but that I thought you might change your mind about marrying me. I can't imagine life without you now. It's as if you have always been here and will always be. Anything different I could not accept."

"Oh Craig, I love you and don't want anyone except you, always. I so wish I had met you long ago and then we wouldn't have these moments of upset. It would have been just us." He held her and kissed her so tenderly yet so passionately.

He took her upstairs and opened the big door. The lights were low and in front of a gently glowing fire was a tray with two glasses and a carafe of wine. Soft romantic music filled the air.

He nestled her and asked, "Is everything okay?"

"I'm okay."

He reached around and unzipped her dress and then unbuttoned his shirt.

On the big shag rug, Craig poured a bit of wine in each glass. "To our love now and always."

"To us forever."

They each took a sip and then could not wait.

Slowly they approached each other not in shyness, but wanting the feeling to last.

"I want everything for you tonight." And he kissed her all over, wanting to give her the most he could in physical love to pair with his emotional love. "Sharon love, just let what you feel flow through your body and heart."

The music danced around them as its spirit created all, a softness, a slowness, a rhythm and a melody. It rose and fell with tenderness. The music seeped into their souls and carried them far away through the clouds where they floated into the night that held them close, the day to look into their eyes and see love reflected. Their passion lasted long and filled with complete desire they reach the spiritual realm of love together.

They rested as one and then Craig pulled a blanket over them.

As they lay in each other's arms and their bodies entwined, he sang to her softly along with the music, *"O mio babbino caro…"*

"What I feel for you physically and emotionally," Sharon said, "I can't put into words."

"Neither can I love, so let's keep expressing our love this way. Words are beautiful, but what could be more beautiful than the feelings that we give each other when we touch and I go in you and it all happens, together. And someday our love will make us a beautiful baby girl."

♫

CHAPTER TWENTY-FIVE

♫

Spring. New life. Small signs were everywhere. The air was fresher. The sky bluer. Each day the sun hung around a little longer. Caught in the shadows were patches of snow that were melting more slowly. In the winter garden snowdrops were in full bloom and dancing lightly in the soft, cold breeze. Nearby crocuses were cracking the dark, dank earth. A lone robin was searching for a worm.

As Craig and Sharon were preparing their dinner his phone rang. "Mom, how are you?"

Sharon saw a big smile slowly come across his face.

To Sharon, "Beth had a baby boy this morning. James."

"Oh wonderful," and she smiled too.

Craig listened for several minutes. "Oh mom we can't we have to work Sunday at church. Our young choir is going to sing and Sharon plays for the service. But why don't you and Bill come up? We have our house in good order and you and Sharon have taught me how to cook."

He looked at Sharon and she nodded her head yes. "She is going to ask Bill."

While they waited he told her, "He weighed seven pounds and seven ounces and arrived at ten-twenty this morning."

He turned his attention back to his mother, "Oh great. Come up Saturday afternoon or whenever and I'll be here. Sharon has to work in the evening."

Another pause, "See you then and goodbye."

"We got our house fixed just in time."

"They will be our first guests. Is this the first time they have been here?"

"No, they came up right after I got here, before school started and I showed them around the campus. Mom wanted to know where I was going to live. Now they don't have to stay in a hotel."

"Why don't you bring them to dinner at the country club?"

"Good idea. We can listen to you play."

♫

Saturday morning Craig and Sharon met with the young people for the last time before their debut. They were so pleased with their progress.

Excitement filled the air.

On their way out they talked with Deacon Ely. "You have worked wonders with this group. You kept them off the street and something to look forward to. I can't thank you enough."

"Thank you Deacon. What Sharon and I like

best is sharing music in whatever way we can."

"I have one last thing." Deacon asked, "Rather sudden, but it has been requested that at the end of tomorrow's service would you close with singing, "The Lord's Prayer." It would be a beautiful way to end the Easter service."

Craig looked at Sharon and smiled. "I think so." And she nodded yes.

"We have been practicing that because later this month we are going to Texas for a friend's wedding, which I am going to close with that piece."

"You will be compensated financially with thirty-five dollars, if that is okay."

"Deacon, I would love to do this for you without…"

Deacon interrupted, "No. I insist that you be paid because you two have worked very faithfully and hard with these kids and have asked for nothing."

Craig just smiled.

"You and Miss Sharon will both have envelopes tomorrow. And we thank you so much."

"On the way to get food for their Easter dinner Sharon asked, "Is this your first job here?"

"Yes. I had a lot in Texas and want to work here too, but with competition and courting you…" They both laughed.

"The vocal exercises that Dr. Westmore has me doing are paying off."

"From listening to you, yes. Wait until your mother hears you tomorrow."

"Let's let it be a surprise."

They arrived at their home laden with food and

decided to cook upstairs, which would be a first.

"I'll bring some dishes up from your cabinet."

"This won't be a fancy dinner, just the usual ham and sweet potatoes and the other stuff we got."

"I hope your folks get here before I have to go home to get ready for work."

As she finished those words the doorbell rang. They looked at each other and smiled.

They welcomed his mother and Bill into their home. They gave them a quick tour, explaining what they had done and what they still wanted to do.

"You have made wonderful progress."

"I'm so glad you got here before I have to leave for work."

"I am taking you to dinner at the club tonight and we can listen to Sharon play."

"Oh honey, that is so sweet of you."

"And tomorrow church is at ten and after we are going to have dinner here. It will be the conventional Easter dinner."

Sharon said, "I must get home and get ready."

Craig handed her his keys. "Take my car and I will drive home with you tonight."

At the club near eight o'clock, Sharon saw Craig and his parents being shown to their table. At her break she joined them for a few moments.

His mother said, "This is one of the nicest dinners that we have had and accompanied with the most beautiful music that I have heard."

Bill seconded her complimenting words.

"Thank you. I have been doing this for four years."

Craig asked, "Have you thought how much longer you want to keep working here?"

"No. I need to help out." She didn't want to say much in front of his mother, but she thought I will have to buy my wedding dress and other things and now my bank account is low.

"I have really enjoyed working here. I don't have to prepare, but just come and play for a while."

They stretched their dinner until ten and on their way home, Craig asked, "Are you going to stay with me tonight?"

"I don't think so. I would probably be embarrassed in the morning."

"Whatever you want. I'll drop you off and then see you tomorrow." A quick goodnight then he joined his parents at home.

♫

After breakfast and just before starting for church, Craig pinned a corsage of white roses on his mother's jacket. For Sharon he had red roses.

In the car she said, "Helen your son and my fiancé is so sweet to get us flowers for Easter."

"Just like his father, he always got me and Beth flowers."

"Mom, I also have something special for you at church."

"Oh, what?"

"You will know."

At church they saw the choir in their Sunday best and totally excited. Craig introduced his parents to

Deacon Ely and the kids, then Sharon took them into the auditorium and she went to the piano.

The service started and after the offering plates were passed, the pastor said to the congregation, "We have a special offering for you and for the Lord. Our young choir that Mr. Jamieson and Miss Heisendorf have so graciously worked with since January will sing unto the Lord and for us."

The choir assembled and their voices filled the auditorium with a heavenly sound. Their hearts were in every note they sang. Their attention to Craig was without question. He held them close until the last delicate tone.

After a moment of silence, they filed to their seats. Sniffles and amens were heard throughout the auditorium.

The pastor took his place and looking directly at the group said, "Thank you. Absolutely beautiful. A message from God in these young voices. Do we now need words?" Although he continued with his traditional Easter message of the resurrection. He held everyone spellbound with words of love from Jesus and that it was for us, you and me.

"As we close this celebration of life everlasting, we have a special prayer."

The pastor sat down and Craig rose and gave a nod to Sharon and he sang, *"Our father which art in heaven, Hallowed would be thy name…"*

His mother knew what he had meant when he said he had something special for her. She was so moved that she had to reach for her hankie, along with many others.

There was total jubilation after the service. Everyone was telling the choir how much they enjoyed their music and Craig as well received many thanks.

At home, Sharon, Craig and his mother prepared the Easter dinner. Bill in the kitchen would have been one too many, so he retired to the sitting room just off the kitchen, but managed to be a part of the conversation.

"Thank you Craig for your prayer in song. It was beautiful. You sounded wonderful," his mother told him. "And the little choir truly moved everybody in the audience."

"They sounded really good. They tried with all their heart and it worked for them."

"I think that was the best they have ever sung."

With everything ready, before they sat down Helen said, "Craig, fill our glasses with wine, I want to make a toast to my children. I am so proud of your work together in music. Sharon, thank you for agreeing to be Craig's wife. Bill and I accept you with love as our daughter. You couldn't be more perfect for Craig and him you."

"Thank you Helen, I too accept you with love and your son is a beautiful man. And I love him unconditionally and will always be at his side. To his wonderful mother."

As they clicked their glasses, Bill offered one last thought. "And to your new home."

They enjoyed their traditional Easter dinner and shared good conversation.

Later Bill and Helen decided that they should start home. Loving goodbyes and, "We're looking forward to another visit, soon."

Craig and Sharon went back down to his apartment to relax.

"Everything went well at church and you sounded great."

"I'm glad. A little high in places but I got there."

"Why don't we bring it down a key or two?

"Tomorrow, now quiet time."

♫

CHAPTER TWENTY-SIX

♪

Time moved the season forward. Each day a little more of spring was in the air. New buds, new birds and new greens. There was much Craig and Sharon had to prepare for. Their house still needed work. They were gathering eclectic furniture for the bedrooms and the back sitting room and were working them over to be fashionable. Some painted, some varnished. Curtains were cut and trimmed to match. Extras were added for comfort.

That spring was breaking, outside work had to be added to the list.

"Isabella said whatever was in the garage we could keep or throw away, and there is a lawn mower. Maybe we can have it serviced and it will go for a while. I will get in there this week because if it turns real warm, that grass is going to take off. Sweetheart, I'm not a novice at these things. I always helped my dad and then my mom after he died. Just a little rusty."

"I know sweetie. Some of these windows need washing. That can be my job."

"Let's plan this out because we are going to be gone during spring break and we want to get all of this done before our wedding."

"I also want to get out my invitations for my recital and order wedding invitations."

"Yes, this week. Our wedding in the little garden, and if it rains, in front of the fireplace. Either can be decorated. And at three o'clock. I have been noticing how the sun is positioned at that time and it will be shaded. Come let me show you."

They went to the doors in the piano room. "We can open the doors and Glenna will play for us and you choose someone to sing."

"Dr. Westmore, without question."

"We need more than just a piano. How about some strings from Dr. Livingston?"

"Is Kevin coming up to be your best man?"

"Yes. I already asked him. He said yes before I finished my question. We'll invite all of the Texas bunch. Most of them teach and school will be out. Our garden can be decorated with flowers and it will be a beautiful place to be married."

They each took a big chair and continued discussing plans.

"I must tell Mr. Heid, and I will ask Glenna if she is interested in moving in. It will be cheaper than the dorm. Her parents are supporting her and want her to go to graduate school. Although she doesn't stay here in the summer, she might like to start classes before September. I would like to."

"Honey, I would like for us to have this summer without too many commitments. Just be together, make love to you every night and every morning, get up late and go when and where we want. It will probably be our last time to have this freedom. We could go see Glenn Gould at Stratford."

"I would like to start classes because I want to finish in a year."

"We can get it all in. Right now back to our wedding. Sunday in our garden. We're going to Texas next Friday morning and to your family on Monday evening. You told them our arrival time?"

"Yes Mom said they would meet us. Who is meeting us in Texas?"

"Kevin. Maybe Sunday we can rent a car and I will show you where I spent most of my young life."

"I would like that."

"So next is Jeff and Sara's wedding. Let's practice their music."

♫

The next day at school Sharon found Glenna.

"Are you going to be here this summer or go home and start in the fall?"

"I would like to start classes this summer."

"Me too, because I would like to finish in a year. And would you play for our wedding?"

"Oh, I'd love to. The date is?"

"Sunday after graduation. Our families will all be here and Craig's friends from Texas are coming."

"That's wonderful. It's working out so well."

"Also would you be interested in my studio? I thought I would ask you before I told Mr. Heid that I was getting married. The only expenses would be rent and telephone. Cheaper than the dorm. And better."

"Hey. Yeah. I would. Let me talk it over with Mom and Dad. They are the ones sending me money."

"You are lucky you folks are so supportive. You have heard my story.

"But you must have a wonderful sense of accomplishment and finding Professor Jamieson."

"You can call him Craig. I'll tell him I told you to, and yes I am fortunate. It has been a great journey. There were times when I just closed my eyes and was riding along and one day opened them, and school almost over and there is Craig. Now I'll start another journey. A very special one."

"Sometimes I wasn't sure I wanted to go on but I thought of my parents and their encouragement. Now it is over, I am really looking forward to graduate school, but I have not found my Craig."

"Oh Glenna, you will. One day you will be surprised."

"I am going to call Mom tonight and see what she thinks. I would like to break away from the dorm. Your little studio is perfect."

Glenna glanced at her watch and said, "I have a class now, but I will catch up with you tomorrow."

♫

A couple days later Glenna and Sharon found each other and she said that she would take the studio.

"I'm excited to have a place of my own. Mom thought it was a good idea to be on my own."

"We're getting married on the twenty-eighth and not leaving for Paris until June second. That will give us time to get me out. You know the basics are included, bed, dressers, couch, chairs. You just have to get linens and small things. I went to the Salvation Army and got some stuff. I had been working for two years, so I had a pittance."

"I think the best thing will be my own bath."

"Karen will be across the hall until September. I have a class now. Tonight I will tell Mr. Heid."

♫

The next two weeks were devoted to doing all Craig and Sharon discussed.

Friday morning, they boarded the plane for Texas. As always he held her hand tightly until the seat belt sign went off. Heads back they talked softly. Not long after lunch they touched down in the land of the Alamo.

Everyone was there to meet them, Kevin, Jeff, Sara, Judy, George....

Sharon was introduced and welcomed sweetly by the girls and all congratulated them on their engagement.

"We're all coming to the wedding. When is it?" George asked.

"May twenty-eight."

"I am anxious to come to New York. I have never been there," Kevin responded.

"Where we are, it is beautiful, even the snow. We had a hefty winter and all Sharon and I could do was cuddle up on the couch."

She looked at him rather surprised. "Honey we are among very old friends and we all know each other very well," and he gave her a quick kiss.

Judy said, "We sure do." She thought how lucky Sharon was because all of the girls at one time or another had been in love with Craig, although he probably didn't know.

Sharon was deep in questions about what they were doing and New York.

Kevin and Craig walked on ahead and Kevin said, "Hey buddy, you know Eileen is here, and she didn't know that you were engaged. She took it hard. Feelings or just surprised, I don't know."

"Oh no! Sharon didn't want to come when I told her she would be here. I hope everything stays calm."

"When was the last time you saw her?"

"At Christmas, we talked. Not really a surprise to either of us. We just were not compatible. She cared nothing about music and I felt she resented that I loved it so much. She didn't like Buffalo and I could only get there on weekends. After school started, I met Sharon and we worked on my competition music and I fell madly in love with her. We never looked back."

"When it happens you know. You had all the time to marry Eileen and you didn't."

"I thought so much about that, if I had missed Sharon."

"She is beautiful and I believe everything else you have said about her."

Kevin said, "I'm taking you to the hotel and

275

will be back about five and we'll go to rehearsal and then to dinner."

After the rehearsal the conversation took off.

"Craig, tell us about New York," George asked.

"Oh it is a great place. I've had a wonderful year and will be there next. Sharon will be in graduate school. Our wedding is in our garden." And for a moment he let his southern drawl swing back into his words. Sharon smiled. She had never heard that before.

"We're all coming. Get us a hotel near."

"Our house is pretty big and my apartment downstairs can hold a lot of you. What is going on down here that Kevin hasn't told me about?"

Sara responded, "Probably nothing."

"Jeff, where is your new home?"

"In the Highland district. Maybe Kevin can drive you over Sunday. We'll be getting ready to take off for Hawaii. Where are you guys going?"

"Paris for two weeks, then a quiet summer. We're also going to Stratford to see Glenn Gould. Judy you would like that. Toronto is close and a beautiful city to visit."

Sharon looked at him and wondered when he had been there. He never mentioned it.

Sara asked, "How are your mother and Bill?"

"Great. They were up for Easter and we fixed our first guest dinner. Sharon taught me how to cook."

"Tell them about your little choir."

They asked about Sharon's recital and school. Craig went on to tell about the campus and surrounding homes, their home.

"Never any trouble. All serious students. We're isolated from the academic campus."

"Kevin told us you won Ohio. Congratulations," Margaret said.

"Thanks. What has your group been doing?"

"We took first in regions and second at state. I was pretty glad."

"Great. How is Reggie?"

"He'll be here tomorrow."

"Sharon spent last summer in Salzburg studying with Dr. Kreutzer."

"That must have been wonderful," Judy replied.

This was how the evening went, a warm exchange of personal happenings. Craig enjoyed himself immensely, he was among friends and Sharon was welcomed as if they had always known her.

After dinner Judy asked Kevin, "Bring Craig and Sharon over to our house for a just a bit."

At Judy and Lee's Sharon spied a grand piano.

"Make yourself at home while I get us drinks."

The guys immediately fell into conversation.

Judy came back with lemonade and soda.

"Now that I've got you here, I want Sharon to play for us and Craig sing for me."

"Oh Judy, what would you like to hear?"

"Anything, just your voice."

Craig said, "Sharon first. She has played at an elite country club for all of her four years, and this year Sunday cocktail hour."

"Sharon," Lee said, "center stage for you."

And he pointed to the piano.

For several minutes she captured them with little jazz and slow melodies. She stopped and smiled at Craig and began to play, "Unforgettable" and Craig picked up instantly and sang for Judy. He went over and sat down next to Sharon at the piano as he continued to sing.

"Thank you. I love you guys. I wish you lived here. We all have so much fun."

It was just a little over an hour at Judy's and then Kevin took them back to the hotel and went upstairs for a few moments.

"I am going to come up as soon as school is out. I'll drive up and you can get me a place to stay."

"You will stay with us. Plenty of room. You will love it there and won't want to come home."

"I need to get out and that will be a good start. Maybe I'll go to Europe this summer. Sara wants us at the church by one, so I'll be here at twelve-thirty."

Craig and Sharon were alone after a wonderful evening with friends, and tomorrow the wedding and more friends. He could not stop thinking what he would say to Eileen.

After a warm shower they snuggled together and talked softly. Their words faded into a passionate good night.

♫

Morning arrived. They dressed and went for a late breakfast.

"Your friends are so nice, and they are so warm

and loving to each other."

"We have been together all through college and never parted. I hope it is all right with you to have Kevin come up and stay with us for a few days."

"Oh absolutely. Does he have a girlfriend?"

"No, not since Sally."

Sharon thought of Karen, but she was taken.

Back in their room they dressed, Craig in tuxedo and Sharon in a pale blue dress that gracefully fell to the floor.

Kevin arrived. "Man you two look beautiful."

"You too buddy."

"Sharon should have seen us in our college days."

"No, I don't think so. The first time she saw me at school she thought I was the new janitor."

Kevin laughed heartily. "Janitor!"

"Oh Craig forget that."

After some folly they went to the church. Craig began greeting friends. He thought again, what am I going to say to Eileen. How are you would sound so trite.

He turned and she was there. She stared at Sharon, but she missed the glare that went through her.

Craig kissed Eileen on the cheek and asked, "How are you?"

She whispered, "I'll tell you later," in a stern voice and moved on before Craig could say more.

He thought, that's over and now I have to sing and need to be focused.

They went with Kevin to where the wedding party, other than the bride and her attendance, were gathering. They all talked happily but softly.

George said to Craig, "I hear Kevin is coming up as soon as school is out."

"Yeah. He'll love it there. It won't be so hot."

"You two, after Jeff now, are the only ones not married. But you soon. Slowly we all got picked up."

They giggled quietly like kids.

They got their cue to gather upstairs for the ceremony.

After Sara and her father reached the altar Craig sang "Panis Angelicus." Not a dry eye to start this holy and beautiful ritual of becoming one for life.

He and Sharon slipped quietly to their seats and he held her hand tightly through the nuptials.

Soon it will be us he thought.

As the ceremony began it ended with Craig singing a prayer. Then the organ began "Mendelssohn's Wedding March" as their recessional. There were many smiles as they exited the church.

The wedding party and family went for pictures and later to the reception.

Dinner over and the band in place the music began. Craig and Sharon mingled to hear how beautiful the music was and then went to dance.

They stopped and went again to talk with friends, when that same girl approached and took Craig's hand and said, "Let's dance."

Not wanting to make a scene, he went.

"Well is this the incompatibility?" she said in a not so nice voice.

"No Eileen, we parted as friends because of each other and no one else."

"I didn't know until I got here that you were engaged. A little young isn't she?"

"Eileen that is not nice. She's an adult just like we are."

"I thought maybe we could start over."

Craig didn't say anything. He knew he didn't have to.

"Please Eileen, let the past be gone and go forward as friends."

"How can you say that after all we went through and did?"

"Eileen, there is more to life than going to bed together and that is about all we did well, and that leaves a lot of empty."

"We were together a long time."

"Well she and her previous boyfriend had been together for seven years, so we didn't set a record."

"You broke them up."

"No, I did not. She came back after Christmas and it had already happened. So there."

"I don't want to hear this!"

"Then why did you ask? Please Eileen, let's not get out of hand. Our life together has passed and we both have to go on."

She left Craig on the dance floor alone. He found Sharon talking and laughing with Kevin and others.

He and Kevin looked at each other and as friends can, looked into the other's mind.

"I kept her safe while you were gone."

"Thanks." His eyes dropped. Sharon could see that he was uncomfortable. She knew that was Eileen.

She took his hand and engaged his eyes to tell him that she understood. She knew how he felt because she had just been through this with Joel.

Craig thought we both hurt someone else to gain our own happiness. Why does this have to happen? It is one of life's ugly moments.

♫

CHAPTER TWENTY-SEVEN

♫

It was a typical spring day in Texas. Young leaves on the trees. Early blooms in the gardens reaching for the sun. A cloud wandering by effortlessly.

Craig rented a car and was going to show Sharon where he had spent most of his life. Home was in the last village in the confines of the larger city.

"It is only half an hour."

As they drove he told her all about what they were seeing. Some industrial sights, other areas were houses and small shopping strips.

"How did your mother meet Bill if he was in Albany?"

"He was down here for the Whittier case that his firm was handling and they met at a party. They had a long distance courtship then finally got married. I think she is happy although she would be happier if my father was here. We are almost there."

A few streets over, he stopped in front of a white colonial with black shutters. It was surrounded with bushes and spring flowers.

"That was home." He gazed at the house without saying more, just in thought.

"It is beautiful and very nice."

"Inside we had the usual's and the times were happy until … but you go on. Then Mom left it all behind to start a new life." His tone changed with his last words.

"You don't blame her do you?"

"Oh no, but it was sad to break the home that had meant so much. She nurtured us, but we were all gone and she decided to go too. Most of her family was in California."

"How old were you when you moved here?"

"Ten. My father was transferred. I had to leave friends behind but made new ones. This bunch will always be friends, even if some live far away."

They drove to where Craig went to high school and then he asked, "Do you mind if I visit my father's grave?"

"Of course not."

They drove a few miles outside of the village and entered the place of rest. Toward the back they got out and walked still further. He stopped and stared at the stone and his father's name. In a hushed voice and his eyes cast upward, "Dad," as if calling him, "I miss you and I love you."

He turned and saw that Sharon's eyes were full.

Softly, "Blink," and he wiped the tears away. "It's okay. It is something we have to accept. Many questions but no answers."

He shook his head from side to side. "It had been raining that day and just as we came out of church the sun came out really bright. And here as the minister was saying the final prayers, it was so quiet, all but several goldfinches in the tree over there were singing their hearts out. I was the only one that heard them. Mom and Beth were so despondent their minds were closed even to beauty around them."

"Honey, in your composition. I remember them."

"They were there."

He took her hand and they walked around among the silence so profound in a resting place that caused them to whisper as they spoke.

He smiled. "We'll go forward together and love our life, our children yet to be and love each other more than even God should allow."

She squeezed his hand in response. "Enough. Let's get back and I'll drive you around the campus and show you where we all tried to keep each other out of trouble. Tomorrow you can show me around your hometown."

Back at the hotel they dressed, Kevin arrived and they all went to dinner at Sara and Judy's parents' home. It was a grand event even though Craig was saying goodbye to friends.

Monday afternoon Kevin took them to the airport and his last words were, "See you in a month."

A little over two hours they landed in Missouri. Mom, Dad and Aunt Katy were there to meet them. Her parents were warm and welcoming but Aunt Katy was overjoyed to see her favorite niece and to meet, the soon-to-be, new member of the family.

The talk was casual on the way home, weather, Texas, the weather in Texas.

When they arrived home their conversation had more substance and dinner was served.

Sharon asked her mother, "Are Allen and Carolyn coming up while we're here?"

"They are. Katy is planning dinner Wednesday."

"Your brother and Carolyn, Jack and Sue. Craig you will get to meet everyone."

"That's great. I know it is a short trip, but we had the wedding and have to be home by Friday. Sharon has to work Saturday and Sunday."

"And to let you know honey," Aunt Katy said, "I received your invitation to your recital and I am coming up. We'll talk about it later, but I wanted you to know."

Sharon's parents looked surprised.

"Someone from this family needs to be there. You have worked very hard these four years and I am very proud of you."

"Splendid." Craig almost shouted. He thought, I am so glad someone has the courage to look jealousy or whatever in the face and acknowledge Sharon's accomplishments. If only her parents were as accommodating.

"That would make me very happy."

Craig thought she was going to burst into tears.

"She is still deciding what she is going to play, but it will be professional status and ready for any stage. Mr. and Mrs. Heisendorf I'm sure you realize your daughter is extremely talented. This summer we're going to look into booking her recitals around New York. They command a nice salary."

Finally her dad broke the silence that her mother never did. "We're proud of her too." Not wanting to let Katy dominate his daughter.

"Thanks." Sharon said in a strained voice. She thought of all of the times they had upset her about wasting her time in music school. If Craig wasn't here I would remind them.

Before Aunt Katy went home, she told Sharon she was taking them to the airport Thursday. "So why don't you stay all night with me?"

Happily Sharon responded, "We can do that."

Sharon's father showed Craig to their guest room and with strong implications, stay here.

Craig lay quietly as his thoughts fought with sleep. Her parents are so tight and uncomfortable to be around. Maybe after we're married they will be different. Being far away it may never happen.

The next day Sharon's mother stayed home. She was busy doing things around the house and not being a part of their visit. Craig wondered if she stayed home to make sure they didn't kiss.

Sharon practiced as Craig listened, after that they escaped and she drove him around to various places of her younger life, school, church.

Wednesday morning early her father drove them over to Aunt Katy's. Craig immediately felt more relaxed. After coffee, she showed them around her vegetable and flower gardens, affectionately touching the new blooms.

Relaxing on the back patio they talked so easily. "I want you to play your composition for everyone tonight."

Craig asked, "Will everyone be interested?"

"Small point. They will listen anyway." Aunt Katy came back fast.

Aunt Katy getting a little more personal asked, "Are you planning on having children. Neither Allen or Jack seemed to be interested."

"We do Aunt Katy. We've talked about it briefly, but I would like to get graduate school over first, then plan. How's that." And she smiled at Craig.

Early in the afternoon Allen and Carolyn arrived. Allen and Sharon held each other tightly and it was obvious they were happy to see each other.

"Come meet Craig."

They greeted each other warmly and Allen said, "Congratulations both of you. God bless. We wish you years of happiness. A big welcome to our family."

Allen and Craig had a wonderful chat while the girls prepared dinner. Allen asked Craig all about school and being a composer. Craig told him about their choir at the missionary church.

Craig learned about Allen's journey as a young minister. They were only a year apart in age and seemed to enjoy each other's company. Craig thought Sharon and Allen are very much alike and like their Aunt Katy.

Soon Jack and Sue arrived and Sharon's parents.

At the table Allen offered a prayer of thanks for

the food and asked for a blessing for Craig and Sharon as they began their journey through life together.

After dessert, they went to the living room and Katy informed them they were going to hear Craig's composition that won Ohio. After a back and forth with Sharon and Craig, Craig won, Sharon would play.

The piano had a beautiful tone and did justice to Craig's beautiful work. After she was finished, Allen went to offer his hand in congratulations to Craig. "Absolutely beautiful. God gave you a wonderful talent to express yourself in music. And I know how talented my sister is and she played it with such grace and love. Music is at God's right hand."

Others also expressed their congratulations, all except Sharon's mom and dad, although her dad shook his head in mild agreement. All her mother could do was smile, sort of. Craig pretended not to notice the absence.

Katy broke the topic and said, "Now we want to hear about your wedding. What can we do?"

Understanding Sharon wasn't his to give, but Craig thought, I am going to make the gesture.

"First, Mr. Heisendorf, I ask kindly for your daughter's hand in marriage. I will keep her within my loving soul all of my life. Protect her with all of my being. Share and give freely of myself and always be at her side."

Everyone was a little surprised, especially Sharon's father, and at first didn't quite know what to say. Then he surprised everyone. "Craig, I willing approve."

His reply brought an air of comfort to the room.

Craig turned her face and kissed her and said, "I love you Sharon." He wanted everyone to know it was not a sin to show affection and was not shy about loving her.

Aunt Katy said, "We're all coming to your wedding. Tell us."

They happily relayed what they had planned and everyone seemed to approve.

At the end of the evening, Mr. Heisendorf got Craig alone and pulled out an envelope and said. "She is our only daughter and we want to be a part, so here is a check to pay for the wedding."

Craig was surprised. "Thank you, but I believe this is between you and Sharon."

"We," awkwardly, "thought you would be in charge of everything."

"No, we are doing everything together, but I think this is between you and her."

He turned and said softly, "Okay."

The evening over goodbyes were offered.

Everyone gone Katy took a deep breath and asked, "How about a glass of wine? You know the others don't drink, not even wine," Aunt Katy said.

Craig looked at Sharon. "I think we would like that." They chatted much more comfortably and it was not just from the wine.

"Honey, your recital is Friday. If I come Thursday afternoon, would that be okay?"

"Oh, Aunt Katy, yes, you don't know how happy I am that you are. Stay at least a few days."

"How about until Sunday?"

"We have two guest room ready."

"Well. I am certainly looking forward to getting up there again and seeing your home. It is getting late and we have to get up early to get you to the airport. Sleeping arrangements. I know what they were at your house Sharon, but they can be anything you want here."

Craig and Sharon smiled and looked at each other and that told Katy what she wanted to know.

Craig rolled her in his arms and thought it had only been two days, but seems like an eternity. She had been so close and yet so far.

Later Thursday, the large plane growled to a halt and they were home. Their whirlwind trip into each of their past lives was over or just beginning.

♫

CHAPTER TWENTY-EIGHT

♫

*S*pring had arrived. Hyacinths, tulips and robins. The purples, blues and pinks were welcome after the long, white winter. Their fragrances filled spots in the air.

The last of four intense years were in sight and they were going to be the best. Sharon's recital, graduation and most important, their wedding.

Friday, their last day of spring break Craig suggested, "Let's stay in our new bedroom these last two days."

"Then when we have all of our family and friends you can stay there and not feel guilty."

"The Texas bunch can have my apartment. It won't be the first time they all stayed together."

"How about starting with a bubble bath?"

"Let's call it a swim and hold the bubbles."

They both laughed and she said, "Okay."

After a small meal, they edged their way to a special evening. Craig filled the new claw-footed tub, that so matched the homes décor. They immersed themselves in the warm water. Facing each other they talked.

"When your recital is over you are through."

"Twenty days free out of four years!" She scooped water on him.

"And to you," the water came back, "this summer lady, we are going to make up for all the years that we did not know each other."

"So much different than the shower. I can splash you better."

"Turn around and nestle in here."

This closeness led them to stronger desires.

"We have been here a long time and the water is getting a little cooler," Sharon offered.

He wrapped the large white towel around himself, pulled her in and they dried each other. She took his hand and led him to their new, white bed. Soft music filled the air.

It began as the flower opens, slowly and gently, and then the last gasp into full-grown beauty. As the waning moon glides across the night sky, their love took them to another place.

♫

Monday morning it was back to school. Sharon met Glenna in the cafeteria.

"How did your week go?"

"Really good. I met all of his friends and he got to meet my family. How was yours?

"Good. I got a car. It isn't fancy, but I told my folks that I was going to sign up to sub and accompany. We got a car so I could get around. For groceries too. And I brought back some stuff."

"Do you want to put anything in the studio?"

"No. It will be okay in the trunk. I'm getting excited about summer and next year. Maybe there will be some new faces in graduate school. It would be nice to date an adult."

♫

Two weeks went by in a flash. Thursday Sharon and Craig went to the airport to get Aunt Katy.

A warm embrace welcomed her to New York.

"We'll give you a quick tour around the campus and see how much you remember."

"I'm not sure I will remember much. I was so focused on getting Sharon settled and then driving home."

At home, they gave her a quick tour of their home and settled her in a guest room.

"You have a bath for each bedroom. That is unusual for a Victorian."

They explained what Mrs. Zachery had done.

"Mom and Bill are coming up tomorrow so you will be able to meet some of my family. My sister had a baby boy at the end of March and will be here for our wedding. Sharon can play her program for all who missed it."

"Oh, it will be so nice to meet your mother."

"Come Aunt Katy, and I'll show you Craig's piano and the garden where we're getting married."

After admiring the piano and talking about the

garden, Aunt Katy asked, "Honey do you have your wedding dress?"

"No. I thought I would do that immediately after the recital."

"Wonderful. Why don't I take you and Karen shopping Saturday and see what we can find."

"Oh, I would love for you to go with me. Maybe Craig can meet with the kids by himself."

After conversation and hot tea in the library, they closed the evening and went into the night.

Friday Sharon stayed home to rest and practice while Aunt Katy listened. Craig came home after his class at ten and shortly thereafter his mother and Bill arrived. Helen and Katy bonded immediately. It was a quiet afternoon and dinner.

They all dressed for Sharon's recital. Her deep red gown accentuated her soft-toned complexion. She did not forget the pearl earrings that Craig had given her, what seemed like so long ago, long before she even knew that he was in love with her.

At school there was a large crowd gathering, they talked, laughed and introduced. Craig took his family into the hall to the reserved seats and then went back stage with her.

"You are so relaxed, I just can't believe you."

"Because I love doing this. I only need a few moments to choose my journey."

"Do you want me to go?"

"No stay, and I want to close my eyes and you hold my hands and I'll find my other place."

Moments passed and he kissed her lightly on the lips. "It's your time now. Good luck sweetheart."

"Thank you beautiful man in my life."

Craig joined his family and the lights lowered, Sharon elegantly came on the small stage, acknowledging the applause with a smile and a gentle nod. Seating herself, she paused and looked into the audience and smiled again. She thought I am saying goodbye to them for a while. She looked straight ahead and found her other world.

Starting with Chopin's "Revolutionary Etude," then two Bach "Partitas" and Rachmaninoff's "Sonata No. 2 in B-Flat Minor" and after Braham's "Ballad No. 4 in B Major" she left the stage for a quick respite and a quick drink of water. Back she continued with a Schubert impromptu and one quick Beethoven sonata before Craig's "Opus."

When he heard the first chord, he knew and quickly looked at the program, for the first time, because he thought he knew what she would be playing. He closed his eyes and once again listened to how beautifully she interpreted his music. Sharon wanted it to be a surprise and it was.

Her program was difficult and beautifully performed. It was obvious she was a professional.

The applause was so great that she happily added one last short Bach as a token of love.

As she was acknowledging the applause she received deep red rose that matched her gown. Helen and Bill sent white and pink was Aunt Katy's color. She threw a kiss to her family in the front row and then went backstage to meet Craig.

Dr. Bernard as in all recitals, came on stage and said, "You have heard one for the ages. Miss

Heisendorf will be in the outer foyer, if you would like to thank her in person. Good night and thank you for coming."

Deacon Ely had brought the choir and they were the first to be at Sharon's side. He took her hand and said, "My lady, I don't have words to tell you how beautiful that was. When you are great, remember us and how we loved you."

"Thank you so much. Never forget you."

She hugged the choir members. "I'm so glad you came. That is special for me. Did I play big enough for you?"

"Yes, yes," as their energy was loosening up.

Others gathered around, Karen and Jim, the bunch from the country club, Glenna, and Kelly.

Among friends and family there was a stranger. He approached Sharon and said, "Good evening, Miss Heisendorf. I was told there was going to be a very special performance here tonight and they were right." He introduced himself. "I am Reginald Goldman from the Brooking Music Agency. I understand you are interested in performing."

Sharon surprised said, "Thank you," and for a moment was lost for words. "Yes."

He handed her his card. "Please call me soon and we can set up an appointment and talk. Your performance was spectacular and professional. It will be a pleasure to represent you, and with that I say good night."

Sharon turned and looked at Craig. "Did you know about this?"

"No honey, I did not."

Aunt Katy at Sharon's side was about to burst with happiness and gave her a big hug.

"Probably your guardian angel, Dr. Bernard."

On the way to the car she stopped and turned to Craig, "I just can't believe it. Am I dreaming?"

"Your dream is reality."

At home friends gathered for a small reception. Dr. Bernard confessed, "I had to invite Mr. Goldman. You are ready for the stage. This is only the second time that I have done this. After you meet with him, you and Craig can decide. But he is a nice man and I know their agency. It is reputable. They only do New York, and that could be a good start for you."

She hugged Dr. Bernard and thought, I don't know if this is proper, but I don't care.

The air was festive then all of a sudden things were very quiet. The choir gathered and Craig gave a pitch and their young voices were directed at Sharon as they sang for her.

When they finished, she thanked them with a big hug. "A most precious gift of song and from all of you is very special. We have had a lot of fun since January. Have you had something to eat?"

They shook their heads no.

She took a hand. "Well then come with me." They filled their little plates and stood by eating like young men and ladies.

Dr. Bernard, Dr. Westmore, and other professors were impressed with the work that Sharon and Craig had accomplished with the group. They had made a difference in their young lives.

♪

The next day Helen and Bill said goodbye early. Craig went to work with the choir and Aunt Katy took Sharon and Karen to look for wedding attire.

Later they arrived back at Sharon's studio. "Our shopping venture has been a success."

"I am so glad I found a dress I really like."

"Ivory silk is so classic," Karen added.

"Aunt Katy this is where I have lived the last two years. Perfect for one. Karen has been across the hall and we have shared a lot."

"Let's get these dresses out of the packages."

They carefully unwrapped them.

"I like the empire waist and it looks perfect on you. The lace jacket is really nice because it secretly serves a purpose without covering you or the dress. The long sleeves are appropriate for a May afternoon," Karen giving her perspective.

"And these little buttons, Craig will have to unbutton them for me."

Sharon looking at the veil that she had selected, "I think this elbow length is not so formal and I like the satin edge. I can gather it at the back of my hair. I didn't want anything lavish or fancy. It's perfect with the dress."

I like your dress too and you looked really great in that shade of green. It is so delicate and spring like," Sharon said to Karen.

"Perfect for outside," Katy added.

"I'll leave you two. Do you have to work tonight?"

"I do and Craig is bringing Aunt Katy for dinner and she can see where I worked for the four years."

When they were alone Sharon asked Aunt Katy, "Would you do something for me?"

"Of course, honey anything."

"Would you tell mom and dad about the agent? I don't want to tell them, because I just don't want to talk to them about it yet."

"Never understood their attitude. They have never said they misjudged."

"No, but it's okay. Until last evening they might have been right."

"You knew and I knew it would work out, but yes I will tell them. You probably didn't know, but long ago I gave your father an earful."

"No, I didn't."

"I want to tell Allen. He always said that I should do what I wanted. Well we had better get home, but first I want to get a dress to wear tonight."

At home there was just enough time to relax and get Sharon to work.

"Sweetie, why don't I take you over and then come back and then we won't have two cars."

Craig and Sharon were on their way and alone after a fast several days. He held her hand and, "I noticed when you play here you don't seem to find that other place like you do when you play classical literature."

"Playing here is fun, but in concert I have to find the spirit of Chopin or Brahms. I have to get into their person, their soul or spirit. I have to be a part of them so I take a little trip before I play. A little psychic journey," and she laughed.

"Do you feel that way when you play the janitors work?"

She took his hand and kissed the palm. "Yes," and with wide eyes, "Yes! And with broom in hand." And then she laughed. "Seriously, when you showed me the paintings that were your inspiration, I got into your soul."

They arrived and he walked in with her and then on his way home.

Aunt Katy was dressed and waiting in the living room.

Craig sat down. "We have about an hour so I'll get dressed." But he started to talk. "It means so much to Sharon that you are here."

"She didn't have her parents, so happily I came. She lost them the moment she mentioned music school. I'll never forget that summer day she rode her bike over to my house, and you saw how far it was. She had been crying and told me everything. I vowed right then I would do all I could to help her. I told her we would find a way. When her scholarship came through I cried with happiness."

"Were her parents convinced then?"

"No, they were surprised and upset, but didn't think she would go."

"Didn't they know their daughter?"

"Then her father refused to bring her. So we packed my car and drove up. It was me or the bus."

"Well she has my total support. I guess I had better change. You are probably hungry, I am."

At the country club they were seated and ordered. Sharon saw them and gave a tiny wave.

"That day we arrived here is so etched in my mind. We were both determined, but I was so apprehensive about leaving her. After being here a few days I felt better. She told me she planned to go to work somewhere, so she would have money for the last two years."

"I was astounded when she told me she made the dresses."

"Oh yes, her mother insisted that she learn to sew and cook. Her sewing machine was among the stuff we brought. She said she made little things for the girls in the dorm for a small fee."

"She never told me that. She knows how to get along in this world."

"She defied her parents, but she believed in herself."

"How glad we are for that."

During her break Sharon joined them for a moment. "Are you enjoying?" she asked her aunt.

"Oh yes, the food is wonderful but the music is more wonderful and so beautiful."

♫

Before going to church the next day, Aunt Katy gave Sharon a little box that was beautifully wrapped.

"Honey this is from Allen for your birthday, and he thought you might like to carry it on your wedding day."

She carefully opened it. A white leather- bound

302

Book of Prayers, engraved *Craig and Sharon May, 28, 1961.*

"Oh, Craig it will be perfect with red roses."

She also handed her an envelope. "I know Craig will help you celebrate and buy something for your new home."

"Oh, Aunt Katy Craig's birthday is in May too, the fifteenth, four days after mine."

"Oh I didn't know. A card will be coming."

"No. Your being here is enough."

After church they saw her off and got Sharon back to the country club just in time.

♫

CHAPTER TWENTY-NINE

♫

The month with all of its activities was moving fast. Craig and Sharon met with Mr. Goldman in the beautiful old Cramer Building downtown. Handshakes put them immediately at ease. Music in the background added an extra touch of comfort.

"I am so glad to meet with you and again your recital was absolutely wonderful." He began the discussion explaining two contracts that he would offer her. "I will be happy with either one you might accept. It will be a pleasure to represent you. Not to be insistent, but I have two cancellations for this fall. Also three summer requests that need to be filled."

They both listened very closely.

"Take these copies and discuss them. Get back to me as soon as you decide. If you decide not to accept either, it has been a pleasure meeting you."

After reading the fine print and meeting with a lawyer, Sharon decided on the limited version for a year. Upon signing, she was booked for recitals at Saratoga, Chautauqua and Skaneateles on the Lake.

Also Ithaca in October and Albany in November. She liked Chautauqua because it was the musical place to be in the summer.

She was ecstatic. She smiled at nothing. Hard work and determination had paid off. That evening Craig popped the cork and their glasses rang a happy tone. A call to Aunt Katy was not forgotten.

Sharon immediately began organizing her repertoire for the recitals. She consulted Craig because of his experience and knowledge. She treasured his input. They were a team.

They celebrated their birthdays. It was just the two of them, it was their intimate connection to life.

Wedding plans were coming together. Florist, caterer and music were completed.

Classes were over on the nineteenth, but Craig had students' grades and work to complete.

♫

School was out in Texas and Kevin was packing his car. He decided to bring many things because he didn't know how long he would be in New York. Two suitcases, radio, record player, records and books. Other personal papers and things were included. A suit, jackets and tuxedo were hanging. For along the way a cooler with sandwiches and fruit. He even threw in his sleeping bag. Map in the seat next to him, he was off.

♫

Sharon was home and around noon on Monday the doorbell rang. She thought, did Craig forget his key or is it Kevin.

"Kevin!" She welcomed him with a big hug and ushered him in.

"Did you drive all night?" She was concerned.

"No, I left yesterday and stayed over."

"Are you hungry?"

"No thanks. I had a big breakfast."

"Craig is at school. Classes were over Friday, but he has to get grades in."

"I know how that is. Are things going okay?"

"Really good, and Craig will be happy to see you again. Why don't you get your things in and then go over to school. He'll be in his office and he can show you where he spent last winter."

Looking around, "Your home is beautiful."

"Oh thank you. I'll let Craig show you everything. I'll tell you how to get to school after you're settled."

Following Sharon's instructions, Kevin walked in the large building and straight to Craig's office. He saw his friend writing briskly and knocked lightly.

"Hey buddy, you made it safely." Their manly greeting of hugs and pats on the back were warm.

"Sharon said you would be hard at work. She got me settled and then sent me over here."

"Yeah, last minute stuff."

"Nice campus. It is bigger than I imagined."

"The academic and medical campus is on the other side of town and very large. We'll give you a tour. How was your drive and everybody there?"

306

"Okay, and they're flying up Saturday."

"I will be through here today and Sharon will have dinner. And this evening Dan Westmore is coming over to run through some music. It will only be about an hour."

"I will stay out of the way."

"No, we're going to listen."

"I'll let you get back to work and I'll drive around a bit and I want to help you with whatever I can. Yard work, inside. What I saw of your house, it's great."

"We have a couple things to do yet."

Kevin left Craig to finish his work. He did some exploring before returning to the house.

Craig finished, went home and found Sharon and Kevin chatting in the kitchen, while she fixed dinner. As they ate Craig asked Kevin, "What are your plans after this. Stay on for a while, at least until we come back from Paris, if you can."

"Everything is open. Stop at Mom and Dad's on the way back, look into a doctoral program, go camping out west." He paused. "I can stay until you get back. I'll take care of your house."

"I would like to paint the stairs leading down here. It is a little dark and we have pictures to put up. And finish some yard work."

After dinner Dan Westmore arrived. While Dan, Craig and Sharon were still in the foyer and in deep conversation, the doorbell rang again. Kevin went to answer.

"Oh!" Glenna said as she gazed at this guy with little wisps of black hair that fell on his forehead, pointing to his dark brown eyes.

Kevin stammered. "They are talking to Dr. Westmore. Can I help you with something?"

"Yes, I am supposed to play for them."

"Oh! OH! I didn't know. I'm sorry. Come in."

"Thank you." And she flashed a sweet smile that exposed the tiny dimples in her cheeks. She took a deep breath. "I'm Glenna."

"Nice to meet you. I'm Kevin, Craig's friend from Texas." And he took a deep breath.

"Glenna, come in." Sharon went to meet her.

"I wasn't sure he was going to let me in, so I introduced myself."

Playfully he said, "I thought you might be selling something. I'm sorry. I'll make it up to you."

Glenna took another deep breath and thought, he is almost as handsome as Craig.

They both took long glances at each other. While she focused on his face, he took in all of her. This was not missed by Craig or Sharon and they smiled at each other, knowing.

"Let's go down and hear you two."

"We got together last week after school."

"Getting to play this beautiful instrument is such a pleasure."

The talk was all about casual subjects. They went through the music a couple times and were satisfied how they sounded. Dan said, "I'll leave you guys and will see you Saturday evening for the final get-together. So happy for you two."

After he was gone Glenna said, "I will go too." Sharon came to her defense. "Why don't we have a glass of wine." Hoping to further the heavy glances between Glenna and Kevin into a friendship.

"Come on back upstairs," Craig said, "and we'll get the wine."

The girls seated in front of the fireplace, Craig and Kevin went to the kitchen.

"Hey guy, who is she?"

"We saw the way you two looked at each other."

"She is really cut and curly blond hair matched her dimple so well. Does she have a boyfriend?"

"Sharon would know about these things. She is a nice girl. I've known her this year. She and Sharon are good friends and were roommates the first two years. She is from Pittsburgh and that is all I know. Go for it." They joined the girls, but had not lost their mischievous smiles.

"Glenna is moving into Sharon's studio for the next year. She has to stay there until after Sunday or she could move in now."

"I can stay in the dorm all of this week. I told the janitor to leave my room intact and I would move Monday."

Feigning concern, Craig said," I didn't get that message."

They all looked at him. "Oh a private joke. Kevin knows, so we'll let Glenna in. When Sharon first saw me she thought I was the new janitor."

"You didn't tell me." And Glenna laughed.

"I'm never going to live that down."

"Kevin, are you a music teacher?"

"No. I teach high school English."

"Very close. Music and literature."

"He just arrived this morning and he is going to help me finish up round here."

"What's on for the rest of the summer?" Kevin asked.

"Sharon's recitals and maybe Stratford."

"What's Stratford?"

"Music and theater, over in Canada. We thought we'd like to see Glenn Gould."

"Oh, that would be special. I'd love to see him," Glenna added.

Craig looked at Kevin with raised brows.

"I signed up for two class this summer. I'm not doing much else," Glenna said.

"I think I'll just go for one since I have been booked."

"Starting in September I hope to work some. I signed up to sub Monday and Friday," Glenna said.

They continued their friendly exchange in the disguise of getting to know each other. An hour or so passed and Glenna said, "I had better go."

"Did you drive over?"

"No. I walked."

"How would you like protection to accompany you back?" Kevin offered.

She smiled. "That would be nice. It is a short walk."

"Do you have curfew?"

"No, school is out, so we're on our own."

When Kevin and Glenna left Craig and Sharon hugged and said, "Why didn't we think? Did you see the way they looked at each other?"

"I did and that is why I asked her to stay and have a glass of wine."

"But he has to go back to Texas."

"She is committed to graduate school."

As Kevin and Glenna walked to the dorm, they talked about school, their families, Texas verses New York. He asked her, "If you don't have any plans for tomorrow evening could we do something?"

"I don't, us seniors are just hanging around waiting to graduate. That is why it is so quiet. Even the cafeteria is closed. I've been eating in my room." There was a heavy pause between them.

"You have known Craig a long time. It seems strange to call him Craig. All year he was Professor Jamieson."

"We entered college together. There is a bunch of us that are still together." Kevin paused. "Tomorrow we could get something to eat? Where do you normally go?"

"The Kitchen Place, it isn't far, it's small and they have good food. We'll go dutch."

He looked at her strangely. "Is that what they do here in New York? I'm from Texas and we pay for our girls when we take them out. What time?"

"You are the busy one, you tell me."

"Five-thirty, then we can do something after."

Kevin ran all the way to Craig's house.

He realized he did not have a key, but the light was still on and he rang the bell.

"A long walk." They just looked at each other with that smile they had so often witnessed before.

Sharon caught up with them.

"I am going to take her out tomorrow night to eat. She seems really nice. Her parents are lawyers."

Sharon said, "I know."

"Nice family."

"I know. I went home with her several times."

"Did you guys plan this?"

"No, but we're all for it."

"A while ago we were talking and she said it would be nice to date an adult."

"I'm that adult that walked right into her life."

"It is late and you have to be tired."

♫

The next day Craig and Kevin painted the stairway and finished the yard work. Before Sharon fixed dinner she asked, "If you are taking Glenna out you had better take a key."

"Yeah, I might stay out a bit late." They all smiled, especially Craig, because he knew Kevin hadn't dated much since he and Sally parted.

Kevin drove to the dorm and went in just as Glenna was coming out.

"I'm glad you came out because I wouldn't know where to find you."

In the car and a few turns they were at The Kitchen Place.

The quaint little eatery was quiet at this hour so they chose a table overlooking the garden.

"After graduate school, do you have plans?"

"Teach or accompany a choir or soloist."

"Your profession is miles away from your

parents. Not interested in law?"

"I like to hear them talk about what they are doing, but to be one, no."

"Is this the first time you have been to New York?"

"It is and so far I like it. I haven't seen much. They are going to show me around."

"How long are you staying?"

"At least until they get back from Paris."

It was pleasant eating together and getting to know more about each other. Finally Kevin convinced her that he was going to pay.

Back in the car. "What now? Is there a park near where we could just take a stroll?"

"Over near the big campus and you can see it."

After driving around the campus they stopped at the park. They got out. Taking her hand they followed the foot path along the river.

"You need a sweater as the sun goes down here. In Texas your never need one."

Across the little wooden bridge and on the path he stopped, turned, and took her face in his hand and kissed her. "I've wanted to do this since I answered the door yesterday."

She smiled sweetly.

They drove back to the dorm and they sat in the courtyard as it grew darker.

"I don't know what Craig and Sharon have planned for tomorrow, but I would like to get together again."

"I'd like that. Why don't you call me? The phone is near my room. Want to watch TV a while?"

He sat in the big chair and she curled up on her bed and they watched, when they weren't talking.

After several programs, "It is late and I'll go."

She walked him out and he kissed her lightly. "It is so nice meeting you, Glenna."

"Very nice meeting you too."

When he got home it was very quiet, Craig and Sharon were out of sight.

♫

The next day they went through their check list for graduation and their wedding. Sharon gathered all her things and took them to her studio. Kevin saw where Glenna was going to live this next year. He also said he wanted to get her something for graduation. After shopping, they picked her up and showed Kevin more of the city before going home for dinner.

"When are your folks coming up?" Kevin asked Glenna.

"Friday morning, and staying until Saturday morning. My little sisters are staying with me in the dorm. They are excited."

"What are you all doing after graduation?" Craig asked.

"My dad is taking us to dinner."

"We're having a gathering, with food. Ask your parents if they would like to join us. Just family."

"Thank you I will. They would like that."

"More personal than a restaurant."

"I can meet your parents, your sisters and little brother," Kevin added

314

"We'll expect all of you," Craig said.

♫

Thursday afternoon, the big plane from the Midwest carrying Sharon's family landed in New York.

They all seemed happy to be here, especially her mother. She hugged Sharon lovingly. Dad was equally as warm.

Jack said, "I have been to New York City, but not up here. From the air it looks beautiful."

Aunt Katy added, "It is beautiful country." To Sharon's mom, "You will like it too."

Allen and Carolyn both looked tired. "We were out most of the night with one of our parishioners. She is very ill and her family wanted us to be there. God's work is around the clock."

"Tonight you can rest. It is quiet here," Craig offered, "and even sleep late tomorrow."

After everyone was settled they were given a tour of the house and garden.

Sharon's dad starting asking questions about the campus, so she said, "Let's all go for a little walk. We can even walk over to my studio."

After the guys saw where she had lived, they went downstairs and Sharon showed her mother her wedding dress.

"It is beautiful honey. It is you."

Sue agreed that it was perfect for her.

"Karen's is pale green. We thought it was a good color for a garden wedding."

They enjoyed the walk after sitting on the plane. The old homes were awake from the long winter sleep and showed their colors in flowers.

Before leaving for dinner Sharon found her parents in her library. She gave them a big hug and said, "I'm so glad you finally made it. Hope you will come more often."

"We're going to do that."

"Next time we'll drive and see the country."

"We're taking all of you to the country club for dinner. It is where I worked for the last four years, not as a waitress, but playing piano for the dinner hour on Saturdays. I also had church jobs."

"Oh, why didn't you tell us?" her mother asked.

"I wasn't sure you would approve. I started right after I got here. I had to support myself for year three and four. I worked the least hours for the most money. My studio was cheaper than the dorm and cooking my own food was better."

"Honey, it seems that you were right. We just couldn't see into the future," her mother finally relented.

"I believed in myself but, I could have been wrong. Things are on their way to working out."

"We like Craig a lot and are anxious to meet his mother and family," her mother added.

"Helen is real sweet and you will like her."

"Well you kids sort of do what you want. Allen told us that he was going to quit the ministry and teach history." Her father offered the news.

"Really!" She wanted to ask, were you as

stringent on him as you were me, but she didn't.

She gave them each a quick kiss. "I knew you would understand." Hoping, if not, she planted the seed.

"I'll go find Craig. Kevin is going to drive his car. He is picking up Glenna."

At the country club they were seated and wine was ordered by several of the group.

Sharon's dad said, "I will have a glass too. Haven't had one in years, and this is certainly a celebration." Her mother raised her eyes in surprise.

"Go for it Dad."

After dinner and before dessert Mr. Kellogg came out.

"Would you like to play for your family? If they live so far away they have never been here."

Craig looked startled and Sharon knew, "It's okay, I told them before we left."

"Oh," he stammered.

She entertained all for about ten minutes and then came back for dessert.

Finally Craig said, "Let's get back, Allen and Carolyn need to get some rest."

He took his family home and then took Sharon and Aunt Katy to her studio.

"You told them."

"I thought I had better since we were going there."

"How did they react?"

"Not too bad, and Dad said Allen told them he was leaving the ministry."

"Oh my, I hope this is not too much for them."

"When they get home they can say what they want to each other. Now we're going to have a great few days."

Sharon walked downstairs and he pulled her in his arms and kissed her and said, "I'll miss you tonight. Two nights."

♩

Friday's dawn was a shadowy mist. As the sun rose, it dried the air and the puffy clouds parted for a bright and happy morning.

It was graduation day, an end but also a beginning, the last comfort before stepping into a life of their own.

Prayers would reach each heart, music to stir each emotion and words to guide, were offered to this vast group. For each student it was personal with their hopes and dreams. Accepting the roll tied with a tiny black ribbon, closed the mini life of joy, tears and hard work, and yes, play.

For Sharon her hopes and dreams had fallen into her arms, but not without a struggle that she felt was over. "Thank you—thank you," she whispered.

Introductions and goodbyes took longer than the ceremony. It was a happy time touched with a bit of sadness. It was bittersweet.

Kevin found Glenna in the big crowd and he said, "Congratulations," with a big hug and kiss.

"Kevin, this is my mother and father."

"So nice to meet you." He extended his hand.

Glenna added, "He is Professor Jamieson's

friend from Texas and is here for their wedding and we have become friends. And Kevin, this is Vickie and Rachel and Stevie."

Kevin shook hands gently with the girls. To her brother, "Nice to meet you young man. We'll have a man-to-man chat about this later."

"I'm on," he said. It was an instant bonding.

"You're coming to Craig's?" he asked her mother.

"Glenna told us earlier, but this is unexpected and I don't have anything to take."

"That's okay.

"We've met Sharon several times and Dr. Jamieson sounds like a very special man."

"He is. We have been friends for a long time. Just come on over. They are expecting you."

"Thank you we will, and I will send her something later."

The caterer had everything ready when the guests and family arrived home.

While eating and enjoying a glass of wine … Craig noticed Sharon's parents were extremely happy and friendly ... Helen and Katy picked up where they left off when they met at Sharon's recital … Kevin and Glenna held hands and her mom and dad smiled … Allen and Carolyn finally got rested and found their place in the conversations … Bill and Glenna's father could not resist talking about their professions, but her mother joined the girl … Karen and Jim joined the young couples for laughs and exchanges … Jack and Sue could not stop talking about the city and how beautiful the neighborhood was … Craig and Sharon mingled among their family and friends adding to the present idea in words.

All wished Sharon and Glenna a hardy congratulations for their effort to make their lives more exciting and richer.

At the end of the evening, Glenna's mother told her they were going back to the hotel. "Kevin will walk with us to the dorm," Glenna assured her.

"Okay darling, we'll see you in the morning and we'll have breakfast together before we leave."

They said goodbye to all and wished Craig and Sharon a blessing for their wedding day.

Slowly everyone retreated to their rooms. Craig took Sharon and Aunt Katy to her studio. Kevin got Glenna and her sisters safely in the dorm.

♫

Saturday midday, Kevin and Craig went to the airport to gather their friends from Texas. It didn't take Craig long to tell them Kevin had a girlfriend. "The same day he arrived."

"Oh no, we're not going to lose you too?" Judy asked.

"Oh." He seemed surprised at the concept, which obviously he had not thought through.

"She is a friend of Sharon's, very nice and you'll meet her."

They took them to the Pickford Hotel to get settled and then home for new acquaintance and renewed friendship. Kevin went for Glenna to fulfill his promise. They welcomed her as they had Sharon.

Finally Craig's sister and her family arrived with baby James. He didn't want for being held for the next two days. It was a loud and fun afternoon.

Later there was rehearsal for tomorrow's special event. The evening closed with food and happy liquid.

♫

CHAPTER THIRTY

♫

Sunday's dawn broke into a magnificent sunrise. This heavenly star answered Sharon and Craig's prayer for a beautiful day. Three o'clock would put its rays just in the right place.

Craig and Kevin met the florist, but requested everyone stay inside as they wanted the garden to be viewed only after it was decorated.

The yard and garden was groomed pristinely by Craig and Kevin a few days earlier. Tall evergreens enclosed the garden from the street. Its natural form with its varied bushes, size and colors, made a perfect setting for their wedding. Hyacinths, tulips and other spring flowers colored the space around the bushes.

"Right here under this old oak," Craig called as they brought the white lattice arbor covered with red roses.

Kevin asked, "Where do you want these beautiful white benches?"

"Right here on the green, but leave a path. A couple on each side. These are for our parents."

"They have a little white chair."

"That's for John. Next to Mother. Where is the pedestal for the ring pillow?"

"They are bringing it now."

"It goes just beyond the kneeling bench, at the edge of the arbor."

The workers quickly finished as Craig and Kevin watched. Along the walk were white lilies and cascading ivy and large cherubs holding candles. Other plants placed with the blooming spring flowers made it complete.

They brought over one last candle. Craig said to Kevin, "A memory candle for my father."

He carefully placed it on a small pedestal among the flowers. "I'll light it just before we start."

Craig and Kevin stood back and admired the work. Their garden smiled with beauty.

"It's beautiful. You two did it right."

"I think I will keep the arbor. It would make a perfect place for a little iron table and chairs."

"After a hard day at school or working in the yard this summer."

"Let's go see how Mr. Heisendorf is doing with the set up. He really wanted to do something, so I told him what Sharon wanted and he said he would be happy to supervise. After all he paid for it."

The tent was up and most of the tables, some had place settings and white lilies in the center.

"This is going to be a beautiful wedding." Mr. Heisendorf admiring what was accomplished.

"Thank you, Sharon will be glad that you like what we planned. Mention it to her."

"I will do that the first moment I see her."

"I think it might be time to get dressed," Craig said to Kevin.

Upstairs in Craig's bedroom while they were making themselves handsome, they reminisced about their long friendship.

"Fate certainly took a different turn. When you left Texas never did I think you would be marrying someone that you hadn't even met."

"It was never a thought."

"And Sally left so fast. After the initial shock, I felt numb for a while, then my protective senses took over and I didn't seem to care."

"It's for the best, but you don't see it at first."

"For some reason other than your wedding, I couldn't wait to get here. Do you suppose it was Glenna? She really got to me fast. Maybe too fast. I don't want to make a mistake."

"You won't. You'll know when to cross that imaginary line. Let's go get Beth to pin our boutonnieres on."

"Then I had better go get Glenna."

When he saw her in her dark-pink, long gown, he looked at her so strangely it made her say, "What?"

He looked away and she thought his eyes were heavy. He took her in his arms and composed himself. "It's because you look so beautiful." Yes, he was thinking that, but also I have to leave.

When they got back, the strings had arrived and were setting up on the flagstone patio outside the French doors. Dan and his wife were also there and all were conversing at the piano.

At two-thirty, the strings began with "Romance" from *The Gadfly*, Saint-Sean's "The Swan" and "This is My Beloved." Glenna alternated with Debussy, Braham's and Delbruck's "Berceuse." The beauty of the music and the garden were one.

Family and friends were assembling and in awe of the garden. "So much beauty in one place, it's heavenly, it's Shangri-La," were some of the comments heard. What they saw and heard was setting the mood for beautiful moments to come.

At three o'clock, and to Glenna's beautiful music, Craig lit his memory candle for his father. Jack and Beth's husband, Josh, also lit the candles the cherubs were holding. The white path that would lead Sharon to Craig was rolled out.

When Craig came back in Kevin said, "Karen called and said they are on their way."

Jim arrived with Karen, Sharon, her mother who had joined them earlier, and Aunt Katy.

Aunt Katy looked into the garden and, "I never dreamed, Do you like it?" she said to Sharon's mother.

"Oh, I am going to cry before we even get started," she said softly.

They were ushered in on the arms of Jack and Josh. Sharon took her father's hand.

As the strings and Glenna offered the recessional of Handel's "Largo," Craig and Kevin took their place under the arbor with Allen.

John began the processional, angelic in his white linen suit that would not be that way for long. He walked carefully with his treasure, placed it on the pedestal, and hurried to his grandmother's side and took her hand. He thought all this was very nice, but he wasn't sure what getting married was all about.

Karen followed, her pale green gown and pink roses blended well with the colors in the garden.

Sharon, in ivory silk, and her father walked slowly on the white path. Her eyes met with Craig's and held tight until her father placed her hand in his.

They all paused and the silence welcomed Dan as he sang Gounod's "Ave Maria."

"Dear souls of our Lord, we have gathered here today to witness my beloved sister, Sharon, and this special man, Craig, in holy matrimony..." Finishing the words of the Lord and from his heart Allen offered the rings and they were accepted.

The strings of a lone cello sang out Elgar's "Salut d'amour." Under the angel blue sky Craig turned to Sharon, took her hand and, "How do I love Thee? My Sharon, I love thy face as it smiles on me. I love thy eyes as they sparkle love. I love thy hands as they touch me. I love your words as you speak to me. But most of all, I love your soul as it has met mine and we are one in love, life and music. My love for you is complete, but it will grow and through my life I will make—I Love You, reach into the endless universe. I'll devote my life to making you happy and caring for you. My first—I Love You—to start this long journey is now." And he kissed her lips lightly.

"Oh love Craig, you are a beautiful man. Every day my prayer to God is of thanks that he sent you my way. I am my heart and it speaks, I love you more each day, each day with more emotions than the day before. I will always be your helpmate and by your side, because I believe in your love and in all that you are. My love is so great I will decline eternity if you are not by my side. May our love always be at peace as it is this wonderful day in this wonderful garden. Thank you for making it so beautiful."

He whispered, "It was easy love."

"By the power invested in me, I now pronounce you man and wife." They knelt as Dan sang a closing prayer to let God flow through their joined hearts.

They rose and Allen took each of their hands in his and said, "Congratulations, and much love, and I have never felt closer to God than in these moments here with you in your beautiful garden."

They turned and looked upon the happy faces with smiles and, yes, some tears and received their applause of approval.

Karen and Kevin were the first to offer best wishes. Craig gave his mother a kiss, then to Sharon's mother, and then best wishes flowed from all. The strings and Glenna played for another half hour while Kevin sat beside her at the piano.

Craig noticed his mother had paused in front of the memory candle. He thought, she is asking, are you watching? It is these moment, when James was born, us getting married and our children yet, that her heart cries for him to be near and be a part of the joy. I just can't imagine her feelings.

The photographer disrupted his thought for, "Pictures." He took many poses in front of the arbor and flower.

It was time for all to make their way to the

backyard where all of the food was waiting. Another string group played for the next hour. No dancing, there just wasn't a place for it.

After everyone was seated, Kevin tapped his glass and got their attention.

"It is time to offer a toast to Craig and Sharon. I have known Craig ten years and I have never seen him happier. We met when we arrived at college, but I will skip that part." Craig smiled and shook his head. "This year while he was here in New York, we talked on the phone many times and he was always excited to talk about Sharon and I thought he was exaggerating. No, she is the special person just for him. They both knew that and that is why we are here today. Join me in wishing them a long life of love and happiness. To Craig and Sharon."

It was an evening of friends and family being together, laughing, exchanging stories, inventing new ones, all in honor of Craig and Sharon's wedding.

Later they went upstairs to change and then return to thank everyone for helping them celebrate their special day. To her father and mother, "Thank you for giving us this beautiful wedding."

To Aunt Katy, "Thank you for being at my side when no one else was there. You will never know how much it meant. We'll see you tomorrow. We want to be back so we can be with you for a while before you leave."

They found Kevin. "We're going to go now."

"Okay. I am going to help Glenna move tomorrow morning."

"She has a key and I boxed up the last-minute

stuff, so just push them out of your way or in the hall. She can put her car in the garage," Sharon said.

"We'll bring your boxes when we come back."

Kevin offered his hand to Craig. "Buddy, it was all very beautiful and I hope the best for you two, always," and he kissed Sharon on the cheek.

Craig and Sharon left the day behind and went to be together in body and spirit. A special love shined on them. The garden, the words to each other, the music and loved ones would be forever in their hearts and imprinted in their souls.

The sun faded, friends and family made their way to another place. Glenna and Kevin walked over to the garden that was quiet and dusk had slipped in.

"What a beautiful spot in this big world." She put her arms around him, he held her close, and they danced to the songs of the universe.

"We don't need music."

"Just each other. So nice to be here with you at the close of this wonderful day. Let's sit," Kevin said.

The sun set completely and the angel blue sky had turned to shadows.

"I don't want to let you go tonight," he said softly to her.

"When there is something as beautiful as today, you don't want it to end."

"That too. But I mean you sweetie."

"It is easy to get caught up in the spirit of the day, but we have to remember it really isn't ours. It's Craig and Sharon's."

"I know but it's hard to separate yourself." And he turned her head and kissed her. "What time do you want me to come over tomorrow?"

"Not too early, everything is packed."

"I believe everyone is almost gone. Let's go inside."

The family and the Texas bunch were just milling around reliving the wonderful day. Kevin and Glenna joined them.

Judy asked, "When are you coming back? We missed you this week. Lee didn't have a golfing partner."

Very lightly he said, "I don't know. I like it here. You all are coming over here tomorrow to stay with us?"

"Yes. Katy said they would have our bedrooms ready."

"Craig and Sharon will be back and we'll have a great time for two days."

"I want to see some of the area," Margaret said.

"I think Craig has a little tour planned. We can pile in two cars and see it all."

Directed to Glenna Jeff said, "Your campus is really nice and big."

"It is like a little village. We call it the Music Box. You can stay right in this area all four years."

"Any plans after graduate school?"

"Nothing definite. Maybe New York for an accompanying job or teach."

Kevin listened closely. He had thoughts he couldn't share with her yet.

"We have to move her in the morning, but we'll be back before Craig and Sharon. Come on over anytime."

"It's late. I think we're all going back to the hotel. Goodnight all."

"I'll drive Glenna to the dorm. It's cool out."

When they got there she asked him to come in.

"Would you excuse me for a moment while I get out of this dress?"

She put on her sweatpants and shirt and felt much more comfortable.

"Oh I wish I had something to change into."

"I can't help you, mine are too small."

"I'll be okay." He sat down in the big chair. "Come sit with me. I wanted to snuggle with you. All day I saw how beautiful you looked and wanted to grab you and kiss you passionately, like this … can we tame the lights?"

Only her night light was on and she went back to the big chair and cuddled with Kevin. They made up for not being near the whole day.

"When I left Texas, I didn't have a dream that I would meet you and be cuddled up here, but it is so nice."

He got up and picked her up and put her on her bed and lay down beside her. "I will be a gentleman. I just want to relax here with you." They were close but their feelings held their place. He thought, I have only known her for a week, god what is two weeks going to be like.

They talked softly. "We'll have a good time tomorrow. We're a fun bunch."

"Everyone seems really nice. Sharon had a good time in Texas. What possessed you to become an English teacher?"

"My mom probably, she is."

"Do you write?"

"Not a lot. Mostly I read and teach. When I get back I am going to look into getting my doctorate. Then college."

"Interesting. Do your parents live in Texas?'

"No in Ohio. I grew up there. I went to school in Texas and stayed on. Craig's family lived close and I went to his house a lot before his mother got married to Bill. On the way home I am going to stop and stay a few days with Mom and Dad."

"Your sisters?"

"One lives in St. Louis the other Chicago."

"When are you going back?"

"I don't know right now." He thought, I did know, but now I really don't since I met you.

Softly, "Oh Glenna, I am getting too comfortable. In a few moments I could be asleep. We got up early and helped the florist. It has been a long day." He wasn't sure she heard him. She is breathing like she is sleeping. She is. I'll stay a few more moments. Those moments turned into another day.

♫

"Oh! Kevin, it's morning!"

"Oh my gosh. How am I going to explain this. Did you cover us up?"

"I did. I got cold and couldn't put you out in the night."

He held her and quickly kissed her. "I'll just slip out."

"Just say you went for an early morning walk."

He laughed. "In my tux."

"We really don't have to explain to anyone."

"No, we don't. I'll see you in a couple hours. Maybe someday we will laugh about the first night we slept together."

"The first time I've slept with a guy other than my little brother." Then she realized what she had revealed.

Oh my, he thought. A quick kiss and he eased out.

He carefully opened the door at home and caught the fragrance of coffee. There was soft conversation on the back porch.

Afraid it might be a parent he slipped upstairs.

He quickly took a shower and went back down for coffee. He found who was enjoying the early sunrise, Aunt Katy and son Jack.

"You are up early," Jack said.

"Yeah, but I slept very well."

"I think we all did. Sue is still up there."

"You won't have jet lag going home. What time do you expect to land?" Kevin asked

"Around ten tonight. Sue and I are staying with mom. Allen is staying with his mom and dad."

"We were just talking about how wonderful everything was yesterday," Katy said.

A few others straggled down for that first wake up. Kevin said, "I have to go help Glenna, but will be back soon."

Back to the dorm he found Glenna refreshed and ready to go.

All of the boxes in the cars they drove to her new home. Boxes upstairs, he helped her unpack, get the bed made, towels in the bath, and what food she had in the cabinet. "Look what my mother sent." She held up *The Joy of Cooking*. This is more than a hint."

"You didn't have an opportunity to cook living in the dorm."

"I haven't done much. We have had a cook after Rachel and Vickie were born and mother worked more."

"We'll learn in this nice little studio."

"I am so glad she got married and vacated it."

"I think we're all done."

"For now. I want to go shopping and get a few more things and food."

"Can I go with you?"

"I'd love to have your company."

"A date, but now let's get back. Craig and Sharon are probably back too. They want to visit before everyone leaves."

They put Sharon's boxes in his car and went back. Craig and Sharon arrived very soon after.

After lunch all of the Texas bunch arrived and the festivities continued until Craig's family said goodbye. Then it was a quick trip to the airport with Sharon's. Hugs and kisses and promises to visit often were exchanged and love you was spoken many times with sincerity by all.

All of the Texas friends found a place for the next two days. Revelry and gaiety exploded. They ate. Sharon, Glenna and Judy took turns playing the piano while others danced. Bottles of wine were emptied.

Margaret and Craig sang duets. In the warmth of the sunlight, they enjoyed the garden although much of the decorations were gone. They packed a lifetime in these two days. No one knew, but it would be the last time they would all be together as a bunch of friends loving, caring and having fun.

Only Glenna had to go home. She asked Kevin, "Where did you learn to dance so well?"

"My sisters were learning and they needed a partner and if I didn't, they would tell mom things that I did not want her to know."

"Sibling blackmail,"

"Yeah, but I did learn to dance."

He paused, "Want some company again tonight?"

"Well," she stammered, "it probably wouldn't be the same."

"No it wouldn't." And he kissed her goodnight.

Wednesday morning they took their Texas friends to the airport.

Sara said to Craig and Sharon, "You will never know how much we loved your wedding and meeting everyone. It was the best. It is beautiful here. I can see why you like it." With a tear in her eye, "You are probably never coming home."

Craig took a deep breath. "Probably not, but we can spend summers together, and holidays."

"It won't be the same, but knowing you and Sharon are happy eases losing you. God love you." And they hugged each other and kissed goodbye.

The same sentiments were echoed by all. They watched from the window until the plane vanished from sight and the days started their journey as a memory

Craig, Sharon, Kevin and Glenna all looked at one another knowing how sad the other felt. A void was in their hearts.

"Well, it's just us now," Craig said, and then to Sharon. "Let's get home and pack. We have a flight on Friday."

♫

CHAPTER THIRTY-ONE

♫

*P*aris in the springtime is magic. Young leaves fill the oaks and maples. Colorful flower carts ready for the gift of beauty. Sidewalk cafés humming and the young man leans in and kisses his lovely. Posters of the latest celebrity and bookstall lines the walkways. The river Seine slips by as easily as wine down the throat. Night-lights reflect gold and silver. Romance is in the air, the romance of Craig and Sharon.

They arrived in the late afternoon and went straight to their hotel. They had chosen a small one and they were not disappointed. No crystal chandeliers, but remnants of gaslight, with electricity piped in. Its old world beauty had today's comforts. They wanted to take a quick nap, but were too excited. They joined Paris in the springtime.

Finding a little café, they enjoyed a light dinner and then they walked, just absorbing the sights of this enchanting city.

"We made a good choice, you think?"

"We did, and I am glad you know some French."

"I can get us around thanks to being a voice major. Do you have the little dictionary?"

She patted her bag, "Easy access."

He held her hand tightly as they walked on. "There is so much to see, I'm glad we made an itinerary."

Each day they got up early and enjoyed a Parisian breakfast, and with cameras and map in hand, started their trek. They laughed. "Nothing like saying we're tourist."

Notre Dame Cathedral was on their schedule for Sunday. As they walked toward it, the sound of the massive organ pulled them in and they went to the front so they could hear the choir. After mass they took pictures and enjoyed the beauty of the church. The rose window peered down as a herald from God.

"Let's brave the steps to the tower," Craig said, "and we can see the bells." Their reward was a view of the endless city.

"When you're up here you think of the *Hunchback...*"

She snuggled close to him. "You sure do."

"This structure was finished in 1260. I just can't imagine that long ago, and with all of the European Wars, it is still here."

After their spiritual experience in and out at the church they walked toward the Eiffel Tower. It looked like lace from the distance. Beneath this landmark, it was a mass of iron and steel, but it had not lost its beauty. One evening they came back late and the base framed the sunset like a protectorate of the golden ball.

They stopped along the way to observe many of the building they had known from history. So absorbed in this wonderful metropolis they carefully followed their map so they would not get lost.

Another day they found the artists in Montmartre just as they would have been years earlier, and it didn't seem so long ago.

Sacré-Coeur stood high above, white and pure, and they rested in her shadow before having dinner and returning to their hotel.

On their way to Père Lachaise, Craig told her where he first heard of the cemetery. "In high school we had a choral selection called "Madame Jeanette" and she waits for him who fell in World War I, until she is old and her hair is white, and they take her to rest in Père Lachaise. It is a beautiful choral piece. Wonderful harmony with five flats and sung a cappella. I must get it for the double quartet."

"So sad, I don't know that one."

"It's at home. Speaking of home, I wonder how Kevin and Glenna are making out."

"Well, I hope they are not making out yet," she whispered.

"He really liked her from the moment that he saw her."

"It will be news when we get back."

As they walked through the stone arch, they knew they were among the greats of music, art and literature. In this city of the dead, their bodies are here but their true remains were found in the notes, paint, and words alive the world over.

The cobblestone streets were lined with chestnut trees and at the side were the mausoleums and life-size sculptures. The gently moving leaves and cheep of a tiny bird was all they could hear. Walking among these works of art Craig and Sharon spoke softly. They hadn't walked far until they came to Chopin's grave. Colorful flowers covered the base. They looked at the monument and then at each other, "Fred Chopin." Craig said and smiled.

"Oh my," Sharon responded also with a smile. "Thank you Fred Chopin, for all of the wonderful music that you have created. You are a favorite." She looked at Craig. "But you are my real favorite."

"Will this have an effect on your little journey when you play him in the future?" Craig asked her.

"Oh it will. I'll forget all about the salons and come directly here."

"You know only his body is here, and his heart is in Poland."

"I didn't know."

He pointed to the muse of music at the top. "Euterpe, and that gives me a place to start a composition. She weeps for the broken lyre." As he spoke he gazed at her in deep thought.

Sharon did not disturb him because she knew he was rolling around a melody along with broken chords. It will be beautiful she thought.

They walked on stopping at others who had enriched our civilization with their creativity.

Another special artist in Craig's life was Camille Pissarro. He had called upon him as he wrote his "Seasons."

Their hotel was not far from Montparnasse Cemetery, so they went there several times. César Franc and Camille Saint-Saëns were at rest there and Craig and Sharon stopped and paid homage in silence.

"It is so nice to come here and close our day among the souls of music."

The most physical exercise they did in a day was to ride their rented bikes to Versailles. The Palace took their breath away. The rooms of the kings and queens and the hall of mirrors offered a look into history, but most of all, they loved the gardens. After enjoying the little village and the sun on the other side of the sky, they rode back and satisfied their big appetites.

They scheduled two days for the Louvre. Each day they walked and were in awe of the world's greatest collections. Craig took notes when he saw something that touched his psychic.

"I always have liked sculpture, but today I fell in love with it."

"I loved Père Lachaise, but this building and its treasures are probably my favorite."

"I have to agree."

Their last day, they took a guided tour of the city. This allowed them to see areas not on their agenda. This final touch made their trip complete.

♫

Far away from the enchantment of Paris was New York where Kevin was watching over everything. He decided to lodge temporarily in Craig's apartment, assuring them that their practice would not bother him. It would be for a short while, until he went back to Texas. He played gardener, mowing, trimming and deadheading flowers. He also had books to read and materials to prepare for the next school year.

He and Glenna were together every day. They welcomed the quiet time. It had been non-stop for both of them since school was out.

One day they took a big shopping trip. She purchased kitchen supplies to go with *The Joy of Cooking*.

She quietly told Kevin, "I really don't know much about cooking, but I am going to learn. I would like a small table and chairs to put in front of the window and we can look down into Mr. Heid's garden when we eat. His flowers are very beautiful. It's even nice in the winter."

They stopped at a second-hand store and found a perfect size table and chairs although they didn't match. The next day they painted them white and placed them in front of the window with little red place mats and a vase with an artificial red rose. "I think it's sweet." Glenna said proud of her creation.

Rugs, lamps, and small tables made the studio feel comfortable. Groceries completed their shopping.

At home they put everything in place and Kevin treated her to dinner out. "Tomorrow we can start our venture in preparing dinner here. I would also like to go back to the large cemetery near the big campus. It needs a longer visit."

Another day they drove to Lancaster Park. After viewing the canyons and small vignettes they enjoyed their picnic lunch.

Glenna practiced at Craig's while Kevin sat on the flagstone patio with novel in hand.

They also started their venture in cooking. Kevin would read and Glenna would make it happen. Most of the time they were satisfied, but hoped they would get better.

They were both alone and they found a warmth in each other and this allowed their friendship to grow.

Although warm, Kevin felt she had put up a barrier between them. She is willing to be close but only to a point. I more than like her, oh god what do I do, because I am not sure she feels the same way. There isn't time for this to play out, so I had better just ask her. Well there is always Texas.

Two days before Craig and Sharon would return Kevin said, "It is a beautiful evening let me take you out to eat and then we can enjoy the park."

The Kitchen Place had become their favorite and as they ate she surprised him by asking, "When are you going back to Texas?"

"I haven't decided yet." He wanted to say you can answer that.

"You like it here."

"I really do. It is not so hot and if I lived here I would be closer to my parents."

He changed the subject, "When do your classes start?"

"July twelve through August seventeen. I would like to go down and visit with my family before they start. I have to fill in for Sharon at church for a couple more weeks.

"What about the country club?"

"No I can't play like she does. Mine is learned and hers is natural."

"Dessert?" Kevin asked.

"Not tonight, thank you."

"Let's go to the park and watch the sunset."

He parked in a quiet spot and they walked to the pond. The mallards swam close hoping they had brought crumbs.

Breaking the peacefulness abruptly, Kevin turned to her. "Glenna, I kiss you and you're warm, but then you put up a strong resistance" Then softer, "Why?" He took a deep breath. "I like you a lot, more that a lot, but I am not sure you feel the same way. I would like to know, because if you don't, I'll get on back to Texas and treat our friendship as over."

She looked away into the pond that held the shadow of the setting sun and stood stoic for a few moments without saying a word or offering an expression.

Kevin thought, I believe I am going to find out what I don't want to hear. Better now than next week.

She turned to him and her eyes were full. "Oh Kevin, what do you think? Do you have to ask? Have a fling with you and then you're gone. That is not me. I let myself like you and then you are gone. I have never been hurt, but I've known girls that have and I don't want to get near that."

"But you haven't answered my question. You have only told me that you want to avoid being hurt."

"In plain English, I don't want to develop feelings for you knowing you're leaving in a week.

That seems clear." And her eyes got bigger and bigger.

"Did you ever think of letting down that barrier that you have just described, if someone loved you?"

"I have been waiting for that special person."

"I hope you are not still waiting because he is standing right in front of you."

She looked at him in slow wonder, "What are you saying?"

"Glenna I'm falling in love with you so fast that it might be over before sunset."

She looked at him and smiled willingly. "I have wanted to hear that since you answered the door, but I was afraid I never would."

He touched her face and she was small in his arms and every part of her body felt his.

"Honey, that is all I wanted to know."

With her voice heavy, "But you still have to go home and I'm in graduate school two thousand miles apart."

"What if I stayed? I have no life there, it all seems to be here now. We can work it out."

He kissed her tenderly and felt her respond like no other time.

They sat down on the bench and she snuggled close with his arm around her. Her stomach was in a knot and his heart throbbed.

"I thought the way we looked at each other that first day there was something. It seemed so telling. Such a nice surprise. Then when I saw you more my feelings grew and fast. But that night we slept together will be one to laugh about. I promise I can do better." And he kissed her lightly.

She only smiled and squeezed his hand.

They sat and felt the other's closeness and watched the ducks swim in and out and watch the sun glide easily to brighten another land.

"I wanted to talk to you before they came back so I would know whether to be off or make other plans."

"It would make me very happy if you stayed, but you have to make that decision. I love you Kevin. I have never told a guy that before, and it is so easy to say it to you. I love you."

"That sounds so wonderful."

"I have never been in love before but it is very recognizable. I want to be with you. I love everything about you. I love the way you were with my parents and siblings. I love the way you and Craig have had such a long friendship. Your friends in Texas were so nice to me. And most important, I love the way you are with me."

"Thank you for your beautiful words."

"Have you thought beyond this moment?"

"Well—it is not too late to apply for a teaching position here, but I had to know if you felt the way I do. Let's sleep on this and see if we both feel this way tomorrow and then we can talk again. You can go back to Texas with me."

"My dad has paid for graduate school. I really couldn't do that. If we didn't make it, I would be there all alone."

"I know and agree, so there is only one other thing to do. I think we had better go. It is a little too dark to stay here any longer."

They sprinted back to his car. He reached over and kissed her passionately. "I feel relieved because when we walked over there I wasn't sure how it would end."

"I couldn't let my feelings out because you would be gone. Over as quick as it began."

"Want to watch TV?"

♫

The next day after holding her for a few moments he said, "I'm here early because I was anxious to know if you felt today like you felt yesterday."

"Even more now, that I know your feelings."

They sat down at the new little table and she poured coffee. "I will apply for a teaching job and we'll wait. I brought my typewriter and a lot of stuff. I just kept saying to myself, I don't know when I will be back. A premonition."

"Dorothy, our secretary at school, has all of the addresses of the districts and their contact people. We'll go over there and in the meantime draft a resume."

"You won't believe this, but I brought a folder of personal things and my resume is in there."

"You knew—you knew."

The next day they got addresses and spent most of the day typing letters.

With letters ready to send out and a dinner ready, they went to the airport to get Craig and Sharon.

Surprisingly their plane was early. They waited

patiently for them to deplane. "Wait till Craig hears that I'm going to stay. He mentioned several times this winter that I should think about living here."

When they all saw each other they had big smiles. Hugs for the guys and kisses for the girls.

"You look great," Kevin said, "and happy too."

"We are. We are," Sharon said with expression.

"We have to hear about everything." Kevin said. "We fixed dinner, but just know that we're just learning to cook."

"We had to go through that. I did. Sharon knew how. Is everything all right here?"

"Real good. I cut your lawn a couple times, but no phone call while I was there. I spent a lot of time with Glenna."

"Did you get settled?" Sharon asked.

"I did and so happy to be there. I am so glad you got married."

"Me too," and Sharon raised her brow.

"Were your happy with Paris?"

"Oh gosh, yes."

"You should try it out."

"Maybe we will." And he glanced at Glenna.

They looked at Kevin and Glenna with straight faces and big eyes.

"Should I ask?"

"I'll just tell you. I am not going back."

"What happened?" Craig asked quickly. "No, I didn't mean to say that."

"We discovered we were in love with each other, but we're going to step back and let everything grow in its natural way."

"That is the best news I could get coming home. You will be here!" He thought Craig was going to shout with happiness.

"We spent today getting resumes out to all the districts in the area, and now we wait."

Sharon said, "Oh Glenna, I am so happy for you. Remember a couple of weeks ago what you said."

"I do and when you least expect." And they had another big hug for each other.

"More important tell us about Paris."

On the way home and at dinner, Craig and Sharon talked about the wonderful time they had, but it was nice to be home.

Craig was slowly getting over the shock that his best friend would be here.

"I have to get back to practicing. This is the longest that I have been away from the piano, ever."

"You'll remember," Glenna assured her.

"Lot of exercises and Kevin will get bored

"After so many years listening to Craig, I don't think so. I have been listening to Glenna. I'll stay with her during the day so I won't bother you."

"Stop the silly talk. You don't know how glad I am that you're staying."

"Let's hope for a job."

It was a short evening. Craig and Sharon went to their bedroom and Kevin took Glenna to her studio and finally came home.

♫

CHAPTER THIRTY-TWO

♫

Summer is a symphony of bright colors. Shades of green are shared among the small bushes and tall trees. Finches of yellow and cardinals of red play at the feeders. Purple hydrangea blossoms hang heavy. Red roses lift their faces to be kissed. The blue, blue sky takes your gaze to the edge of the universe. Sunrises and sunsets choose from day to day how they will begin and end their pallets.

After the excitement in the spring, Craig and Sharon were back to reality as the summer began.

Craig started a new composition and reworked old melodies. He spent so much time at the piano that Sharon got out her bike and rode to school to practice. She did not want to disturb him.

Tchaikovsky and Rachmaninoff concerto's lay open on the library table, for her to begin the next phase of her career. Mr. Goldman asked her to prepare should there be a cancellation. Sharon didn't need to be at the piano to memorize, so her library was a perfect place to work. She had given up playing at the county club, but either she or Glenna would play for church and the young choir was turned over to the main director.

She converted one of her bedrooms into a sewing room and was busy making herself summer attire for her recitals.

Although busy it was a relaxed summer and they slept late and loved much.

Kevin spent most of these days with Glenna. Being avid readers they would curl up on her couch to delve into Faulkner or Hemingway, but soon they would be in each other's arms.

Kevin was waiting for results from his many resumes. They were all anxious.

Glenna was falling into a routine of living away from the dorm. No curfew, food of her choice and yes her own bath. She enjoyed "practicing" cooking as she called it. The summer would give her time to get this new craft started. She practiced piano at school every day and Kevin went with her with a book tucked under his arm. They spent time listening to classical music. Kevin had a vast knowledge because of living with Craig for so many years.

Several evenings during the week, and Saturday or Sunday, they would all get together for a movie, or the art gallery, picnic or just TV. They never wanted for a lively conversation, mostly about music or literature. Kevin's interest in current events entered occasionally.

♫

One evening Glenna was very excited. "I talked to Dr. Bernard today."

"Tell me," Sharon getting excited too.

"He has had a request from Mr. Goldman for a quartet, and he asked me if I was interested."

"That's great. I can see that you are."

"He told Dr. Bernard he has several requests for a group to play at various venues in the fall. So Dr. Bernard got in touch with Dr. Livingston and they remembered your wedding and how nice we sounded. So he is going to get us together."

"Is he going to use four strings?"

"He didn't say, but I hope so. Also he said he wanted to have more student recitals during the year."

"At our last piano department meeting he briefly mention that. The performance student could always use the experience."

"When is your quartet getting together?"

"I think as soon as he can find everyone. I don't think Emily is here, but she is going to summer school. Also he thinks he has a temporary accompanying job for me, just for the summer. I have to check back."

"Where?" Craig asked.

"The Sudbury Choir."

"Nice group. I thought about trying out but I have been busy. There are several good choral groups here."

"You have been at the piano early," Kevin said to Craig. "What are you working on?"

"Probably what you heard was "Euterpe." I don't know whether I am going to call it that. On top of Chopin's grave was the muse Euterpe with a broken lyre. I think it's going to be short, a respite piece. All of this inspiration is coming and I have to get it down."

"Before I left yesterday I heard a long stretch. Gosh it was beautiful."

"I was doing some reading and Sharon, Euterpe supposedly invented the flute."

To Kevin. "She also plays the flute."

Mentioning the flute brought back thoughts of Joel and their long friendship, but it slipped away as quickly as it came.

"The broken lyre symbolic of Chopin's death and his break with music," Craig said.

Kevin added, "I love the myths. They are so rich in symbolisms."

"Symbolism in literature and great for writing music. The muses play above the clouds. Their musical instruments are string, wind and percussion. They have power. Broken lyre, broken chords, broken life. The Greek musicians called upon her to assist in their writing music. She must have heard me because I am getting a lot of inspiration. But then again, I think it's Sharon," and he kissed her lightly. "You are my muse."

"Most likely," Kevin added.

"You have a lot to work with. I will be anxious to hear it. I just love your work," Glenna added.

"Thank you. Judy called yesterday."

"Did you tell her I have applied for a job?"

"No I didn't. I thought you could do that when everything's together and I didn't want to be the one to make her cry."

"You're going to Skaneateles with us. We'll go

down early and come home after I play. It isn't far."

Glenna responded quickly. "Oh absolutely."

Kevin followed. "I want to see more of New York and more important, my first Sharon recital."

"You'll love Sharon and the village is nice."

"This will be our first visit. I have been here four years, but too busy to get very far from the Music Box."

"Glenna, you and Sharon are taking instructions this summer, what is your other class?"

"History of Opera. I think it is going to keep me busy. When I signed up I hadn't met Kevin."

"Just tell me and I won't bother you."

"You can read while I am working or prepare for classes."

"For somewhere."

"Opera," Craig said. "Every other year they do one?" When do they present it?"

Glenna responded. "Last time it was right before February break. Two nights and well attended."

"Dr. Westmore has been working with the choruses. That is why I helped out with the girls' glee club and quartet. *Hamlet* is a nice one to do. It is not as heavy as some of the others. Next year I am going to be involved officially in vocal a little more, but composition comes first."

"The second year we were here we both played for opera rehearsals. I liked that."

Glenna asked, "Are you entering a competition this year?"

"I believe I am going to do California Open. That is a big one, but not until March so I have time to do a new one, or I have wanted to play "Virtuoso in E" and I can play it myself. Sharon won't have to bear the stress."

"Oh yes I will. You know I feel right along with you."

This is how their evening conversations went, music and more music. When Kevin and Glenna were alone they talked a lot about books. She had managed, through her four years, to get in several advanced literature courses. They discussed opera librettos. She was surprised that he knew so many. She could tell he had spent many hours studying and reading literature of all kinds. She was happy to find out that he had taken piano lessons at a much younger age, because his sisters did. She thought, maybe I could encourage him to begin again.

♫

The last week of the month Kevin received two calls for interviews. The first was junior high. He dressed in his navy summer suit and found his way. After, he went back to Glenna's.

"I would prefer high school, but I can't be choosy right now."

Two days later he went for the other, high school. Back at Glenna's he seemed discouraged. "I wasn't fond of the gentleman that interviewed me. He was old and didn't even hardly look at me. Just talked around me. I just pretended not to notice. At least it has relieved a little stress."

"Put on your shorts and shirt on and join me

and I'll get some lemonade."

He joined her and told her more about the two interviews between sips of the cool drink.

"Don't worry yet. There is still a lot of time. Maybe you should look for an apartment just to be ready. You don't want to stay with Craig and Sharon?"

"No. If their piano wasn't downstairs it would be different. But it is and wouldn't give either of us the privacy that we need."

"Please don't be discouraged yet. I don't like to see you this way," she said softly.

"I don't want to be and I still have a job in Texas and may have to wait for an opening here."

"Oh no. I don't want you to go back."

"I don't want to."

Later his spirits lifted.

The next afternoon they scoured the area for him an apartment.

"I want to live near you and would like to be near where I work too, but I only know one." They found several that he liked.

Glenna had accepted the summer position of accompanying the Sudbury Choir. It would be only for the summer. The rehearsals were Thursday evenings. Kevin waited for her at her studio.

♫

The first week of July they celebrated the holiday with a picnic at the lake. Kevin's first glimpse of Ontario of the Great Lakes.

It was the first time Sharon had been to the lake

since being there with Joel last September. They were at a different beach, which made remembering not so strong.

"Toronto is just over the way. Great city. Maybe we can get over there before school starts. And Niagara Falls. Maybe when we go to Stratford we can stop there. You are living in a nice area."

"And we went to Lancaster Park while you were in Paris. It's gorgeous out there."

The day ended with one last swim in the cool lake waters as the sun touched the horizon.

The next day Kevin got another call for an interview. Looking handsome, he went to meet a Mrs. Travers.

He went back to Glenna's and got into comfortable clothes and she got the lemonade and he started. "I feel better about this interview. She seemed to be a very nice lady and I got the feeling that she was glad to see me. I would be a Madison West High and not too far from here."

"I know where it is." She snuggled close. "Keep going."

"We talked about what I've done and she told me what I would be teaching. We talked about Texas, Ohio and New York, real nice conversation."

"Did she ask you anything about your personal life?"

"She did, and I told her my best friend was a professor at the music school and my fiancée was here also. I stretched a little, you don't mind."

"No." And she smiled sweetly.

"We'll get there sweetheart. Also what was

encouraging, she said they wanted more men in their English department like myself because we would be a good example for young males students to expand their reading skills."

"That sounds great," she said softly as she continued to listen.

"That was all the important points and she said that the next step would be getting a call from the head of the English department. She didn't say that I would, just the next step. So here we are waiting again."

"But this sounds very promising."

♫

Monday of the next week, Kevin got the call that thrilled him and got him hopefully closer to employment here. Same blue suit, he went to central office of the Lakefield District, Mrs. Traver's district.

"Mr. Werner, do come in. I'm Mike Crawford and this is our English headquarters." And he sort of laughed as he offered his hand. "I am so very glad to meet you. Mrs. Travers was delighted with the conversation she had with you. You are moving here from Texas. You are from Ohio and went to school in Texas, have masters, three years' experience in high school, service duties are satisfied. Seems you are ready to go forward unencumbered."

"Yes sir, I am."

"Mrs. Travers was truly impressed with your resume and she told me to hire you. And I do say she, in all of the years, has made excellent selections for our teaching staff. Before I spend time telling you about specifics, which I think she did, I am offering you a one year contract. That is standard procedure. You know the pay scale and where you would be located, so could you provide me with an answer, or do you want to think it over, or decline completely."

"I have thought about it since I talked with her, and it would be my privilege to accept your offer."

"Thank you, Mrs. Travers will be happy. I am going to have Betsy type up your contract while I get your material and go over it with you." He came back and gave Kevin everything he needed to start the year, books and scheduling.

"Also the reading list for the senior English classes." And he handed it to Kevin. "We ask our staff to select from this list because if a parent comes in and objects, all you have to do is send them to us. And we have one or two during the year. We do not want to inhibit our teachers, just protect them. And should you have any books that you would like to see on this list, just write a short paragraph and send it along and it will be looked at."

Kevin glanced through the list and said, "It looks large, and at first glance a very good one."

"Your principal is Mrs. Ann Garrison and she has asked that you come over before August first and also prepare your reading list until Christmas vacation so the books can be ordered."

"Is there a particular time to meet with her?"

"No, she said just walk in and that she would be in or close to her office all day.

They completed their discussion, Kevin signed his contract and was on his way. He was so excited he wanted to run to his car and drive fast to get to Glenna's. He thought, I had better tell my parents I am living here now.

At Glenna's he took two stairs at a time and she heard him and opened the door. He grabbed her and swung her around and kissed her long.

"This has to mean good news."

"I can't believe I have been so lucky. I signed a contract for a year. School is Madison West."

"Oh honey, I'm so glad and excited," she said.

"Now I can be with you, get an apartment. I have to go back to Texas and ship stuff. Home is here."

"What do you have to ship?"

"Just personal stuff, books, no furniture. My little place was also in a private home, but Mrs. Campbell furnished everything and kept it going for me. She cleaned, changed my bed so I have to get everything for an apartment She also had dinner waiting. I moved there after Craig came here."

"Sounds like the motherly type."

"She was, me and an older lady lived there and she took good care of us. I hope I can get a place by August first. How was your first class?"

"Okay, just piano instructions, but tomorrow is the opera class. That will keep me busy."

"Well, I am going to be busy preparing. I have all my textbooks. They are in the car and I want to get busy on the reading list. Go see my new principal. Pinch me honey, to see if I am awake."

"You are. Craig will be happy too."

"Aren't we eating together tomorrow? I'll get a bottle of champagne."

"Yes, and going to Skaneateles Saturday for Sharon's recital."

The next day while Glenna went to her opera class and practiced, Kevin scouted for an apartment. The one he liked did not have an opening until September, so he picked up Glenna and they went to Westphalia Gardens, his second choice. This was smaller but had laundry facilities for each building and a garage.

"You'll be happy with a garage this winter."

"It has the usual, a galley kitchen and appliances, but no other furniture."

They both felt it was a good choice and that he could move in August first.

"Next week, will you go with me to pick out a few pieces of furniture and maybe we can use them in another apartment or house when we get that far."

After their busy day, they picked up a bottle of champagne and, with their other contributions, they went to Craig and Sharon's for dinner.

When Craig saw the champagne he said, "Let me guess. You're in."

"The man upstairs is really taking care of me." Handshakes for congratulations and a pat on the back. "Welcome to New York."

"High school?" Sharon asked.

"Madison West. I couldn't be happier." And he hugged Glenna again.

She said, "And there is more."

"I signed for an apartment at Westphalia Gardens, August one."

"No. I am going to miss you," Craig said.

"It is just down the street. Could still be in Texas."

"Let's get the bubbly open," Sharon said. "This is a real celebration."

After emptying the bottle and laughs and dinner history Glenna said, "We should be going."

"What time are we leaving Saturday?"

Sharon responded with the information. "It is at the Webster Gallery at eight o'clock and they said someone would be there at six so I could play the piano and dress."

"One o'clock will be early enough. We can also have a light but leisurely dinner."

♫

They arrived in Skaneateles in the afternoon. The gentle lake beckoned and they found a large bench and sat quietly chatting as the gentle lake breeze swirled around them.

"This looks like an affluent community."

Glenna responded. "It is. Retired folks. Summer homes and they have summer theater."

"This is so peaceful," Craig said, "I hate to leave but we had better get something to eat."

They walked back to the main street and found a small restaurant for a light dinner. After, they went to the gallery and an attendant showed them to a dressing room.

"Mrs. Jamieson, if you will come with me, you can play the piano for a few minutes."

Craig said to Kevin, "Why don't you two

362

occupy the dressing room while we check out the piano."

"I have to put on my tie and jacket. We can handle that together."

They went in and before anything they hugged each other, not forgetting a passionate kiss. Kevin put on his tie and jacket. In the little bath, Glenna fixed her make-up and brushed her teeth.

"I didn't bring a tooth brush."

"After kissing me like you just did, a tooth brush is nothing. Here."

She added a colorful flowered scarf to her navy linen chemise and slipped on her high heel sandals.

"You look like you just stepped out of *Vogue*."

She smiled. "Thank you and you by my side."

"Here we are dressing together much like our first night sleeping together. We're going to do it right one of these days."

She just smiled.

"Ready?" He took her hand. "Let's let Craig and Sharon have their dressing room."

They were just coming back and Craig looked them both up and down. "You two look ravishing."

"Now it's our turn," Sharon said.

In the dressing room, Sharon put on newly made black top and white skirt and she too had black high heel sandals. Craig found his tie and jacket.

They waited for the eight o'clock hour. Near seven-thirty the attendant knocked lightly on the door. Craig answered. "Is there anything I can get you? I brought water for both of you. If not I will be back when we get the audience settled."

Alone Craig gave Sharon a light kiss as not to mess up her lipstick. "I'll go find Kevin and Glenna and will see you after. Good luck sweetheart. Your first recital as a professional."

She smiled and asked. "Is it real?"

He echoed her smile and shook his head, "Yes, it's real."

She sat in the straight chair and focused and started her "journey" before she touched a key. She found a small salon in Paris where Chopin might be. The tall narrow windows draped in red velvet and the Pleyel at the side of the room. I like this thought better than visiting his grave.

A light knock on her door told her it was now. She walked on the small stage, to a welcome applause. She nodded gently and smiled.

They sat close enough to the front that Craig could see she was away on her little "journey" as she came on stage.

Her fingers called upon compositions of Chopin, Beethoven sonatas, Debussy, and others for the first part. After a fifteen-minute break, she played for another hour. The audience was elated and asked for just one more. She played Craig's "Interlude." She wanted him to be a part of the recital also.

Benevolence was shown with white and pink roses. She nodded gently to thank the audience and threw a kiss before exiting the stage. She returned to her dressing room and a few minutes later there was a light knock. Answering, she found the attendant. "There are several people that want to thank you personally. Would you see them?"

Softly she asked, "Yes of course. Who are they?"

"Mr. and Mrs. Bradley, he is the mayor, and Mrs. Redford, she is director of the summer theater."

She went with him backstage to meet them and they thanked her and told her how much they enjoyed her performance.

Approaching, "And this is my husband Craig and friends Mr. Werner and Miss McCaffrey."

"So nice to meet all of you." Mrs. Redford asked, "And what was your encore selection?"

"A composition of my husband's."

"It was wonderful. Do you have more?" she asked Craig

"Yes. I am composer-in-residence at the music school and will be giving a faculty recital sometime next year. I could send you a schedule. There are many beautiful recitals by our faculty during the year."

"That would be great." She opened her purse and handed him her personal card.

"Our little community is very much into music and theater. Maybe you could honor us with your music here. Do you work with Mr. Goldman?"

"No, just Sharon."

She turned to Kevin and Glenna, "Are you musicians as well?

"Glenna is also a pianist and I teach high school English."

They all wished each other a good evening.

"Now it is our turn." Glenna gave her a big hug. "It was so beautiful it brought tears to my eyes."

Kevin took her hands in his and said, "So

beautiful it took my breath away and may God grant you many more." And he kissed her on the cheek.

Craig just took her in his arm. "Beautiful darling. Shall we be on our way home?"

"Me and Glenna have the back seat." On the way down the girls rode there and talked and laughed constantly, while the guys chatted about Texas and other stuff.

In the car Craig said, "Honey over here close to me."

"One moment. You in the back seat close your eyes while I get out of this skirt and into shorts."

"You're safe," Kevin assured her.

Sharon moved close to Craig as he drove and they talked softly about the day and hopefully coming back.

Glenna was in Kevin's arms and he took off her sandals and pulled her close. They talked and caressed each other, but kept their closeness within reason.

They got home and Craig said, "We'll go home and then you can take Glenna home."

♫

All of the excitement was behind and the new week was going to be just a mundane day-by-day.

Kevin called Glenna. "I would like to go the big bookstore downtown. Craig said it's The Village Reader."

Happily she consented to go along.

Kevin arrived and kissed her long and with an

emotion that almost kept them home.

"Do you know the way?" he finally asked.

"I do. Let's go while we can."

They found the store and were lost for the next hour among the shelves filled with words. They replenished their reading matter. "Let's go back to my studio and have lunch and then I can go practice."

After her class Wednesday, Glenna checked her mailbox and found a note from Dr. Livingston. He wanted the quartet to meet Thursday at one o'clock.

The next day everyone arrived and there would be four strings, Emily violin, Josh violin two, Jack viola, Will cello, and Glenna completing with piano.

She hurried home to tell Kevin.

"We discussed that we would be working for Mr. Goldman as a group and we would be paid. Everybody liked that and complied. He gave us music to work on. And we have four requests to play before the end of the year."

"Where would you be playing?"

"Right here in the city. Three are for the dinner hour at the convention center the other at the Medical Auditorium for a doctor's symposium. I can't believe I am actually working for money. I can buy my own Christmas presents this year."

"When are you getting together for practice?"

"This summer until classes are over, Tuesday, and Thursday at one."

"How is Dr. Livingston to work with?"

"Really nice, so is Dr. Bernard, Dr. Westmore, Dr. Jamieson, but not Dr. Peterson. Nobody likes him. He is a good musician, but can't relate to students."

"You kids are tough, but I am excited for you."

Friday Kevin went to meet with his new principal.

Glenna waited at home and he soon returned.

"I felt like I was talking with my mother and that is good. We had a good conversation about many things. We were getting to know each other and me the school. She is from English before becoming a principal so we could relate."

"Did you like her?"

"I did, first meeting and I felt she liked me. She also liked my reading selections and would order books. I am anxious to meet some of the other staff."

♫

The weekend passed into the last week of July and Kevin called Glenna early.

"Hi Sweetie. Love you today."

She responded with stress and he asked her, "Are you all right?"

"Not exactly, but nothing serious."

"Why?"

"I have a belly ache."

"Didn't something not agree with you?"

"No, not food, just what we girls have to put up with once in a while."

"Oh, I understand. I have two sisters. I was going down to get my car registered and maybe buy some stuff for the apartment. But if you don't feel like going, I will come over and comfort you."

"Are you sure you want to?"

"Yes. I'll be there soon."

He knocked lightly and then opened the door with the key that she had given him and called, "Glenna."

"Oh I'm here." She walked out of her bedroom in her oversized sleeping shirt.

"Honey you look tired."

"I am. I woke up in the middle of the night and haven't slept since. I feel like the day looks outside."

"Yeah, it is pretty gray and rainy, so let's get you back to bed and I will go with you, and will be a gentleman." She thought when is this gentleman stuff going to stop?

He took her hand and they went back into her bedroom. He kicked off his shoes and lay down with her and cradled her in his arched body.

"Try to relax." He felt her lurch with a pain.

"Does this happen all the time? Did you take something?"

"No, just once in a while, and yes I did."

He gently massaged her belly through her shirt and then he lifted it up and his hand was on her warm body.

Oh god she thought, that feels so good.

He gently massaged her stomach and then slowly his hand slipped easily to her small breasts that were full and tender.

For the next hour he tried to make her more comfortable and finally succeeded. She slept as he cradled her close, but he only dozed.

He had taken another step closer to making love to her, but he was nervous. He thought, how do I make love to her? What does she expect? How far do I go? New to me and especially to her.

After she slept for a while, she showered and went into the kitchen where he was fixing a little lunch. She put her arms around him. "Thank you for helping me feel better."

"Just call me anytime."

"I warmed the soup that we have left over from yesterday. It will help on this cool rainy day."

"You are so sweet, but you didn't get to the DMV."

"There is tomorrow."

The remainder of the day slid by and she went to practice later with Kevin by her side.

The next day they went to the DMV and shopped for dishes, sheets, towels, and a few other things that he needed for his new apartment.

The remainder of the week went by on schedule.

♫

Tuesday, Kevin and Glenna went to claim his new residence. They took the things they had accumulated.

The next day he went back to wait for the furniture and telephone man. After her class she joined him.

"Oh, I see the furniture is here, How about the phone? I didn't know whether you could leave, so I brought something for us to eat."

Kevin pushed his books to the side and they ate

370

at the new table. "I was looking at my calendar this morning and if I fly to Texas tomorrow, I'll have Saturday to pack and Sunday to say goodbye, ship Monday and fly back Tuesday."

"That's a good plan."

"I want to be settled when school starts."

"Do you have a TV?"

"I do, but it is old and I might leave it for the next person. Put shipping money toward a new one."

"You brought your record player in May and a lot of books and records."

"And I have more."

"I think when I get the phone connected, I will make reservations and call Judy."

"I'll take an empty suitcase to fill and I have another one there and ship everything else. Mostly clothes, books and records."

After she helped him get things put away, they made a list of what he still needed. They closed the day by just being together.

♫

CHAPTER THIRTY-THREE

♫

Kevin was on his way to make his break from Texas. Leaving friends behind was hard, but to be with Craig and Sharon and the love of his life had made his life complete. Friday morning Craig, Sharon and Glenna took him to the airport.

"Did you say Lee was picking you up?" Craig asked.

"Yeah, I called from my new phone, and yes Judy cried. I did feel bad, but she wished us well."

They announced the boarding call. He said a quick goodbye to Craig and Sharon and a loving kiss for Glenna. They waited until the plane took off before they left.

On the way home, Sharon asked Glenna if she wanted to come over for dinner.

"No thanks, I think I will get caught up on my opera class and practice a lot, especially my quartet music. I love it."

"I'll be anxious to hear you again," Craig said.

"I'll get him on Tuesday and he'll probably

want to see you and tell you all about everyone there."

"Why don't we plan dinner Tuesday?" Sharon suggested.

"Okay, call me and tell me what you want me to bring."

They dropped her off at her studio and without Kevin she felt lonely. She thought, how fast you can bring someone into your life to fill a void that you didn't even know was there. I love him so much.

♫

Tuesday, after quartet practice Glenna was off to the airport. Kevin's plane was due at two-fifteen. She hurried because she felt she would probably be late, but he knew she had practice. She parked and went to check what gate he would arrive. Gate six, but there was a delay for one hour. Delays at the airport were common and almost expected. She had *The Winter of Our Discontent* to occupy her waiting. With a cup of coffee she found an out-of-the way place to read. Later she went to check the board and found another delay, one hour. She went to the ticket counter to inquire. There were other people asking the same questions. Why the delay? The answer was no information at this time.

Glenna called, and Sharon answered the phone. "Have you heard from Kevin?"

"No. Why?"

"His plane keeps being delayed. It was due at two-fifteen and it's now four-fifteen and no plane and no information. I asked if he was on 1276 and where was it. Did it leave Texas? There seems to be a blackout of information."

"Let me get Craig."

Glenna told him everything she knew, which was nothing.

He thought for a moment then said, "Let me call Lee and see if he got on and if he knows anything. Give me the phone number where you are and I'll get back to you."

Glenna talked to an elderly couple waiting for their son and another lady waiting for her husband. Everyone was growing more concerned as the hours passed. They would take turns going to the ticket counter for information. She walked to the big window and watched as planes were leaving and arriving. She had an idea.

She went to check the board for all planes coming in from the west, maybe they were rerouted, but after several arrived he was not on any of them.

She went back to be near the telephone and everyone had someone to call. Finally it became free and she called Craig.

"Did you find out anything?"

"No, but Lee took him to the airport this morning but did not wait because he had a doctor's appointment, but he is going to see what he can find out and call back."

Waiting and not knowing is awful, she thought. Her body began to feel the anxiety and her head felt tight. Has the plane crashed? Oh god, no.

Lee called Craig back and as they talked, Sharon could see the color leaving his face. Oh no, she thought, something awful has happened.

All Craig could say was, "See what you can find out and call back as soon as you hear."

Craig hung up the phone and stared for a moment into some faraway place.

"What did Lee say?"

"There was an accident, two planes collided. All traffic in and out of the airport stopped. The runways were receiving ambulances and other emergency vehicles to get people to the hospital or somewhere, but apparently there was no fire which could have made everything even worse."

Sharon held him and she could feel that he was cold and trembling. She tried to comfort him, knowing they did not have all of the information.

"What do we do?"

"Lee is still trying to find out which planes were involved in the accident. They have to inform next of kin before releasing a lot of information to the public."

"What should we tell Glenna?"

"Let's wait until we hear more from Lee."

After a while, they decided to go to the airport so they called Lee back and gave him the phone number and they called Glenna.

"We are coming out."

She started to cry. "Craig, what has happened?"

"Honey, really, I don't have anything definite. We'll see you shortly."

She was crying as she left the phone and several people caught up with her and asked if she had found out something. Everyone was anxious.

"Maybe, I don't know. My friends have been talking to Texas and are coming out." She was near sobbing and they all managed to comfort her and each other.

Finally Craig and Sharon arrived and found the group. Glenna asked, "What do you know? Please tell me."

Others gathered around and Craig with no color in his face explained what he knew. He was stammering and obviously very upset.

Glenna was crying, "Oh no, if he's hurt I am going down."

"We'll all go."

She walked away and Sharon went with her, crying too. "I just found him, I can't lose him."

"Honey, we don't have all the information."

Craig finished answering questions that he didn't have good answers for and then went to be with the girls.

Sharon asked again, "What do we do?"

"Wait for Lee or they will get something here."

Another hour passed and people were checking the ticket counter or calling.

Finally the phone was free a few minutes, but rang again. An elderly gentleman answered.

He held up the phone and looked at Craig and said, "It's for you."

Sharon and Glenna went too.

"Really," the girls did not think that sounded good, but were silent.

Craig asked, "You don't know which one?"

He listened, "Okay buddy, if we leave this phone we'll call."

Craig relayed the information to the group. "Apparently there is a lot of wreckage on one of the runway. He heard all of the people are in the hospital or somewhere," and his voice cracked. "But a bit of good news, some of the planes that were delayed and were in position have been able to take off, apparently around two or three o'clock. Maybe they didn't release 1276, that's why they haven't said anything. Let's check at the desk and tell them what we have heard."

Glenna heard him say that and she turned cold again and prayed silently.

An airline agent said "I'll try to get some more information and will let you know immediately when I have something definite." He went to the back office.

More time passed. It took a while for him to get information, he too had to wait.

Later an announcement came over the loud speaker. "Will those waiting for flight 1276 gather at the end of the ticket counter."

A few moments later the agent came out and said, "I wanted to make sure I have the correct information before passing it along. I apologize for the delay, but I have good news."

Glenna gripped Sharon's hand.

He relayed what most knew, there had been an accident causing the delay. "There were lives lost and each life is precious, but I understand it could have been worse." He paused. "The good news, around two o'clock they began releasing planes and 1276 was one of them. It should be arriving within the hour."

Glenna heard nothing more, but hope was confirmed. She put her hand over her face and cried. She thought, he has to be on it or he would have called Lee or Craig.

Craig said, "This has been a terrible afternoon for all of us."

Glenna wiped her eyes, "I must look a mess."

"No honey," Craig said, "you look beautiful, and Kevin will be so happy to see you he won't even notice. He has to be stressed out too, knowing an accident was so near and the waiting."

Everyone talked softly to each other and was definitely more relaxed.

Glenna said to Sharon, "Go with me to the ladies room and see if I can fix my make-up."

"I can't imagine how you felt, but I know if I lost Craig I would be devastated. I don't look very good either."

They went back and milled around with everyone else. No one seemed to sit, nervous energy kept them moving. They waited.

Finally the announcement came, 1276 has landed and will be arriving at gate twelve on the east ramp. Everyone slowly made their way to the arrival.

Again they waited. Craig saw Kevin first and raised his hand and Kevin answered back with a wave. He inched through the crowd of anxious people and reach for Glenna. She took his face in her hands. "We didn't know where you were all day. We've been frantic."

He could see that she had been crying and tears were ready again and he took her in his arms and she buried her head on his shoulder.

"Oh Glenna, I love you darling. Marry me."
She nodded her head and softly said, "Yes."

Craig and Sharon both heard him and Sharon
started to cry and said, "We're marrying brothers."

Kevin and Glenna held each other for what
seemed like hours with their eyes closed and the world
locked out. At this moment their souls came together.
They released each other and Kevin looked at Sharon
and then Craig in a bewildered way.

"Oh buddy what happened?" Craig asked as he
took his hand and gave him a pat on the arm.

"Oh, it was awful. There was a collision?"

"Yeah, we finally found out."

"I didn't see it happen. I had my nose in a book,
but could see everything after that from my window. I
knew you guys would be worried. Ambulances and
emergency equipment was all over. You thought any
minute there could be an explosion or fire, but thank
God there wasn't. That's why we couldn't leave. I
couldn't call, I'm so sorry."

"You don't have to apologize," Glenna
followed.

"We didn't have any information, what planes
were involved until about an hour ago. Lee and I have
been talking back and forth and they couldn't find out
much either."

Kevin could see they had been upset and still
were. Shock takes a while to relax.

"They didn't tell you. We left around two."

"No," Glenna said, "that is why we have been
so worried." And her breath caught and she started to

379

cry. "We imagined all sort of things happening to you."

He reached for her. "Honey, as I watched that terrible collision I said if I get back okay we're going to get married tomorrow. I knew people had been badly hurt and some probably died and would never be able to say, I love you again. Oh, it was awful. I really meant what I just asked, will you marry me?"

"My answer is still the same, yes." And she managed a smile.

"One moment life is so great and it can change without warning. I want to make every minute of my life count and you have to be in it." And he hugged her so tightly.

Craig and Sharon heard all of his tender words. Sharon started to cry and turned to Craig and buried her head in his arms.

When they all gained composure, Craig said, "We have to call Lee. I don't know whether he knows your plane took off. The phone isn't busy let's call him now. They have been upset too."

After Craig and Kevin got off the phone, Craig said, "Let's get your baggage and go home."

"I double if anyone is thinking about food."

"My salad and dessert are still in my studio, but I'm not sure I can eat yet."

"We all have to settle down, so why don't you two stop over and we'll have the casserole and save the salad and dessert for later. We can make it quick and congratulations, you two, we heard it all."

They smiled at each other and Kevin gave her a quick kiss on the cheek.

Kevin asked her, "Want a little casserole? By the time we get there we'll all feel better."

She handed him her car keys.

At Craig and Sharon's he suggested, "Everything has been said. Maybe if we don't talk about it we'll feel better."

Kevin agreed. "I think so."

"Tell me about everyone in Texas."

"We all got together Sunday evening at Sara and Jeff's. They cooked out. They wished you guys were there."

Small conversation back and forth pushed the evening into late. Kevin said, "I want to get my girl alone." And he looked lovingly at her.

She had relaxed and smiled more easily.

"This weekend is Stratford. "We are all anxious to hear Glenn Gould," Sharon offered.

"Goodnight buddy, this whole thing gave us a scare. We were all on the next plane to Texas to be with you."

"I'd do the same. Love you guys."

"We love you too," they said together.

♬

The evening wasn't over. At Glenna's holding her gently in his arms, "I'm sorry everyone had to hear me propose. Not what I planned sweetheart."

"Oh Kevin, I love you and I heard your beautiful words. No one heard except Craig and Sharon and they are so much a part of us." She paused. "Don't leave me tonight. Don't ever leave me."

381

"I hadn't planned to and I'll always be here for you. I missed you so much these five days."

Trying to ease things he said, "I didn't bring my pajamas." That made her laugh.

"You are not going to need any and no sleeping in your clothes," And that made him laugh.

"I don't even own pajamas, but I do need a shower. It's been a long day."

Looking deeply into her eyes. "Will you join me?"

The warm water rained down on them as they were playful and talked quietly. Kevin felt relaxed as Glenna was not at all inhibited and he could feel her strong desire.

"I have never been this close to anyone before." Her heart was beating wildly.

"I will always make love to you in a gentle and reverent way. Yet I will not leave passion behind. I love you so much, I want to swallow you up."

Her hands on his body, "To help you find that passion and I want every second of tonight imprinted in my being, it will be so beautiful."

He turned her around, cradled her in his body and caressed her breasts and stomach and where no one else had touched. "This is only a small part of what I can give you," he said softly.

She turned and smiled, and she put her arms around him. "I need to know all those wonderful things—now."

They dried each other, he took her hand and to her blue bedroom where she found love for the first time and him knowing, he had waited for the right girl.

As the near full moon floated in and out of the night clouds their passions were entwined. Eager for the other to know and share their physical love.

They slept in gathering arms until the break of day.

♫

Sunrise was in their hearts as well as the eastern sky as they loved again. They cuddled close and talked quietly. She pushed his hair back and said, "You were wonderful. I won't forget you as my first love, my only love."

"Oh Glenna, sweetheart, you have made me so happy. I've been wandering around aimlessly for a long time looking for you and it happened when I least expected. I opened the door and there you were."

"I was surprised too."

"In Texas in May I felt a bit lonely and when I started for New York, I immediately felt so much better. I thought it was after a year of teaching was behind and the break would be welcome. See a new part of the country, be with my best friend for a while. Craig couldn't say enough about everything, Sharon, school, the city, the tall green trees. He even liked the snow. He was so right and then there was you."

"I haven't even dated seriously these four years."

"You knew I would be here someday."

"I have piano instructions today and I'm glad it's later."

"I'll take you over and pick you up and have

lunch together, or do you want to practice?"

"I'll practice and then you can pick me up. When do you expect your things from Texas?"

"Next week while we're waiting go with me, and I'll get all of what I need so when that stuff comes I can get settled. I need a bookcase and whatever is on the list."

"Also next week is my last class and I would like to go visit my family. When school starts we're all going to be very busy."

"It's okay with me."

"I'll check with Mother. We could go Friday afternoon and come back Monday morning."

A late breakfast and Kevin drove her to school and went to Craig's. He was practicing and Kevin knocked lightly. "Yes," not knowing who it was. Kevin popped his head around the door and waved, not expecting him to stop but he did.

"Yesterday was quite a day. Did you come home last night?"

"No, I stayed with her. The first time we stayed together."

"I didn't mean to inquire."

"Have we ever kept anything from each other?"

"I don't think so."

"We were upset and we both needed each other. I have wanted to love her since I answered the door, but actually it was not the first time we slept together."

"Do I follow?" Craig was bewildered.

He told him about falling asleep in the dorm.

"You missed a good chance."

"No. It would have been too soon. I really liked her and didn't want to mess things up. You guys have to come over to Westphalia Gardens. We'll have dinner for you as soon as I get settled. We're almost finished and I will be out of your way."

"Hey, don't talk like that. Couldn't be happier that you are here and we got our girls, that is the best part."

"Everything has gone so well, I can hardly believe it. I want to get her a ring soon to make it official. We can then tell our parents. Where is a reputable jeweler?"

"Kesslers, downtown."

"About Stratford. I am anxious and Glenna is ecstatic. She said it was a Bach concert."

"Go early Sunday and stay Sunday night and come back Monday via Niagara Falls. It's about a four-hour drive. Sharon will make reservations."

"One room for us, obviously."

"I hear the plays are wonderful. We'll have to get to some of them. We'll have to go to Toronto some weekend, that is a special city. Eileen and I went when we first got here."

"For so long we thought it was going to be Eileen and Sally. Overnight things changed and so much for the better.

"Strange how things work sometimes."

"Eileen was at Sara's Sunday. Her date was a really nice guy and she's glad she's back. I talked to her and she never like it here. She wished me well. I'll let you get back to practicing. I'll probably be staying

385

with Glenna, but I'll see you in between and talk about Sunday."

♫

CHAPTER THIRTY-FOUR

♫

Music was in the air as they drove across the big bridge into Canada, customs only inquiring about citizenship. The industry along the harbor front in Hamilton created an interesting skyline. Only Craig had been this way before. In Stratford they registered at the motel as Mr. and Mrs. C. Jamieson and Mr. and Mrs. K. Werner. Back in the car, Kevin said to Glenna, "For this weekend you are Mrs. Werner. We can practice."

They bought box lunches and went to the riverfront to eat and then to the concert. The excitement among the four was infectious. The performers held them spellbound. Glenn Gould was the one they mainly came to hear. The three who also played piano appreciated this clarity of tone, each note was crisp, his touch determined.

After the concert, they walked along the rivers' edge and watched the swans and mallards swim their way for food.

"He certainly gets lost, as you do Sharon, as he

plays," Craig said. "Although you're not as physical."

"So I noticed."

"This is a day for our diaries," Glenna added.

"Dr. Kreutzer heard him in Salzburg and I can see why he is so great."

"Are these summer concerts only?" Kevin asked. "We should come and stay all season."

"That would be great, but we live among musicians that are just as great and I'm holding one of their hands this moment."

At dinner their conversation was completely about the concert.

"What a nice day. A beautiful ride, beautiful music, wonderful food, but most of all wonderful friends."

Monday morning they had breakfast in town and enjoyed the specialty shops before heading to Niagara Falls.

The spectacular geologic sight held them in a trance as they watched the water race uncontrollably over the falls. They enjoyed both American and Canadian sides and after lunch drove home.

Kevin said, "I am loving New York more all the time."

♫

Glenna had her last class and quartet practice until September. Their program was established for their fall engagements.

They finished shopping for Kevin's apartment and readied for their visit to her parents. They had stayed together at Glenna's studio since he came back from Texas. They found their love for each other and did not want to let it go.

"What are we going to do when school starts and I have to stay at my place?"

"I'll stay at your place with you, but while we're at Mom and Dad's we'll have to miss a few days."

"Did you tell your mother?"

"No. How about this weekend?"

Kevin's shipment from Texas arrived and he decided to put everything in order later.

Friday afternoon early, they were on their way to Pittsburgh. Not a long drive but the day was hot.

After twist and turns guided by Glenna, they arrived at her large, brick, two-story house. Her mother and siblings were there to greet them. Glenna and her mother embraced each other in a tender and loving way. She also gave her sisters and brother big hugs. Kevin offered his hand to her mother and she took it in both of hers. "We're so glad you could come."

A gentle handshake for Rachel and Vickie and a big man-to-man for Stevie.

"Do come on in. Your father had a late meeting, but will be along soon."

Glenna took Kevin's hand and brought him along into their large and beautiful home.

"Before we settle for cool drinks, show Kevin to the guest room."

Stevie had to go along. He wanted to show Kevin his room and coin collection. Glenna sent him on ahead to make sure everything was in order. "We'll be right over."

"When should we tell them?" she asked.

"Let's wait until tomorrow. I'll find an opening."

She agreed and they went to Stevie's room.

By the time they got back downstairs her father had arrived and greeted his daughter and Kevin.

Greta, their housekeeper, had cheese and crackers and cool drinks.

Her mother asked, "Tell us about your quartet and classes."

"It is a quartet of five." And she laughed. "But we sound wonderful and have six jobs until Christmas. Dr. Livingston said possibly more. My opera class was a lot of work, but I loved it." As she told them about Kevin coming back from Texas and tears filled her eyes. "It was awful waiting and not knowing."

Kevin put his arm around her to help quell her anxieties as she was reliving that day.

Her mother added, "It can be awful," thinking of some of her own experiences.

Her father asked Kevin about his new teaching position.

"I am looking forward to starting school."

"He has to report on the fifth."

"English is my favorite subject," Vickie announced. "I love to read."

Kevin asked Vickie and Rachel what they had been doing this summer.

Rachel responded. "We went to music camp for a week and sports for a week and some short trips around the city. Mom took us."

Glenna told them about Stratford and Sharon's recital in Skaneateles. As they talked they realized how busy they had been. At dinner their conversation continued.

Her mother offered, "Greta is preparing dinner for us tomorrow so I can be with you for the day. Your first visit is special."

"Oh Mother, that is so sweet of you to ask her."

"Thank you," Kevin added.

After dinner, which was long, Kevin and Glenna went for a walk.

"You have a beautiful family. Your mother and father are so warm to each other and their children. I know you will be the same with ours."

"It is easy when you love. You will be a wonderful father too."

The evening was still warm as they knew the sun was setting, but hidden behind the tall trees.

"Did you bring a book?"

"Of course. Three. Ones that I want to use this semester. I have the first four weeks already prepared but I have to move ahead. Let's go back."

♫

The next morning Glenna and her mother prepared breakfast. Kevin could see how close they were. She had been an only child for so long, adding to the affection.

In the afternoon they all went to an art festival. It had something for everyone.

At home Glenna asked Kevin, "Could you wear a tie? Mom wants this to be a special dinner."

"Of course I can. That is so nice of her."

Grandmother arrived and hugged everyone. They gathered, and her sisters were in lovely summer dresses. Stevie also in shirt and tie. Glenna wore her dark-pink gown that she had worn at Sharon's wedding. Her mother lovely in beige.

Greta served and the conversation was warm and personal. They went over all that was happening in upstate for grandmother.

After dessert everyone was having tea, and for Kevin it seemed like the right moment to relay the good news.

"Mr. McCaffrey, this has been a wonderful day and a wonderful dinner together. You have a beautiful family."

He looked puzzled for a moment then thought Kevin was just talking about the nice day they had experienced together. He smiled, nodded his head and said, "Thank you. I love them dearly."

"I have a request," Kevin paused and took a deep breath, "I am asking for your daughter's hand in marriage. I love her beyond words and will forever keep her at my side and in my care."

Everyone seemed surprised except her mother. Her sisters had broad smiles.

"This is not a surprise. We could see at graduation that something had happened, and quickly for both of you. We are so glad you didn't go back to Texas. You have my permission and blessing, but I will reserve the final word for Glenna."

She was the most surprised of all and tears were in her eyes. When she gained her composure, "Thank you Daddy." Gazing into his wonderful eyes, "Yes, Kevin I love you very much and want to be your wife."

Kevin stood and reached for her to stand. He pulled out of his pocket a Marquise diamond and slipped it on her finger. "With love forever my darling Glenna. 'When I saw you I fell in love, and you smiled because you knew,' not mine, but just too appropriate to pass it by."

He kissed her lightly and held her tightly for just a moment. Everyone had a tear. Grandmother went to Kevin. "You are such a wonderful young man that Glenna has chosen and we welcome you to our family. Ann, Mark, we have five children. And Vickie and Rachel your husbands have a hard act to follow."

"But Grandma, I haven't even had a date yet."

They all joined in congratulating them and Vickie said, "We think you are so cool."

Glenna asked, "This was not spontaneous?"

"No, I called your mother and she said she would see that it happened."

"No one told me either," her father added.

The evening closed with Kevin in the guest room and Glenna in hers. Not their choice.

Monday morning early they said goodbye to everyone and were on their way home. Arriving at Glenna's studio....

♫

The remainder of August was as busy as the first part. Craig and Sharon accepted new private students to begin in September.

They had their initiation dinner at Kevin's new apartment which was a success in every way.

All four went to Chautauqua for two days. Sharon's recitals were again well accepted.

Kevin and Glenna did not go to Saratoga, but went to visit his parents in Ohio. His sister, Rennie, was able to break away and visit also. It was a nice few days. Kevin had not been home since Christmas.

They accepted Glenna warmly and wanted to know about wedding plans. They explained they hadn't had time to talk about that, but would soon.

Back to spend the Labor Day weekend with Craig and Sharon and get ready for a new busy school year.

♫

Summer closed. The trees spread their shade and flowers threw their fragrance to the wind. They had not received the message of impending fall. This had been a special summer for these four young people. Craig and Sharon's marriage and Kevin and Glenna finding each other when they were looking the other way. Their futures were as bright as the evening star in the twilight sky. Their careers in the arts were heard.

When life is young and beautiful, there are no thoughts that cloud the days as they drift and sometimes race by. Life opens and closes doors. Now life had opened all the doors they had touched.

    …but sometimes the wind blows one shut all too early in the day….

♫

PART THREE

♫

the soul wanders again

CHAPTER THIRTY-FIVE

♪

*S*eptember is the twilight of the year, but it has its beginnings. Spots of burgundy and rust have sneaked into the trees, saying fall is about to begin. Mums are the new flowers. School begins with new friends and new teachers. A refreshing breeze was blowing in.

The four knew they would be very busy, but decided to get together every Saturday evening for dinner.

One evening at their home Craig said to Sharon, "I have finished "Euterpe." Want to hear it?"

"Of course. I know you have been working hard, but I can't hear from upstairs."

As they went to the piano she asked, "What are you going to call it?"

"Euterpe Weeps." It is for you sweetheart, in memory of our visit to Père Lachaise."

He sat down at the piano and she put her arms around him and kissed his neck. "Thank you. Now that you have sent little prickles all the way, take a chair."

He chose a minor key for this lament that death had ceased this wonderful music. Sadness emitted from every measure. Euterpe's tears fell on the strings of her broken lyre striking a cold and mournful tone. This soul had taken his music to be with God and the hurt is deep. Her grief was cast for an eternity.

"It's wonderful. I wouldn't change a note."

Craig and Sharon arrived at one of the Saturday dinners and Craig held up a bottle of champagne.

"Let me guess," Kevin paused and thought, "Gee, I don't know."

"My publisher is releasing five of my compositions for sale."

Glenna heard that and said, "I am going to be the first to add them to my collection of sheet music, with an autograph. That is wonderful."

"That is the greatest. My famous friend."

"We're glad," Sharon responded happily.

Glenna asked, "Have you decided about California?"

"Not yet. I have two others that I am finishing and it could be one of those or "Virtuoso in E."

"That is my favorite."

Kevin opened the champagne, Glenna served the hors d'oeuvres and they toasted.

Craig, after a sip asked, "Glenna how was your first quartet performance? I slipped in last week and heard you guys practicing. Sounded wonderful."

"He always slips in and listens. I hope he didn't sneeze," Sharon added.

"Every time I see Mr. Sanderson I want to laugh, but I can't. He would think I was laughing at him." Glenna reminded Sharon. "The performance was great. We got a lot of applause and attention although everyone was eating. We have another next week at the same place."

"This might work into something that you didn't expect."

Kevin asked Sharon, "When is your Ithaca recital?"

"Last Saturday in October. Hope you guys are going with us."

"We are," they both responded.

♫

The next week at school Sharon asked Glenna if she would go home with her. Glenna drove over.

"Come on in the library."

"Is something wrong?"

"Yes, very wrong. I think I might be pregnant." And she broke into tears.

"Oh, that's not wrong, that's wonderful."

"I want a baby, but not right now. I may not make it through grad school. I may not be able to accept recitals."

"You're not sure."

"Everything is pointing in that direction."

"I noticed you didn't drink your champagne the other night."

"I hope Craig didn't notice."

"I don't think he did, he and Kevin were engrossed in something. If you are it will be okay. She will be beautiful and talented. Craig will help you. We will help you. It's really wonderful."

"He can't stay home while I am traveling around the country playing. What am I going to do?"

"If you are you will accept it and love every minute." She paused. "That is what I'm afraid of, getting pregnant now. Loving Kevin is so wonderful."

"Why don't you get married soon?"

"I am thinking Christmas. Mother is talking about a big wedding, but it would be mostly their clients and friends. I don't want that. I have to get serious with her. If I got pregnant it would not be a good example for my sisters."

"Please don't tell Kevin that we talked because he will tell Craig."

"Never, and he would. You are going to have to tell him soon."

"I know, but first I have to get use to the idea myself." And she continued to be a little tearful.

"No Sharon, it's not over. You and Craig are going to have a beautiful baby alongside you as you work on your careers. My mother had me and she went right back to law school."

"I have to get myself together before Craig comes home."

They continued to talk, Glenna trying to convince her how wonderful having a baby would be.

The next day Sharon and Glenna met again in the cafeteria.

"I hope you are feeling better."

"No, it was all I could do to keep from screaming out at Craig, not at him, but to him. I know it's not his fault. It took both of us. Oh, god don't let me do that. I love him so much."

"Just take a deep breath before you speak."

"I know. I will be careful."

"Well, maybe you aren't. Why don't you see the doctor and then you will be sure."

"Craig is going to start thinking and asking questions, but now he has his mind on finishing his two compositions. I'll see what next week brings. Did you talk to your mother?"

"I did, and told her I did not want a big wedding and maybe Christmas. I could tell she was disappointed, but she seemed to accept. I didn't tell her why, but I am sure she can read between the lines. We each have our own place, but stay together almost all of the time. I'll call her this weekend and hopefully she is used to the idea and we can do some planning."

Kelly joined them so they stopped the very personal talk.

Another day while Sharon was preparing dinner and Craig was going through the mail. "Oh honey, oh my. Sharon, come and look."

"What! What!" Joining him in the back sitting room.

"Sweetheart, a letter from *New Music Magazine.* They want to do an article on me and my music."

Sharon was instantly happy and forgot what she felt was a problem.

"They want me to contact them if I am interested and they will come out and do everything here. What do you think?"

"Oh Craig, that would give your music

wonderful exposure. Do it. And school too."

"I'll pass it by Dr. Bernard, because they will want information about school."

"He'll go for it. He will insist you do it."

"And you will certainly be mentioned as an up-and-coming concert pianist."

That upset her immediately and she blurted out, "No, my career is over!" and she started to cry.

"Honey your career has just begun."

"Begun to be over." And she covered her face with her hands.

He reached and pulled her in his arms. "What are you talking about? Did you hurt your hand?" Slowly and meticulously he asked, "Sharon love, what is the matter?"

"I think I might be pregnant." And she kept crying.

"Oh! Oh!" was all he could say.

"Oh Craig, I want a baby, but not yet."

"You said might, then you haven't been to the doctor?"

"No, but I am so late it almost has to be."

"Don't cry, that is the happiest news and we knew our love would make us a baby."

"Craig, how can I have a career with a baby? I may not get through grad school."

"Of course you will. Honey I am here to help. Please don't cry over something so wonderful, but you must see a doctor."

"I will in a week or so."

"Before we go to Ithaca. We have to know. Oh please darling wife don't cry," and he wiped away her tears with his bare hand.

"Let's get back to the magazine."

"We will, but this is more important. Let me help you with dinner."

When evening was over, they snuggled close in their bed and she had calmed. They talked softly, Craig trying to convince her there may be no turning back. He rubbed her belly thinking that it would grow and one day a baby. My happiness has to wear off on her. I suppose it is easy for me because I have obtained many of my goals.

"I can't accept any engagements after February."

"It will be a tiny blip in your career and that little blip will be a beautiful baby. Once she is here you will forget all about how upset you are. Next week a doctor."

She reached for him, feeling bad about being distressed, kissed him passionately....

♫

Craig met with Dr. Bernard about the magazine article and Sharon kept her doctor's appointment.

Dr. Bernard, as suspected, thought it was wonderful for Craig and his music and school. Craig contacted them and being just down the road in New York City, they would drive up soon. They wanted it to be the April issue next year.

Craig went to the doctor with Sharon and when she came out smiling, he wasn't sure what it meant.

She whispered, "Yes."

At home she put her arms around him, "I am happy about it, although it's not quite real. I am going to be a mother and you a dad. That sounds so good."

"Love, you keep making me so happy. Don't forget, I will be here for you every moment. I want to be involved in every part of her life."

"But it may not be a her."

"I will it a little girl."

"Next May we'll know for sure."

"May is our special month. Our birthdays, her birthday, our wedding day."

"I am not going to let my belly get in my way and I have decided to carry on normally from this day until she comes."

"Now we can tell everyone. Aunt Katy will be happy and your mom and dad's first grandchild." He paused. "We can still make love?"

"Oh yes."

They closed the month by going to Erie to Karen and Jim's wedding. They had not found a house so they stayed at Cumberland and they all saw each other often.

♫

Early in October the magazine crew arrived in the town. They first visited the campus. Cameras were in Craig's classroom, on students coming and going and the historic neighborhood. It created a flurry of excitement.

The crew went home with him and took shots of him composing at his piano, playing. Discovering that Sharon was an accomplished pianist they added her with Craig at their piano. They took close-ups of his music. Everyone was pleased with all of the photos, but they did not know what would be used.

Sharon at his side, Craig took them into the library to discuss the text. He gave them a short history of his musical life, his awards, and a list of composition published and those coming soon.

He shared with them some of the techniques that helped him reach deep for those beautiful tones.

"Do you have children?"

"We are expecting our first child in May." And he smiled lovingly at Sharon.

"You call this the Music Box."

"Fondly, yes. The entire neighborhood and campus are a little community. Most of the professors live within these confines."

He also asked Sharon about her musical life and plans. She answered reluctantly.

This was a daylong process and the crew wanted to know where they could have dinner. The Kitchen Place was always a good choice. They even took pictures as everyone was enjoying their food after the long day.

Kevin said while eating, "My famous friend. Since I have been in New York it has been nonstop excitement," and he squeezed Glenna's hand.

♫

Over Columbus Day weekend Kevin and Glenna went to Pittsburgh to begin their wedding

407

plans. Glenna and her mother agreed she would have a small wedding, but a big reception.

Sunday they came back and had dinner at Craig and Sharon's.

"Tell us about your plans."

"There is a small chapel in the back of our church and it will be there. It is a perfect size for family and close friends and on the twenty-seventh. We shopped for dresses and flowers. You and Craig will provide the music and Mother is going to see if she can engage a string quartet. There is a piano and a small organ. The reception is at Casa Loma and we planned the menu. They will provide the music for dancing."

"You did a lot."

"Mother made all the appointments and it went well. At Thanksgiving we can finish."

"We can stay with Beth," Craig said, "and you said Judy and Sara are coming."

"I talked to Judy and she said yes. They didn't know about anyone else."

♬

The last weekend in October, they packed for overnight and were on their way to Ithaca for Sharon's recital. She did not feel well and was worried that she would be sick and not be able to meet her obligation. It made them nervous. Glenna was near tears with worry.

The ride down made her feel even worse. They checked in at the hotel and went to rest.

After, they had a light dinner and went to Bradford Hall.

Sharon said, "I feel so much better now. I'll be all right."

"Does anyone know about having a baby?"

"We don't," Kevin responded, "but we will by May." That brought a laugh from all.

At the hall Craig stayed with her backstage until she went out, and she assured him that she felt fine and please relax.

She wore her black silk dress that she had worn at the winter concert last December. He told her again how beautiful she looked. She thought, I can still wear this in Albany and then I'll have to make some fat clothes.

During intermission Craig took her water.

She played without flaw and he could see that she still took her little journey. That made him happy.

After playing Craig's "Interlude" as an encore, she accepted pink roses from the Arts Council.

They attended a reception in another area of the Hall, getting to bed rather late. Morning was not rushed and after breakfast they were on their way.

Sharon was okay until they got home, but then was sick again. She wouldn't let Craig call the doctor because she felt this was a natural and would pass.

By Tuesday morning she was very weak and Craig did not listen to her and called the doctor. "Come in immediately."

"You are dehydrated and other things that we see in the first months of pregnancy. Take her directly to the hospital."

There they started what was necessary to get her strong again. For two days she lay quietly and rather unresponsive, but they assured him there would be no harm to their baby.

Craig was violently worried. The nurses had to insist he go home at night, where he would pace the floor and think of her every moment.

On the third day he arrived after school, and she was sitting in the chair, looking better and greeted him with open arms. He couldn't have been happier to see her that way. What was even better, she requested that he bring her a score to study.

"I feel so much better and don't need to waste this time just sitting."

One evening after Craig had gone home, she lay quietly thinking what if I lose our baby? The thought frightened her. Oh god don't let that happen. I really want her. Please forgive me for being so distressed. It was a surprise. I know I can manage her, Craig and a career.

While Sharon was in the hospital, Craig spent all of his free time with her, even bringing his own food. Glenna and Kevin also had been there a portion of every evening.

Her illness passed, she resumed her schedule that included making fat clothes.

♫

The days slipped into November and winter was on the horizon. Snow could be any day. Out came winter coats and boots. Kevin's wardrobe had to be replenished with heavier clothes.

The week before Thanksgiving they all went to

Albany for Sharon's recital. They stayed with Craig's mother, as Kevin had done so many times before. She felt well and played beautifully. It was well attended and many of Bill and Helen's friends and his colleagues were there. Helen was proud of her son and his wife. They said goodbye the next day and Helen assured Craig and Sharon the turkey would be waiting next weekend.

Kevin and Glenna would be in Pittsburgh.

After Thanksgiving Craig finished the two compositions that he was working on. He thought, now I have to decide what I am going to play for California. Then I can release the others for publication.

♫

December made its appearance with snow, but one day it could be warm and the next day start snowing all over again.

Craig invited Kevin and Dan Westmore to go caroling with him and the double quartet and following tradition, ended up at Craig's home. Sharon and Glenna fixed hot drinks and little sandwiches. Jennie Westmore joined them to complete the group.

The winter concert was as big as ever, but only Craig was involved. He composed short selection combining the glee club and the double quartet. It was enjoyed by all.

The winter concert closed the semester, but Kevin had four days of classes before he and Glenna could leave for Pittsburgh to celebrate Christmas and be married.

Glenna moved her things into his apartment. It was not crowded, but they could have used more space.

All of Craig's family would be celebrating Christmas at Beth's home, in Pittsburgh. They celebrated in the traditional way. Santa visited for John and his little brother and ironically no one saw him.

The next day they all went to the airport to get their friends from Texas. Only Jeff, Sara, Judy and Lee were able to make the trip. Craig took them to the hotel while Kevin and Glenna waited another hour for his family from the west.

Later they all gathered at Glenna's home to be reacquainted and make sure everything was in order for tomorrow.

♬

The second day after Christmas at eleven o'clock they all gathered at the Chapel. Its interior was white and gorgeous with the decorations of red roses, white lilies, and to remember the holiday, poinsettias and holly. Candelabrum lined the aisle. The string quartet offered solace as family and friends gathered.

Craig was best man, but stepped out of the role and offered vocal inspirations as Sharon accompanied.

Glenna's ivory gown was offset by her sister each in a different shade of dark green. The small organ sang out as Glenna and her father walked to meet Kevin. Their vows were exchanged with love that neither could have thought possible last year at this time.

After pictures a grand reception awaited them. Dinner and dancing filled the afternoon and then Kevin and Glenna were whisked away to the airport to spend a few days alone in New York City.

Early the next morning, Craig and Sharon returned home with their friends from Texas. Jeff drove Kevin's car, hoping there would be no snow. Kevin and Glenna would return to join the festivities of welcoming in the new year. They wanted to be with their friends at this special time.

♫

CHAPTER THIRTY-SIX

♫

*T*he new year opened as the snow fell gently on the old Victorian neighborhood. Gaslights flickered brightly as evening crept in along the snow-covered walks. It could be yesterday or very long ago. The white landscape kept young and old from going far.

Kevin and Glenna settled in his apartment. A house would have to wait until spring. He went back to school as a married man, disappointing most of the girls. He had been their new heartthrob.

Of Sharon's new students, one had a natural ability as she did. Teaching her was very rewarding and guided her along the same path that had led her to, what she considered success. She also had a recital at the Medical Auditorium and the musicologist wrote a raving review for the newspaper. Another excitement for Sharon was a scheduled performance with the Philharmonic next November. A copy of Shostakovich's "Concerto in F Major" lay open on her piano. Her graduate recital was scheduled for April and she decided on an all-Chopin program.

Baby things were sewed with love. Glenna requested and received a sewing machine for Christmas. She was excited to add sewing to her new craft of cooking. She was also working on her graduate recital that would be in May.

While the girls sewed every other Sunday afternoon, Craig and Kevin watched basketball or something and then they would have dinner together.

The other Sunday afternoons, Dr. Bernard began his recital series and Glenna's quartet would open. Craig had heard them in practice, but for Kevin and Sharon it was the first other than the wedding.

The series had been well advertised which attributed to a large attendance. It was a great Sunday afternoon for those who loved music. Many in the area just bundled up and walked over.

Kevin's principal, Mrs. Garrison, and several of the other teachers attended and he proudly introduced his bride to everyone.

One day after classes Sharon went to Craig's office and it was closed. Just as she started to Dorothy's office she saw Glenna.

"Craig's office is closed."

"Dorothy couldn't find you, so she found me and I am supposed to take you home."

"Why?" with concern in her voice.

"He left just after lunch. He felt he had the flu."

"Oh my gosh. Can we go now?"

Glenna dropped Sharon off, but did not stay.

"I'll see you tomorrow."

Sharon hurried in and found Craig in bed.

"What's the matter? When did this happen?"

"After lunch and I went back to my office and felt very warm and my stomach upset."

"Maybe it was something you ate?"

"Something hit me fast. I think it might be a bit of the flu. Don't come near me. I don't want you or baby sick. I thought I would come home early and rest and I'll be all right tomorrow."

"I'll let you rest. Want some hot broth?"

"Broth would be about all, thank you."

"I'll be up later." And she gave him a quick kiss on his cheek.

She didn't sleep with him that night. The next morning he felt even worse. She wanted him to go to the doctor. "Just the flu and it will go away. I have to get better, I have my faculty recital soon."

He recuperated just in time for his performance.

Helen came up and stayed a few days. As she sat at his recital with Kevin, Glenna and Sharon, she was not only proud of her son's accomplishments, but that he and Kevin had found such wonderful girls to share their lives. Her thoughts went back to their college days when Craig had brought him home. He was always considerate and thoughtful. I was glad to be his home away from home.

The school presented many wonderful musical events, but the opera was one that everyone looked forward to seeing. After much hard work, *Hamlet* was ready for the world. Two nights and it would be over.

Kevin suggested that his two senior reading classes attend. He scheduled reading the play so they would enjoy it more. Almost all of the students came.

Another English teacher and again his principal were there to chaperone. He hardly needed anyone else. All he had to do was walk, look, and they quieted for him.

All four went both nights and Saturday Jim and Karen, who was still at Mr. Heid's, joined them. After, they gathered at Craig and Sharon's and had another wonderful discussion about the arts.

Everyone was so busy the days became yesterday, unnoticed.

Craig was working very hard on "Virtuoso," often staying up late and getting up early. This schedule didn't lend well and he had the flu again. This time Sharon insisted that he go to the doctor, which he did. Craig did not mention that he had been ill earlier. It didn't seem to matter. The doctor told him what he suspected, build up his immune system, rest, and medicine to control his symptoms and time will heal. He took it seriously, soon he would be going to California.

♫

The snow had mostly melted and the wind was blowing in spring very fast. The long cold winter was on the edge of history.

Kevin and Glenna were planning their belated honeymoon for July. Paris beckoned them and they were also going to spend a few days in Venice.

Glenna would be out of school a month before Kevin so she decided to look at houses. But this was a few months away. There was a lot of excitement before summer.

Everyone was anxiously awaiting baby who would be here in about a month. The thrill was growing everywhere. Missouri, Albany and Texas. It would be the first baby among their friends in Texas and Sharon's family.

"Virtuoso" was ready. The last time he played it for Sharon, she thought it was perfect and felt that he would receive another award. They both knew if he gets any mention at all, and with the magazine, it would put him in great standing as a contemporary composer of piano literature.

Time came to pack and they drove him to the airport. They wished him the best.

Since it was so close to the time of the baby arriving, Kevin and Glenna stayed with Sharon. They all felt better, especially Craig, that she would not be alone.

He arrived in Sacramento after a stop in Chicago. It was late and he would have to adjust to the time change quickly. That night he missed Sharon terribly and at breakfast even more. He thought, I must keep my head together for now. I'll be home soon.

Early the next afternoon he played. He was pleased with his performance although he missed a few notes, only Sharon could play to perfection.

It had been a strain and he had pains in his stomach, but felt it was just nerves. He had noticed a museum near the hotel so decided to spend the remainder of the afternoon there to relax and enjoy that playing was over. He called Sharon before he went to bed and told her all and that he would see her tomorrow.

The next morning she went to the airport. He embraced her lovingly. He told her all about the flight, one not so good and kept thinking about Kevin's experience in Texas. The museum.

"I missed you every minute and having to do everything alone was awful."

"There is a surprise for you at home."

"Well, I know it isn't a baby."

She laughed. "No, but I'm sure it is a copy of the magazine. I didn't open it."

At home they snuggled up on the couch and he opened the big thick envelope and slowly pulled out the magazine.

"Oh my god, I am the cover boy. They didn't tell me."

"Oh honey it's beautiful."

They had captured Craig playing his Bechstein and looking up, eyes wide and far away. A lock of his dark blond hair almost in motion.

They exchanged contented smiles. She kissed him warmly and said, "I am so proud of you and love you so much."

"My sweetheart your accomplishments, I am also proud of and I love you so much."

Craig opened the magazine and read aloud. "The very talented and handsome Dr. Craig Jamieson graces our cover. He…"

They read the entire article and were pleased with both text and pictures. He was glad they had included one of him and Sharon, after all, she was his best critic and muse. The enclosed letter stated it would be issued next week.

He took her in his arms and whispered, "I missed you so and glad I am back which is more important. Feel like going upstairs?"

"I always feel like going upstairs."

Later Kevin and Glenna came home and joined the excitement.

Glenna asked, "Will you autograph my copy?"

"Of course."

"You are going to get a lot of that, starting with your girls' glee club."

"I hope you told Judy," Kevin asked.

"I did."

"I will call and remind her," Kevin added.

"It is a nice write-up," Sharon followed.

Soon after having dinner Kevin said, "We took good care of them, but we should be going."

"And I appreciate it very much. It made me feel so much better knowing you guys were here."

♫

A week later on the day that the magazine was everywhere, Craig received a letter stating that he had received the highest award for his "Virtuoso."

Dr. Bernard had also received the information from California and a package of magazines. "This is such a wonderful habit we're getting into."

There was total excitement around school. Craig was busy all day receiving congratulations from students and professors.

Sharon and Glenna waited in the hall. "He so deserves every bit of the praise. He is so talented."

"I agree. He works very hard," she paused. "I have to give my graduate recital next week. I hope I feel okay."

Hoping to encourage, "You will, you have another month."

"Yeah. I hope I make graduation exercises."

"I hope you do too."

"Your recital, are you ready?" Sharon asked

"I am and excited about it."

"It is in the middle of the week. Are your folks coming up?"

"They are planning on coming, but Dad may have a trial."

"They can stay with us."

"My sisters will bring their sleeping bags and bunk in our living room, but Mom, Dad and Stevie would love to. It's not going to be too much for you?"

"We'll put Craig and Kevin to work."

"They really appreciate your hospitality."

All things settled down and Glenna's recital was wonderful. Parents and husband were equally proud. Sharon's graduate recital also went forth also without incident. They did not have a reception, just Kevin and Glenna, Karen and Jim joined them at home to close the evening.

Before the month close, Craig and Sharon went shopping for their nursery. He had painted the small room a soft green and they planned around that color. They had received gifts from their friends in Texas, family and other friends. They were well prepared. Helen found a beautiful handmade cradle they could use anywhere.

421

After the distress at first and the months of waiting, they were both excited, they soon would be three.

♫

CHAPTER THIRTY-SEVEN

♪

*M*ay gently nudged spring into place. The garden outside the piano room was filled with rainbow-colored flowers playing among the greens. This was the month of blessings and they were all celebrated and graduation day was tomorrow. Baby waited.

Sharon was uncomfortable but she was glad that she could be there. Craig stayed as close as he could and Kevin stayed close to him.

After the ceremony friends and family gathered at Craig and Sharon's. It was a catered event but Helen and Glenna's mom took charge and everything went very smooth. They insisted Sharon relax, graduating was strain enough for one day. Sharon's family would be coming when their grandchild arrived.

After all of the bedrooms and kitchen was in pristine condition everyone slowly said goodbye. Sharon decided she would just sleep and sleep.

Sunday morning she woke to a few pains. She

decided not to tell Craig until the last minute because he would get too upset. They were mild and could be just an upset stomach. She had coffee and that did not stay down. She dressed and went to play. Craig would not bother her and if the pains got worse he would not know for a while. She knew it could be a long time, even tomorrow.

The four had planned to watch television in the afternoon. When they arrived she managed to get Glenna in the kitchen alone. "I am having labor pains, but they are not bad, but getting more intense. I haven't told Craig."

"Oh! Why not?"

"He will get upset and I don't want to go to the hospital too early."

"Well, think about telling him. We will stay if you want us to."

"Please do."

In the late afternoon they had sandwiches and salad and Sharon did not eat.

"Why are you not eating," Craig asked emphatically but gently. "Please tell me."

"Honey, be easy, but I am having labor pains."

"Oh my god, when did they start?"

"This morning."

"Oh no! Let's get you to the hospital!"

"See Glenna, I told you he would."

"Craig, please listen to me. They are not real close together. When they are we can call the doctor."

"Oh my god, don't put me through this agony."

"Who has the agony?" Sharon came back but they all laughed.

"It's not every day that we have our first baby."

"Let's settle down and we'll watch television and I will keep you informed."

Craig rubbed her belly and hoping it would relax her and maybe me too, he thought.

Kevin asked, "You want us to stay?"

Quickly Craig answered, "Oh yes, I can't go through this alone."

"Please dear love, relax. Millions of women have had babies."

"But I don't want it to be in the car."

"It won't be. First babies always take a while."

"Not always," Glenna added. "Mom says I came fast."

As they watched television their minds somewhat gravitated to the shows, but Sharon's mind was totally on her pains. She noticed they were getting stronger and closer together.

"Craig, you can call the doctor."

"Oh god what a relief."

The answer was go to the hospital. Kevin drove because Craig was too upset.

Her pain was written on her face. She said, "See you guys later with my surprise." With kisses they relinquished her to the medical staff. Her doctor was already there and that eased her mind.

The three went into the waiting room and as fathers in waiting, Craig could not sit still. There was only one other man, a mother and sister. They managed to talk and that helped the anxiety. Even with conversation the hours passed slowly.

Craig said to Kevin, "If you want to go, it could

be morning before anything happens."

"We'll wait. It is not late."

Later Sharon's doctor came through the door and said. "Mr. Jamieson, congratulations, your wife has presented you with a baby girl."

Craig turned white and looked as if he wanted to cry with happiness.

"Are they okay?"

"Beautiful, Sharon did not have any trouble. I think she arrived at seven pounds six ounces. Nice size." And glanced at Craig's hair, "And blond curls."

Craig was speechless, but smiling.

Composure for the three took a few minutes and Kevin said, "Congratulations," followed with a pat on the arm and handshake.

"Congratulations," Glenna managed to say wiping her eyes and gave him a big hug.

"When can we see them?"

"When they are ready the nurse will come and get you."

This was the longest wait of all, although it was only about a half hour.

At her room Kevin said, "You go in and we'll wait here for a few moments." He put his arm around Glenna and they walked to the window, gazed out into the night and watched the blinking lights near and far.

He looked at her. "I guess we're next. This has been a good introduction."

She smiled lovingly and nodded yes.

Craig walked quietly into Sharon's room and she was wide-awake and smiling. He took her in his arms and kissed her a hundred times. My love for you is so big and I am so very relieved that both of you are okay and it's over." Choosing his words. "I know it wasn't easy for you. I know you were concerned that you would make graduation and I know you were uncomfortable. But when I wasn't near you I worried so much I think I made myself sick. So glad it is over."

She put her fingers to his lips. "I sensed your concern but it is all over now. Love you for giving me a beautiful baby girl. Wait till you see her. I think she is a little you."

He wiped her eyes and she his. A moment of love to remember. "They are going to bring her in shortly. What time is it? Did Kevin and Glenna go home?"

"No they are waiting in the hall."

"Tell them to come in. I'm fine."

They both gave Sharon a big hug and offered love and congratulations.

"You held her."

"I did, for a moment. They will bring her in shortly." And shortly it was when the nurse arrived with tiny Holly Rose. Craig took her and could hardly see her for the tears. They pulled the blanket back and they all gazed at their little bundle of joy.

"Look at her hair, it's beautiful."

"I know," said Sharon, "that is what I noticed first too."

"Her tiny lips are moving. She is singing." That brought a gentle laugh from all of them.

"She's precious," Kevin added.

"The doctor said it went well," Craig asked.

"It seemed to. They gave me a spinal and I was

awake and she came out without any trouble."

"That's great. Some girls stay there for hours," Glenna added.

"I do feel lucky, and Craig you didn't need to get upset at all."

"Next time I won't."

"That will be a while."

They each held Holly Rose for a while and then the nurse came back for her and said visitation hours were over.

Kevin and Glenna said goodbye. "We'll wait for you in the hall."

"I'll be here first hour tomorrow and stay all day." Lovingly they kissed each other. "Until tomorrow."

Craig went home and called everyone with the wonderful news.

The next day Craig arrived early with a dozen red roses as an expression of his love.

♫

After five days in the hospital, Craig brought his favorite girls home. In the next days there were visitors, Dr. Bernard among them. Kevin and Glenna stopped in every day for a few moments to see if they needed anything, bringing dinner several times.

Bill brought Helen with many gifts for her new grandbaby. She saw Craig had everything under control so she only stayed a few days.

So Sharon could gain her strength, Craig was doing everything, including caring for Holly. He bathed her, changed her, prepared her bottle, although Sharon usually gave it to her. He also got up in the night with her, but after two weeks she started sleeping through.

As Craig did all of these things for her, he sang lullabies in French, Spanish or English. She responded in her own little way, each time different. It made him exceedingly happy.

Later in the month Sharon's mother, father and Aunt Katy arrived. Baby Holly had unlimited attention for two weeks. Her parents were proud, but Aunt Katy was overjoyed.

By the time her family left Craig did not feel well, but did not mention it to Sharon. He began to think his stomach pain could be an ulcer. The last several months had been stressful, Sharon graduating, competition and mostly her and baby.

Kevin still helped him with the yard work, but he would soon have his own. Craig had confided to him that he hadn't felt well for a long time and promised him he would go back to the doctor. He did.

Just too much stress at once, and the doctor gave him a bundle of vitamins and medication for relaxing. He asked him to check back in about a month.

Sharon was becoming concerned, but with the doctor's assurance, her thoughts went back to Holly.

Kevin was out of school and now summer was for everyone. They asked him to sign a two-year contract.

Glenna was hired as a substitute accompanist in the school district for the coming year. Both employed, they felt better about going forward with buying a house. Glenna had found one she liked. Four bedrooms were necessary and an alcove for a grand piano. It was centrally located which meant it was not far from school or Craig and Sharon.

A new home and a belated honeymoon it was time for celebration. Everyone could have a glass of wine and toast the good things happening.

Sharon had rehearsed with the Philharmonic several times. A new conductor would be arriving in September. He had been a guest conductor several times, but she had never met him.

But on the agenda now was her first recital since Holly Rose was born. Kevin and Glenna had returned from their honeymoon and willingly stayed with her.

Sharon worried all the way to Syracuse about leaving Holly. Craig worried about her performance.

"Glenna is a natural mother. She said she helped with her sisters and brother."

"I know and I have complete confidence in her and Kevin as surrogate parents, and that is what we will be for their kids. The first time is hard."

Craig thought, I feel the same way, but we will get used to leaving her.

"If leaving upsets you so much, and if you want to give up performing for a while, sweetheart you have my blessing."

Give up! That sounded awful. I thought my struggle was over. If I cancel what I have scheduled, I will never get another offer. She was silent for several miles.

430

"Kevin is probably rocking Holly right now."

"She'll miss him not singing to her."

Knowing she was distressed he took her hand, "Think only of playing today and we'll work out everything else when we get home."

In Syracuse she played her all Chopin program to a packed Crouse Auditorium.

They arrived home late, Holly sleeping in her cradle as Kevin and Glenna watched over her and television.

♫

CHAPTER THIRTY-EIGHT

♫

Summer was closing for Craig, but it was always exciting getting ready for a new school year. He had been selecting new music for his glee club. They would be singing for the Sunday afternoon performance series and he wanted music that would do justice to their beautiful voices.

He had a special feeling for his double quartet. The blend of their voices was as if they were from the same biological family. It was an intimate group and all of the students would be back this year. Selecting music was exciting only exceeded by hearing them sing. He was also developing new techniques for his composition students, new ways to spark the creative spirit.

He wanted to skip competition this year and devote time to only composing. Winning three prestigious awards and the magazine article would give his music enough exposure for now.

Between bath and bottle, he composed, in the brightest key he knew, a "Kinderszenen," for Holly

Rose. He had transcribed her coos and bubbles, her wiggles and noises into notes. It was a one-page representation of her, for her. At the end of the music he signed it, Love Dad.

He thought, I can add more "scenes" as the years go by. I will play it for Sharon, and Holly will be listening as she kicks her chubby little legs and waving her tiny hands at the noise her dad is making.

For one of his compositions this year he had chosen *"Thatched Cottages at Cordeville"* painted by van Gogh in 1890. He painted *Cottages* ... and many others in a few months. It was thought he might have had a premonition of his death. Craig saw the painting at the Louvre on their honeymoon and immediately felt inspired by what it offered him. Sharon found a big print and he hung it in their piano room between the two big chairs, to gaze on while creating.

The painting, in shades of blues, the color of tranquility and spirituality, defied every stroke of his brush. The spinning clouds, the distorted trees, and the waterfall evoked turmoil in natures soul. In desperation, the white sun struggled to free itself from the angry clouds. Sections of the earth and the fences were also in motion. Even the roof of the cottages were waving, but beneath, was the frame of a solid, placid home.

Already bars of music were running through his mind and he was anxious to turn this tempestuous work of art into another form.

As Craig and Sharon's life was getting back to a normal routine, they grew even closer. They made love more passionately and looked more deeply into each other's soul. They talked about getting away for a weekend before school started, but why....

...they could walk hand in hand in their little garden ... they could have a candlelight dinner in their beautiful dining room ... in their claw foot tub they could pretend it was a big pool ... they could lay on their rug in front of their fireplace with music all around until the flame was swallowed ... they could go to the park and watch the sunset or they could look out their bedroom window and watch the foggy dawn turn to a brilliant sunrise. They could do all of these things at home and they would be near their beloved Holly Rose.

♫

One day Sharon was helping Glenna get settled in their new home, while Kevin was helping Craig in his yard. They were looking forward to having that beer on the back porch and talk about their wonderful lives and the coming school year.

Craig was gathering sticks out of the way of the lawn mower when he rolled to the ground.

Kevin looked up and said, "What was that?" Then he saw Craig's head sink into the grass. He realized he was not funning around. Kevin rushed to him and tried to help him up and then realized he was unconscious.

"Oh my god, Craig what's the matter?" he asked in vain. I have to get help but I can't leave him. Just then he caught sight of Mrs. Bedford, the neighbor, and yelled, "Call an ambulance quickly.

Something has happened to Craig. I can't revive him."

When they arrived, Kevin quickly told them what had happened and said he would go with him, but he had to call his wife. He made the conversation short, because the ambulance would not wait.

The girls arrived at the hospital and Sharon was quietly frantic when they found Craig in the emergency room, and Kevin by his side.

She gently put her arms around him and said, "Honey, what happened?"

Kevin told her. "I have not left his side and he was unconscious until we arrived here."

Craig was obviously still dazed, but slowly becoming more responsive. He asked softly, "What happened? The last thing I remember was reaching for that stick." Kevin finished the scene.

Still holding his hand, Sharon was gazing at him in disbelief. Did he have a stroke? Too young for that. It's not too hot. "We have to find the cause."

The nurse came in and asked everyone to leave, she needed to do blood work and other tests. Soon they were back with Craig.

Later the doctor came in. "Mr. Jamieson, we would like to admit you just for the overnight. We need to run more tests. Probably tomorrow you will be able to go home and wait for results."

Glenna suggested to Sharon, "I'll go get you something to eat, and then take Holly home and Kevin can come back for you later."

"Holly should go home. Will you get her ready for bed? But I don't know if I want anything to eat."

"I'll go to the cafeteria and get you something

light, then we'll go."

"Let me hold her just for a moment." Kevin placed Holly in his arms. With a smile he gazed at her and in a very weak voice and sang. "*Lullaby and goodnight, With roses bedight...*" She looked at him and her little lips starting moving. Sharon and Kevin watched with soft smiles.

♫

The next morning early, Craig called Sharon. "Honey, they are releasing me, can you come?"

"Holly is still sleeping, can Kevin come?"

They arrived several hours later in good spirits. But Sharon thought something strange, a little too happy, a little forced. She questioned him, but he just said they were waiting for more test results. She accepted his answers and was glad he was home.

The remainder of the day was quiet and Craig played the piano, wrote and rested.

The day closed and after making love they lay close and talked softly. "You have made me the happiest man alive. I could never imagine."

"Honey, I was the one so blessed. God dropped you right in my arms and I'm going to hold you so tight and never let you go."

"You will have a long career. I hope our little Holly plays like you do."

"I do too. It will be so much fun developing her. You will teach her to sing?"

Craig did not answer her question. "It is so sweet how she wiggles her lips when I sing to her."

"I know. She is trying to do the same thing you are doing."

Craig fell asleep for a moment. Sharon was concerned that he might have passed out, he loved me so passionately. He woke momentarily and whispered, "Good night love."

Sharon heard the distant thunder and saw the faint flashes of lightening, hoping it would stay far away. It gradually moved closer and stronger. It passed as quickly as it arrived, but left a hard rain in its wake. She snuggled close to Craig and joined him in sleep.

♪

Kevin called early the next day and said they would bring dinner around five o'clock, if that's okay.

The day was quiet and Craig rested, but he wanted Sharon near. There was concern in his heart and worry on her face, but they laughed and played with Holly.

Kevin and Glenna arrived with dinner. Sharon added a salad and they ate in their dining room by candlelight and soft music. Later, retiring to the back room they continued their chatting and laughing, but concern for Craig hung like the morning storm cloud. Sharon noticed, but thought it was mostly her imagination or worry.

Finally Kevin said, "Glenna my love, we probably should be going and let these good folks get some rest." And he got up and stretched.

"It is still early," Craig responded and as he got up he collapsed, but Kevin caught him and eased him to the floor and grabbed a pillow for his head.

"Glenna, call the ambulance!" he said firmly.

Sharon kneeled beside Craig and was holding his head in her trembling hands. "Oh god something is so wrong. Oh Craig, honey what's wrong?"

Kevin ran for wet cloths and Sharon put them on his face. Glenna rubbed his hands. It seemed like forever, as they waited for the ambulance. Sharon was near tears, but she knew that it was not the time to cry. Craig needed her. He slowly opened his eyes just as Kevin opened the door for the medics.

Softly he said, "Sharon I love you."

"Honey we're taking you to the hospital and I love you too. You should not be passing out. Something is wrong." Craig did not answer but took her hand.

"Sharon you go with him, and I'll drive over and Glenna will stay with Holly."

At the hospital, they looked at his records and admitted him immediately. Every minute Sharon was closer to breaking into sobs, but she still held back.

They got Craig settled and wired him up to a monitor. He was more alert and asked Kevin, "What happened."

"You got up and passed out, but I caught you before you fell and now you're here."

"Why is he wired up?" Sharon asked the nurse.

"The doctor will be here in the morning and he will have more of his tests back and will go over them with you."

"I feel better now," Craig said.

"Why has this happened and twice?"

438

"In the morning maybe we'll know. Until then I'll just lay here and be waited on."

Standing by his bedside the three chatted softly about not much, just idle words.

"Have you started on your new composition?" Kevin asked knowing that he had.

"Some. Few individual passages. I'm anxious to get back to it. I really like what I have in mind."

"It is going to seem strange for me, not going back to school. How many years has it been?"

"Holly is a career," Kevin offered. "How many engagements do you have for fall?"

"Three recitals and the Philharmonic in November. Is Dr. Livingston going to keep the quartet together?"

"He wants to. They all like playing together."

Sharon was talking and listening, but her other self was worrying about Craig. The nurse came in and Sharon asked, "Could I stay all night?"

"Of course. I'll be here until midnight."

"I'll sleep in the big chair. It looks comfortable all stretched out. I will be close if you need anything."

"It's okay. Go home where you can rest."

"No. I wouldn't sleep at home."

She turned to Kevin. "Would you please stay with Holly?"

"Sharon, we're here for anything you need."

Craig and Kevin looked long at each other.

"Glenna loves taking care of her."

"Stay at our house. It will be easier. Glenna knows where everything is."

"We'll do that, and it's getting late and I'll go.

Call if you need anything."

He took Craig hand and said, "Out of that bed."

"I will. Hey buddy, it has been a great run."

"Yeah." And Kevin left quickly because it was more than his soul could hold.

Sharon moved the big chair close and they talked as the hours passed. He dozed and she too felt sleep was near. He stirred several times and Sharon was awake immediately and up to see what she could do. He took her hand once and held it tightly until he relaxed and fell into sleep again. Back in her chair for a few more hours.

♫

It was very early and the sun was rising for one more day. Craig moved around and Sharon was immediately awake and at his side.

"What time is it?"

She glanced at her watch. "Almost seven."

"Nobody gets up too early around here. Honey get in bed with me." He said softly.

"They might not like finding me here."

"Honey, I don't care what they like, come on, up here."

She kicked off her shoes and carefully eased herself next to him and put her arm across his chest. She felt his heart and it seemed to be beating very slowly.

"I feel so cold and you being near makes me feel warm," he paused. "I am going home today."

They lay quietly for a few moments.

Craig started to gasp and said, "Dad." In that instant she did not feel his heart beat at all. Within seconds nurses rushed into the room followed by a doctor. Lights on and they yelled at her and literally threw her out of bed and she almost fell to the floor. Frantically they started CPR on him as others rushed in to help. It was too late, with her arm around him he had slipped into eternity.

Sharon was standing in the corner sobbing just as Kevin entered the room and saw all of the turmoil.

He rushed to Sharon, "Oh my god, what is going on?" and he turned white.

Sobbing frantically. "I was next to him and I felt his heart stop. He said, "Dad." Oh Kevin I think he's gone."

The nurses and doctor kept working with him.

"Oh no," Kevin uttered. "Oh no, not yet."

He took Sharon in his arms as they cried uncontrollably

The doctor came over to them as the nurses continue to hopefully revive Craig. "I believe we have lost him. He was a very sick man, as you know."

Sharon screamed, "No! I didn't know. Why! Why! He's too young to die! Why did he!"

The doctor looked at Kevin and asked who he was. Kevin said, "Their best friend and I knew that he was very sick. They told him just a few days ago."

Sharon rushed to his bedside and took his face in her hands and said, "Oh Craig, oh Craig, where did you go! I can't live without you. We need you. We need you." She cried uncontrollably.

Only one nurse remained. Kevin walked

slowly to his bedside and stared in disbelief at the man who had been his friend for over ten years. He thought me too, what am I going to do without his friendship. I have put it all in him and now he is gone.

Sharon caressed his warm chest and hands as to remember the last touch of her greatest love. She kissed his peaceful lips.

"Kevin why was he so sick and I didn't know?"

Kevin choked up said, "He wanted to spare you as much heartbreak as he could. He said there would be enough after he was gone."

"I don't understand why he died," she asked pathetically and her breath catching.

Kevin said to the nurse, "Can someone tell his wife of his illness." The nurse left and soon the doctor arrived.

"I am the doctor on the floor and if you want to wait until his specialist comes, and I understand he is on the way."

"Tell me now, just something."

The doctor explained that Craig's cancer had advanced with them not knowing just how much. This kind takes you before you even know that you are ill."

"Cancer," she said slowly. "His father had cancer and it sounds like the same kind."

"It could be. It is thought presently that it is hereditary, although we need much more study to say emphatically."

She spoke so softly and her eyes seemed to wander. Kevin was afraid that she was going to pass out from the shock.

"Stay with him as long as you want. My dear, I

am so sorry. These things are out of our hands medically and spiritually. We'll be close by."

He left, obviously emotionally disturbed.

Sharon went to his side again and touched the little smile that his lips would hold for an eternity. "Oh I wish I had known. I could have prepared."

"Did you tell Glenna?"

"I did, because she found me crying so hard that she had to know why."

She put her head back on his chest to hold every sensation that would have to be timeless.

Kevin paced and would come back and gaze fondly, shaking his head, questioning why.

"I want to be next to him for just a little while," she said as she got in bed with him. Kevin said nothing. He put his arms around both of them.

In her muffled voice, "This can't be real. Please tell me I am dreaming and will wake from this awful scene."

"Honey, it is real. I hoped it was a dream too. I'll leave you alone with him for these last few moments."

She lay quietly next to Craig's lifeless body. She touched his face and chest as she sobbed. "Wake up Craig. Honey please wake up. Oh God I hate you for taking him. You have Chopin, Brahms, Schumann. You don't need him yet, but I do."

She did not think past these moments that turned into almost an hour. Kevin looked in often to make sure she was okay.

After a while he went to Sharon. "Honey, maybe we had better go."

She shook her head. "Never. I want to go with him. Life will not be life without him."

"I know honey, we have been friends and gone through a lot together and I don't want to give him up either. But it is out of our hands." He waited. "We should go. He is with God."

Slowly she got out of bed, turned and kissed his lips one last time. "Whatever I do I will always love you more." She pulled up the sheet covering his chest.

The nurse came in and said, "I'll take you to the sun room." The sun beamed in brightly, but their hearts were dark with grief.

"I just can't believe this has happened. He is so young."

She looked into Kevin's tearful eyes and asked, "You knew?"

He nodded his head yes. "The morning I brought him home he told me, but I don't believe he thought it would happen so quickly. He was upbeat about treatment, but he told me there is a letter in your strong box, should you need it. And I suppose you do."

He looked out the window with a deep and hurt expression on his face. "You will have to make arrangements. We'll help. Helen will help."

"Oh, she is going to be so hurt. Did Glenna call her?"

"She did and she is coming up today."

"And to find him gone. Oh god love her as his mother. Ease her pain."

"Helen is special. She was so good to me while in Texas. She so graciously kept my parents many times when they visited."

"Little Holly will never know him. I am so glad I have her. I wanted to wait, but thank God she is here. Every time I look at her I will see him. He will live in her forever. She'll never hear him sing to her again."

"Shall we go?"

♫

At home Sharon said, "I'll read the letter, maybe he has some last wishes that we should know about."

Sharon came back and she was crying so hard she asked Kevin to read it to her. With her head in her hands and tears washing her face, she listened.

"My darling Sharon,

You have brought me happiness that I cannot put into words but I tried to show you every moment that I could. I have hurt you now. It is the last, the very last thing that I would do, but I was not given that choice. It was made for me.

I only found out a few days ago that I probably inherited the gene that caused my father's cancer and it has attacked my body and plans to take me too.

I decided not to share this with you because should I have six months, I did not want the pall of death hanging over our wonderful life. Please understand. I may not get to say goodbye so I thought I would put it into words and you could read and reread.

I have accomplished much in my short life and I am grateful. More special than anything was finding you for my love and our beautiful baby you gave me.

So much I wanted to do this all over again, but I had to leave you, Holly and our music.

In this short wonderful life, I am thankful music was in my soul and darling Sharon, you understood and shared this passion because you have it too. Our souls are one and can never be separated. When you play my music make your journey to my spirit.

Giving up this great happiness with you and Holly is so very hard. I will try with every ounce of my spirit to be with you when you want me near.

Never feel guilty if you, and I know you will, fall in love again, but when you are old and gray and close your eyes for the last time please ... please find me in eternity. It would not be everlasting happiness without you at my side.

Soon, put your sadness behind and think of all the happy moments we had together and treasure the love that I have placed in your heart.

Don't let this have a gap in your performance commitments. Play for me. I will be listening and will send roses.

So for now ... good night sweet love and goodbye for just a while.

Now for things not so maudlin. I have an insurance policy that my beloved father took out for me when I was seven. Never thinking that you would need it so soon, I just failed to mention. It is very generous. It will provide for you and Holly, that I can't. Your spiritual soul mate Craig"

♫

CHAPTER THIRTY-NINE

♫

*G*rief was far reaching. Tears fell from those who love him and those who loved his music. Expressions of sympathy came from everywhere. Flowers massed their home and school. Notes of condolence crowded her mailbox. Food filled her kitchen. And in a blink it was all over. It was just Sharon, Holly and Aunt Katy who stayed to help her through the saddest time in her life.

Sharon's eyes were hollow. Her smile retiring. She wasn't in denial but disbelief that she could lose Craig so soon in her life. Why, stressed her mind and still no answer.

She welcomed sleep. She could dream and Craig was always there. She saw him walking on the foggy dune, but as she neared he faded away. Another sleep found him at the water's edge and she tried to run to him, but her legs would not move. There were others, but he was always just out of reach. When she woke she realized there was much truth in her dreams.

Awake she would sit in their garden and meditate trying to reach him. She placed a memory candle where she could see when she played. Some days she hated God for taking him. He was so good, his life so promising. He did not deserve this. Silently she would tell him what Holly did today. In her library she would imagine he was downstairs playing his beautiful Bechstein. When she played his music she took her little journey to his spirit. It was easy because his soul was still with her.

She thought, I love the most beautiful man in the world and he was handsome too.

After crying herself to sleep many nights and reaching for Craig every morning, she got up one morning and went for coffee. Aunt Katy was rocking and giving Holly her bottle. Sharon joined them. They chatted a while when Sharon said, "Aunt Katy, today is the day that I am going to look forward. Crying has not brought him back. I have no choice but to accept. It's just Holly and me. My why question will never be answered, so I am going to stop searching. I can't shut my life down. I know I will be sad for a long time, but I am going to embrace life and smile through my tears." She paused. "How is that for starting the day?"

"Oh honey, I am so glad to hear you say that. I knew you would in your own time."

"I am going to work very hard at it."

"You are a strong girl. I knew that when you decided piano as a career."

"Yeah." And she looked down into the garden. "This is the first time I have had to surrender and that has been hard, especially to death. Let's have Glenna and Kevin over for dinner tonight. We haven't seen them for a couple days. I know Kevin is grieving too. Maybe we can all have a glass of wine and get silly together." She paused again and looked into that angel blue sky that so graced their wedding day. "When you love too much you get hurt too much."

♫

September was into itself. Schools were starting at various times. Aunt Katy had decided to stay until after Sharon's Philharmonic concert, which was November third. She was also preparing for her recitals in Skaneateles, Syracuse and here in the city at the Medical Center Auditorium.

One day when Sharon and Aunt Katy were attending to household things and Holly, the phone rang. It was the new Philharmonic conductor's secretary.

"Dr. Bremmer would like to meet you. What arrangements would you be able to make?"

Sharon thought, that I won't have to go out maybe he could come here.

"My Aunt and I would welcome him at my home. We are just off the music campus. You have my address."

"Yes I do and I am sure he would be agreeable to that." Sharon knew he was thirty-one years old, young for a major orchestra. From New York City. Had conducted orchestras in Florida and Minnesota, but that was all she knew.

Later in the week, Dr. Bremmer arrived

dressed looking like he was ready to hike the nearest mountain. She welcomed him and introduced her Aunt.

Aunt Katy excused herself. "I will look after Holly."

"She is my little one."

"And how old is she?"

"Just five months."

He thought, oh my, the little one just lost her father. "I understand you just lost your husband and you have my deepest sympathy. I read *New Music Magazine* and was very impressed."

"Thank you. We liked it."

"It is so very nice to meet you Mrs. Jamieson. Dr. Saxon, as you know has been rehearsing the orchestra and said you are very talented and play the Shostakovich beautifully."

Again she said. "Thank you."

"It is certainly understandable that you haven't rehearsed with them the last few times. That brings me to the question, do you feel that you will be able to play in November?"

"Oh yes, I am sorry, I just couldn't make the last few times."

"That is good to hear." He paused. "Are you going to continue performing or make teaching your career?"

"Performance has always been my goal."

She thought, now I am going to ask the questions. "You were in Minnesota and Florida before accepting the position here. How do the orchestras compare?"

"From what I have heard and the few rehearsals, this is the better orchestra. Having the school with the best talent is an advantage."

"I knew the students and they loved to be called to play."

After one more sip of lemonade he said, "Thank you for having me and I will see you next Tuesday. I want to devote the entire time to the Shostakovich."

Life went on and it was better, but it would never be the same. They had dinner with Kevin and Glenna often, but the empty chair was glaring.

The winds of fall had touched the leaves and they were falling fast. Her life was busy and she liked it that way.

Her recital in Skaneateles, Kevin and Glenna insisted on taking her. She was happy they offered. It was bittersweet with memories of a happier time. Craig's absence was heartbreaking for all of them. Syracuse was the same. Aunt Katy stayed behind with Holly.

♫

CHAPTER FORTY

♫

Saturday of the Philharmonic concert was a bright, crisp November day. Bill and Helen had arrived to be with Sharon on her concert debut and to see Holly Rose. She was just seven months old, happy, active and spirited as her mother.

After dinner the car arrived to take Sharon to the concert hall. Her last request was that everyone be filled with happiness and everyone tried.

The last person filled the packed auditorium and the program was ready to start. The Shostakovich was to be performed after intermission.

Sharon waited quietly in the room where she mentally passed over her music.

She was at peace with herself and the world. She knew Craig's spirit was just a breath away. She was happy to be performing with a major orchestra. She thought, I am going to be okay.

Wearing her long black dress, she entered the stage with Dr. Bremmer and they gracefully bowed to a grand applause. She noticed at the side of the first row an empty chair. She smiled. He's here.

Dr. Bremmer brought down his baton and the wild flight began. Her fingers flew through the allegro with such velocity they appeared she was chasing the speed of light. Each note clear as the ting of crystal. The andante she switched to a delicate firmness that makes the beautiful melody sing. The closing allegro, she returned to the speed required to make this composition exhibit its intended design. Switching from the extremes showed her absolute control of the keyboard.

Acknowledging the audience's appreciation, she received three bundles of roses. She took them to her room and looked at the cards, pink from Helen and Bill, white from Glenna and Kevin and the red, a blank card.

She smiled. "How did he do that?" she said softly out loud.

Kevin and Glenna had a reception for her at their home and invited close friends, the new conductor among them.

When Dr. Bremmer arrived Sharon went to greet him and introduced him to everyone. He was very cordial and seemingly glad to be invited.

As he chatted with Kevin he said, "Mrs. Jamieson has made me proud. She played beautifully. I could not have ordered a better performance. Her natural ability plays an important part in how she can get through this spirited piece."

"Her performances are all on a grand scale. A very talented lady and loves every moment."

"Does she play Liszt?"

"Glenna said she is working on some."

"This is a wonderful music scene here in the city. I have been to a couple faculty recitals. I believe Mrs. Jamieson has a recital at the Medical Auditorium later this month. I will be in town and am planning on attending. I understand your wife is playing in a string quartet?"

"Yes, and they are performing at the Medical Auditorium the first Saturday in December."

"I will be there if I am in town."

Dr. Bremmer made his way around talking music or literature or about his new orchestra.

♪

Late Sunday morning they took Aunt Katy to the airport. She had been at Sharon's side through her crisis, but it was time to say goodbye until Christmas. Loving kisses and tearful hugs and she was off.

On the way home, Sharon reminisced about how her aunt had helped her through so many upsets.

"I remember so well the first day I met her and you. I thought she was so sweet and kind," Glenna said.

"So much has happened from then until now."

♪

Sharon's recital at the Medical Auditorium was a mix of romantic composers and she included Craig's "Virtuoso in E." It was a very cold evening, the hall was full but not overflowing. She played from her heart and smiled through it all. After her encore, she went back to her room and was gazing out the window into the dark night, when there was a light knock on her door. She thought, Glenn or Kevin and I am ready to go. It was neither. It was Dr. Bremmer.

She welcomed him in and left the door open and he extended his hand. "It was a wonderful recital. Piano is my instrument so I know how difficult those selections are and you played each beautifully."

She smiled easily and said, "Thank you, you are too kind."

After a few more words he asked, "May I escort you home?"

"Kevin and Glenna are here for me. Thank you."

"Perhaps some other time. Again I enjoyed the last hours immensely. Good night." He smiled, turned and left.

She thought, I don't want to get involved with him. I like him but no ... no ... no ... not yet.

At home she tucked Holly in her crib and went to be alone one more night.

♫

Thanksgiving was in Albany. Sharon packed Holly's big bag and a little one for herself and they drove the thruway. Beth and her family were there to enjoy the big dinner. It was very very hard, for this would be the first holiday season that Craig would not be with them. Christmas would be even worse.

Sharon was back a few days when she received

a call from Dr. Bremmer asking her if she would be interested in performing a Rachmaninoff concerto at the end of the season.

"Yes, I would love to."

"Could we talk about this over lunch? They are pressing me for a program."

"Lunch would be nice. Where could we meet?"

"Daisy's. I have heard it is nice, about twelve-thirty, Thursday."

Oh no, no, no, she thought again, but I do want to play.

The following week she met him at Daisy's. He was dressed as casually as he had been the first time.

They started by discussing the weather, but quickly turned to music where they both were comfortable.

"Which Rachmaninoff are you familiar with or like the best?"

"I know two, three and four quite well."

"Your favorite?"

"Three.

"Let me think it over and get back to you, but I see no reason why we can't."

He knew at that moment that it would be the third concerto, but he wanted an excuse to call her again.

She thanked him for a delightful lunch and they each went their own way.

Glenna had stayed with Holly and Sharon was glad to have company for the remainder of the afternoon.

"His actions and words are so much like when Craig slipped into my life, then maybe I am reading too much into it."

"I remember when I asked you if you and Dr. Jamieson were dating and you said, I don't think so. That was too funny." They laughed about other things from their time of knowing each other.

"Come on home with me for dinner."

♫

CHAPTER FORTY-ONE

♫

The snowy, cold winter came fast and was making itself at home for the duration. Sharon's heart was even colder. She didn't have any engagements until next February, but was waiting for Dr. Bremmer to call about the Rachmaninoff. She was also making plan to go home for Christmas.

She was giving Holly her baby food, which she called lunch, when her phone rang. It was Aunt Katy and she was crying and could hardly talk.

Awful thoughts ran through Sharon's mind. Had she been diagnosed with a dreaded disease? Was it Jack? Mom? Dad? Allen?

"Honey I hate to tell you this over the phone, but your father has died."

"Oh no! What happened to him?" her voice choked.

"We don't know for sure, but your mother said he had awful chest pains, and by the time the ambulance arrived he has passed. That was about two hours ago. I rushed to the hospital and found her devastated. I'm glad I got there. It broke my heart too. He's my baby brother."

"Did you call Allen?"

"Just moments before I called you and they were leaving immediately."

"He won't get to see Holly. Not another funeral. Oh Aunt Katy, this is too much. I'll come down tomorrow. Allen will be there tonight."

Sharon spent the remainder of the day planning and making phone calls, among them one to Dr. Bremmer's secretary. "Tentatively, I probably will not be back until after the new year."

Shortly after, Dr. Bremmer called. Hearing his voice she thought, he is going to tell me I have been replaced or something.

"You have my deepest sympathy and I am so sorry that you were so far away. When are you leaving?"

"We're flying out tomorrow morning."

"Do you have a way to the airport?"

"Glenna has already offered. Thank you."

"Perhaps you would like to know that the "Third" is what we'll be playing. And we can start rehearsal when you get back. Again, I am so sorry, and it is hard to say Merry Christmas, but I extend to you the best holiday season that your heart can hold."

Sharon added the score to her bag to go home.

Changing planes in Chicago, Holly became very restless. It was all strange and the noise scared her. After they boarded for St. Louis, the stewardess took her and her mood improved.

Sharon thought a lot about her father and

home. She could not think of home without thinking about Joel. He wouldn't be home yet, his two years are not up. Mother said she heard he was going to get married. I won't have to see him. Her thoughts rested.

In St. Louis, it was cold but no snow. Allen met her and instantly took his niece in his arms and kissed her tiny cheek. "She has grown since August. I love her blond curls. And I can't wait, we found out three days ago that Carolyn is pregnant."

"Oh congratulations. We had given up on you two. Did Dad know? And what happened to him?"

"He did. He has a massive heart attack. From what they told mother and it took him instantly."

"Oh I hope this is the end of our sadness."

"To add this to what you have been through."

Arriving home, she embraced her tearful mother and she took Holly and held her close. She was happy to see both of them.

"I suppose Allen told you everything."

"He did."

"Tonight only the family will be with him. Tomorrow afternoon and evening will be for friends and Tuesday the funeral."

"It is a hard time in life." Sharon was speaking from experience.

"I have everything ready for Holly, a crib and playpen. It was something we could do early and a good thing we did. Your father was so excited that you were coming and now you are here, he doesn't even know."

That evening the family gathered to be with Mr. Heisendorf. The next afternoon Sharon greeted family, friends and friends she had known in high school. Most of them seem to know all about her. She wasn't sure where they got their information. Some congratulated her on her Philharmonic debut. Her music teacher, who had helped her get her scholarship, was even more informed.

"You have made our music department proud and I read *New Music Magazine* about your husband. I am so very sorry and now your father. Things are not very fair in life." He wished her the best and went to say a few words to her mother.

After their dinner break, friends were soon arriving to express condolences and the hour grew late.

Sharon and Allen were looking at the cards on the beautiful flowers when she heard softly, "Rose of Sharon."

Startled, she grew flushed and gazed into the banks of flowers, she knew who it was before she even turned around.

She turned, "Joel," held out her hand, and he took it and expressed his sympathy.

"It must have been a shock to all of you."

"It was. I didn't think you would be home yet!" And it was a shock seeing him.

"I saved some furlough time until the end. There wasn't much to do where I was. Going to San Francisco by myself wouldn't be much fun either."

They just stared at each for a few moments.

Very uneasy he said, "I am so sorry about your husband. I hope you have found peace."

"Thank you. I have."

"When did you get here?"

"We flew down yesterday morning."

"We. Someone came with you?" The *we* hit him hard. He thought, am I too late again.

"My baby and me."

"Oh! Oh!—I didn't know—oh a baby. You have a baby." He paused again to right his demeanor. "A boy or girl?"

"A little girl, Holly Rose."

"Oh, I didn't know."

Sharon saw that he was surprised and felt bad for him that he showed his feelings so strongly.

"Congratulations. How old is she?"

"Eight months." She paused. "I heard you were to be married."

"My mother told me about the rumor. I have no idea where it started."

He thought, get married when I am still in love with you, Rose of Sharon.

"Mr. Jacobs is gone, I'll go talk to your mother."

Sharon greeted another elderly couple and more high school friends. And not a surprise, Joel's mother and father.

"Oh Sharon darling, our heart goes out to you losing your husband and now your father."

She smiled, trying hard not to cry.

"I see Joel is talking to your mother, have you talked to him?"

"Yes we chatted a bit. He seems well."

"He is, and glad to be home."

You have our sympathy dear and, I am sure we'll see you later."

Joel came back to Sharon and they went on with their conversation, joined by old friends from the band.

"How long are you staying?"

"I planned to be here for Christmas so I'll just stay on until after New Year's."

"Mom and Aunt Katy will enjoy Holly."

"I would like to see her too," Joel said quietly.

"She is very sweet. Although I am prejudice."

"You have that parental right."

"Tomorrow is the funeral. Call me after that and come over some day. Are you working yet?"

"Some, but I still have to get discharged. I believe everyone is going, so will I."

He kissed her on the cheek and looked long into her big, dark eyes, hoping she would remember.

♫

Several days after the funeral, Joel called. "I thought if you were ready for a visit I would come over."

"Please do. Holly is in gay form this morning. She is happy and that makes me happy."

Joel arrived and Sharon welcomed him in.

"I hear her."

"Yeah she is really loud today. All of the attention. Mom just left. Mrs. Berger invited her to lunch. She hesitated, but I told her to go."

"Come on in and meet Holly."

Holly was in her playpen and as Joel walked into the room she held up her arms for him to pick her up. And he did. She patted his face and nose and waved her arms, squealed and made other noises. He thought, she is so pretty. I only saw him once but I believe she looks like her father. For sure the blond hair and blue eyes. Skin tone like Sharon's. She should be our baby.

He talked to her softly about visiting grandmother, Aunt Katy and her pretty dress. She listened intently.

"Aunt Katy stayed with me for a while and loved taking care of her. Allen and Carolyn are going to have a baby. We gave them up."

"Congratulations to them."

"He gave up his ministry and is teaching history in high school."

"He did. Why? He seemed so well suited."

"He said he could do God's work by teaching and helping the students."

"Your parents probably felt bad about that."

"Yeah I don't know what was said, but I think I broke the ice by going off to music school without their permission." She paused. "You hold her like you are experienced."

"Remember I am Uncle Joel five times over."

She smiled. "How are your family? Your dad? They looked well the other evening."

"Good. I could see that he aged while I was gone, but health wise, okay. He wants to retire. It will take me a while to get things under control."

"How was your stay in Korea?"

"Very lonely, but I had to go."

He put Holly back in her playpen.

"How about a sandwich? We still have food."

"If it's not too much trouble."

After they had lunch Sharon gave Holly her bottle and she went to sleep.

"What have you been doing musically?"

She told him everything and what was planned for the coming year. As Holly napped in the playpen, Joel and Sharon talked about the two years they had not seen each other. Craig was not mentioned by either.

As the afternoon grew later, he decided he should go. She walked with him to the door. "Maybe some evening I could take you to dinner. You don't have to consider it a date, but just to eat."

"Okay. We still have some catching up to do."

The next few days Sharon practiced and studied the Rachmaninoff and welcomed friends who stopped by to see Holly and her mother.

Joel called. "How about a fish fry tomorrow? I haven't had a good one since I left. Mom says The Cove is still open."

When he arrived the next day, he went right in to see Holly. She held up her arms again for him to pick her up.

"I hoped you dressed warm, it's really cold."

"I have. I am going to ease out while mother distracts her."

He took her hand as they walked to the car.

"The Cove has the best fish fry this side of the Mississippi," and they talked on and on. Sharon noticed herself sincerely laughing at some of the stories Joel had brought home.

He remembered Glenna and she told how she and Kevin met and it was love at first sight for both.

"I came down so suddenly I didn't have my Christmas shopping done. I'll have to do it here."

"I haven't finished either. Maybe we could go together. There is a new mall on the north side of the city that Mother talks about. Would you be interested in checking it out? She said there are lot of different stores to choose from."

"Maybe we can get it all done in one day. Mom will stay with Holly or Aunt Katy."

They spent the whole day shopping, and for the time Sharon forgot her present and past sadness. Joel suggested dinner, but she felt she should get back to Holly. Some other time.

Holly was doing just fine and they had dinner with her mother at home.

"Are you going to put up a tree?"

"Oh yes. It is Holly's first Christmas."

"How about dinner at the little French restaurant on Eleventh Street some evening?"

Saturday they drove into the city to enjoy the wonderful food and distinctly French atmosphere. Quaint with candlelight, they dined looking like two in love. Joel so wished

"You are going back after the first?"

"I have to. I have students and I have rehearsal with the Philharmonic, soon."

"Are you planning to stay in New York?"

"I haven't thought about going anywhere else."

On their way home he took her hand. She thought, I know he is going to kiss me and if I encourage him it might send a message that I'm not sure about.

And he did, but it was gentle. He took her face in his hands and said, "Rose of Sharon I missed you," and kissed her softly. "The first time I have kissed anyone in two years. When do you want to get your tree?"

"Tomorrow, if that's all right."

"I'll be over to get you in one of our trucks. A little one."

After much difficulty choosing a tree they arrived home. Sharon's mother had the decorations out and they got busy with eggnog and made it beautiful. Holly watching every move everyone made.

♫

Joel and Sharon enjoyed each other's company at his home and hers, at the movie and another special dinner. They spent Christmas day with their families, but Joel joined them for dessert as he has many times before.

Secretly Sharon's mother was glad she was seeing him. Maybe she would come home. She was sorry that her daughter was so far way.

"New Year's Eve my sisters are coming and the children will be there. It will be just our family. My mother and I would like to have you and Holly join us."

"Did you explain to your parents why we parted?"

"I did. Shortly after I left I wrote mother a letter

and explained everything and that it was my decision."

"She wrote back saying that she was very sorry and sad, and that I was wrong. I suppose I was, but we can't undo the past."

"Are you sure you want a baby for New Years?"

"Yes, the kids will love her."

"My mother wants to go to a church gathering so that would work out."

"We're having a late dinner and waiting for the ball to drop."

Holly Rose loved the attention from Joel's nieces and nephews. Sharon wasn't sure who was more enamored.

It was a very nice evening, seeing everyone again and when the midnight hour struck he kissed her lovingly. Sharon felt a bit sad, but she was glad to be with Joel and his family. He took her home and carried the sleeping Holly and put her in her crib and they went back to the kitchen for a hot chocolate.

"You are leaving Saturday, so could we have one more evening out. How about Wednesday, but I would like to see you every day. Come over and play with Holly. She is so sweet. You must love her so much."

"Oh, Joel you don't know until you have your own child how much you can love."

"My sisters say that. Mom too. It's really late. I hope we haven't disturbed your mother."

Saying goodbye he kissed her softly but very warmly and said, "I still love you Rose of Sharon. I'll call and be over tomorrow, if that is okay."

At dinner Wednesday there was candlelight and it was very romantic. He took her hand. "Sharon I meant what I said, I still love you. I would like to start over or just pick up where we left off. I want to marry you, if not now when you are ready."

"Oh Joel, are you sure? It has been two years and a lot has happened."

"The two years has just been a gap for me. I know for you it has been much more. If you haven't found peace, I'll wait. Your baby will be our baby."

Sharon thought, she can never be your baby, she is mine and Craig's.

"I've fallen in love with her too, and she needs two little brothers to grow up with."

"Oh Joel, I have enjoyed being with you so much, but all of this is a surprise. I thought you were still gone and I wouldn't see you."

"Like before, I will not be possessive of your career. I love you for being so determined and will not stand in your way. Having our own business, I can get away with you for concerts. Most of all we loved each other and I want us to be in love again."

All she could say was, "Oh Joel."

He was glad that she did not say no.

He took her home, stopped his car, and moved over to her and kissed her and she responded warmly.

"I have said a lot tonight and all from my heart. Getting reacquainted won't be hard. It is not as if we have to start at the beginning."

She smiled in the dark car and thought of their love and making love to him.

"I'll even move up there to be near you so we

can be together until you say yes." He paused. "Or say no."

♫

Saturday morning Sharon and Holly were ready. They said goodbye to her mother who was glad Joel was taking her to the airport because she did not like to drive that far.

"Extra baggage for a baby wherever you go."

"I wish I was going back with you."

"It would be nice to have your company and help, but I will be okay."

"You probably aren't coming home soon."

"No, not until summer."

"May I visit?"

With a smile she nodded her head yes and she thought, it will give me some time to clear my mind.

They sat waiting for the boarding call. His arm around her and they talked softly.

"Sharon, you know how short life can be. Every day must be special and treasured. Maybe I have overstepped and there is someone else in your life."

She took his hand. "No Joel there isn't, just Holly."

There was silence between them and both were staring out into space, wondering who would speak next and what they would say.

It was Joel. "There is no joy in being alone. We both know that. Joy is being together. We're both very young and hopefully have many years ahead and I want mine to be with you. I hated life after I lost you, and I don't know what made me act the way I did."

"Oh Joel, that was long ago. It would be nice if we could always do everything right. I don't fault you. I was afraid I would lose all I had worked so hard for. I thought we could wait, but you saw it differently."

"We are where we are and I want to start over because I never stopped loving you. I wanted you to know that."

The boarding call was loud and maybe too soon. He took Holly as they got up.

Through the gate, he took Sharon in his other arm and kissed her lovingly. Holly patting his face and then he kissed her cheek and her chubby little hand.

"I'll see you soon?" He took it as a question as it was meant to be.

Joel watched the plane until it was a tiny speck, further and further away. He thought, I hope I haven't opened the sadness that I didn't intend to. He walked outside and the wind was sharp on his face. Driving home he was so lost he forgot to turn on his heater.

♫

She arrived home and her house was cold and she felt more alone than ever. She called Glenna and they talked about their holidays and she told her that Joel was home and they saw a lot of each other.

"Joel. Oh Sharon."

She made a fire in the library, with soft music and with a glass of wine, she thought of "Euterpe Weeps," my song. Did something deep in his psychic draw him to this representation of death? We saw many paintings and sculptures, but he chose this one.

Did he have an omen of his short life on earth? Euterpe's grief is cast for an eternity. Do I want mine to be? I have memories, but you can't kiss a memory, you can't make love to a memory. I believe I have always loved Joel somewhere in my heart, but if I marry him, I will be leaving Craig behind.

Will I ever be ready to leave him behind...?

♫

ACKNOWLEDGMENTS

In LIFE we receive experience and knowledge from family and friends, the neighborhood and world. Add imagination and you have fiction that becomes a novel.

Composers and their music that stirs the emotions into Words

My son who read and corrected those pesky typos and misspelled words.

Quotes from Shakespeare and Arrigo Boito

Editor Nina Alveraz

The author lives in Upstate New York

Other books by author:

Fiction: *After Sunset*   2013

Non-Fiction: *Freddy's Book*   2015